Praise for Ed Ruggero's
gripping novel of West Point
THE ACADEMY

"The atmosphere of the Point, the history and the mystique, are featured players in this steamy tale of political intrigue and Army politics, set expertly in a milieu Ruggero knows intimately."

—Amazon.com

"Ruggero . . . knows how to keep his readers hooked. . . . For an inside peek at the school and its inhabitants, you couldn't ask for a better vehicle than *THE ACADEMY*. . . . Fascinating."

—*The Daily Sun* (GA)

"The academy itself seems to be the main character as civilians and military struggle with its motto—*Duty, Honor, Country*."

—*Library Journal*

"An absorbing tale. . . . a neatly plotted conspiracy."

—*Kirkus Reviews*

Books by Ed Ruggero

The Academy
Breaking Ranks
Firefall
The Common Defense
38 North Yankee

Published by POCKET BOOKS

ED RUGGERO

THE
ACADEMY

POCKET **STAR** BOOKS
New York London Toronto Sydney Tokyo Singapore

This book is a work of fiction. Names, characters, places and incidents are products of the author's imagination or are used fictitiously. Any resemblance to actual events or locales or persons, living or dead, is entirely coincidental.

A Pocket Star Book published by
POCKET BOOKS, a division of Simon & Schuster Inc.
1230 Avenue of the Americas, New York, NY 10020

Copyright © 1997 by Ed Ruggero

Originally published in hardcover in 1997 by Pocket Books

ISBN: 0-671-89171-5

First Pocket Books paperback printing December 1998

10 9 8 7 6 5 4 3 2 1

POCKET STAR BOOKS and colophon are registered trademarks of Simon & Schuster Inc.

Cover art by Steven Assel

Printed in the U.S.A.

Dedicated to
The Long Gray Line
for its nearly two centuries of service
and all the years that lie ahead
and to the
Class of 1980
my extended family

AUTHOR'S NOTE

At about the time I began writing this novel, I attended a conference at West Point. Some of the conference members were recent graduates of the Military Academy, others had already celebrated their fiftieth reunion. I listened to the older men as they talked about the Battle of the Bulge, about the Korean winter of 1950–51, about second tours in Vietnam and building the Army in Europe, about friendships forged at West Point and still flourishing half a century later. I was overwhelmed. How could I ever fit all this history, all this emotion, all the experience and love and loss between the covers of a single book? I called my editor, who wasn't surprised to hear that I was intimidated. "It's difficult to write about things we care deeply about," he said. "Write anyway."

I received encouragement from other quarters. Phil Caputo, who had written so beautifully about his Marines, told me that I must simply "write the story, the truth will come out." Author Tom Carhart, USMA '66, told me to write what I wanted to write, and "anybody who doesn't like it can write his own damn book." But it was my former boss, Colonel Peter Stromberg, Head of the Department of English, who put it best when he told some graduates who'd

AUTHOR'S NOTE

asked about the book, "We must remember that fiction arises from conflict, and that conflict implies villains as well as heroes."

West Point is a complex organism. I have taken liberties with the minute details of organization, staffing and even regulations. There are, for instance, four "D" companies in the Corps of Cadets. Only one is mentioned here. Noncommissioned officers, I am happy to say, play a much greater role in training the cadets than they did in my day (or in this story). These small details change all the time at West Point. As I told some classmates after I watched the induction of the Class of 1998: the big things remain the same and being a plebe still isn't fun.

I would like to thank Joe and Joanne Cox, who generously provided me with a second home on my visits to West Point. Thanks also to John and Angela Calabro, and Peter Stromberg. To Gus Lee, who wrote with such passion and power about West Point—take big bites. Thanks also to Danna Maller, who gave me a completely different perspective; to Andrea, a patient and generous reader; and to Mark, whose blood runs gray.

As always, I owe a great deal to the efforts of the people at William Morris Agency and to my editor, Paul McCarthy.

And thanks to Marcia. For everything.

This is a fictional story set at the United States Military Academy. No single character is based on any individual I've known in the twenty-plus years of my association with West Point. But the concerns, the dedication, the fears, and the selflessness are all true.

30 December 1996
Swarthmore, Pennsylvania

Strengthen and increase our admiration for honest dealing and clean thinking, and suffer not our hatred of hypocrisy and pretense ever to diminish. . . . Make us to choose the harder right instead of the easier wrong, and never to be content with a half truth when the whole can be won. Endow us with courage that is born of loyalty to all that is noble and worthy, that scorns to compromise with vice and injustice and knows no fear when truth and right are in jeopardy.

—from *The Cadet Prayer*

THE
ACADEMY

PROLOGUE

THE UNITED STATES MILITARY ACADEMY
WEST POINT, NEW YORK

MAJOR TOM GATES, UNITED STATES ARMY, USED HIS PARADE
ground voice to dress down the linen closet before him.

"I don't think it's asking too goddamned much," Gates
bellowed to the empty upstairs hallway, "to expect to find a
goddamned towel in the goddamned linen closet."

He stood before the bare shelves, his voice bouncing off
the unflappable, white-painted wood. He slammed the
door.

"Am I being unreasonable?"

He was alone in the house; the histrionics felt good.

"But *no,* we wouldn't want anything to be someplace
where we could actually *find* it, now would we?"

He dragged the hamper out from under the bottom shelf,
went to work with both hands, flinging dirty children's
clothing to the floor. No towel. He left the hallway and
stomped down the stairs, his sneakers squeaking on the
landing. In the living room, just where he expected to find
them, the towels were balled up with other clean laundry—
underwear, socks, washcloths, what looked like a fitted
sheet—an undifferentiated mass of cloth. He pulled out a
towel and rubbed it over his face; a tiny red child's sock
stuck to his heavy beard like an elongated sideburn.

1

"I know what you're up to, Kathleen," he said, addressing his absent wife.

For spite, he threw the wet towel back on top of the pile of clean clothes.

The problem was that he pushed her: the more he griped about the house not being tightly run, the more she let things go. If he made a comment about the laundry not being done, she'd leave it around the house. If he complained that she spent too much decorating their quarters, she'd go out and buy a dress. Dealing with her twisted the laws of physics: action produced an exaggerated reaction. Gates knew she was hardheaded when he married her, he'd just never imagined he'd have to hold his tongue for so long, or that he'd do such a poor job at it. And now, with plenty to be done around the house, she was out *shopping*, kids in tow.

"Probably looking for some more freakin' dried flowers or something," Gates said as he opened the refrigerator and pulled out a tall beer bottle, working his way through a six-pack.

Tom Gates loved his wife. He just wished she weren't so much of a goddamned civilian.

Gates was beginning his first year as a Tactical Officer at the United States Military Academy, responsible for the discipline, military training, and daily lives of the hundred and ten cadets in his charge. Although he was not a graduate of West Point and so did not know much about how the Academy was run, he had been a highly successful field soldier. He believed that the cadets—and maybe even West Point—could learn a lot from a grunt: about leadership and combat, about hard work and tough training, about what it meant to be a real soldier in green instead of a toy soldier in gray—all things that couldn't be found in schoolbooks. He had no clear vision of how he would do this, but he was clear on the need, clear that he was perfectly suited for the job.

Gates went out to the tiny front porch. His neighbor, another major who taught in the Foreign Language Department, was cutting his grass on this Friday afternoon. Gates stared in disgust at the loose rolls of flesh hanging over the elastic band of the man's shorts.

The other man looked up and waved, mouthed something Gates couldn't hear above the roar of the mower.

"Fat slob," he said, raising his beer and smiling.

His neighbor eased back on the throttle; the noise dropped off sharply.

"How's that?" he said, cupping his hand to his ear.

"Great job," Gates said.

The other man nodded and hit the gas.

That's what the easy life here can do if you're not careful, he thought, patting his own flat stomach. Tom Gates looked like some advertising executive's vision of the ideal soldier: six feet, two inches tall, wide at the shoulders, with square-cut good looks that, along with lively green eyes, were the best gifts of his Irish-Scottish-English heritage. Lately he had taken to looking at old pictures of himself, then studying—in secret—hairline, jowls, crow's feet for evidence of slow betrayal.

He looked out over the roofs of the quarters across the street, up the long valley of the Hudson. In winter the narrow defile of Storm King Mountain would channel the cold winds, rattling windows in the house and keeping the kids inside day after day, driving their mother to distraction and the kind of hopeless irritability still known in the Hudson Highlands as cabin fever. But now, late in the summer, the air was thick and moist, smelling of grass and laurel, oak and pine that clung to the slopes all around him.

Gates had put off his daily run until the evening. He hadn't meant to grab another beer—his second, he thought, or maybe third—because it would be tough to run hard with all that sloshing around in his belly. But he wasn't about to miss his outing either, wind up like his neighbor the French teacher.

Gates went inside.

He traded the empty bottle for another and also pulled himself a tall glass of water, which he drank all at once in anticipation of losing a pint of sweat on his run. He looked at the clock in the kitchen—like everything else in the room, it was decorated with cows—and figured since he was going running anyway, he might as well go just before Kathleen came home. That way, by the time he got back she'd have the kids bathed and in their pajamas and ready for him to come in and sweep them up in the air and kiss them, their sweet little bodies smelling of powder and fresh cotton.

Yeah, that'll help her out if I'm not in the way, he thought. "What a guy," he belched to the Hereford cookie jar.

Gates went into the closet in the storage room, just off the kitchen, where he kept his uniforms. Here the cows and the potpourri and the flowers stopped. This was Gates's corner of the house, and it could have been a model for a training manual. He'd even shown it to some of his cadets when they came to visit the house, not to brag, just to show them that he paid attention to the small stuff. But he caught the condescending little smiles they traded with each other when they thought he couldn't see.

The uniforms rested in order from most formal to least formal, tunics buttoned, trousers crisply folded on wooden hangers. On the floor, his shoes occupied a sharp rank, all of them stored toes out, laces tucked in. His battle dress uniforms, the camouflage shirts and pants most people pictured when they thought of the Army, hung in neat rows, sleeves rolled down, shirts and pants on the same hangers. Because they tended to fade, Gates marked each set with an alphanumeric code as soon as he bought it. He always wore trousers A-2 with blouse A-2; that way the trousers and blouse were evenly faded. God is in the details.

Up on the top shelf, his gray physical training shirts were folded with a symmetry any clothing store would envy, all of them stacked with the ARMY logo evenly turned out and visible from the front. On the right-hand side of that shelf were his nonuniform running shirts. Kathleen had bought him some pieces she insisted on calling "exercise wear," shirts and shorts with flashy, colorful logos of running shoe companies or sportswear manufacturers. Gates much preferred his black shirts with the gold Ranger tab re-created across the chest, or the souvenir from his days as a paratrooper: *Death from Above: Kill 'em all and let God sort 'em out.*

He put on his maroon tee shirt with the outsized master parachutist wings, sipping from the bottle as he pulled his running shoes out. He dropped his big frame into the narrow doorway of the storage room and laced up. That finished, he sat enjoying the rest of his beer.

The problem was that the cadets didn't seem like soldiers to him. When he was at Fort Bragg he liked to visit the barracks on the weekends, maybe take a six-pack with him. He could always count on finding some of the men shooting baskets on the outdoor court, or along the company street polishing their shiny, souped-up muscle cars. The soldiers were unpretentious, even unsophisticated, young. Tom Gates always had something to talk about with them. The cadets, he figured, sat around talking about philosophy, probably in that West Point jargon that eluded him.

He'd been in the Army thirteen years, a half dozen posts and dozens of jobs, and he'd done well enough for the assignments board to recommend him for this high-profile job. He knew his way around soldiers, knew the coin of his trade. Yet six weeks at West Point had proven him to be an outsider. He'd somehow left the Army behind; he felt as if he'd abandoned his post. More than that, he was beginning to feel as if he'd just boarded a sinking ship. There were persistent rumors throughout the Army that powerful members of Congress were maneuvering West Point onto the budget chopping block. Here at the Academy, the rumors were a tragic chorus, a cacophony.

Gates tried not to spend too much time questioning his choice of assignments. He arrived ready to work, and if he didn't feel like part of the place yet, he was determined to bull his way in.

"I oughta call the barracks," he remarked to the cow on the clock. "Take some of those kids on a run."

He drained the last of the beer, pushed himself off the floor, and went to the phone. The first number wasn't working, so he dialed his company's orderly room. One of the new sophomores, on duty as the Charge of Quarters, answered.

"This is Company D, Cadet Schwimm speaking. May I help you sir or ma'am?"

"Schwimm, you goddamned tree-hugger, this is Major Gates."

The one hundred and ten cadets in Gates's D Company

represented thirty-nine states, and he tried to associate their homes with their names. Schwimm was from Oregon.

"Are you standing at attention while you're talking to me?" Gates growled.

"Airborne, sir," Schwimm barked. The cadets had already adopted the boss's paratrooper vernacular.

"Good," Gates said, smiling. It was all a game, but what the hell. The cadets liked to be messed with every once in a while; it gave them stories they could brag on when they went home on leave and wanted to tell their civilian friends how tough West Point was.

"I'm looking for Cadet Holder," Gates said. "His phone's not hooked up yet. Find him; have him call me back. If you don't find him in ten minutes, you call me to report, got it?"

"Wilco, sir," the cadet on the other end of the phone said, slipping into the clipped speech of military radio.

"Out here," Gates obliged, hanging up.

Gates sat on the living room floor and stretched his legs across the carpet, touching his toes once, twice. He went back into the kitchen, saw that only five minutes had elapsed, and pulled another beer from the refrigerator. Chances were the seniors were all out of the barracks and he'd wind up running alone anyway, so one more beer wouldn't hurt. After dark, he could run as slowly as he wanted.

Cadet Wayne Holder stood in the middle of his spartan room in a wing of MacArthur barracks, practicing the manual of arms with a cadet saber, symbol of his rank. His roommate, Alex Trainor, sat on a footlocker at what he judged was a safe distance away, giving commands and offering advice.

"How did you manage to get through the summer without learning this stuff?" Trainor asked. Just weeks earlier the seniors had traded the rifles carried by the under three classes for the sabers carried by firsties—for cadets first class. They were only days shy of the beginning of the academic year and the fall parade season.

"I told you, I faked my way through my first three years here," Holder said, pulling the shiny blade straight out of its scabbard, pointing it at the ceiling at a forty-five-degree angle. "I don't see any reason to change that approach now." He flashed his roommate a sidewise grin.

"Show over substance," Trainor said.

"I like to think of it as charm and personality," Holder responded.

Five ten, curly blond hair worn at the limit of cadet regulations for length, handsome in a sun-ripened way, Wayne Holder looked like what he was: a California surfer dropped temporarily into cadet gray. Trainor could imagine him, board under one arm, some sort of trendy Eastern medallion on a leather thong around his neck, laughing easily with admiring young women in bikinis. Trainor, shorter, slightly built, with straight, dishwater hair and the flat-vowel tones of eastern Kansas, tried not to waste energy envying his friend.

Holder brought his hand to his side, pulling the blade toward him so that it rested alongside his arm, the tip next to his ear.

"If those things were sharp," Trainor said, "you'd be doing a Van Gogh imitation out on the parade field."

"If I don't get this down by the parade on Monday," Holder answered, "it won't matter how sharp it is; mess up and Gates will stick it up my ass."

Holder had a particular reason to be concerned about his performance. He had been chosen as the cadet commanding officer—or CO—of his company, which meant he would be in front of the formation on the parade field, painfully visible to the thousands of people in the stands, including the cadets who graded each company's performance as well as the ranks of Tactical Officers who watched their charges from the reviewing stands. Major Gates had told Holder and Trainor, who was executive officer and second in command, that he expected D Company to win the drill streamer, the trophy pennant for the company flag.

"It's occurred to me that he kept me on as CO," Holder said, "so I'd screw up right away and he could just kill me early in the semester. Get me out of the way before football season even started."

"He just went along with Ryder's choice, is all," Trainor said.

Captain Ryder, their Tactical Officer for the previous two

years, had selected the cadet chain of command before he changed jobs at the beginning of the summer. An easygoing artillery officer, Ryder had been a known quantity. Gates was intense, untested, and thus a bit frightening. The cadets called Gates Major Mercury—as in mercurial—for the sudden temper he'd already demonstrated.

"Present . . . *arms,*" Trainor commanded.

Holder brought the handle of the saber to his chin, sweeping the weapon upward in a graceful arc. When he brought it down again, the tip of the weapon clanged on the floor.

"Do that on the Plain," Trainor said, referring to the parade field, "and you'll be marching away while your saber is stuck in the ground."

"I heard that happened to some chick last year," Holder said. "She was too short and every time she brought the point down it got stuck in the grass. *She* graduated."

"She didn't have Gates as a Tac."

"I've got it," Holder said. "I'll challenge him to single combat."

He held the saber before him in a two-handed grip, feet spread, knees flexed as if preparing to fight.

"You'd better take him seriously, Wayne. He means business."

"Not in the plan this year, buddy boy."

"What isn't?"

"Serious. No room. We're *firsties,* man. This may be as good as it ever gets."

He brandished the sword from side to side, parrying the thrusts of an invisible foe.

"We've got cars, and privileges—free time just like people in real colleges. And it's almost football season. Home games—it'll be babe city around here.

"Besides, you know I'm not going to let something as boring as responsibility interfere with my enjoying senior year."

Holder put the blade in its scabbard, unbuckled the sword belt and stored it in its rack. Trainor shook his head. He had returned from his brief summer leave thinking that perhaps Wayne had grown up and into his role as one of the leaders of the Corps. He'd been disappointed.

Wayne Holder was a fourth generation West Pointer, a bona fide member of the nearest thing the Army had to an aristocracy. If he was at all impressed with his lineage, he hid it well.

In a world of starch and polish, Holder was always a little rumpled. His uniforms didn't seem to fit him well, his haircut always drew a second glance from inspectors, his shoes and brass belt buckle were clean but never radiant. He invested almost as much energy and forethought into elaborate practical jokes as he did in his studies. Yet for all that, it seemed to Trainor that Wayne's flippancy was not just beach boy insouciance. Underneath the disdain for regulations, some part of Wayne Holder was struggling to become a leader. People liked him and wanted to be near him, but it wasn't leadership. Not yet. He would grow into the role, eventually. Trainor suspected that fact scared Wayne Holder a bit; he handled it by pretending he didn't care.

"Ryder and I would have gotten along well," Holder said.

"Yeah, neither one of you liked to shine your shoes," Trainor interrupted.

Holder looked down, then stood on one foot and rubbed the toe of his shoe on the back of his pants leg.

"Ryder and I shared philosophies. . . ."

"Now it's a philosophy?"

Holder went on, ignoring the interruption.

"The military stuff—the Mickey Mouse stuff of shined shoes, shiny brass and all that, is a distraction."

"From what?" Trainor wanted to know.

"Huh?"

"If you say it's a distraction, that implies that you know what it's a distraction from, that you have a focus."

"You've been reading your leadership manual a little too much lately," Holder said.

Trainor let the sarcasm slip by. The outgoing Tac had made them roommates because he knew that Holder, who had natural leadership ability, needed counsel. New lieutenants had their sergeants; Holder had Trainor. The Kansan was near the top of the class, academically. He was somewhat naive—even for a product of the sheltered environment that was West Point. His family was from the conservative—though not militant—religious right. He didn't curse; he tried hard to control his anger and his tendency to look on the great bulk of his peers as unwashed and in need of saving. He had done his share of proselytizing as a plebe, until a roommate—tired of the harangues—had offered to make a martyr out of him through the quick use of a third floor window. Though he had toned his delivery, his ardor had not cooled.

"Right now I'm focused on getting through Monday's parade without stabbing myself, OK?"

The door to the room was wide open in the hope some sluggish breeze might pass through. The sophomore—yearling in the cadet vernacular—who had taken Gates's call rapped on the thick wood.

"Major Gates just called," Schwimm announced. "He wants you to call him back right away."

Holder nodded his thanks, then followed the younger cadet into the hallway.

Holder took the message form Schwimm held out and dialed Gates's home number.

"Sir, this is Cadet Holder," he said, trying to sound pleasant, upbeat, but at the same time martial.

"Holder," Gates said. "What are you doing down there?"

"I was practicing my saber manual, sir."

"Are you kidding me?" Gates said.

"No, sir," Holder said. With almost any other officer he knew—certainly any one of his instructors—Holder would have joked about what this said about West Point. How many other college seniors spent Friday evening practicing drill? He wasn't sure Gates would get it.

"I want to go on a run," Gates said after a pause.

I'll alert the media, Holder thought. "Yes, sir," he said.

"Who's around the barracks?" Gates said. "What firsties?"

Most of Holder's classmates were enjoying their new privileges. There wasn't much to do near West Point—a couple of movie theaters if you didn't mind driving twenty miles to the nearest town of any size. But the senior cadets had been hanging around the barracks for three years; it didn't take much to entice them to leave.

"There may be a few of us around, sir. Cadet Trainor is here."

"Round up all the seniors and have them outside by MacArthur's statue in fifteen minutes. We're going for a little spirit run."

"Spirit" was an all-purpose adjective in Academy jargon that appended itself to anything that had to do with extra work. If it was supposed to be good for you and wasn't fun, it was called "spirit."

Holder hesitated. There seemed something wrong with Gates's voice—timing, tone, inflection—something was off.

"Uh . . . I don't know how many I'll be able to round up, sir. Lots of folks have already worked out today and . . ."

"I'm not asking for fucking volunteers, here," Gates barked, suddenly angry. "Get those people out of the barracks. I'll meet you down there in one five."

Holder gave the only response available to him.

"Yes, sir," he said.

Trainor came up behind him.

"What did he want?"

"We're going on a little run with the old man," Holder said, hanging up. "He wants all the firsties who are in the barracks to meet him outside at MacArthur's statue in fifteen minutes."

"What the heck is that?" Trainor asked. Although it was certainly within Gates's right to call them out of the barracks, the officer was violating a cardinal—if unwritten—rule: don't mess with people's free time.

"What are we, the Eighty-second Airborne Division rolling out on an alert?"

"We might be before the year is out," Holder said.

"If he starts this stuff now, what's he going to do during the academic year? We gonna practice fire and maneuver during study barracks?"

"No," Holder said, still thinking about Gates's voice, about how quickly the officer had snapped at him. Gates clearly was not used to being questioned, but there was something more than that.

"You want me to go around to the rooms?" Trainor asked, shaking his head.

"Those are my orders," Holder said. "And I wouldn't dream of thwarting Major Gates."

He leaned against the wall.

"Schwimm," he called.

The CQ—a combination receptionist, guard, and glorified messenger—approached the two seniors.

"Cadet Trainor will be going around to all the firsties' rooms here in a few minutes, rounding people up for a spirit run with the tactical officer."

Schwimm raised his eyebrows, which was as close as he would come to saying out loud, "What the fuck is this guy thinking?"

"Cadet Trainor and I want every first class cadet who happens to be in his or her room to join us at MacArthur's statue in ten minutes for this run. Of course, any cadet who is not around when Cadet Trainor and I knock will miss out on this opportunity."

Schwimm gave a puzzled nod, but he wasn't comprehending.

Trainor spoke, leaning in conspiratorially.

"He wants you to go around to the firsties' rooms ahead of me and casually mention to them that they're about to be given an invitation . . . and there's only one way to avoid the invitation."

"Oh," Schwimm said. He scrambled away down the hall.

"Give him two or three minutes," Holder said.

Major Tom Gates drove slowly through the tight streets of the officers' housing area known as New Brick. There were dozens of children about, bicycles and tricycles cluttered every sidewalk, plastic toys covered tiny lawns, balls and water pistols and skates lay about like colorful detritus. This was a community with a skewed demographic. Only married couples could live in post housing, and since housing was grouped by rank, the neighbors were about the same age—child-bearing age. This was a fertile community. Certainly there were couples who did not have children, but they were the exception, and the jokes about the need to "produce warriors for the next generation" had a ring of advice to them. Gates, ever the romantic, had referred to the birth of their second child as "punching out our quota."

Gates was halfway down the hill toward Washington Road, which would lead him to the barracks, before he realized he still had a beer in his hand, an open container, and wouldn't the Military Police love to catch him like that. Such a transgression could be a career-ending move at West Point, where staff and faculty lived under a microscope. The Academy didn't just teach order and discipline and almost-Victorian propriety, it force-fed those virtues, demanded them back at every turn. They animated the statues, shined from the stones, anchored the great rock itself.

Still, Gates liked to have a little fun now and then. Flaunting the rules just a bit was a sign of good spirit, a little *panache*.

He looked around for other cars and, seeing none, took a swig from the bottle.

That's something the cadets are missing, he thought. *That kind of spirit; they think the whole thing is about coloring inside the lines. They need coaching, is all.*

As difficult as the course of instruction was at West Point, it didn't harden the cadets in ways that Gates thought they needed to be hardened. He had been surprised when, while observing basic training for the new class of cadets during the summer months, he had stumbled across a "Stress Reduction Class" on the training schedule. Curious, he'd gone to the gym, eventually finding his way through the maze of rooms in that city-block sized building to find fifty new cadets lying flat on the hardwood floor, listening to a relaxation tape while some tweedy civilian psychology type—*who the hell was letting these people in?*—talked to them in a cooing singsong about letting go of their anger.

Gates had fantasized about throwing a hand grenade simulator into the big room, shouting, "Do you think the enemy cares if you're fucking stressed out?"

His job, he decided that day, was to help his cadets toughen up, be flexible, learn to take it and dish it out. Not many of them, he knew, would ever see combat. But the ones who did would thank him; he was sure about that.

Not that it was going to be easy. When he first met the seniors from his company, he told them how much he loved the infantry, the bloody-knees business of soldiering. A couple of them had given him tight little smiles.

"The smug bastards," he'd said to Kathleen later on. "I

wanted to grab them and shake some sense into them. What the hell do they know about the Army?"

"They're kids," she'd answered. "They think they know everything, just like kids everywhere."

Gates drove down Washington Road, the professors' houses on his right keeping watch on the river valley as they had for a hundred and fifty years. These great stone and brick affairs, with their big screened porches, for the most part housed only two people apiece. The professors, all full colonels, had done their time, and so got the privileges. But in the meantime, young officers and NCOs were crowded into tiny homes, two or three children, one bathroom, bedrooms so small, one of Gates's friends had remarked, that you had to go out into the hallway to change your mind.

He drove around Trophy Point, the green expanse of the Plain off on his right, and parked near the soccer field. There wasn't much traffic here; he drained the last of his beer so that it wouldn't spill on the floorboard of the car when he put the empty in the back.

Gates took a deep breath and walked along the path that skirted Trophy Point, the bluff just above the Hudson. The view was magnificent, with the river rolling out of the mountain-gated valley to the north, crouching between hills green and misty in the summer humidity. In six weeks, Gates knew, those slopes would glow red and orange and yellow. Trophy Point, now quiet, would be overrun in the autumn season of visitors—football games and reunions, parades and tailgate parties. A million and a half visitors a year came here for the pageants, for a piece of the history, for a view of this river and a chance to see where the nation's most famous battle captains were schooled. But for these weeks at the end of summer, this was a quiet, if not a private place to watch the river.

Gates checked his watch. He was a bit early, so he sat on one of the stone benches that lined the walkway, letting his fingers hang over the edge to trace the deep-carved letters bordering the two-inch thick slab. Integrity. To the right another low bench, its ends preaching Honor. And there were more, another dozen or so, Gates guessed, around the curved walkway marked by the upturned tails of cannons— prizes from nineteenth-century wars carted back to this place, the trophies of "Trophy Point." The benches marched in an easy rank, like a line of skirmishers across the gentle slope. Duty and Service, Valor and Dignity.

Though he did not often use such words, these were the very things Tom Gates felt when he was among soldiers.

He heard a car pull up, doors opening and closing. A detail of Military Police prepared to lower the flag at the end of the duty day, just as they did here every afternoon. Gates watched as a lone bugler found his spot a little off to one side. The sergeant in charge positioned his troops—two on the lowering lines, one at the retreat gun, another in the road prepared to stop traffic. Gates looked up the hundred and fifty feet of the great white pole to where the garrison flag rolled over slowly in the summer air.

The sergeant checked his watch, nodded, and the bugler extended his arm and instrument above his head, twirling it once, twice, three times. Then to his lips for "Retreat."

This was Tom Gates's favorite time of day, when a bugle signaled the end of duty, reminding him that his service had been marked by many such days, not all of them quiet, not all of them happy, but all of them, he felt, invested in a good cause, a good fight.

The cannon cracked over the river. Gates was not in uniform, and so was not supposed to render a hand salute; but he was caught up in the moment, in the light-headed feeling that seemed the evening's gift. He raised his right hand, touching fingertip to eyebrow, watching the flag come down, framed in the tree branches. The quicksilver notes of "To The Colors" rolled across the roadway and the grass, bouncing lightly off the buildings and the hills, clear and bright as truth.

Yes, it was all worthwhile, he thought, comforted by the ritual. This was what he wanted to show the cadets, this was what he wanted them to feel. But he was not a poet; he didn't trust himself to speak of service, dignity, pride, all the things he carried deep in his soldier's heart. All he could do, he told himself, was live that way so that others might see him.

He would take them out on a run, he decided, a hard run. Most of them had probably hit the gym already that day, which would even the score a bit. He wanted to show them what the old man could do. He wanted to get out on the road, bullshit with them, talk about assignments, the Army, Ranger school, all the things he knew and they didn't. He would show them that they were part of something larger, something that would outlast all their petty concerns. Then they would feel as he did, or he'd know why the hell not.

Wayne Holder and Alex Trainor stood inside the low granite walls that formed a portico around the statue of General Douglas MacArthur. What had seemed like a good idea in the barracks—giving the other firsties enough warning to clear out—suddenly didn't seem so great now that they were outside and alone.

"Think he's going to be pissed?" Holder asked. He nervously fingered the back of his neck, where he'd had Trainor trim his hair with an electric razor. He hadn't taken the time to get the haircut he needed, and seeing Gates always involved an inspection.

"No doubt," Trainor said. He was leaning against one wall, studying General MacArthur's faraway stare caught in bronze.

They were interrupted by the sound of retreat. The two young men stood straight, quiet because they had been trained to be quiet and respectful, watching with mild interest the flagpole and the little ceremony just across the parade field. When the last notes faded, they resumed the conversation.

"You don't seem too worried about it," Holder said, trying to sound calmer than he felt. He took his cues from Trainor, who seemed mature beyond his years. Holder looked up to his roommate, who would make a fine leader if he stopped taking himself so seriously. If Trainor thought it was OK to be cavalier about this, that was good enough for Holder.

Trainor shrugged. "What's he gonna do? Bend our dog-tags?"

"Hello, men," Gates's voice boomed at them. "Where the hell is everybody?"

He came toward them with long, powerful strides, up on the balls of his feet, his tee shirt with the big silver paratrooper wings stretched tight across his wide chest.

The cadets saluted and waited until Gates had returned their salutes before explaining.

"Turns out we're the only firsties around, sir," Holder said.

"Is that right?"

Gates lost his smile and looked over their heads at the wing of the barracks behind the monument, where Company D lived.

"You boys wouldn't be trying to bullshit me, now, would you?" Gates said. He was smiling again, but there was no mirth there. Holder studied the big man; there was something odd about him today, about the way he carried himself.

"Could it be that you told everybody to get lost?" Gates asked.

He didn't wait for an answer. He knew the cadets wouldn't lie to him, and he didn't need their admission to make his point. Judging by the way they were squirming, their eyes shifting around nervously, he'd guessed right.

"You little . . ." Gates began. He took a breath, gathered himself. "I'm going out of my way here . . . devoting some of my free time, time I could be with my family."

That part wasn't exactly true, Gates knew. He was here to avoid the bath-time bedlam, but why worry the details?

"And you think you can turn me down?"

Predictably, the cadets said nothing.

"Get the underclassmen out here," Gates said coolly.

"Sir?" Holder ventured.

"Did I fucking stutter?" Gates said. He still smiled, but his anger surged closer to the surface. He pointed at Trainor. "Get up there in the barracks and roll out every cow and yearling you see. Leave the plebes alone."

Trainor lingered long enough to give Holder a puzzled glance, as if asking the other cadet what he should do.

"What the hell are you looking at him for?" Gates snapped. "*I* told you to get up in the barracks and shake out every soul in there. You read me?"

Trainor saluted, squeezed past Gates in the narrow opening to the monument's wall, and jogged to the ground floor of the barracks.

Holder was staring at him now, Gates noted. He walked

out to the sidewalk and began to stretch his legs. The moment was gone. No camaraderie now, no easy banter.

Fuck them, Gates thought. *I served with eighteen-year-old paratroopers who were more interested in learning what I had to teach.*

"Come here," Gates said.

The cadet moved quickly. That was good. Still jumping.

"When I was a lieutenant," Gates said, "my commander used to make us all go to the club on Friday afternoon for Happy Hour. You didn't have to drink, and you didn't have to stay late. But you had to show up, had to socialize a little bit."

Gates sat on the ground, one leg out before him in a runner's stretch, grasping the toe of the shoe with both hands, tanned forearms stretched tight.

"You know why?"

Holder shook his head. "No, sir."

"Because it gave you a chance to talk to people, open up communications, you know? Which might make it easier when you had to work with these guys during the week. I mean, if you could stand at the bar and talk to some guy you didn't necessarily like—no pressure on—next time you had to call him to ask for something, things would go a little easier. And it gave you a chance to get to know people, figure out how they might react when things got dicey."

Later, Holder would think it was Gates's mentioning the club that helped him put things together. The cadet took a step closer to Gates, drew in a deep breath.

Gates had been drinking.

Oh, shit, Holder thought. *Now what do I do?*

He had to figure out a way to keep this little spirit run from happening. Not that Gates was drunk enough to run them all into the river or anything, but it wouldn't do for the underclassmen to be roused out of the barracks by their Tac, only to see that he was half in the bag.

Alcohol was the great taboo. Take any infraction of the myriad rules that governed the lives of the cadets and the staff, add a little alcohol—no matter how tangentially— and even a minor sin became apostasy.

"Sir, I don't think we should go on this run," Holder said.

Gates, who'd relaxed somewhat in his reverie, looked up quickly, a sharp scowl on his face. Major Mercury.

"The fuck you say?"

Gates didn't use foul language around the underclass cadets. It was soldier patois, but he used it around a few of the seniors as if to say "We're in this together."

"I don't think it's a good idea to go on this run, sir. I mean, we're taking the underclass cadets out on their free time—kind of taking their free time away from them, not giving them much choice, you know. If we'd planned ahead. . . ."

Holder was stumbling badly and he knew it. And Gates knew it, too.

"I'd be glad to go on a run with you, sir," Holder tried, changing tacks. "It would give us a chance to talk about the company, about classes starting next week. . . ."

"What's your problem?" Gates asked. He stood up, moving closer to the cadet. Gates, at six two, was four inches taller and forty pounds heavier than the younger man. He leaned in closely; Holder tried to step back, bumped into the low wall, could go no farther.

"What are you trying to say, Mister Holder?"

"Mister" was the form of address for plebes, the freshman who would have no identity for a year. Holder didn't miss the significance.

"I just don't think it's a good idea, sir," Holder tried one more time. He wasn't afraid of Gates—Gates wouldn't hurt him physically. Up until a moment ago, he had been afraid of what Gates could do to him. It would be a long senior year if the officer who had the most say in Holder's life decided to dislike him. But even that feeling was fading away.

Holder knew the smart move here. Gates was an officer; he had all the experience, all the rank, all the weight of tradition and law behind him. All of Holder's training made him want to say, "Yes, sir."

But he couldn't say it.

It would be no big deal. Trainor would drag a couple of sophomores out of the barracks, and they would bitch and moan, but that's what they did anyway. Maybe a couple of them would guess that Gates had been drinking. More likely they'd just assume that this was another side of his personality they hadn't seen yet. Bizarre. A little too tightly wrapped. He and Trainor could smooth things over. Could be that no one would even notice.

But it would be wrong.

"Sir," Holder said, his voice a little shakier than he wanted it to be. He tried to swallow, but his tongue moved like cotton in his mouth. "I don't think it would be right for the underclassmen to go with you . . . because you've been drinking."

Gates stood up straight, and Holder's first thought was that he didn't want the cadet to be able to smell his breath.

"Who the hell do you think you're talking to, Holder?" Gates said. The muscles at the base of his neck knotted tight; his jaw barely moved when he talked. "I'm doing you a goddamned favor by not kicking your ass right back into the barracks and taking those stripes away from you, understand?"

There were a few seconds where Holder felt panic. Maybe he'd misread Gates. Maybe Gates hadn't been drinking—after all, why would someone like him risk career-ending censure by pulling such a stupid stunt?

But Gates didn't immediately deny it either.

Holder had been right. And he hoped that would be enough to save him.

"I'm sorry, sir, and I meant no disrespect."

Gates inched closer. Now Holder was leaning backward over the wall, the granite pressing the backs of his thighs. He looked around quickly to see who might be watching. They were in one of the most public and highly visible spots on the cadet grounds: an entire wing of the barracks looked down on them from across the street, they were thirty yards from the front door of the Superintendent's quarters.

What a show, Holder thought.

"You goddamned priss, Holder," Gates said. White spittle trembled at the corner of his mouth, threatening to spray Holder.

"So you're one of those fucking pansy West Pointers who think everything is supposed to be sweet and clean and touchy feely. The Army ain't like that, Holder, and the world ain't like that. It's messy out there."

"That may be, sir," Holder said, fighting to keep his voice even. "But for right now, all I know is that I believe you've been drinking, and it wouldn't do the underclass cadets any good to see you show up at the barracks like this."

Gates was thinking about how good it would feel to smash this punk right in his pretty-boy face. Gates dropped one shoulder, a sudden move, and Holder flinched. Then Holder leaned back on the low wall, sat up, and swung his legs over, dropping right into the bushes on the other side. He came to attention, right there with the evergreen shrubs wrapped tightly around his legs, looking ridiculous. But he saluted sharply, said, "Good evening, sir," then started back toward the barracks.

Gates was so surprised he didn't know what to do. He wanted to call out to the cadet, but something made him think Holder might not stop. Gates looked at the six-story building above him. There were no cadets visible in the windows. But that didn't mean no one was watching.

Gates put one big hand on the wall and jumped it like a low fence. He jogged after Holder, who had gone into the sally port, a one-story opening that led like a tunnel to the quadrangle within the barracks. There was a set of big double doors leading off the sally port and into the building; Holder was reaching for the handle when Gates caught up to him.

"I didn't dismiss you, you little dipshit," Gates snarled, pushing the door shut with one hand. "And let me tell you something else; you're here to learn from me."

"I don't think it's a good thing to learn sir," Holder said. His eyes had gone flat. His voice was even, Gates noted, without that slight tentative note he'd had just a few moments earlier. If he wasn't so angry, Gates might have appreciated Holder's courage.

"I think it would be a bad idea for the cadets to see you like this."

Gates couldn't believe this; he was being defied by a twenty-one-year-old cadet whose only experience of the Army had been hanging around other West Point cadets.

Neither of them saw, through the narrow glass in the door, Trainor reach the landing inside. Trainor, talking over his shoulder, did not see the two men outside. He stepped up to the door and shoved at the bar to open it.

Outside, Gates thought Holder was trying to pull the door open. He used his strong right arm and most of his weight to push hard against the opening door. With his left hand he shoved Holder away.

Holder, surprised, stumbled backward, lost his balance. There was a cry of pain, but not from Holder. Gates looked at the door; he had used all of his two hundred and twenty pounds to slam it on Trainor's hand.

Gates let go immediately, then pulled the door open. Trainor fell to the floor, his arm held in front of him. Holder scrambled over, pushing in between his roommate and the stunned officer. Trainor was moaning, the two sophomores who'd been on the steps behind him were cemented in place.

"Call an ambulance," Holder told them.

One of the cadets turned for the hallway.

"Is it that bad?" Gates asked.

Holder, who was blocking his view, moved aside a little. Trainor was on the floor, knees and forehead pressed to the cold stone. Gates could hear him breathing in short, rasping breaths. Three fingers on his right hand were twisted and bloody; yellow and red tendrils of flesh spread out from the mess. Trainor was squeezing his wrist with his good hand.

Holder removed his tee shirt and wrapped Trainor's hand, as much so the injured man wouldn't see what had happened as to stop the flow of blood.

"The ambulance will be here in a few minutes," one of the yearlings reported.

"Good," Gates said. "Go out front and meet it, flag it down."

The yearling didn't move, and Gates wondered if the cadet had heard him. Then the sophomore looked at Holder.

"Go outside and make sure they see you," Holder said. The cadet turned immediately.

Now a crowd was gathering, a dozen or so cadets, most of them in their gym uniforms. The ones in the closest circle were looking at Trainor's hand, which had bled through Holder's shirt. On the fringes of the circle other cadets were whispering. Gates, seated on the floor, felt as if he should chase them away. But he wasn't sure they would listen to him.

"Go upstairs," Holder said to the second yearling from Company D, "and get me another tee shirt from my locker. I'm going to the hospital with Alex."

The younger cadet looked at Gates for one beat, two, then turned and went upstairs, taking with him, Gates thought, God only knew what story.

CHAPTER 1

WAYNE HOLDER PACED BACK AND FORTH IN FRONT OF THE WIDE
door of Exam One just inside the Emergency Room entrance at Keller Army Hospital. He couldn't see much of
Alex Trainor—just his cadet-issue gym shorts and beat-up
running shoes—so he was watching the doctor, the one
wearing the flip-flops. The ambulance crew had taken one
look at Alex's hand down at the barracks and had radioed
the hospital; the doctor in sandals, who stood with his back
to the door, had been on call. Holder could see, through the
open back of the doctor's sterile gown, loud gold shorts and
a tee shirt with big red letters that said "Doesn't Play Well
With Others."

A nurse came out of the room carrying an aluminum
clipboard.

"How is he?" Holder asked.

The nurse, a black man wearing the silver collar insignia
of a first lieutenant and a nametag that said "Speers," spoke
without looking up from the notes he was taking.

"Must have been a big door, huh?"

"Yeah," Holder said. "And a big guy pushed it, too."

The nurse stopped writing. "You his roommate?"

"Yes, sir," Holder said.

25

"Well, the docs are talking about whether or not he needs an operation on his hand. It might mean going down to D.C., to Walter Reed. They're better equipped for this stuff."

Holder, a little dizzy, leaned back against the admissions counter. "That bad, huh?"

"Did you close the door on his hand?" Speers asked, thinking that the kid felt guilty about causing the accident. The cadet looked up as if startled.

"No, it wasn't me. I mean, I was there and everything. I saw what happened."

"Was it an accident?" Speers asked.

The question was a simple one, really, and all Holder had to do was say "yes." And there was Speers, ready to believe it was an accident, ready to write this off as another instance of horseplay in the barracks. It happened all the time. In spite of their grinding schedule, or maybe because of it, cadets still found the energy for rough games and practical jokes; they fell down stairs, twisted ankles, broke bones. Holder even remembered a cadet falling out of a second-floor window of the barracks during a particularly energetic pep rally.

"Lieutenant Speers," one of the doctors called.

"Be right there, sir," Speers said over his shoulder. Then, to Holder, "Is there something you want to tell me about this?"

Holder hesitated. He wanted to say that his Tac had been drinking and they'd gotten into a little shoving match and the officer had pushed the door shut at just the wrong time and now he was afraid that Major Gates ("Did I mention that we call him Major Mercury?") was going to take all this out on Holder and at the very least he'd be pissed at Holder for the whole year and . . .

"Lieutenant Speers," the doctor called again.

"Don't leave," Speers told Holder as he went back into the examining room.

Holder heard the lieutenant say very clearly to the attending doctors, "There's something going on here."

Kathleen and the kids were already home by the time Tom Gates pulled to the curb in front of his quarters. He reached onto the floorboard of the back seat for the empty he knew was there; he found two and a plastic bag. He put the bottles inside the bag and carried them around behind the duplex, slipping them into the trash. Then he walked into the back door.

Kathleen was at the kitchen sink. "Hello there," she said.

Gates slumped into a kitchen chair without answering.

"What's wrong?" she asked, drying her hands on a towel and turning to face him. She used the back of one hand to push a strawberry blond curl out of her eyes. Born Kathleen Moira McDade, her inheritance included the creamy complexion of her Irish ancestors, a tiny chin she found small for her face, sky-blue eyes and—on occasion—the temper that had made her police-officer grandfather both scourge and protector of his Boston beat.

Gates told her about slamming the door on Trainor's hand.

"Ouch," she said, pulling her shoulders in tight, scrunching her face with the imagined pain. "So you feel bad, huh?"

"Yeah," Gates said, his eyes on the table before him. "I messed up."

"It was an accident, right?"

"Yes and no," he said.

Kathleen got that calm look she had when she was taking charge. She sat at the table, folded her hands, and listened while Gates explained his call to the barracks, his feeling that Holder and Trainor had thwarted him.

"So what?" Kathleen scolded. "You should have known that the cadets wouldn't want to give up their free time, especially on the last Friday night before classes start. Why did you want to push them?"

"They defied me, Kathleen. I guess I could have asked if anyone wanted to go along, then it wouldn't have been such a big deal. But I told them to round people up. When they didn't, they were challenging me."

I could live with you a hundred years, Kathleen thought, *and never come any closer to understanding why you think the way you do.*

"So how did this lead to Holder getting belligerent with you?"

"He accused me of drinking," Gates said after a pause. It

would do no good to waffle, Kathleen would always find out the truth.

"Were you?" she asked. Her tone wasn't accusatory. There would be no "I told you so's" from this woman. Gates could sense the change in her. Kathleen Gates perceived a threat to her husband's reputation, and hence to his career. If he'd made a stupid move, that would affect her whole family. With the instincts of a mother bear, she pulled herself together, sharpened her senses. The threat was out there; she took charge.

Gates didn't see problems as his wife did. He tended to break things down into opposing camps: he stood in one, someone else stood in another. Kathleen was politically savvy; she understood shifting alliances, intrigue, influence, the nature of human frailty and desire. She would have been at home in the court of the de Medicis.

"I had a beer before I left. I suppose he might have smelled it on my breath. But this kid was making a big deal out of it in that self-righteous, smug little way they all have."

That's it, Kathleen thought. *We're back to the us–versus–them mindset. He doesn't like them because they're West Pointers, or because they have opportunities he didn't have.*

"Did you admit that you'd had a beer?" she asked. Very cool. She didn't have to shove her husband aside to take control. It was the natural order in their marriage: they played to each other's strengths. When their problems called for a battering ram, Tom stepped up. If they needed a feather touch, it was Kathleen's turn. They both appreciated the balance.

Gates tried to re-create the conversation in his head. He couldn't remember saying anything like that to Holder; he wouldn't admit such a thing to the little prig, anyway.

"No," he said.

"What, exactly, did you say to him?"

"I told him I was doing him a favor by making myself available. That he should be happy that I was willing to spend my free time on his development. I told him about how Colonel Grier used to make us go to happy hour, just so we'd get used to talking to people in the battalion, even people we didn't like. Told him what a good thing that was, that it opened up communication."

Kathleen remembered those Friday afternoon Happy Hour gambols when her husband was a lieutenant, when he'd come home at midnight, smelling of spilled beer. She made him sleep on the couch a couple of times, or the floor if he couldn't make the couch. She'd always felt bad the next day, and she waited a long time for him to act like an adult. After one night of his drinking she let him crawl into bed with her, fully clothed. An hour later he woke to go to the bathroom, but instead of finding the toilet, he had simply stood in the corner of their room and pissed on the floor. The next day, Kathleen had gone to visit her parents, staying for a week. When she got back, Tom had painted the bedroom and installed new carpet. She never mentioned the incident, but she decided that day that her husband might never grow up. And since she couldn't afford to wait, from that day on she didn't hesitate to take over when Tom's techniques were too heavy-handed.

"Anyway, he walked away from me, just blew me off, like he had better things to do. I caught up with him in the sally port, told him that the world wasn't always such a neat place, that people weren't always as polite as they might be at West Point. That the real world was a little tougher."

Kathleen looked at her husband. There was no trace of drunkenness in his storytelling, but she allowed that the facts might be a little skewed. He had pulled himself upright, thrown his shoulders back while recounting his story of how he'd handled a little mutiny, showing off for her even now. He was such a little boy, sometimes.

"Why did you say that?"

"What?"

"Why did you say the world isn't always neat and clean?"

"Because it isn't. These kids live in this sheltered environment and then they go out into the Army and . . ."

"That's not what I meant," she said patiently, as if explaining things to a high school student who should be bright enough to follow the argument.

"What was the context? Did you say that because the way you were acting wasn't neat and clean? Can't you see that he might have taken that as an admission that you had been drinking, but you could excuse that because in the real world sometimes officers do show up drunk at the barracks?"

"I wasn't drunk, Kathleen."

Kathleen let out a long breath. She could hear the children playing upstairs. The quarters weren't as big as the ones they'd had at Fort Campbell, but they were nice, and they were at West Point. No matter how much Tom complained about it, there was a lot to be gained, some definite career advantages, to an assignment here. He would meet some of the most talented people in the Army, if he could just get by the fact that they didn't spend all their time in the field. She looked at him, his big face close enough to touch.

Her husband was a muddy-boots soldier, more at home in the field, laboring under a heavy rucksack and the demands of running a complex tactical problem than he was at the political skirmishes fought over linen and silverware at the Officer's Club or at the homes of senior officers. At Fort Bragg, at Benning and Campbell he'd been successful, the one they came to when things were tricky. Here, Kathleen knew, amid the spit and polish at West Point, he felt a little like a stevedore at dance lessons.

Kathleen Gates had pushed him to take this assignment, because she believed he could develop the savvy he needed to reach the Army's highest ranks. He had a natural instinct for soldiering, all he needed was a little coaching. What's more, he deserved to succeed. He was the most honest man Kathleen had ever known, and if he was a little rough around the edges, he had a great heart—not a gentle heart, but a true one. And she loved him, good qualities and bad.

"I want you to go upstairs and get a quick shower. Change into something you can wear down to the hospital," she said.

Gates was nodding.

"You have to go visit this kid, Trainor, see how he's doing—I'll even come with you if I can get a babysitter."

Gates left the table and started up the stairs.

"Make sure you use mouthwash," she said to his back.

When she heard the water start, Kathleen Gates went to the refrigerator. She had bought a six-pack of beer last night; there was one bottle left standing in the cardboard holder. She took the bottle from the package and laid it on its side on the bottom shelf. Then she went to the recycling bin and removed two bottles. Tom never rinsed the bottles out, so it was easy to determine that he had put them in there this afternoon. There was a third bottle in the sink. She walked out the back door and opened the trash can, pulling the plastic bag containing two more empties from the trash. She put the five bottles inside, then put that sack inside another, covering the top with other rubbish. This done, she walked through the gate that separated her yard from her neighbors'. She opened their trash can and stuffed the bag down the side.

Tom Gates would not deliberately lie to anyone. But if there were no empties to count, he could probably convince himself that he'd had only two that afternoon.

Captain Tim Breitland, on duty as the Officer-in-Charge, walked over to MacArthur Barracks after the cadets on duty at Central Guard Room told him that an ambulance had taken a cadet to the hospital.

"Call Keller," he told them, "and see what you can find out about this guy's condition."

Breitland was, like Gates, a Tactical Officer. Like Gates, he was also an infantryman who'd spent most of his time with the paratroopers. He wore his hair in the high and tight, close-cropped buzz that paratroopers wore. Below average height, with the thickly muscled chest and arms of a weight lifter and the booming voice of a drill sergeant, he liked to walk into the barracks wearing the gold and black brassard with its big "OC." The OC was the commandant's representative, the off-duty-hours voice of authority in the cadet area, dispenser of what the cadets called "quill," citations for sins against regulations, which were legion. He liked to watch the cadets jump.

Breitland walked along the apron, the concrete formation area that faced the Plain between the parade ground and the barracks, then into a sally port that led to north area and the D Company barracks. Some cadets, their heads and arms outside second and third floor windows as they watched a basketball game on the outdoor courts, saw him coming. Breitland could see them disappear inside as they went through the hallways warning everyone in the barracks that the OC was coming. Breitland, feeling a little like a feudal lord, imagined the cadets on six floors of barracks checking their rooms, making themselves scarce as he entered the building.

He wasn't sure which floor D Company was on, so he entered the hallway on the first floor. Four cadets in gym uniform were on hands and knees in the hallway, using green paint to letter a large piece of cloth that had started out as a bedsheet. They leaped to attention when they saw Breitland.

"What floor is D Company on, men?"

"Third floor, sir," one of the cadets answered.

It was common practice for cadets to produce signs during football season, banners that fluttered from barracks windows during pep rallies. Some were clever, some artistic; many of them showed a caricature of the opposing school's mascot undergoing gruesome torture—Notre Dame's Fighting Irish leprechaun under the treads of a tank, for instance. The Commandant's position was that they all had to be in good taste. "Something you could show your Mom," he'd told the cadet commanders.

Breitland stepped to the side, walking gingerly in the space between the sheet and the wall until he could read the lettering.

**BARRACKS FOR SALE:
122 RMS / 12 BA; RIVER VU. INQUIRE WITHIN
BRUCKNER COMMISSION REALTY**

"You plan on hanging this outside?" Breitland asked.

"Just on the north area side, sir," one of the cadets replied, describing the interior quadrangle.

"You guys have new careers planned for after they shut this place down?"

One of the cadets looked at his buddies, then ventured, "Real estate speculation, sir."

Breitland, who was as worried as Gates that he'd chosen an assignment that was going to send him down with the ship, said, "You guys are a laugh a fucking minute."

He left the cadets standing at attention and walked to the

third floor and the Company D orderly room. A crowd of cadets in gym gear snapped to attention as he opened the fire door and stepped into the hallway.

The Charge of Quarters, the only cadet in class uniform, saluted.

"Sir, Cadet Schwimm reports," he said.

Breitland was a little surprised to find so many cadets—there must have been fifteen or twenty, hanging around the CQ desk. Ordinarily, since there was no academic work to be done, the underclassmen would have been out running or playing ball at the gym, or anywhere other than where they had the chance to run into the OC.

"At ease. I understand you sent a cadet to the hospital," Breitland said after returning the salute.

"Yes, sir," Schwimm said.

"Is the CO around?"

"He's at the hospital with Cadet Trainor, the one with the smashed hand."

"How'd his hand get smashed?" Breitland asked.

None of the cadets had left, Breitland noticed. In fact, it seemed that a few of them had moved a bit closer.

"It got smashed in the door downstairs," Schwimm answered.

"Bad?"

"Pretty badly, sir," one of the cadets in gym uniform added.

Breitland turned, thought he recognized this cadet; maybe the kid was on a varsity team.

"Did one of you knuckleheads close the door on him? You got it in for Cadet Trainor?" Breitland joked. "Maybe a power play?"

A couple of the cadets smiled. A few, including Schwimm, did not.

"Major Gates closed the door on his hand, sir," Schwimm said.

"Oh," Breitland said. "Is that what you're doing over here in D Company instead of handing out demerits?" Breitland laughed at his own joke.

This time not a single cadet joined in the humor, and Breitland thought that maybe the kid's injury was pretty bad and he ought to lay off the levity.

There was a disconcerting silence in the hallway. Breitland looked at the cadets around him. Some of them looked away, a few smiled—embarrassed little grins as if they were all in on some big joke. They seemed to be hanging around waiting for something to happen, waiting for someone to speak first.

"Schwimm, is there something I should know?" Breitland asked.

Schwimm's mouth opened in a not-too-shabby imitation of a carp out of water. Before any sound came out, another cadet spoke up.

"Sir, I'm Cadet Carey, the First Sergeant."

Breitland turned to face a cadet about his size, a handsome black kid with an air about him that said, "I'm in charge." Breitland noticed the other cadets parting to give this one some space.

"You know what happened downstairs?" Breitland asked.

"Sir, I've had a chance to talk to some of the cadets who live on this side of the building," Carey said, indicating the side that overlooked MacArthur's statue. The hallway, already quiet, grew quieter still, as if the cadets were holding their collective breath.

"Maybe we should talk in here, sir," Carey said, indicating his room.

"Hello, Wayne," Kathleen Gates said.

Holder was sitting on one of the vinyl couches in the tiny waiting area just off the Emergency Room lobby, feet up, staring at Weather Channel graphics and wondering if Alex's injuries might be severe enough to keep him from getting commissioned. He didn't see Kathleen Gates come in.

"Hello, ma'am," he said, standing, looking for her husband.

Kathleen took his hand, held it in her own while she spoke.

"I'm sorry about what happened," she said. "Tom is very upset about the accident."

Her hand was warm and dry; Holder could smell her perfume, very faint, or maybe it was only shampoo. He was conscious of how she leaned forward when she spoke to him, held her eyes wide, almost as if she were waiting for him to agree.

"Is Major Gates here, too?" Holder asked.

"He'll be along in a minute; he's parking the car," she said. "Have you spoken to Alex?"

"No, ma'am. . . ."

"Please call me Kathleen," she interrupted. "Ma'am makes me feel so old."

Holder only nodded. He couldn't imagine himself calling this woman by her first name; she was married to The Time Bomb.

"They still have him in there; two doctors are poking at him. The nurse told me they're thinking of sending him down to Walter Reed."

"Oh, my," Kathleen said. "It must be a pretty serious injury."

Holder shifted his weight uncomfortably from one foot to the other. Kathleen took his elbow and steered him onto one of the couches. She had on a long sundress; when they sat, the folds of the dress—all cool cotton—touched his leg. Holder felt as if all the nerve endings on that side of his body were sounding an alarm. He watched the double doors for her husband.

"Tell me what happened down at the barracks," she said.

Holder had met Kathleen Gates for the first time only two weeks earlier when the Gates hosted a barbecue for the new seniors at one of the picnic sites by the football stadium. Holder and his classmates had noted what a pretty woman Kathleen Gates was, although to them—only a few of them over twenty-one—she seemed ancient at thirty-two. Up close, he could see tiny laugh lines at the corners of her mouth, little tracks by her eyes when she smiled. Her lips were thin, but deeply colored next to her pale Irish complexion. Her scoop-neck sundress showed no cleavage, Holder noted, but did show a spray of tiny, pale freckles across her chest.

She was smiling at him now, but her gaze didn't waver. She wanted an explanation, and she was clearly used to getting what she wanted.

Holder looked around again. *Gates must be parking the car in Queens,* he thought. *Either that, or she told him to stay out in the car for a few minutes while . . .* he had a sudden flash that Kathleen Gates was here for damage control.

"Didn't Major Gates . . . uh . . . didn't Major Gates tell you what happened?" Holder managed. He needed time to figure out what to say to her. He never assumed for a moment that he would tell her everything. But he was cognizant, as were all cadets, that he must never lie. The cadet Honor Code—which stated simply that a cadet will not lie, cheat, or steal or tolerate those who do—made that decision clear-cut. He wondered if Kathleen Gates would use this against him, push him into a corner knowing that he wouldn't lie to cover up his version of the story.

"Tom told me that you two were at the door to the barracks and that Alex was coming out just when Tom pushed the door shut."

He left out the part about shoving me, Holder thought.

"Yes, ma'am, that's pretty much what happened," Holder said. His mouth tasted like ash.

"Kathleen." She smiled, waiting for him to respond.

"Kathleen," Holder obliged.

He had been in the waiting room brainstorming how his showdown with Gates would go: a big, messy fight right in the emergency room; some minor intrigue, maybe some threats about how miserable Gates could make Holder's senior year, with a Faustian bargain in the works. But this— the soft, subtle approach from another quarter—this was something else.

And three hours ago your biggest problem was learning saber manual without stabbing yourself in the foot, he thought.

"What I didn't understand," Kathleen Gates said as she smoothed the pleats of her dress, "was why Tom was closing the door if you were going in."

"I guess he didn't want me going into the barracks," Holder said, catching himself just before he called her "ma'am" again.

"Was Tom upset about something?" she asked.

She knows the whole story, Holder thought. He felt

trapped, and he suddenly realized that he'd rather deal with Major Gates. At least with the direct, head-down, take-no-prisoners approach Gates favored, Holder knew there was a war on.

Holder saw Gates hurry through the big glass doors. The cadet stood, taking a step away from Kathleen Gates. He looked down at her on the couch, noticed again the tiny lines beside her eyes, even though she wasn't smiling now. He said, "I'm not sure. You'll have to ask Major Gates how he was feeling at the time."

The Superintendent's quarters, a handsome center-hall brick classic that is one of the oldest buildings on West Point, sits just across an expanse of lawn and garden from MacArthur Barracks. Lieutenant General Patrick Flynn happened to be standing at the side door of his living quarters, in the rear portion of the house that was mostly a museum, when the ambulance took Cadet Trainor to Keller Hospital. He went to his study and phoned Central Guard Room.

"This is General Flynn," he said to the surprised cadet who answered the phone. "Did someone just get taken to the hospital in an ambulance?"

"Er . . . uh, yessir," the cadet said.

"Anything serious?" Flynn asked. He tried to imagine the cadets in the guard room, sitting around after calling for an ambulance, not sure yet as to what happened, when the highest ranking officer on post calls and demands to know the story.

They must think I know everything that goes on.

"I'm not sure, sir. I mean, we haven't heard the details. The OC went over to check, though. Shall I have him call you when he returns?"

"As long as it's before twenty-two hundred," Flynn said. "If it's serious, he can call me later than that."

The cadet had recovered somewhat and seemed a bit sharper. "Will do, sir."

Lieutenant General Patrick Flynn was not an impatient man. When he saw the ambulance pull away on the road between MacArthur Barracks and his quarters with its lights on but siren off, he figured it must not be too great an emergency. But he was at home, a little bored and used to having people do what he told them to do.

It was nearly a half-hour before his phone rang.

"Flynn here."

"Sir, this is Captain Breitland calling from Central Guard Room. I'm the Officer in Charge today, and the cadets here told me you wanted a report on the cadet who was taken from MacArthur Barracks in the ambulance a little while ago."

"Thirty minutes ago," Flynn said.

"Yes, sir," Breitland said. "The cadet's name is Trainor. He had his hand smashed in the door at the entrance to the barracks."

"Is it serious?"

"Pretty serious," Breitland said, "yes, sir. I talked to one of the doctors at Keller; they're thinking of sending him down to Walter Reed. He might need surgery on his hand and I guess there are some people there who have a lot more experience."

Flynn was in his second-floor study, looking out the window at the expansive walled garden below; the glass reflected his image. He was fifty-one years old, five seven, deep-chested, with a rich voice and martial carriage that telegraphed his role: he was a man used to giving orders. He kept his thick gray hair cropped close. In private, he wore reading glasses. In public, he still exuded the physicality that, when he was a collegiate wrestler, had earned him the nickname "Bulldog."

Flynn was only in his second month as Superintendent, or Supe, as he was called by everyone who wasn't speaking directly to him. He'd had numerous tours of academic departments and staff sections, but it was unlikely that he'd met even one quarter of the active duty personnel at West Point. He couldn't place Breitland's name or voice with a face.

"How did it happen?" Flynn asked.

"Well, sir," Breitland said, "I haven't had a chance to talk to the injured cadet or the second cadet and the officer who were there. But I have talked to a few cadets who were in the barracks adjacent to MacArthur's statue."

"And?"

"I wonder if I could speak with you in person, sir," Breitland said.

Flynn was behind his enormous desk early the next morning, his chair turned backward so that he could look out over the Hudson River from his office window high up in the stone tower of Taylor Hall.

Lieutenant General Patrick Flynn, the first Superintendent in West Point's nearly two hundred year history who was not a graduate of the Military Academy, had been appointed to appease critics who claimed that West Point was a closed, elitist society. Such complaints were nothing new; in fact, the criticism had been a part of the Academy's history since the first handful of graduates joined their regiments in the early nineteenth century. The novelty that had led to Flynn's appointment was something called the Bruckner Commission, a Congressional study group with a mandate to cut a wide swath in government—particularly Pentagon—spending. West Point was a fat target, especially if critics succeeded in defining it as a training ground for elitists.

The Chief of Staff of the Army, Flynn's boss, believed that installing a Superintendent who was not a West Point graduate was the clearest signal he could send Congress about the Army's concerns: we are about our mission, Flynn's appointment indicated, not the preservation of the status quo. And since this assignment was traditionally followed by retirement, Superintendents could make decisions based on what was best for West Point and the Army, without having to consider the next job or promotion.

Patrick Flynn, with none of the political flamboyance that marked so many of his ambitious peers, was a perfect fit for the job. Over the course of a nearly thirty year career, he had earned a reputation for scrupulous honesty. Once given his marching orders, he was single-minded and determined and could be ruthlessly efficient. Flynn's father had once said his son had gotten only "an Englishman's share" of the romanticism and sentimentality of his sprawling Irish-American family. Flynn supposed that was true: he loved the soldiers he'd commanded and, on most days, he could say that he loved the life he'd chosen. But he also knew his shortcomings; there were parts of his makeup that fell short of altruism. When he found selflessness in others, he was pleasantly surprised, but he did not expect it.

He had been known, on St. Patrick's Day, to sing a few drinking songs. He loved his God, feared and respected his church, honored his parents. But he had also read Machiavelli, and he had seen that combat brings out the very best and the very worst in the human condition.

Flynn swiveled his chair around at the sound of approaching footsteps. The Commandant of Cadets, a brigadier general responsible for the military side of cadet life, came through the outer office. Since Saturday wasn't a regular duty day, both men were dressed casually: Flynn in khaki pants and a golf shirt; the Commandant, Anthony Moro, in stone colored shorts and an open collared shirt.

"Morning, sir," Moro said.

"Come in, Tony, have a seat," Flynn said, gesturing to one of the leather couches. He came from behind his desk and took the chair next to Moro.

"You talk to the OC this morning?"

"Last night, sir. I guess Captain Breitland didn't want to wait."

Although he'd left New York City over thirty years earlier to start his life as a West Point plebe, Moro still carried, without apology, the thick accent of his native Brooklyn. The cadet humor magazine regularly featured a character named "Gangsta," who favored white ties, black shirts, chalk-striped suits, and a wise-guy movie patois. Moro had one of his favorite cartoons framed in his office.

"Gates?"

"I just finished talking to him, sir, over at my office. The cadet, too," Moro said.

"And what's their story?"

"That there was a little misunderstanding about a spirit run. Seems that Major Gates called the company and invited the firsties on a run. . . ."

"On a Friday afternoon?" Flynn asked.

"Gates can be a little enthusiastic sometimes, sir," Moro said. "Anyway, Gates expected to see a crowd when he got there, and there were just two cadets, this kid Holder, who's the cadet company commander, and his executive officer, Trainor, the one whose hand got smashed.

"Anyway," Moro continued breezily, "Gates thought he'd told them to roll everyone out of the barracks. The cadets thought it was voluntary. So Trainor goes back inside to get some other cadets, some of the underclass. Gates and Holder start walking back to the sally port and the door, and Gates is explaining how Holder misunderstood him—the run wasn't voluntary. Gates said he wanted to emphasize his point by slamming the door. Trainor was coming out just then and had his hand in the door. Wrong place at the wrong time."

It was, Moro knew, a simplistic explanation, but it served his purpose. Order and discipline within the Corps of Cadets were his concern, his professional responsibility; he didn't want Flynn taking that from him just because a few people had gotten out of line.

"What about all these stories the cadets told Breitland? That Gates had been drinking?"

"Well, sir, Breitland got his stories second and third hand through the cadet first sergeant. All the cadets in the barracks knew for sure was that Gates and Holder got into it pretty heavy. Not one of them was close enough to Gates to say he'd been drinking."

"Except Holder," Flynn said.

"Except Holder," Moro agreed.

"And what did Cadet Holder say?"

"Holder said Gates smelled like he'd been drinking and that he seemed a little agitated. Holder told me he didn't think it was a good idea for the underclass cadets to see their Tac like that, or to even suspect that he might show up at the barracks in that condition. He said he suggested that just he and Gates go on a run."

"What did Gates say about this drinking business?"

"I sent Holder out of the room and asked Gates if he'd been drinking. He said he might have had a couple of beers during the course of the afternoon but that he wasn't impaired and certainly was not drunk."

"You believe him?" Flynn asked.

"I believe that neither Major Gates nor Cadet Holder would lie to me, sir," Moro said.

Flynn noted the slightly defensive tone and the fact that Moro hadn't exactly answered the question.

"I think we're talking here about degree," Moro continued.

Flynn studied the Commandant. He and Moro had never worked together before; their paths simply had not crossed. Moro had a reputation as a slogger—not flashy, not brilliant, but reliable, dependable.

"If you want a job done in some new way," one of Flynn's peers had told him, "don't give it to Tony Moro. But if you want a tough job done the same way it's always been done, he's your man."

"That only works up to a point," Flynn said. "Gates shouldn't have gone down to the barracks, for what was essentially something in the line of duty, after he'd had even one beer. He was wrong. Period."

"Right, sir," Moro said.

"OK. What happened next?"

"Breitland said that one of the cadets who lives right above the sally port reported that Gates was loud. This wasn't a calm exchange. It sounded to this cadet like Holder was getting an ass-chewing and he walked away."

Flynn paused, leaned forward.

"You're telling me that a cadet walked away while the officer was dressing him down for something?"

The picture was a little hard for Flynn to imagine. From their first day at the Academy, cadets' lives were suffused with discipline. Six weeks earlier Flynn had watched some new cadets learning the only four responses they were allowed during basic training: "Yes, sir"; "No, sir"; "No excuse, sir"; and "Sir, I do not understand." Although not a West Pointer himself, Flynn had known hundreds during his career. Not once did he remember any of them reporting that as cadets they said things like, "Sir, I'm afraid I just don't agree" or "Ma'am, I'm just not comfortable with that."

"Yes, sir," Moro continued. "At least, that's the story Breitland got from the first sergeant, kid by the name of Carey."

"One cadet saw this?"

"No. Two or three cadets told Carey about the same thing."

Flynn sat back in his chair, the leather creaking under him.

"Is this Holder kid a moron?"

"No, sir. He seems intelligent, if a little laid back for a company commander."

"So if he's not stupid then he must have believed he was right."

"Exactly, sir," Moro said. "Which is why I'm inclined to let Holder off with just this morning's counseling session. The problem with Gates is there's no way to determine, at this point, if he was drunk. No blood alcohol test; no other witnesses."

Flynn paused, looked out the window again. "But Gates had been drinking. He lost his temper and slammed some cadet's hand in the door."

"I don't believe he was a raging lunatic, sir," Moro said. "He was upset with Holder."

"If he'd been completely calm, would this other kid have landed in the hospital?"

"It's still a possibility," Moro said.

"I'm not so sure," Flynn said. But it was the Commandant's problem, and he wanted Moro to handle it.

"You think maybe there was more to it and Gates told Holder to keep his mouth shut?" Flynn asked. "I mean, Holder has to live with this guy for a year, right?"

Moro wrinkled his dark eyebrows.

"I suppose that's possible, sir. But I don't think that's the case. As I said, Gates is a little too enthusiastic sometimes, but that's about the extent of it."

"Does he have a drinking problem?"

Moro shifted his weight almost imperceptibly. The selection process for Tactical Officers was rather involved. Every candidate met the Commandant.

Do you think I'd hire a drunk for this job? Moro thought. He shook his head.

"How are you going to handle this?" Flynn asked.

"I told the cadet that he has an obligation to follow legal orders. He doesn't have to *like* the orders. And while it was admirable for him to want to protect Major Gates's reputation—not saying that Gates needed protecting—Major Gates was a big boy and certainly understood the consequences of his actions. I told Holder he should defer to the judgment of his superiors."

"What about Gates?"

"I told him he should have stayed away from the barracks if he'd had even one beer; that in his position, the appearance of impropriety is as dangerous, sometimes, as improper behavior."

"Anything else?"

"Based on his admission that he had at least one beer, I'll most likely give Gates a letter of reprimand, sir. He exercised very poor judgment."

"A career-ending move," Flynn commented, standing and walking to the big window casement. Reaching the window, he turned to face the commandant. "Are you going to relieve him of his duties?"

"Not unless he proves ineffectual," Moro said. "The other thing is I'd rather keep this quiet with the Bruckner Commission due here soon."

"So because the Bruckner Commission is breathing down our necks you want to handle this differently?"

"I want to proceed cautiously," Moro said.

The Superintendent moved to his chair behind the big desk and sat down. The massive piece was as big as a judge's bench, and that was the effect, Moro thought, Flynn was looking for.

"Lamar Bruckner is on the lookout for anything he can use to get his name in the press," Moro continued. "The hearings he's promised in the media are nothing more than sound bytes in his reelection campaign."

Lamar Bruckner, a flamboyant, publicity-hungry Senator from Texas and head of the investigating commission that bore his name, was sometimes referred to as the "new Joe McCarthy" for the zeal with which he went after what he termed the "enemies of the taxpayers."

"We have critics in Congress who would love to close this place," Moro continued. "Some of them think that we don't need West Point, or any of the academies, anymore. Others complain that we turn out elitist toy soldiers. Others—and I think this is where Bruckner fits in—just want a little free press. Attacking West Point provides that. I don't think Lamar Bruckner cares about West Point one way or the other, but he's carved out this role for himself as the taxpayers' champion, and we're a target of opportunity.

"Bruckner doesn't care about issues, doesn't deal with studies. I doubt if he cares about what we accomplish. He cares about Lamar Bruckner and he deals with hype. The messier the better, because that's what'll get his face on the news."

Flynn understood Moro's position. It was the same with most of the staff and faculty. Just as war was a multifaceted art: logistics, intelligence, operations, strategy, deceit, ruse, smoke—so, too, was surviving in a republic with limited funds and an endemic mistrust of the standing military. The problems began when the political maneuverings over-shadowed everything else.

"West Point is here to serve the Army by training these cadets, Tony," Flynn said. "The Army doesn't exist to support West Point. Nor should we become so enamored of our jobs here that we think that self-preservation is our main concern."

"So if you thought that closing West Point was in the best interest of the Army, that's what we'd do."

"Yes," Flynn said without hesitation. "But I don't think that's the case. The hard part of our job is to make the country see what West Point contributes. I mean, it would be easy if we could just say, 'Give us the money.' But no organization—especially the military—can do that any-more.

"If we do our job and do it well, all the rest will take care of itself."

Flynn had made his point as succinctly as he could, and he watched Moro for some reaction. He knew what his critics were saying: the new Superintendent was merely the lead spear carrier for the enemy at the gates.

"Now I know that the folks on the Academic Board think I was sent here to open the gates for the pinko left-wingers who want to see this place turned into a real estate development," Flynn joked.

The academic board, consisting of the heads of the

various departments as well as the Dean and the Commandant, was the seat of power at West Point. Even the Superintendent, who had ultimate authority, couldn't afford to cross
swords too often with the board.

"The Trojan Horse," Moro said.

"What's that?"

"Someone has been passing around a little drawing of the
Trojan Horse," Moro said. "You see it everywhere: bulletin
boards, in offices, on e-mail, in the barracks. There's no
commentary with it, but I suspect it has something to do
with your appointment."

"Well, if I were worried about people liking me, I'd have
gone into some other line of work," Flynn said.

Flynn watched Moro, whose expression was tough to
read. Interested. Unconvinced, maybe.

"We can't let ourselves be distracted by this Bruckner
Commission," Flynn said. "This isn't about damage control
or keeping a lid on a scandal. This is about doing the right
thing."

"Bruckner will think it's about scandal, sir," Moro said.
"And he'll try to make it look like this mess—or any
mess—is representative of the academy. He's no better than
a tabloid journalist. It's all well and good to keep our eyes
on the big prize, but we can't fail to notice that the other
side is fighting dirty."

"There's a lot to think about," Flynn said. "We're talking
about a man's career, for one thing. Whatever we choose to
do also sends a message to four thousand cadets and the rest
of the Army. Think about those things when you decide
what to do with Gates and Holder."

"I'll keep you posted, sir," Moro said.

"Good," Flynn said, standing to end the meeting. Moro
rose, and the two men shook hands. As Moro made his way
through the big outer office and down the stone stairway,
Flynn wondered how the younger general would react to his
stance.

Flynn believed the Commandant was not like the other
senior people on post. The Dean and the professors who
headed the academic departments—and thus made up the
powerful academic board—were in place until retirement.
Some department heads had spent more than half of their

thirty five years in uniform right at West Point. Though this was good for institutional memory and consistency, it did not do much to bring fresh points of view on board. It would be easy for such men to assume that their most important task was not training cadets but protecting West Point. Moro was still an up-and-comer, determined to make his second star and to command one of the Army's combat divisions. His ambition would influence his choices, but he was also concerned about the Army beyond the academy walls, the field Army to which the young brigadier would soon return. Today's cadets would be the lieutenants Moro would later command. The Commandant, Flynn hoped, had enough imagination to see through the wide-angle lens.

The Superintendent sat on the ledge of the big window, looking south down the river valley. There were a half-dozen small sailboats skating circles on water that looked like hammered steel. Out in the channel, a tug pushed a set of four barges toward Manhattan.

When he first talked to the Chief of Staff about this job, Flynn's mission was clear: he was to pilot the Academy as it planned to meet the nation's needs in the twenty-first century. What the nation's needs were was a little less clear.

"Whatever else you want to say about the Cold War," Flynn had once heard a colleague remark, "it gave us focus."

When he'd first learned of the Bruckner Commission, Flynn had anticipated that it would prove a distraction. Now the commission's work seemed to embody all of the uncertainty facing West Point and the nation; it overshadowed everything else. At West Point, the threat of massive redesign—or even the closing of the Academy—was all anyone talked about. It was as if the fabric were unraveling in many places; Flynn first had to bring cohesion back to West Point before he could lead it anywhere.

Flynn turned off the overhead lights. Just before leaving, he studied the portraits of his predecessors, which lined the walls. Each of them had faced their own special challenge, and each had found some solution that had, at least, allowed West Point to continue its mission.

Flynn hoped someone would be able to say the same about him someday.

He walked downstairs and into the small courtyard, out through the archway with its medieval portcullis. The air was clear, cooler than it had been in a while. He passed some tourists, readily identifiable by their white socks, sneakers, cameras on straps, maps from the visitors' center. Some cadets walked by, recognizing him and snapping energetic salutes. They were in a happy limbo: summer training was over, and the pressures of the academic year had not yet settled upon them. For this weekend, at least, all looked peaceful. Flynn knew another story.

The Academy was at odds with itself. In every office, every barracks room, every classroom and set of quarters the debate raged: What is West Point? What should it be? The staff and faculty, the family members, cadets and civilian employees were all concerned about their individual careers and about the fate of the institution in which they had invested so much. These fears played out in conflicts between people who were ostensibly on the same side: between colleagues, between friends, between subordinates and superiors, between husbands and wives. The splintering and divisiveness rolled across West Point like a smoky civil war. And always, just beyond the gates of this once impregnable fortress—the enemy gathered in his camp.

Brigadier General Tony Moro left Taylor Hall, crossed Thayer Road, and made his way behind Bradley Barracks to the access road that ran behind Washington Hall. Most of the building was taken up by the cadet mess: six wings, three stories tall, with soaring cathedral windows. Three floors of classrooms, auditoriums, and offices were piled above that space. Moro passed a dozen or so cadets on his way to the back entrance; he took the elevator to the fifth floor, threaded his way through the classroom areas occupied by the language departments to his office at the front of Washington Hall.

The Commandant's office was huge: a sitting area big enough for two couches and an overstuffed chair manned the corner by the fireplace. Resting like twin sentinels on the mantle were two bronze studies of Eisenhower by the sculptor who executed the larger-than-life statue that gazed out over the parade field. Under one of the five big windows—more arches and leaded glass—a wooden conference table sat ringed by ornately carved, straight-backed chairs. The general's desk, crammed in a corner as if an afterthought, was awash in paper.

Below his windows were the broad stone steps of the front entrance to the mess and the wide concrete expanse called the apron. During the twice daily formations, one half of the Corps of Cadets filled that space, drawn up in gray ranks. On his first visit to the office, Moro had joked with his chief of staff that all he needed was a little balcony to feel "like the Pope on Easter Sunday."

Just beyond the apron, a huge bronze Washington gazed from horseback over the Plain and its rim of stately elms and oaks and, always, the dramatic backdrop of mountains across the river.

Moro dropped his keys on the desk and picked up the telephone. He went to his personal directory for the private, unpublished number of the Dean's quarters.

"General Simon."

"It's me," Moro said.

"Just a second."

Simon's quarters were only a few hundred yards from where the Commandant sat; Moro could hear Simon close a door for privacy. When he picked up the phone again, Simon asked, "What happened?"

"He all but told me to give this Gates a letter of reprimand," Moro said.

"And then he goes running to the Bruckner Commission and it's all over the news that we have drunken officers fighting with cadets," Simon said. "Wouldn't Bruckner love that sound byte."

"We'd be putting the whole Academy at risk," Moro said. "But Flynn doesn't seem to think it matters. He says we should just do our jobs as if nothing is happening and the rest will take care of itself."

"That's just great," Simon complained. "He wants to put his head in the sand."

"I told him about the Trojan Horse cartoons," Moro said.

"What did he say to that?"

"He made light of it, you know. Big joke."

"That's because he knows it's true," Simon said. "He was

either sent here to help the Bruckner Commission dismantle the place, or he was sent here to make it easier for them just because he's so incompetent that he couldn't possibly get in their way."

Moro waited while Simon thought about what would come next. Although the two men wore the same rank, Simon was senior to Moro. Simon had been a major and an instructor in the history department when Moro was a cadet. The Commandant deferred to the Dean.

"What are you going to do with this Tac . . . what's his name?"

"Gates," Moro said. "I bought some time. Maybe we can just keep it quiet."

"We can't afford to do nothing, in case Bruckner's flunkies find out," Simon said. "You could tell him that you're preparing a letter and just leave him hanging."

"Right," Moro answered. "Until we figure out what to do with him."

"With him and Flynn," Simon said. "It's a risk, but it's one we might have to take to get Flynn removed."

Moro was silent. He looked out across the parade field to Trophy Point, its impossibly tall flagpole, the crisp red and blue of the flag.

This is how it sounds, Moro thought. *We won't use the word mutiny, of course. . . .*

"Are you there, Tony?"

"I'm here," Moro said. He had wanted to help Simon; he had thought Simon the best man—more so than Flynn—to help West Point through this tough time. But he had not anticipated that it might be at the cost of loyalty.

"We can't fight this battle with Flynn in the way," Simon said.

"I . . . uh . . . I'm not sure how far we should go," Moro said. "There's a lot at stake here."

"Yes, there is. That means we have to dare great things," Simon said. "Unless you want to be known as the last Commandant of the U.S. Military Academy."

When Moro didn't respond, Simon said, "Don't worry about it. Sleep on it and we'll talk later."

When the two generals were off the phone, Simon went

back to his study with its killer view of the Hudson. He was reading Freeman's *Lee's Lieutenants.*

"Somebody has to be sure, Tony," he said to himself. "Somebody has to decide what to do."

He opened the book and very soon was back riding with a long-dead Army in the wet woods of Virginia.

CHAPTER 2

Tom Gates felt exposed, almost naked, as he made his way along the narrow gravel path in front of the reviewing stands beside the Plain. It was the same feeling he had driving across the flat of the Kuwaiti desert, wondering if some Iraqi tanker had him in his sights, wondering when the incoming would start, knowing that he might be shot at any time.

He wished that he were imagining the attention he was getting; he wished his paranoia was merely the result of a guilty conscience. But the fact was his peers and even the cadets around him knew what had happened in the sally port; it was as if everyone around him could actually see the sword that hung over his head. There were—he was sure of it—sensational stories flying from company to company, office to office, all at his expense. He wondered what they'd made up about him: that he and Holder had come to blows, that he was stinking drunk. The fact was that the truth was bad enough.

At least if I get relieved I won't be around to listen to all the crap, he thought. He wasn't consoled.

"Hey, Tom," one of the other Tacs had said to him as the two men climbed to the high tiers of aluminum seats to watch their companies perform in this first parade of the academic year.

"Some of my cadets said that you and your company commander got into a pissing contest on Friday night."

Gates figured the cadets were also saying he deliberately slammed the door on Trainor's hand. He didn't want to answer the follow-up questions, so he didn't answer the first.

Gates found a seat next to one of the other new Tacs, a quiet captain named Curry who had the good sense to keep her mouth shut.

"Joanna," Gates said in greeting.

"Tom," Curry said back. Nothing else. No questions, no funny looks. Gates sat down and waited in silence for the parade to begin.

Kathleen had shut him down, saying no more than a dozen words to him after leaving the hospital on Friday night. He knew from experience that this was as much to punish him as it was to give her time to plan their next move. She would sit down with him, maybe after dinner this evening, and tell him what he should do to protect himself, to cover his tracks, to minimize the damage he'd done to his career. Her motivation was her love for this man, with all his imperfections. But when it came time for action, she could be as coldly calculating as her husband could be bullheaded.

She'd sneak up on him, dropping a casual comment during dinner that perhaps, if he felt like it, they could talk about what had happened. Tom Gates thought her indirect approach a result of her being unsure, of her looking for his agreement, some consensus as to what they should do. He did not understand his wife as well as she understood him. She knew that anything else—a direct approach: do this or you're on your own—wouldn't work. Tom Gates liked to think he was in charge, or at least an equal partner in the couple's decisions about what was, in effect, their joint career.

Kathleen Gates knew it was a joint venture too. Tom Gates was in charge of screwing up, she was in charge of bailing him out.

"I guess you heard about what happened last night," Gates finally said to Curry.

She nodded.

"I suspect it's one of those stories that has several different versions," she said, smiling.

Gates relaxed a bit. She wasn't patronizing him, he saw, and he'd brought it up because he felt like he might burst if he didn't talk to someone.

"Each one better than the last, I imagine," he answered, trying a smile himself.

He turned to face Curry. The two officers had arrived at West Point just this summer and had gone through much of their orientation together. Gates, whose experience with women officers was limited, had spoken to her on several occasions and had been surprised to find that she was as much the professional soldier as any of his male colleagues. He felt as if he'd discovered something new, but he thought it best to keep his surprise to himself.

Curry was a few years junior to Gates, with a stocky build that reminded him of the best field hockey players in his high school. She was not pretty: her black hair was short and thin, her face broad. Her teeth seemed too big for her mouth and she went around, most of the time, with a very serious expression. But when she smiled, Gates noticed, there was a bit of mischief there.

"When I was at Fort Hood, a couple of my women friends and I used to make a joke out of collecting all the outrageous stories about us that circulated around post," she said, turning to face him. "For a while my husband was calling us the 'Lesbian Surfer Nazis.' One of the women threatened to get tee shirts made with that logo."

Gates smiled at the story when Curry did, even as he thought of all the times he'd spread stories about women in uniform.

Apparently Curry, now watching the parade field, was not going to ask him what had happened last night. Gates had started the conversation thinking he wanted to tell someone his version, now he wanted nothing more than to joke about it without having to explain himself. He wanted to let it go for a few hours.

Below where he sat, Gates could see some senior cadets

with clipboards who were prepared to grade the performance of the cadet companies. Gates was glad he didn't have to do anything other than watch. As the band marched to its position on the far right of the line, stepping to the sound of a solitary stick on the rim of a drum, Tom Gates let himself be mesmerized by the ceremony, the surety and comfort of ritual.

Wayne Holder stood in the shade of the sally port, holding his saber just below the hilt, point down, while another cadet wrapped a thick rubber band around the slick handle.

"This will help you hang on," Chris Dearborn said as he worked. "Did you wet your gloves like I told you?"

"Yeah," Holder said, flexing his fingers and stretching the white glove on his right hand. All the cadets wore the gloves, which looked good from the stands but had a tendency to stain quickly—orange from the leather slings, black from the rifle oil, or, in the case of the seniors, a dingy gray from years of use. Holder had bought several slippery new pair; he hoped he wouldn't drop his saber.

Dearborn, a junior and the company guidon bearer, held that flag against his body while he worked. He and Holder would march—Dearborn a step behind and to the left—in front of the solid square of the company formation. Dearborn would use the flag to relay Holder's voice commands. In the days of smoky battlefields, when ranks of soldiers faced each other at short range and hammered away with inaccurate rifles, the guidon—literally, "guide on"—was a marker on which the soldier depended for instructions: stand here, face this way, prepare to fire, advance, retreat.

Holder noticed that Dearborn stuck his tongue out of his mouth, wrapping it across his upper lip, while he worked.

"You remember what to do if you see the flash of sunlight on metal out there in the stands, right?" Dearborn asked without taking his eyes off the task at hand.

Holder, distracted by his roommate's medical evacuation and already nervous about his debut on the parade field, didn't remember this from drill; the thought that he'd forgotten something added to his mild—but growing—sense of panic.

"What? I don't remember anything . . ."

"That just means," Dearborn interrupted, "that Gates is up there with a sniper rifle. You see that flash, or even the muzzle blast . . ."

"I hit the ground?"

"Negative," Dearborn said, shaking his head. "I hit the ground, you cover me with your body."

"Thanks, man."

Dearborn, tall and thin, always gave the impression that he was slumped forward a little bit. Even in the dress gray uniform the cadets wore in the winter—nicknamed the iron lung for the way it yanked back the shoulders—Dearborn looked more like a descendant of Ichabod Crane than of MacArthur and Patton. His blond, almost white hair was as unruly as straw. His face was narrow, pinched, and marked at the jawline and beside his eyes with scars from the acne that raged there during the long stress test that was plebe year.

More than a few of Holder's classmates didn't think much of Dearborn.

"If you look up geek-a-zoid in the dictionary," one of them had commented, "his picture is there."

Dearborn parried the unkindness with a sharp wit; his physical awkwardness was matched by an intellectual agility that allowed him to run circles around most of his tormentors. He had a gift for antagonizing people.

"I hope I don't drop this thing," Holder said again. His lack of skill on the drill field was legendary. As a plebe, he had once knocked off his own hat—the tall, black "tar-bucket" the cadets wore in the fall and spring—right in front of the reviewing stand. His squad leader had made him jog out onto the Plain, his rifle held diagonally across his chest at high port arms, immediately after the last company had cleared the field. Some Boy Scouts grouped in the stands that day had applauded him.

"Don't worry about it," Dearborn said. "Concentrate on giving the commands. Not many people will notice if you drop your saber, but everyone will catch on if you march the company into the stands by mistake."

"Full of encouragement," Holder said.

"As always, my liege," Dearborn answered, bowing from the waist.

The company in front of them stirred. Holder could hear the band out on the Plain. He checked his watch, which he wore with the face turned on his wrist—an affectation he'd picked up that summer hanging around real soldiers at Fort Benning. He took his place centered on the front rank, facing the underclass cadets, his back to the bright hole of the sally port that led to the parade field.

"Company . . . atten—*shun!*"

The hundred-plus cadets in front of him came to attention, weapons at order arms, the rifles' butt plates scraping concrete. The sally port, which magnified all sounds like a tunnel, became quiet. In the front rank, Rebecca Hollings, a junior and one of the squad leaders, winked at him and mouthed, *You'll be fine.*

Holder smiled in thanks and turned to the front, ready to march out onto the Plain. He had marched in dozens of parades here, only tolerating them. Now he wished he'd paid a little more attention to how the company commanders had done things out there on the wide arena of the parade ground. Alone in front of the formation, he felt like a soloist who wasn't quite ready to perform.

Don't think about it too much, he told himself. In less than a year, he and his classmates would leave this field for the last time, marching out into the June sunshine for their own graduation parade.

"Wayne . . . *Wayne!*"

It was Dearborn, interrupting his reverie.

"What?" Holder said, looking over his shoulder.

"Turn around."

Holder put his right toe just behind his left heel and executed a sharp about face. *Not bad,* he congratulated himself.

When he turned around, most of the thirty or forty cadets whose faces he could see among the front ranks were smiling broadly at him. He'd forgotten to have them shoulder their weapons.

"We could march like this," one of the squad leaders in the front rank said, lifting his weapon a couple of inches off the ground. "It'd be a first, but hey, we'd be trendsetters."

"Right shoulder . . . *arms!*" Holder commanded.

The rifles came up almost as one.

"Looks a little ragged there, D Company," Holder said. "Let's try to keep up with the high standards I've set so far, OK?"

Holder turned around, somewhat comforted by the laughter behind him.

Just let me hold it together for thirty minutes, he prayed. He looked out onto the parade ground, framed for him by the stone arch. This was another in the long series of tests West Point had thrown at him. He did not enjoy the challenges, even those at which he excelled. He didn't hate the many hurdles that made up his cadet experience, but he didn't love them either.

He had once heard Trainor describe the time at West Point as a love-hate relationship. The intense experiences could cause either reaction—both on many days—but almost always there was some emotion. Holder did not feel that way. He kept things in check, he did not invest himself fully. He liked to think that the distance he kept made him a little more mature, but he'd never told anyone that. Easier to play the beach boy. Sometimes he felt like an impostor; not caring about consequences was not the same thing as having the confidence in a decision, not the same thing as courage.

He had a feeling that before this incident with Gates was behind him, he was going to be tested. He hoped Trainor—who'd been taken to Walter Reed, the big military hospital in Washington—would be back soon. Holder knew he was going to need some help.

They came out of the sally ports in solid blocks of white and gray, issuing smoothly into the sunlight in company-sized formations like dozens of slow-moving limousines. At this end of August, the viscous, humid air of the Hudson Valley rode each pair of shoulders like an unseen pack. Yet the cadets were *sharp*—the word came easily here—in their thousands, crisp, polished, shoes glistening black, cross belts starched stiff and blinding white, breastplates like individual suns on their chests. They moved in arithmetic precision, gliding across the grass, all those legs like parts of a single machine, arms swinging forward and back, white gloves marking identical arcs; mind-numbing uniformity wherever he looked. Tom Gates drew in his breath involuntarily.

Gates watched D Company emerge into the sunlight, thread its way across the grass, and take its place in line. Smooth. Looked good. Holder hadn't even screwed up yet, as far as he could see.

Kathleen Gates couldn't get the tandem stroller holding her two children through the crowd watching the parade, so instead of trying to join Tom in the stands, she pushed it up to the chain that marked the edge of the field. To her right were Quarters 100, where the new Superintendent lived, and Quarters 101, the somewhat smaller home of the Commandant.

She looked to her left as she nudged the stroller just under the chain—so the children would be able to see—and saw Tom talking to a woman in uniform. Kathleen stood on her toes and saw that it was another Tactical Officer, a homely captain named Curry.

Now what is he talking to her about? she wondered.

She had met Curry at a reception for new Tacs. Bad teeth, bad hair, a weight problem waiting to happen, and a lop-sided smile. Yet Tom had said something complimentary about her, Kathleen remembered, but she couldn't recall what it was.

Well, it certainly wasn't about her looks, Kathleen sniffed as she looked about.

The Saturday morning parades were a fall ritual at West Point. Once home football games started, the crowds would grow to the tens of thousands; fans came early to watch the spectacle on the Plain. Many of them would then have tailgate parties in the hour or two between the ceremony and kickoff. Kathleen was looking forward to entertaining some of their friends from Fort Bragg who had promised to come up this season. The various souvenir shops, on and off post, sold all sorts of decorations in Army colors—black and gold—pins, stadium blankets, sweaters, little brooches in the shape of the Army mule. Kathleen had seen some of the women on post outfitted in these trinkets. Some of them looked festive—nothing wrong with joining the fun and showing a little school spirit. Some looked downright ridiculous.

Just then a middle-aged couple passed Kathleen. The woman wore a too small tee shirt that said "West Point Mom." The man, predictably, wore a shirt that said "West Point Dad." The cadet son or daughter, Kathleen thought, would probably die of embarrassment.

Kathleen was studying these representatives from middle America when she noticed the two well-dressed women following them down the walk. Roberta Flynn, wife of the Superintendent, and Faith Moro, whose husband was the Commandant, were ten yards away from Kathleen and headed her way.

Kathleen had been introduced to both women just a few weeks earlier at a welcome coffee for new arrivals. Bobbie Flynn was fifty or so, Kathleen had guessed, a petite, elegant woman with thick silver-gray hair and a lovely smile. She made time to talk to as many of the hundred or so women and men at the reception as cared to wait in line to meet her, Kathleen had noticed, and she'd been as gracious to the last as to the first. Today she wore a beautiful white linen suit: jacket with modest V neck above three wide buttons and a pleated skirt. She looked as cool as the big white house from which she'd just emerged.

Faith Moro wore a summery dress and beads covered in orange silk. She was taller than Flynn and every bit as graceful; the two women fairly glided along the walkway.

And why not? Kathleen thought. *Their husbands are the most powerful men on post. Everyone knows who they are, and everyone defers to them.*

Indeed, as they walked, Kathleen noticed faculty and staff, spouses, and even cadets greeting them warmly. They were like the fine ladies of the castle, coming down to mix with the commoners.

"Hello," Kathleen blurted out when they were close to her.

"Hello," Bobbie Flynn said. Moro said nothing, but smiled. The women did not remember her.

"I'm Kathleen Gates," she said, a little too breathlessly,

she thought. "I met you at the reception for the newly arrived staff."

The two women had slowed down but had not stopped. Kathleen stuck out her hand as if grabbing at someone from the bank of a stream.

"My husband is a new Tactical Officer," Kathleen continued.

She experienced a moment of panic when she realized that these women might have already heard the story—or a version of the story—about what had happened between Tom and his cadet. The incident had taken place just past the corner of Bobbie Flynn's garden.

Faith Moro shook Kathleen's hand; then Bobbie Flynn did the same.

"And how are you enjoying West Point so far?" Flynn asked.

Kathleen saw Moro look past her to the grandstand. No doubt their husbands were waiting for them; maybe the whole parade would be held up for them. Yet here was Bobbie Flynn talking to her as if she were the most important person at the Military Academy.

"Well, there's a lot to learn about how things work at West Point," she said to Flynn. "My husband, just like General Flynn, didn't go to school here either."

Faith Moro looked at her sharply, just for a second, and Kathleen thought that perhaps she'd gone too far in trying to ingratiate herself with Bobbie Flynn.

But Flynn smiled and touched Kathleen on the arm.

"Yes, I'm finding that there is a lot to learn—but Patrick says we'll just muddle through and act as if we know what we're talking about," she said, smiling. "Now, if you'll excuse us, I believe our husbands are probably wondering where we are."

"Yes, of course," Kathleen said, "It was . . . it was nice talking to you."

"Good-bye," Faith Moro said.

Bitch, Kathleen Gates thought as she watched Moro's back.

But she wasn't really angry. Bobbie Flynn had been as gracious as a queen. She had everything Kathleen Gates wanted. She and her husband were at the very center of things here. People spoke politely to her, hospital orderlies and grocery clerks and the wives of all the old Colonels who'd been around forever. She lived in the biggest house. She had a *servant*. Kathleen had heard Tom refer to her as "Mrs. General Flynn."

And I'm going to be Mrs. General Gates someday, she told herself as she turned back to the field and the gleaming parade.

Wayne Holder turned around and faced the company as he moved them into final position. This was the part he was most worried about. During drill the previous week, the helpful cadets on brigade staff had strung a long cord, staked at either end, to mark the final line for the companies. Marching backward to watch his formation, Wayne Holder had tripped over the cord and landed, unceremoniously, on his rear end. As if that weren't bad enough, for the rest of the drill period, whenever he turned to face the front, he presented his grass-stained backside to the cadets in formation, who had commented every single time: "Nice grass stains."

This time he managed to pull off the maneuver without mishap. He turned to the front and found he could see the people in the stands looking at him. They were not indistinct shapes, as they had always appeared from the rear ranks or the middle of the company's block formation, where he'd often been sent to hide his poor marching skills. Now there were people up there in the stands. He could even see Gates near the top of the section closest to where he stood.

Behind Holder, the predictable chatter started.

"Over there, two o'clock, two o'clock," an insistent voice hammered through the ranks behind Holder. "Red dress. RED dress, getta load a that!"

"Dead ahead, twelve o'clock. Hot damn; *she's* not gonna drown floatin' face down."

"God bless America, men, God *bless* America!"

"Yowza. Stand up, honey, *please*. Is that dress as short as I think it is?"

The women in the ranks were a minority, but Holder

thought he could hear Rebecca Hollings *tsk tsk* at these antics. Some of the yearling women, Holder knew, countered with their own comments on the men in the stands, vying to see who could be more bawdy. To his left, the next company was led by a woman who commanded silence in the ranks. Other women cadets, perhaps even most, tolerated the behavior as indulgent sisters might ignore the immaturity of younger brothers.

Holder forgot himself for a moment, glancing around the stands, moving only his eyes. The commentary moved on, rapid fire. So much to appreciate. The stands were full of them. The country was full of them. Bathed, perfumed, brushed, painted. Young and succulent.

"Check out that major leaguer in white, section H."

"It's a great country, men."

Suddenly the cadet battalion commander in front of him was echoing an order that Holder had somehow missed. The other company commanders' timing was perfect; they echoed the commands in unison. Holder was a second behind. He tried to drag it out, but the effect was even more ragged.

"Ord . . . errrr . . ."

He heard Dearborn groan.

"Pay attention, man," Dearborn said.

"ARMS!"

Behind him, the rifles came down together. The company could save him, Holder thought for a moment until he saw Gates, off in the distance, shaking his head.

All through the first stages of the parade, when his job was merely to stand still and raise and lower the guidon, Chris Dearborn spent his time worrying. He worried that Holder wouldn't pay attention, he worried that the senior would drop his saber. He worried about what had happened to Trainor and what would come of the showdown between Holder and Gates. He wasted no psychic energy fretting over academics and the year that was about to start; for the most part his studies came easily to him.

But the central star in the spinning galaxy of his concerns was this: he worried that Gates was going to put him on the boxing team.

A month earlier, at Fort Benning to earn his parachutist wings, Dearborn had committed a cardinal sin. In the doorway of the thirty-four foot tower, from which the students practiced exiting an aircraft, Dearborn had locked up in fear. Solid. A sergeant had to talk him away from the door while dozens and then scores of other students came around for their second turns and waited on the steps behind him, sweltering in the Georgia heat and their impatience and their heavy uniforms while the sickly sweet smell of the paper mills across the river in Alabama made them nauseous.

He had finally jumped, flailing for purchase in the air and struggling against the harness that lowered him to the ground, a graceless marionette. Dearborn, as he said later, "became a name" that day. For the two weeks remaining of their training the sergeants made a point of asking every cadet, identifiable by their Academy-crest shoulder patches, "Are you the West Pointer who froze in the tower?" Every time a black-hatted instructor asked the question of one of his classmates, Dearborn became more infamous, more reviled. At night, in his hot bunk, Dearborn considered that the others might have rallied around a more popular classmate. If it had happened to someone like Holder, the other cadets would have been supportive, would have banded together in an us-versus-them mindset.

Not so with Dearborn. Dearborn the geek-a-zoid. Dearborn the loser.

It was just a rerun, he'd told himself, of his first two years as a cadet. Every success in academics had been his whenever he set his mind to the work; every physical success eluded him. The four horsemen of plebe year physical education—swimming, gymnastics, boxing, and wrestling—each had its own torturous climax. There were towers high above the pool; rings and bars flying over the gym floor; sweaty, frightened classmates across the boxing ring, on the wrestling mat. They jumped, they hung suspended, they grunted and twisted and pounded their passing grades—point by point, it seemed—out of each other's flesh.

Dearborn knew he had bucked the trend, defied the statistics, just by being admitted. He was not one of the ninety-six percent of his classmates who had earned varsity letters, not one of the sixty-two percent who'd been team captains, Eagle Scouts, heroes of the Four H. He'd run one desultory season on his high school's slovenly track team, and he'd barely passed the physical aptitude test administered to all candidates. Dearborn sometimes wondered if he'd been admitted because, in this place of winners, someone had to lose. He was the equivalent of the blocking dummy, the scrub squad, the walking training aid.

Now Gates was making noise about "intestinal fortitude," and another cadet had heard something about Dearborn winding up on the intramural boxing team—which would be Gates's way of helping him train the undeveloped muscle that was his physical courage. Dearborn was afraid of becoming Major Mercury's project.

Of course, Chris Dearborn could have quit at any time during those first two years; his grades were a ticket to any college in the nation. He knew he was smart enough. What he didn't know—what kept him in the battle with the Department of Physical Education (DPE)—was whether he had the heart to stick it out at West Point.

In the back ranks, plebes were being mildly harassed and ordered to tell jokes no one ever laughed at. Wayne Holder could hear the buzz from where he stood.

"Lock your knees, close your eyes, hold your breath, and think about home," one of the yearlings was telling a big plebe who was famous for passing out during a summer parade.

The pattern repeated itself down the line of companies. The parades were boring, the cadets had to amuse themselves. Holder wasn't surprised at the murmur behind him. He knew that even the most boisterous and immature of his charges was smart enough to keep the noise level below what might be noticed in the stands. Holder would have been surprised to know that one comment kept repeating itself, from company to company down the line, playing on a virulent rumor that lingered over the Academy all summer.

"Hey, mister," an upperclass cadet called. "Did you tell

your Mom not to rent your room out? You'll be back home in a flash when they close this place."

"Pass . . . in . . . review!"

Four thousand cadets, their gloved hands at the muzzles of their rifles, rattled their bayonets, a glittering sound like the applause of tiny hands. The parade was nearly over. One by one the companies wheeled out of position, down the runway of trampled grass and past the reviewing stand to receive the salutes of the gaggle of luminaries in the Superintendent's party. Wayne Holder marched his phalanx of windup soldiers without incident. They turned their heads instantly on the command "Eyes right!" then back again, moving as one, on "Ready, front!" And all the while they kept in step, ranks and files aligned, rifles perfectly canted. Thirty-inch steps, nine-inch arm swings. Just so.

Chris Dearborn saluted with the guidon, holding the heavy staff parallel to the ground as he marched, a wooden vector pointing the way from the field. The hours of drill with the unwieldy pole were paying off. He held the correct distance from Holder, matched the voice commands with the practiced flourishes of his flag. Up to the sky, down along his arm until the pointed bottom of the shaft rested in the brace he wore at his waist. He made it without incident, amazing himself.

Now came the part Chris Dearborn loved.

After the company had passed the reviewing stand, they marched in a straight line toward the Superintendent's quarters, visible above the gleaming bayonets of the company in front of them, like a white confection amid the dark green of the surrounding trees. In front of him, the last rank of the company ahead moved in a gentle rhythm set by the bass drum that was off behind him now. All across the Plain, every time the deep note sounded, hundreds of left feet found the grass again.

D Company always cleared the field near the end of the parade, just when the band began playing "The Army Song," which came last by tradition. The rolling, repeated strains had become the music of his youth. Dearborn breathed in the smells—grass, rifle oil, polished leather, and brass—drank in the sunlit view. All of it filled him, expanded him, pushed at his limits until he felt larger than his daily concerns. It was here that his strongest emotions clashed, love and hate coming together, like knights in a clanging joust.

This was when Dearborn felt most strongly the connection to those who had preceded him on this field. Eisenhower had marched here, and Patton; Douglas MacArthur had been the First Captain and had led the Corps in parades. It was on this field that Grant rode in mounted reviews, as did Stuart and Custer and John Bell Hood and Sherman. Cadets sworn in on this field fought at Gettysburg and Bastogne, at the Marne, at Chickamauga. The Army flag trailed, from its point, scores of battle streamers that were simple testimony to what American soldiers had borne through two bloody centuries. It was on this field that Chris Dearborn felt connected to all of them.

Here he didn't have to worry about boxing, about airborne school, about the fact that half of his classmates would remember him for years as the guy who froze up at the tower door. Here he didn't have to hate; here he was above all that, a part of the Long Gray Line.

Captain Jacqueline Timmer, sitting in the stands next to her husband, played absentmindedly with an envelope in her hands. It held a letter from the man who wanted to be her lover.

"See that guy over there?" Rob Timmer asked her. "The big one who's practically sitting by himself? That's Tom Gates."

"Is he the one who got into a fight with his company commander?" Jackie Timmer asked. She pressed the envelope—standard business-sized government issue—between her palms, imagining she could feel heat there.

"The very one," her husband replied. While Rob studied the big major who sat some two sections away from them, Jackie Timmer watched her husband and wondered if he'd even noticed the envelope. Perhaps, she considered, she secretly hoped he'd ask her what it was, as if this were some kind of test he didn't even know he was failing.

But he didn't ask, just as she expected. In the next instant she wondered if she'd brought it along for some little thrill.

"He was in the advanced course with me," Rob continued. His attention was divided between Gates and the parade, which was unfolding before them.

Jacqueline Timmer was a second year instructor in the English Department, thirty years old, tall, with the lithe body of a runner. The first thing most people noticed about her was her hair: thick, auburn and glossy, it was one vanity she indulged. Cut bluntly at her jawline, it held her face in a rich frame. Her features were long and, she thought, too angular. She had been a beautiful young woman poised on the edge of great adventures with young men when she came to West Point. She handed over that identity and much of her sexuality with the little suitcase of civilian clothes she turned in when she became a plebe some twelve summers earlier.

Now Timmer spent her days in front of rooms full of cadets. If anyone had asked her, she would have admitted that the young men stared at her, watched her with hungry eyes. She attributed this attention to hormones; the cadets were, for the most part, sex-starved adolescents. She would have been the last person to think herself beautiful. Her husband's compliments tended to concern athleticism, as if he were her coach.

"Your legs look toned," he'd say after they'd gone on a hard run. Or, "Looks like you've dropped some body fat. That should take a half minute off your two-mile run time." He might tell her her hair looked nice, but "nice"—which was as enthusiastic as he got—to him meant easy to care for, as in "after working out."

Rob Timmer was a man focused on performance, on tangible, objectifiable measures he could name. He was handsome, in a severe, Nordic way. Sharp featured, hard muscles like flint, he carried almost no body fat; in his running shorts he looked like a skinned rabbit.

"It must be tough," Jackie said. "Waiting around, not knowing what's going to happen to you."

Rob laughed, a patronizing little guffaw.

"I'd say we're all in that boat," he said. "In case you haven't noticed, everyone around here is running scared."

Rob was right; everything was in a tumult. Her peers—who had taken two years out of their profession to pursue graduate degrees—weren't sure they were going to have a job a year hence. The cadets weren't sure West Point would be around long enough to graduate them. It was all anyone talked about, a concern that consumed everyone's attention, like a war. All bets were off. People were doing crazy things.

"I'm going down there to talk to Colonel McNamara," Rob said, indicating one of his department's professors sitting below them in the bleachers. "I have a few questions for him."

"Fine," Jackie Timmer—Jack to her mostly male colleagues—said. She and her husband wore the same uniforms: short-sleeved green shirt, darker green pants with the black leg stripe of the officer corps, shiny black shoes, thin garrison caps to which were clipped the symbols of their rank—a gold oak leaf for Major Rob Timmer and the silver railroad-track bars of a captain for Jackie. Although Army regulations allowed for a tasteful ring or two, some small earrings, Jack Timmer wore no jewelry beside her runner's watch and her West Point ring.

When Rob moved away Jackie looked around the bleachers. There were plenty of people she knew in the stands—West Point, like most Army posts, was a small community—but no one within a few yards. She turned the envelope toward the sun, tapped it to slide the contents to one end and tore it open.

In contrast to the government-issue envelope, the note inside was written on a rich, cream-colored sheet of thick stationery. At the top of the page, her given name, the one her father—who'd adored her—always used when everyone else used a diminutive.

Jacqueline . . .

Layne Marshall was a civilian professor in the history department; Timmer's classroom had been next to his for the whole of the previous semester. Handsome in an eastern prep, milk-fed way, he wore his sandy hair on the long side, at least compared to all the short-hairs surrounding him. There was a deliberateness about him, in the relaxed southern cadence of his speech, in his loose-limbed walk, in the way his smile slowly overtook his face. A Rhodes scholar who wrote books about colonial America, he seemed to Jackie the polar opposite of most of his uniformed colleagues.

He was charming and romantic and in pursuit of Jacqueline Timmer, who had not been pursued for a long time—had not been pursued at all, perhaps, except by boys, and that in another life. She did not know what to make of the attention, she knew nothing other than it was exciting, electrifying, wicked.

> *I saw you the other day on your way from the gym to your office, moving with the grace of a lioness. I have to tell you that I lost my train of thought, lost what I was saying to dear old Captain Berndt, who was too quick and so saw me watching you.*
>
> *At the end of last semester you promised to have lunch with me, to tell me all about your summer playing soldier, and I plan on holding you to that promise. Let's meet. Call me. Tell me when. I'm at your disposal.*

Jackie Timmer had told Marshall that she'd have lunch with him because he had insisted, because he had asked her upward of a dozen times, flirting with her, playing with her, trying to wheedle her into bets that he could then lose or win—the payoff always being their lunching together. Finally, at the end of last term she'd said yes. The fall was impossibly far away, Marshall was headed back to Louisiana and what she imagined was a string of old girlfriends, sororities full of broken-hearted college girls. She had wanted him to forget her and she had wanted him to think about her, to dream about her as she dreamed about him. He had, it seemed. Now she didn't know which prospect frightened her more—that she might see him or that she might let him slip away.

Jackie Timmer had planned a lunch at the Officer's Club, where the sight of them would stir some talk, perhaps, but where she could always find another colleague to join them, dissipating the attention they might garner.

She really wanted to meet him at Painters in nearby Cornwall-on-Hudson, a town as picturesque as its name. The restaurant, in a generously proportioned old house, was decorated with the work of local artists; canvas and sculpture lined the walls, filled the alcoves. There were broad windows and tiny alcove tables for lovers. It was perfect; it would never do. For although they were less likely to see someone they knew at Painters, if they did it would be obvious that they were trying to hide.

The tinny voice of the public address system asked them to stand for the national anthem. Timmer shoved the letter back into the envelope and came to attention, heels together, feet at a forty-five degree angle, thumbs pressed to the sides of her legs just behind the seams of her trousers. At the first notes she brought her hand up in salute, fingertip just at her right eye.

It was at this very place her life had taken its shape. She could look out on the Plain, on the thousands of cadets before her, and remember that she had charted her course right here: circumspect, pathologically self-examined, straight as the gleaming silver swords flashing in the ranks.

Above the massed companies of cadets, above the Plain and the long gray expanse of barracks behind them, the Cadet Chapel dominated the hillside, a huge metaphor come to life in cut stone, standing guard over everything below. From here in the stands the whole of the Academy appeared just as rock solid, its higher calling as clearly visible as the chapel looming above the assembled cadets. Duty, Honor, Country, the motto said. It was on her ring, it was in her heart.

Shoulders back, head up, the picture of a model soldier. And just at that moment, when she responded properly, in the prescribed way, as she did in everything in her life, when she looked for all the world like exactly what she was—a successful career soldier—just at that moment she became afraid that she might lose her way, afraid that she might sleep with Layne Marshall.

Brigadier General David Simon spent part of Saturday afternoon in his office, talking on the telephone with his counterpart at the Naval Academy. Over the years—Simon was in his eighth year as West Point's Dean, Nick Foster had been Navy's Dean for ten—the two men had met dozens of times. Simon thought Foster a bit self-righteous, but there was no denying his intellect, and the man had proved useful on occasion.

"Yeah, Admiral Chichester expects that we'll be next on Bruckner's list," Foster had told Simon. Chichester was Superintendent of the Naval Academy.

"He isn't ready to close the gates, but he did have me put together a couple of contingency plans, alternate designs for a smaller Naval Academy. That way, if the people in Washington win the battle to cut us back, at least we'll be ready with a plan—a plan we developed—that will look after what we think are the Academy's and the Navy's best interests."

Simon's first reaction had been that Chichester was capitulating, but then he saw the wisdom in being prepared. If the Chief of Staff of the Army told them to restructure, they'd be more likely to get what they wanted if they had a plan on the shelf.

The idea had come to him all at once.

"How big would the Academy be under the new design?" Simon asked.

"One half to two thirds what it is now," Foster had said. "Probably a two star for Supe."

Simon wished Foster hadn't made the comment about a new Superintendent; better no one knew what he was planning.

West Point would be smaller, so the Superintendent's job wouldn't need to be a three star billet. A two star, a major general, would do. And of course it would make sense to have someone who knew the Academy intimately. Someone with experience, with impeccable credentials as an academic and a leader.

Someone like David Simon.

Flynn would have to go, that much was clear. And if he went amid some turmoil, it would be all the more important to have someone close by take the helm.

Simon sat back in his chair, looked out the window at the long Hudson below, and allowed himself a smile as his course became clear.

CHAPTER 3

ON MONDAY EVENING WAYNE HOLDER SAT WITH HIS FEET UP on the desk, his back to the wall, carefully tearing the feeder strips off the side of a computer printout. On a top bunk a few feet away Chris Dearborn lay on his back, reading a paperback novel he held above his face.

"You have, like, homework or anything?" Holder asked.

"I . . . *like* . . . did it," Dearborn answered in a mocking singsong.

"Don't get smart with me," Holder said, balling up a sheet of paper and flinging it at Dearborn's head.

"Or what? You won't let me help you with your papers anymore?"

"Cute," Holder said. "Very cute. I only let you help me so that you'll feel worthwhile, to give you some reason for being alive, breathing perfectly good air that some scum-sucking dog could be using instead."

Dearborn rolled over onto his side, toward Holder, but did not take his eyes out of the book.

"Speaking of getting rid of oxygen wasters, is Gates going to kill you? Maybe a nice garroting to start the academic year off right?"

73

"He stopped me in the hall this morning, said we're going to be working together so we'd better put this behind us."

"You believe him?"

"Sure," Holder said. "I guess. The Comm chewed me out pretty good. I don't think there'll be any more official action."

"How's Alex?" Dearborn asked.

"Alex had surgery yesterday and it went well; he'll be back in a few days. Maybe Gates will just wait for Alex to get back before he fires me and puts Alex in charge."

"Someone who already understands pain, you mean," Dearborn said. "And threats. Let's not forget threats."

"I'll tell you," Holder said, "Kathleen Gates grilled me in the emergency room."

Dearborn lowered the book to the bony cage that might, someday, support a chest.

"Mrs. Major? She of the strawberry hair and the sky-blue eyes? The perfect woman? My Helen?"

"You think she swallows?"

Dearborn let fly the paperback at Holder's head. Holder dropped his feet to the floor and ducked, laughing.

"You're lusting after a killer's wife," Holder said. "No margin in that."

Dearborn swung his legs over the edge of the bunk. They were pale down to the knees; from there down—where the skin hadn't peeled—they were an odd salmon color, left over from a sunburn he had endured while in Georgia. Where other people's legs were made up of tissue, muscle, bone, an elegant and sophisticated product of evolution, Dearborn's had the aesthetics of cardboard tubes. His feet were oversized, with prominent bones like the pipes of a tiny church organ. His toenails were as thick as an old man's.

"Lust? Lust? Our relationship has transcended mere physical desire," he said. "But of course, I wouldn't expect you to understand such a concept."

Dearborn raised eyes and thin arms to the ceiling; he was on.

"Oh, beautiful Kathleen, forced to spend your days yoked to that beast, your mate in name only, just as I am left to cast my proverbial pearls before these gray-clad swine."

Holder smiled.

"You two soulmates or something?"

Dearborn dropped his chin. "Verily."

"Good," Holder said. "Next time you're around her, why don't you give her a big wet kiss, a slip of the tongue, maybe put your hand on her ass. That way Major Mercury can concentrate on killing you and I can graduate."

"I think Gates has my number anyway," Dearborn said, retrieving the book and flopping back on the bunk.

"Because he knows about your torrid affair with his wife?"

"Because of what happened down at Airborne."

"Hey, you finished the school, you got your wings," Holder said, trying to sound reassuring. "What are you worried about?"

"Gates thinks I'm a pussy."

Holder swung his feet back up onto the desk. Dearborn's two roommates were gone, at the gym or the library, presumably. Dearborn needed a little reassurance, a little counseling, and now was as good a time as any. The issue, Holder knew, wasn't what Gates thought; it was what Gates could do, and it was about what Dearborn thought of himself.

"You want to tell me what happened in the tower?"

"You sound like a shrink," Dearborn said.

"Just playing sensitive; women love that shit."

Dearborn rolled his long frame off the bunk and walked the few paces to the sink. He looked into the mirror and pressed his hands to his head to flatten out the errant cowlicks that stuck out at angles like unruly pennants. Nothing changed, as far as Holder could see, but when he finished, Dearborn winked and pointed at himself in the mirror, clucking his tongue. The show never stopped.

"What can I say? I froze up," he said, still looking in the mirror.

"You know how there comes that moment, that second, really, where all you have to do is step off, or jump, or let yourself go? Doesn't matter if you're talking about the high dive or the parallel bars or the boxing ring. Well, I missed that second."

Holder knew there was more to the story. He'd heard versions from other juniors in the company.

"So one of the blackhats comes up and starts talking me through the procedure. A pretty good approach, actually. He was just talking, calmly going through the drill with me. Then he got to the point where he said 'Go' and I didn't go. He did it again—a patient man—and I almost got it. But by that time there were twelve or fifteen people right behind me, waiting for their turns. And it must have been a hundred degrees inside that friggin' tower. Everyone was watching, you know?"

Dearborn's voice had dropped. Holder could hear, in the hallway just beyond the closed door, three or four other cadets laughing at some joke.

"But you jumped, right?" Holder asked.

"Actually, the blackhat kind of pushed me. One way or the other, I went out the door. It never happened again, but for the rest of the week the instructors kept calling me 'Tower Man.' I mean, they were just goofing around and all. It was a joke at my expense, but it was a joke.

"Now Gates thinks I need a little character building experience," Dearborn said. "Like the company boxing team."

West Point's intramural sports program dwarfed those of colleges with four and five times the student population for one simple reason: all cadets who did not play intercollegiate sports were required to play intramural. Douglas MacArthur, Superintendent from 1919 to 1921, had decreed "every cadet an athlete." Those cadets who were less athletically inclined, such as Dearborn, were apt to say that while a general can make every cadet play sports, a regulation cannot an athlete make.

As part of a year already destined to be a painful one, all male plebes—freshmen—endured twenty lessons of boxing; so, in theory at least, all cadets possessed some minimal skill as boxers. In practice, when it came to fielding a company boxing team, there were cadets who volunteered, but frequently the ranks were filled with draftees. Plebes, who had only passive roles in their own destinies, were often cannon fodder for the sport. Every once in a while, a well-meaning Tac would encourage an upperclass cadet to participate.

"I got killed in plebe boxing," Dearborn continued. "Bled all over every bout, a red fountain. It got to the point where everyone in the class who needed a few points wanted to fight me. I got a C minus for the course, a few charity points above summer school."

"I thought they gave good grades for bleeders," Holder said. "The sight of blood excites them."

Holder remembered Dearborn, who was a class behind, as a plebe, always struggling with the Department of Physical Education. Cadets called DPE "the Department With a Heart" because it was heartless, and said that "if DPE taught sex, it wouldn't be fun" because that was a safe bet.

While other regular Army personnel at West Point wore standard uniforms, the DPE instructors had their own special outfit: black pants with name and rank embroidered on the waistband, tight-fitting gray shirts. No hats. They looked like the kind of men and women one saw running the nicer suburban health clubs, but they roamed the gymnasium like some Special Action Group, and in the collective imagination of cadets and former cadets, they were uniformly cruel.

"I'm gonna get killed in there," Dearborn said.

Holder remained quiet; it was probably true. It was also true that if Gates decided Dearborn was going to box, there was precious little the cadets could do about that.

"You gotta suck it up, man," Holder said. It was a lame comment, and he knew it. But it was all he could offer.

Dearborn walked to the window and looked outside, bracing his bony knuckles on the window casement.

"Think they're doing this at Notre Dame? Think the juniors at Michigan State are worried about some thirty-five-year-old asshole putting them in a ring to get the shit beat out of them?"

"Not bloody likely," Holder said.

"Maybe one of those Bruckner Commission snoops will ask me what I think about the athletic program, and I could tell how it's run by a pack of sadists."

"Except that they'd come to get you," Holder joked. "A

bunch of guys in black hoods would show up in the middle of the night. . . ."

"The interview results are confidential," Dearborn said.

He was still facing the window, so Holder couldn't see his face, couldn't tell how serious the junior was.

"Oh, well," Dearborn said, turning away from the window and showing a lopsided, insincere smile. "Ours not to reason why. . . ."

Not for the first time Holder wondered why Dearborn put up with all the obstacles West Point put in his path. He was one of the smartest cadets Holder knew; he had trouble because he was not the most agile, the most personable.

While West Point attracted some of the brightest students in America, they were not the same kids who would have gone to Harvard or MIT. They were the kind of students who did well at Penn State and the University of Texas, kids who could divide their time between the athletic field, the frat parties, and the library, who could balance. Dearborn belonged in a library somewhere, or a laboratory; DPE was always trying to convince him of that. And while Gates may not have had something similar in mind, the effect would be the same. Gates, no doubt, looked on boxing as an opportunity for Dearborn, but the junior would get his face punched in every time. He would be beaten down and more and more convinced that he didn't belong in this world that, for all its aspirations to be Athens, was an American Sparta.

When Dearborn turned around, smiling his fake smile, Holder felt sorry for him for just a moment.

"Ours but to eat hair pie. . . ." Holder replied.

"Let's look at that abysmal paper again," Dearborn said, back to business, back to his mocking tone, the mask in place.

Holder had come to Dearborn's room for some help with what he knew was a boring paper. Among his other academic talents Dearborn was the best writer in the company; other cadets beat a path to his door whenever term papers or writing portfolios were due. The engineers, in particular, the cadets whose academic muscle was wired into their programmable calculators, into their humming, throbbing oversized PCs, those numbers crunchers all made the pilgrimage. Dearborn held court from the top of his bunk, mixing advice on sentences, paragraphs, and punctuation with comments and barbs about the writer's genetics, lineage, potential as a sentient being. He was obnoxious, he was crude; he was the guru, the man, the ultimate term paper savior.

"All you did was put a checkmark next to this first sentence," Holder complained. "What's that mean?"

"It means that any college senior who would write a sentence like that is probably a moron. Tell me, did your parents have the same last name before they were married?"

"Funny."

"Read me the sentence," Dearborn said.

Holder shifted his weight in his seat, feeling a little bit like a student called upon to give what he knows is going to be a wrong answer. But there was no stopping; this was how Dearborn worked, and Dearborn was the best.

"During the period 6 June 1944 to 5 May 1945, the casualty rate for junior infantry officers in front line units in the European Theater averaged. . . ."

"Stop right there," Dearborn said. He was staring out the window, a look of mild disgust on his face, as if he'd caught the scent of something unpleasant.

"It's possible that sentence could be more boring, but it would take me a long time to figure out how."

"As usual, Chris, you're the soul of tact."

"You paying me to sugarcoat the truth or you want me to help you?"

"OK, OK," Holder said.

"You've seen this?" Dearborn asked, reaching across Holder and pulling a thick book from the shelf above the desk. *The Register of Graduates,* published by West Point's alumni association, listed all Academy graduates and their biographies in tiny letters on page after page that chronicled two hundred years of the Academy's—and the nation's—history.

"Why would I use that? The paper is supposed to be on the problems with keeping unit strength levels up after D-Day, especially among junior officers."

As he spoke, Holder felt as if he were defending himself.

Dearborn had a sleepy look about him. His hair was smeared on the back of his head where he'd been lying on the pillow. His tee shirt, once white, now reduced to the uniform dun color that seemed the specialty of the cadet laundry, had a big tear under one arm so that Holder could see, if he didn't avert his eyes, a sprout of wiry hair under Dearborn's armpit. It wasn't a pretty sight.

"Yabbada, yabbada, yabbada," Dearborn said, his eyes sleepy. "Statistics aren't interesting. You want your paper to be interesting or boring?"

"This isn't creative writing," Holder said, a little peevishly.

"Fine," Dearborn said, dropping the big book on Holder's lap. "Just keep in mind that your instructor has—what?—fifty of these things to read. Make sure that yours is as much like all the rest as you can make it."

He turned back toward his bunk.

"OK, OK," Holder said. "You're right."

"That goes without saying," Dearborn said, turning back to the desk and standing by Holder's shoulder.

"Part of the problem, Wayne-O, is that you only see this as a history paper; as far as you're concerned it's about something that happened a long time ago."

"Isn't it?"

Dearborn shook his head. "It's all of a piece. You, me, Gates."

He hooked his elbow on the top bunk.

"Because of this stupid Bruckner Commission everyone is running around trying to figure out what West Point should be, and it's all right there."

"Here?" Holder said, placing his hand flat on the cover of the book.

"Right," Dearborn said. "Open it to the Class of . . . let's say . . . 1941."

Holder did as he was told.

"What are the first things you notice when you look at this page?"

Holder wanted to ask what this had to do with his paper and his troubled opening sentence, but he'd found in the last two years that Dearborn usually knew what he was talking about, even if he did make the point in as obnoxious a way as possible.

"Some of the names are in italics," Holder said.

"Those are the guys who died. What about those entries, the ones for grads who are dead?"

Holder studied the page.

"The entries are real short."

"The entries are *really* short," Dearborn corrected him. "Let's put adverbs with those adjectives, shall we?"

"OK," Holder said pleasantly. "Those entries are *really* short, asshole."

"Much better," Dearborn said. He turned back to his bunk and climbed awkwardly up the side, plopped onto his mattress, the springs protesting. Holder knew Dearborn was about to disappear again into whatever paperback he was reading; he wanted an answer while the answers were close by.

"So what?"

"So there's your first sentence," Dearborn said. Then he was back in the book.

Holder looked at the page in the *Register*. The entries were encrypted, a more specialized jargon, even, than the military argot. The page read:

12620 *Francis Joseph Troy*
B-NY: Inf: Kld-Alsace France 25 Jan 45 CPT CO CoF
242 Inf 42 Inf Div, a-27:
PH: Ob-Fa 67.

Holder flipped back and forth to the key, then began to read out loud, translating the ciphered entries as he read.

"Francis Joseph Troy, born in New York, Killed in Alsace, France, 25 January 1945. Troy was the Commanding Officer of Company F, Two Hundred and Forty-second Infantry Regiment, Forty-second Infantry Division. He was twenty-seven when he died."

Here Holder paused. Captain Troy was less than five years out of West Point when he died pushing the Wehrmacht out of France. That was only six years older than Holder as he sat in the barracks room, worried about a history paper.

"Purple Heart, obituary published in the fall 1967."

Holder looked up. Dearborn was still reading. Outside

the barracks he could hear the sprinklers in the Superintendent's garden, a steady, almost metallic sound of water spraying. A couple of small moths battered themselves against the desk lamp.

Just under Troy was Edgar Clayton Boggs, killed on Luzon in the Phillipine Islands, two weeks after his classmate and half a world away. Boggs was twenty-six.

Down the page, Robert Harold Rosen, a captain in the 505th Parachute Infantry Regiment. Killed at Nijmegen, Holland on 20 September 1944. Rosen was twenty-eight. In the page's middle column, a tiny entry—just longer than one line—for William Gardner, who went ashore at Omaha Beach with the 116th Infantry and died on D-Day.

Holder scanned the smallest entries. William Annesley Kromer was killed at Moircy, Belgium during the Battle of the Bulge. Twenty-seven. Harvey Lee Jarvis, Junior, missing in action over Ploesti in August 1943. Twenty-six-year-old Thomas Edwin Reagan was killed in Normandy in August 1944. Hector John Polla survived the Bataan Death March only to die of wounds on board a prisoner-of-war ship in January 1945. Hector was twenty-eight.

Holder felt something stir inside him, a note struck with the resonance of a dirge. These were men who had marched the same parade field, had worn the same uniforms, had spent the same long evenings watching the Hudson roll past. They were far away and as close as the smell of wet grass drifting through the window from the Plain. When he tried to picture them, he saw only black and white, as in the newsreel footage they watched sometimes in history class. He wondered who had mourned for these men, who had missed them for years, who missed them still.

He held the book in his lap, ran his thumb over the page, over the long, long list of names.

"Well?" Dearborn said, breaking the reverie.

Holder looked up; the junior was watching him from the top bunk, his hand propped beneath the side of his face.

"Well what?"

"You got that sentence yet?"

Holder dropped his feet to the floor and pulled his pencil from behind his ear. At the top of the first page he wrote as he spoke out loud, "The first thing you notice, when you look at the war classes, is that so many of the biographies are short."

Dearborn nodded. "Pitifully short," he added.

Tom Gates put the black telephone in the middle of his desk and stared at it for a long moment before picking up the receiver and dialing his home number.

"It's me," he said when Kathleen answered.

"You getting ready to come home?" she asked.

"In a few minutes, I guess." He paused, breathing slowly. Out in the hallway he could hear a group of four or five cadets, all of them talking at once.

"I got a call from the Commandant's office," Gates said. "They're drafting a letter of reprimand."

He waited for Kathleen to say something, but she wanted all the facts.

"It'll go in my official file, which means I won't get promoted the next time around."

And this is what it sounds like, he thought. *The end of a career.*

"Are they going to relieve you?" she asked. He could hear, in her voice, that she was on the verge of tears.

"No," Tom answered.

"Then there's some hope," she said quickly. "You still have a chance. I mean, right up until the promotion board meets and sees the letter, or right up until they pick another assignment for us."

"That's only a matter of time, Kathleen. They're not going to pull the letter."

She was crying now, and Tom Gates felt his own eyes well up for the pain he had caused her, for all the repercussions that would come their way. He looked up and noticed he'd left the door to his office open. He wondered if any of the cadets in the hallway could hear him.

"You're always telling the cadets 'never give up.' Well, we're not giving up," she insisted. "We've got to do something."

"There's not much we can do," he said.

"I'm not going to sit here and kiss ass for two or three years just to be forced out of the service," Kathleen said sharply.

"You're getting your Irish up," he said, smiling into the phone. He had always loved the fight in her.

"I love you, Tom," she said. "You don't deserve this. We've worked too hard and too long and we're not going to take it lying down."

"What choice do we have?" Gates said.

"Leave that up to me," she said. "In the meantime, you just try to stay out of trouble."

And with that, she hung up. No good-bye, no see you later, hurry home, stay away. Just a click.

Tom Gates put the phone in its cradle. As much as Kathleen loved him, and no matter how many battles she was willing to fight for him, he couldn't see a way out of this jam.

He pulled a sheaf of papers out of his in-box and several disciplinary reports—small white sheets that listed infractions of regulations—fluttered to his desk top. With a few strokes of his pen he meted out stiff punishments to cadets who'd been sleeping during morning inspection, or whose shoes were not well shined at formation, or who'd been caught out of their rooms after Taps. He would do his duty up until his last hour in uniform, whether that was days or decades away.

Unlike her husband, Kathleen Gates wasn't going to be content to let things run their course. Kathleen had seen, firsthand, how a few unexpected turns could ruin a career. She had been a sophomore in college, studying mass communications at Penn, when her older brother had his fifteen minutes of fame. Unfortunately, the spotlight was not flattering.

Lieutenant Brian Patrick McDade and his Navy SEAL team were training in Honduras—really nothing more than a thin cover story for their real mission in neighboring Nicaragua: a reconnaissance of possible sites for invasion by American forces. As it turned out, they didn't do much, just walk around on some beaches and in the woods for a while. But the President's aggressive policies were attracting attention at home.

The press developed a few uncertain leads about American military personnel crossing the border into the sovereign country of Nicaragua. An American journalist found and confronted McDade while the Navy men were in Honduras, the invited guests of that neighboring country. The writer began following and photographing the Americans. Thinking, perhaps, that he might provoke a comment from the closemouthed naval officer, the journalist picked a fight with McDade, the smallest member of the team. It was both McDade's good fortune and his biggest mistake that he slugged the reporter in Honduras. That little fact of geography allowed the Navy to deny that the commandos were headed for Nicaragua; it was Brian McDade's personal misfortune that he ever laid a hand on the civilian. The story made the wires, and McDade—a Naval Academy graduate whose family had been serving in uniform since the Civil War—was called home in disgrace.

The White House, eager to put out the fires, left a few of its staff members out in the cold. The most notable of these was a Marine Lieutenant Colonel who admitted without apology that he had lied to Congress. The most forgotten of the victims in this sudden shift in policy was the Navy Lieutenant with the bad temper.

Every year Kathleen invited her older brother to visit her family at Thanksgiving, at Christmas, in the summer. And every year Brian agreed to meet his sister for one dinner in some nearby town because he refused to set foot on a military reservation.

And Kathleen Gates had done more than watch her brother's heart break. She developed a hard, cynical spot, a callus on the spirit. She would not forget how quickly the service, the Navy her brother loved, had turned on one of its own. More than that, she was determined that nothing similar would happen to her husband. In protecting Tom, she was protecting herself.

As she undressed for bed, she thought about a conversation she'd had that weekend with her brother. She had called Brian to tell him what had happened and to ask for advice on what she might do. Brian was smart, if unlucky, and had always been able to come up with a scheme or two.

"The Academies are vulnerable right now," he'd told her. "All these Congressional weinies snooping around have everybody nervous. I talked to a buddy of mine recently who's down at Annapolis, writing policy for the Superintendent's office. He said Navy is coming up with some contingency plans in case they're ordered to downsize."

She had been tempted to ask what any of that had to do with her and her husband's latest screw-up, but Kathleen had kept quiet, figuring that Brian was going somewhere with this. Her mother had always told her that she was the devious child, but Kathleen thought Brian was the sneaky one.

"If they somehow wanted to keep a lid on what happened, you know, because of all the attention . . . that might help you," he said.

"It looks like they're going to deal with this quickly," she'd said. "One swift kick and it's all over."

"That's as it stands now," he'd said. "But if there were other developments. . . ."

Kathleen had been quiet then. She had tried to imagine what other developments could take advantage of the fact that things at West Point were touchy right now, but she kept being distracted by the talk of downsizing.

"If they cut West Point, Tom might be out of a job anyway."

"Maybe there'll be a place for him in a smaller institution," Brian had answered. "But first things first."

As she lay on her bed and listened to the sounds of summer night outside the window, Kathleen turned the problems over in her head. It wasn't as if she could get Wayne Holder to be silent; he and Tom had already talked to the Commandant about what happened Friday night.

She rolled over on her side. It was hot in the room and she pulled her nightgown up above her waist.

But suppose there was something else the administration wanted to keep quiet, she asked herself.

There was nothing, of course. But that didn't mean she couldn't create something.

CHAPTER 4

JACQUELINE TIMMER WAS THE PICTURE OF THE PROFESSIONAL soldier as she walked down the long hallway of the classroom building. She greeted each of the several score cadets who said hello to her, confident that not a single one would have guessed that she was on the prowl.

There was a small paper sign outside each classroom in Thayer Hall, the massive riding hall turned academic building, that gave the name of the professor who used that room. Timmer had checked the east hallway and was now cruising the west, books and garrison cap under her arm, greeting cadets and former students, nodding hello to the always-frightened plebes who rendered the obligatory "Good morning, ma'am" as she passed.

She found him near the south rotunda. He hadn't pulled the shade on the door and so she could see him, sitting on the desk, hands wrapped around one knee, a long leg cocked up as he leaned back, listening to a cadet. She could not hear him respond, but she saw him laugh with the students. He was wearing khakis and a short-sleeved shirt. His arms were tanned; the little blond hairs there were bleached almost white, soft against the hardness of his forearm. She lingered for a moment, not the least concerned about the cadets and officers in the hallway who saw her standing before this door, mooning like a junior high school girl.

"Hello, there, Captain Timmer."

She turned around; it was her husband.

"Hello," she said, trying to sound casual.

"Your classroom at this end of the hallway?" he asked.

"No, actually, it's at the other end. I saw Layne Marshall in there and thought I'd wave."

"Oh," Rob said, peering into the room. No surprise, no comment. Just "oh."

"Are you teaching this period?" she asked, trying to create a conversation out of nothing. She turned and began to walk down the hallway, steering Rob with her.

"Yeah, on the other hall."

Side by side now, they fell into step with each other. Jackie always wondered, when that happened, if Rob did it consciously.

"Hey, troops."

They turned around to see Major Jon Hillard, a philosophy professor and Jackie Timmer's officemate, striding down the hallway behind them. In contrast to the other instructors, who wore the summer uniform of short-sleeved green shirt with no tie, Hillard was wearing his class "A" dress greens, complete with black tie, long-sleeved shirt, and heavy green jacket weighted down with the decorations and awards that read like a text of Hillard's career so far.

"Ah, the Timmer family," Hillard said, smiling a gap-toothed smile. "How they hangin', Rob?"

Jackie laughed. Jon Hillard was one of the brightest philosophy professors on the English Department faculty; he was also a rough-cut soldier. He prided himself, she believed, on keeping that contrast as sharp as possible, mixing quotations from Shakespeare and the ancients with the bawdy humor and ribald commentary that marked the speech of many soldiers.

"Dressed for the occasion, I see," Rob Timmer said.

As far as Jackie Timmer knew, Jon was the only instructor at West Point who wore his dress greens to class on the first few days. Most of the other faculty members, and not a few of the cadets, thought he was showing off. He did have an impressive catalog of achievements there on his jacket for all who knew the code: a combat patch from the First Infantry Division's action in Desert Storm, with a bronze star he won in that short, brisk fight. Parachutist badge, Ranger tab—he was a walking encyclopedia of the Army's badge-producing schools. At West Point, where it was cool to be understated about one's awards and decorations, Jon Hillard came to class on the first few days of every semester as a walking advertisement for the Army.

"The little peckerheads don't really know what this place is about," he told Rob. "They're so caught up with how many papers they have to write this semester and when their lab problems are due that they forget that we're here to train soldiers."

"You make it sound like teaching philosophy is tank gunnery," Rob Timmer said.

Jon put his arm around Rob's shoulder. They were a study in contrasts, Jackie Timmer thought. Where Rob was tall and lean, Jon was short and thick, a bull to Rob's gazelle. Rob Timmer was handsome, in an ascetic sort of way. Jon Hillard was stone ugly. His head, round as a melon, was shaved. He had thick, rubbery lips; his nose—broken twice during his years bouncing around inside tanks—twisted sharply to the left. In contrast, he had a beautiful voice. Once Jackie had sat next to him at chapel and had been so surprised at his rich singing that she had stared at him, plainly amazed that such a pure note could ring from a misshapen bell.

Jackie Timmer suspected that her officemate didn't like her husband.

"In fact, Rob old buddy, it's philosophy and their study of English that gives them the tools they need to name their beliefs. And that's the first step in developing a value system, you see? Just as you need a mathematical language before you can seek to advance that discipline, right?"

"Right," Rob said, squeezing out from under Jon's hand. Jackie knew that Rob would complain later; at the moment she was glad Jon had shown up and taken the limelight away from her standing outside Marshall's classroom.

"A dispatch from headquarters for you, my queen," Jon

said, fluttering a yellow message slip at Jackie and bowing slightly at the waist. Rob had said—more than once—that Jon had a crush on Jackie; Jackie maintained that Hillard thought of her as a little sister.

As he handed her the note, doors up and down the hall began to open, spilling a tide of gray uniforms headed for the next class period.

"Ah," Hillard said, pulling his books tightly under his arm, throwing back his bald head and thrusting his chin forward. "Cry havoc, and let slip the dogs of war."

Rob stood staring at Hillard's short, wide back as he moved up the hallway, barking and scattering cadets out of his way.

"What's with that guy?"

"That's just his personality," Jackie Timmer said, opening the note in her hand. "He's an individual," she said, putting a little more emphasis on *"He's"* than she meant to. Rob Timmer didn't seem to notice.

"Oh, damn," she said, reading.

"What is it?"

"A summons, this one from the Dean," she said. "I have to go over right after this class."

"Does it say what for?"

"Oh, no doubt something of earth-shaking importance," she said testily. "They probably need someone to stand around while some film crew takes more pictures of the Hudson River or a parade, or someone to explain to reporters, for the umpteenth time, just how the Honor Code works. I could just scream."

Jackie Timmer was not unused to calls from the Dean, from the Public Affairs Office, or even the office of the Superintendent. Photogenic, articulate, and successful, she had become an unofficial spokesperson for West Point. The Public Affairs Officer, a fat Lieutenant Colonel who was a little too chummy for comfort, told her, "I wouldn't bother to wheel you out for every photo opportunity except I'm not as pretty as you."

"It might not take too long," Rob offered, taking the note from her hand.

Jackie Timmer narrowed her eyes at him. "It isn't that, and you know it," she said.

They'd been through this before; Jackie resented the fact that she'd been made—in Jon Hillard's words—a "spokes-model" for West Point. It wasn't the time away from her duties; in fact she didn't mind having something to do every once in a while besides grade the endless stacks of cadet essays, and she did occasionally meet a big name television celebrity. The problem was with her peers.

In the shrinking Army, career soldiers were hard pressed to come up with ways to make themselves noticed, to differentiate their good performance from the good performances of their comrades. It was no longer enough to be competent; it was no longer enough even to be stellar; one had to be stellar and self-aggrandizing. Jackie Timmer did not seek out the publicity, she had it thrust on her. But jealous peers wouldn't accept that, and it cost her among friends and colleagues. Rob reminded her that people who snubbed her over such a thing weren't true friends anyway; she knew that to be true and was self-confident enough to live without their approval. But she didn't seek the notoriety; she didn't want it.

Rob wanted it for her, for what it could do to advance their linked careers as West Point's most visible officer couple. What benefited her benefited the man who was married to her.

"Hey," Rob said, his enthusiasm grating his wife, "maybe it's about the Bruckner Commission."

"Oh, wouldn't that be great," Jackie said, noting the bitchy tone in her voice.

"I can go in and mix it up with the most inflammatory thing to reach West Point since news of the firing on Fort Sumter."

"This doesn't have to be a bad experience," Rob said. There was a little too much of the lecture in his voice.

"This could be some major positive exposure. If West Point goes away, you may be in a position to help us . . . see which life boats are working as the ship goes down."

As Rob spoke Jackie could see, over his shoulder and a long way down the hallway, Layne Marshall emerge from his classroom. There were two or three cadets sticking close to him, listening intently. Marshall stopped in the center of the corridor, using one hand to sweep his thick hair off his forehead as he spoke to the cadets, who stood around him in identical poses, books in their left hands, feet together, erect, attentive, enthralled.

"I'm just a little tired of being Miss West Point," Timmer said.

"Isn't that Mrs. West Point?" Rob asked, trying to salvage a little humor.

Jackie looked at him, offered a halfhearted smile. "I suppose."

"Gotta run," he said, looking at his watch. "See you later."

He chucked her on the arm; they would not kiss while in uniform, not with hundreds of cadets around. A little peck on the cheek wasn't a peck on the cheek at all, but a Public Display of Affection, something else reduced to black and white.

Jackie was often tempted to kiss her husband anyway, flaunting the rules just to see what he would do.

Rob walked down the hall without waving. When she turned around, Marshall was also gone. She was both disappointed and relieved.

"Captain Timmer, so nice to see you again," Brigadier General David Simon said as he stood and motioned her toward a chair in front of his desk. The Dean's office was in the same stone tower as the Superintendent's, two floors down. Its decor—oak paneling, polished floor, desk as big as a lifeboat—conveyed the same messages of permanence, steadfastness. Simon was about Timmer's height, five eight, with round glasses, quick, birdlike eyes, and a shiny pate fringed by salt-and-pepper hair. His hand, when she shook it, was dry and cool.

Jackie Timmer had been in his office at least a half-dozen times over the past year, either to be briefed on some public relations project or to brief the general on what had happened with this or that visitor. She always had an uncomfortable feeling she associated with car lots, as if she were about to be sold something she didn't want to buy.

"How did your first class go?" Simon asked as he dropped into his seat.

Timmer settled back in one of the leather armchairs.

When she leaned back, she found she was looking up at Simon. She scooted forward and pulled herself up straight, her legs tucked demurely in front of her and crossed at the ankles, so that she could look him in the eye.

"Fine, sir. I had the plebes this morning, and there's always that horrible smell in the room."

"Smell?" Simon asked.

"It's a combination of the new uniforms, the sweat—they're always running, always late, always near panic—and fear, I guess. We always tell the new instructors in the English Department to expect that the classroom is going to smell bad for a while, until the plebes get the hang of coming to class."

"Interesting," Simon said. "I'll have to stop by and visit sometime."

Someone else's class, I hope, Timmer thought.

General Simon's unannounced classroom visits were the kind of experiences that made great stories years after the fact, although there was nothing humorous about them while they were happening. An historian by training, Simon would frequently launch into some soliloquy about the historical context of whatever the cadets were studying. There was a story about one history instructor whose class was completely overtaken by Simon, who talked for nearly the full period about how the careful student of history may recognize the beginnings of significant trends and historical periods even as they are occurring. When the Dean left, the instructor escorted him into the hallway. The captain returned to find that some cadet wit had written on the board, "Dear Diary: Today the Hundred Years' War started."

"Let me get to the reason I asked you to stop by," Simon said. "As you know, we are expecting visits by members of the Bruckner Commission over the next few weeks. The Commission representatives have free access, of course, to interview anyone they want, anyone who wants to be interviewed. That's the best way to ensure they get a fair picture of the Academy. Senator Bruckner is also—well, obsessed might be too strong a word—is also very *concerned* about preserving the confidence of the people interviewed. And I think that's a good idea as well. If people had to worry about the command looking over their shoulders, they might not give the most forthright answers. Does that make sense to you?"

"Yes, sir," Timmer answered.

"So we don't want to interfere with the committee's work in any way, or even create the impression that we're trying to influence answers." Simon was nodding slightly as he spoke, as if to encourage agreement, a nervous movement that he didn't seem aware of. Timmer found herself nodding as well.

"The Superintendent's position is that the Academy can stand up to the closest scrutiny. We have nothing to hide. Nothing at all."

Simon looked at her for a long moment, then looked down at his desk, though he didn't seem to focus on anything there. Timmer got the impression that she was watching a poorly staged dramatic pause.

Where Simon had been confident before, he seemed hesitant now.

"While the interviews will do a great deal to shape how the visitors report on West Point, they'll spend only an hour or two—tops—with any of the people they interview. A much more important relationship will develop between the interviewers and whatever officer works with them over a period of weeks."

There it is, Jackie Timmer thought. *Nursemaid to a bunch of Congressional aides. If the Academy can stand on its own merits, why are we so paranoid about the visit?*

"That, as I'm sure you guessed, is where you come in. I'd like you to keep me apprised of whatever you see and hear in connection with the Bruckner Commission," he said. "I've already talked this over with your boss. He's concerned about how much time you'll have to devote to this. He wants to make sure—and he has a valid point—that it doesn't interfere with your teaching duties. I told him I thought you could handle it."

He was still nodding, almost imperceptibly, but now Timmer found it annoying to the point of distraction.

"In fact," he went on, nod, nod, nod, "this might be a good opportunity for you to develop some personal contacts with Congress, contacts that could serve the Academy well in the coming months and could help your career, too."

You sound like my husband, she thought.

He was smiling at her now, as if he'd just given her a gift. Jackie Timmer was tempted to ask if she had a choice in the matter, but she suspected she knew the answer to that. The Bruckner Commission visit was the biggest fire going; she'd just been drafted as a firefighter.

"I'll do my best, sir," she said.

"I knew you would," Simon answered, still nodding.

She's a beauty, that one.

Simon wondered if she knew it. He had met her husband once, an instructor in the math department. Like her, the man was all strong limbs and clear eyes and sharp, handsome features. Unlike her, he was dull as an old knife.

Simon kicked back in his chair after she'd left, thinking about the way her legs moved under the green of her issue trousers, of how her hair shifted when she'd given him a snappy salute, standing, feet together, back straight, in front of his desk, a soldier with a mission.

In the mid-seventies Simon had been one to resist the coming of women. An instructor then, he had joined in the chorus predicting the end of the institution, clamoring that a few women in gray would change everything. He'd been proven wrong, and lately had come to think that not only did the coming of women not hurt West Point, their contributions far outweighed the silly little traditions— mostly boys' school stuff—that had gone by the wayside.

And they're so lovely to look at, too, he thought.

Simon picked up the phone to call Tony Moro, but then replaced the receiver. He wanted Timmer to get used to the idea that she was his pipeline to the Bruckner Commission. He wasn't yet sure how he was going to use her, but somehow she was going to help him implement his plan to get rid of Flynn. Moro might be squeamish about using Jackie Timmer to embarrass the Superintendent; Simon did not share those reservations. Flynn was ready to lie down and give away whatever the civilians wanted. What the hell kind of fighter was that?

"Anything he brings on himself is his own doing," Simon said out loud.

His conscience was mildly assuaged, but he pushed the phone away.

Better to play this hand close to the vest, he thought. *I'll tell Tony Moro only what he needs to know.*

Jackie Timmer had no idea how to stop being the Academy spokesperson, the point in these little jousts with the media. She didn't think she was capable of deliberately doing a poor job, although that would be an easy out. She was tired of it, tired of Rob always looking over her shoulder, weighing the advantages for their careers of all the extra work she was doing. She was tired of the Dean and the Public Affairs Officer drafting her. It wasn't that she minded the workload. That all evened itself out after a while anyway, as all junior faculty members drew extra duties, in addition to their teaching loads. And if she got to visit New York occasionally, if she was interviewed on a morning news show or escorted a famous journalist, that had to be more interesting than playing chaperone to some old class back for its fiftieth reunion, arranging bus transportation and visits to the Cadet Mess, and listening to the old codgers complain that the Corps of Cadets had gone to hell.

So what are you whining about? she thought.

What indeed.

Suddenly she didn't like being watched so closely.

Jackie Timmer was the precious only daughter in a family of five. It had been her idea to attend West Point once she was old enough to realize that her father, a minister, did not have the means to send all his children to college. When a guidance counselor suggested she look at West Point, she didn't think she fit the profile the Academy sought. She'd been wrong. In fact, she had been, from her first weeks at West Point, a successful cadet—a good cadet. She was exactly what the Academy wanted: athletic, competitive, straight and narrow. Inexperienced, ready to be molded.

Athletics made her competitive; being the only girl in a house full of boys made her used to standing out; being a minister's daughter conditioned her to being watched. All of that had continued after her arrival at West Point. Gifted athlete, easygoing personality, a natural beauty, she drew admirers like a flame draws moths. She was the dream of the mythmakers who handled recruiting, the spin doctors who put together the catalogs that went out to America's high schools. They adopted her early; for a few years her picture appeared in nearly every print and photo release the Academy sent out.

Come to West Point, the photos of Jackie Timmer said. *Come here, look like this.*

It was the same philosophy that sold clothes and cars and any number of other products, and if it didn't seem appropriate for West Point, well, no one asked her opinion. The attention had perplexed her at first. In the crucible that was plebe year, it had helped sustain her; she was never wanting for friends. But there was a cost to minor celebrity, one that she was only becoming aware of lately. Public figures don't have private lives.

She had been a star on women's track during her days at the Academy; later, a successful platoon leader, then a general's aide when she was a lieutenant at Fort Lewis.

She had thought her marriage would give her a private life, a place where she was free to fail, free to be something short of perfect. Her mistake was in choosing a husband who did not understand that need. She loved Rob Timmer, and she knew he adored her; but she had questions he could not answer. He would never understand the cost of constant scrutiny.

Rob was almost pathologically optimistic; everything that happened to him, he believed, happened for a reason. Everything had the potential to help him improve. His desk was covered with aphorisms, index cards printed in his neat, steady hand, a soldier's *vade mecum.*

Make do. Lean forward in the foxhole. What doesn't kill you makes you stronger. Discipline is the soul of an Army. Duty is the sublimest word in our language.

Jackie Timmer was no longer a believer. Somewhere along the way she had lost that optimism, like something fallen out of her field pack on the way to this spot.

The little mission from General Simon was another infringement, another something that Rob would see as an opportunity but that she felt was an imposition. She knew she would be good at it. She knew she would charm whatever crabby dilettante the Bruckner Commission sent to stir up things at West Point. Male or female, she could win them all over, and it didn't take an effort. She knew that was a talent, she knew that many people envied it, that it could serve her alma mater well, that it was a gift that she had to use, as her father would have said, to the greater glory of God. Sometimes it felt like a plague.

She smiled at the cadets who saluted her on her way back to the office. She greeted two of the professors, full colonels, who were coming out of the building as she came in, flashing her gigawatt smile, a mouth full of straight white teeth, pretty, professional—a small-breasted, short-haired Barbie in uniform.

She walked directly to her empty office—her officemate was still teaching—and closed the door carefully. She set her books down on the desk and walked to the window. Below, the Hudson crept past in summer sluggishness. The mountains just across the river were sheathed in humid air; it was as if she watched them through tulle.

Captain Jacqueline Timmer looked out at the beautiful view below her office window and sorted through the building blocks of her life. She had a career she loved, students who adored her, an emerging talent for writing that was developing even as she taught others the craft. She had a kind, handsome husband who loved her as best he could. She had a notoriety that was the envy of many, wit, charm, intelligence, looks, health. She had everything she'd sought, and now she wasn't sure she wanted any of it.

What she did want was a chance to choose her own path, not what someone else expected, not what someone else needed. Not what looked good or played well in the media. Just something that was gloriously, selfishly hers. She pressed her forehead to the cool glass and was standing that way when Jon Hillard came into the room behind her.

"Well, what did they stick you with?" he asked.

Good old Jon. Lovable, ugly, and more sensitive to what she was thinking than her own husband.

"I have to escort the Bruckner Commission people around," she answered without turning to face him.

"And let me guess, you don't consider this a plum."

"Bingo."

"Your husband will," he said, dropping his books noisily to the desk.

Jackie lowered her head, hiding a smile. She often wondered if Jon's dislike for Rob was jealousy. Jon had once told her that she and he were soulmates. Through a tongue-loosening, truth-finding haze of four or five beers at a department function, he'd confessed, "In another place, another time, another life, we would have made a great couple."

For just that instant, he had been a poet. Not a teacher of poetry, not a borrower or a glib thief, but a poet.

"Of course," he'd joked almost immediately, "in that other life, I don't look like a troll."

Just before he'd pulled back into the protection of self-mockery, she'd leaned over and kissed him on the cheek.

Jon came over and sat on the desk nearest the window; she sat down next to him, her leg just touching his. He had removed his heavy coat; there were half moons of perspiration under each arm. The top edge of his shirt collar was dark with sweat where it dug into his neck.

Timmer swung her feet back and forth under the polished wood of the work station; each of them also had a bookcase and a computer desk. The walls were covered in framed prints, photos chronicling the careers of the tenants. Hillard's section of the white wall sported a poster of an Abrams tank, a pencil drawing of one of the huge monsters churning a cloud of dust, the long snout of its main gun pointed at the viewer like a dark, deadly hole. The drawing was superimposed on a map of Kuwait and Iraq.

Above Timmer's desk there was a framed print of the castle at Heidelberg, where she'd spent a two-year tour and where she'd met and married Rob. He had given her the print, which was not a very good one and was poorly framed, and she'd hung it in her office out of a sense of duty.

"So now you're pondering all you have going for you, right? Somewhere in the back of that pretty head you hear your father's voice saying, 'Count your blessings, dear.' Am I right? Beauty, brains, students who love you, an officemate who's crazy about you."

She couldn't help but smile at him, this ridiculous looking man who was so happy just to be near her. He reached up and touched her elbow, gently, with the tip of a single finger.

"And that's what pissed you off, isn't it?"

"Fuckin' A," Timmer said, smiling now, laughing.

Jon was smiling, too, but there was a sad shadow there.

"I have an idea, let's tell the Dean to fuck off."

"Sounds great."

"Yeah," he said, jumping down from the desk. He was right beside her now; she could smell his breath, smell the heavy odor of sweat.

He picked up the telephone and began speaking, his voice dropped to a husky, breathy whisper—Marilyn Monroe on steroids.

"General Simon? Yes, this is Captain Timmer," he cooed into the handset. "I've considered your offer and I think you should contact my agent. I mean, if I'm so good that you can't make a move without me, don't you think you should throw a little something my way, you bald-headed old bastard?"

Timmer laughed out loud; she could feel her tense shoulders loosen.

"And another thing, about this tiny office I have over here. I was thinking we could switch . . . that's right. I'll move over there to Taylor Hall and you can come to Lincoln Hall and share a space with my clever officemate, the erudite, handsome Major Jon Hillard."

Hillard set the phone back in its cradle.

"He said it all sounded good, except the part about sharing an office with me," he said.

Jackie put her arm on Jon's shoulder. He was a few inches shorter, and she let her arm lay loosely, wrist at his collarbone, fingers hanging relaxed on the top of his back.

"Thanks, Jon."

"Hey," Hillard said, shifting, suddenly uncomfortable. "Who loves ya, baby?"

CHAPTER 5

KATHLEEN GATES WAS LEANING OVER THE DESK IN HER HUS-band's office, finishing a note she was leaving for him, when Wayne Holder knocked on the open door.

"Afternoon, ma'am," he said.

Kathleen straightened, put one hand on her hip and gave him an exasperated look.

"I mean, Kathleen," he corrected himself, smiling woodenly.

Kathleen Gates rattled him. He'd told Dearborn that she was the meat-eater in that family, and there was an edgy air of danger about her. As he looked at her now, smiling from behind the gray metal desk with the ridiculously outsized MAJOR TOM GATES nameplate, he wondered if being around her felt dangerous because she was the forbidden fruit.

"I'm looking for Major Gates."

"Really," she said, tossing her hair back over one shoulder, grinning as if this were some sort of joke both of them were in on. "Me too."

"He may be out running or playing at the gym; his athletic bag is gone," she went on, turning a palm up in a see-for-yourself gesture. Then she locked in on him with those startling blue eyes. "Would you like to leave him a note, or shall we just rifle his drawers looking for contraband?"

"Nah, I've already done that," Holder said. "Nothing interesting there."

When Kathleen replied, "You've got that right," Holder realized he'd been joking at her husband's expense—and she'd gone along with it, a kindred spirit.

Kathleen let her eyes run the length of him; he saw it clearly. He was dressed in his gym uniform: black shorts with gold, block-lettered ARMY; gray shirt with his name printed above the Academy crest.

Yes, she's definitely getting an eyeful, Holder thought. He crossed his arms over his chest and rolled his shoulders, a gesture he'd seen young women do when he and his buddies stared at their breasts. He didn't feel threatened, exactly, but he didn't feel protected.

Wayne Holder knew a few things about young women, about the college girls who came to home football games, about the nineteen- and twenty-year-old sisters of his buddies, the ones he got fixed up with on leaves, on fall weekends. He would have guessed that he knew a thing or two about older women; he would have imagined that interaction with a thirty-year-old would be different only in a matter of degree from flirting with a twenty-year-old. Kathleen Gates was disproving his theory if only with her ability to make him squirm.

Behind him, the door was wide open, the hallway filled with cadets. Gates's office sat at one end of the bottom floor, tucked away with the offices of two other tactical officers. Because it was past the stairwell and at a dead end, no cadets walked by. But they were close, which made her little flirtation—if that's what this was—even more dangerous.

Holder wished he'd already written the note, bringing it from his own room. He could have left the paper on the desk and beat a quick retreat. But he hadn't anticipated that Kathleen Gates would be guarding the throne room.

"Yes, I do need to leave a message," he said, advancing on the desk, trying to sound casual. He stood in front of it; she slid a pen and paper toward him. As he looked down at the blank yellow space, Kathleen put both her hands on the desk top between them and leaned forward. There was a rush of citrus smell as he caught her perfume. His eyes clicked upward; in spite of the fact that he was concentrating just as hard as he could on staying cool, collected, he stared for a millisecond too long at her breasts. Looking up, he met her eyes and she smiled at him.

Caught you, the smile said.

"Forget what you were going to write about?" she asked.

"I . . . uh . . . I could stop back after I get my car from the parking lot," he managed, putting the pen down on the still-blank page, straightening almost to attention.

"Oh, headed out tonight?" she asked. "Who's the lucky girl?"

"Just some of the guys going to the movies," Holder said, suddenly feeling a little dull.

In fact, he and his friends had been excited about their new privileges as seniors—weeknights out on the town. Their peers at civilian colleges had been enjoying these freedoms for years, of course. The cadets satisfied the imbalance by adopting a smug sense of having come a harder route. Now, at the threshold of their last year, West Point grudgingly handed them privileges afforded most high school kids. When he and a couple of his friends planned to go out, they'd felt as if they'd arrived, as if they'd grown up. Now, standing before this woman with the disconcerting smile, Wayne Holder felt a little juvenile.

"I *love* to go to the movies," Kathleen said, moving around to the front of the desk. Holder was glued in place. Normally, such a comment from a young woman was a ploy: invite *me* to the movies. Could it be that obvious with Kathleen Gates? Holder felt as if he'd stumbled into the middle of some game whose rules he didn't know.

What the hell is she doing? he thought.

"Uh . . . what have you . . . like . . . seen lately?" he asked, his command of the language melting as she drew near.

"Absolutely nothing," she answered. "Since I've had kids I've joined the ranks of the cinematically challenged."

She had drawn close, leaning her backside on the forward edge of the desk; he was still facing it. She wasn't touching him, but he could easily have lifted his hand to her face, to her hair. Holder, wooden as a puppet, held his arms at his sides; he wanted to touch her, he wanted to run. There was a silent moment that bothered her not at all; in fact, Holder thought, she seemed to be enjoying his discomfiture.

"So tell me, Wayne," she said. "Do you run all the way to the parking lot for your car?"

"No way," he said, relieved to be able to answer a direct question. "It's way up behind the stadium." He jerked his thumb over his shoulder, pointing vaguely in the direction of the football stadium and its hillside parking lots, where cadet seniors were allowed to park during the week.

"You have the runner's legs for it," she said, looking down.

Holder tried to swallow. Outside in the hallway a cadet complained, distinctly if unimaginatively, "Those fucking dick-lickers over in the math department are screwing with us already."

Holder felt a little embarrassed. Kathleen Gates didn't flinch. He started to speak when something brushed his leg, startling him; he jerked back. When he looked down, her empty shoe lay on its side on the floor. Her bare foot was arched like a hook where she had caressed his calf.

"Jumpy, Wayne?"

She slipped her shoe back on and turned away from him. She was thus facing away from the door when her husband walked into the room.

"Well, well, well," Major Gates boomed. "Plotting a mutiny, I'll bet."

Holder snapped to attention, his face hot. "Good afternoon, sir," he said. Kathleen Gates, safely on the other side of the desk, smiled.

Gates walked behind the desk and kissed his wife on the cheek. Even as she lifted her face to be kissed, Kathleen kept her eyes on Holder.

"At ease, Holder. What do you want?" Gates asked, looking hard at the cadet.

Holder fought the urge to wipe a bead of sweat from his hairline.

"I stopped by to see when you wanted to get together with the plebes, sir."

"I'll have to let you know. My calendar for next week is in a state of flux right now."

"Roger that, sir," Holder said, ready to bolt for the door. "I'll stand by, then."

He nodded at Gates, then at Kathleen. "Afternoon, ma'am."

"Let me know how the movie turns out, Wayne," she said.

"Yes, ma'am," Holder said, backpedaling. "I certainly will."

When Holder had gone, Tom Gates sat down at his desk. "You know, half the time that little prick doesn't seem so bad."

"He's just a kid," Kathleen Gates said. She stepped behind her husband's chair, put her hands on his shoulders, rubbed her fingers at the base of his neck. Tom Gates tilted his big head forward, a puppy wanting to be scratched.

"I heard that the Bruckner Commission will be interviewing next week," she said.

"Mmm," Gates answered, his head lowered now.

"I also heard they'll interview people who ask to be interviewed."

Tom Gates sat up quickly.

"Forget it, Kathleen."

She pushed down on his shoulders, gently coaxing him to lean back in the chair.

"Oh, Tom," she said. "What are you afraid of? I think I could contribute to the commission's work. They should hear from an outsider." She ran her fingernails over the short hair on the back of his head; Gates remained stiff.

"Kathleen," her husband said. "You're the last person on post I'd describe as an outsider. You have this Army thing wired."

"Well, I know how things work," she said. "And that's a good thing for you. This commission visit might prove just the thing to save your career."

"What's that supposed to mean?"

"I'm not sure yet," she said.

Best not to get Tom any more worked up about this. Big bad warrior that he was, he didn't really have the stomach for the skirmishing that lay ahead of them. Tom Gates was still naive enough to think that people behaved as they did for good reasons, that people mostly told the truth, that hard work was rewarded. He had the luxury of believing all that, Kathleen thought, because she had a clear take on things as they really were.

Now that the stakes were so high, the obstacles so huge, Tom especially needed someone with a clear vision of how the world really worked. Thank God he had Kathleen.

I have an idea, she thought. *And Mister Holder will help us out just by being a healthy young male.*

Tom Gates settled against the back of the chair and she reached one arm around his chest, nuzzling his neck.

"Kath*leen,*" he said. He was uncomfortable with the display of affection, but his wife didn't act this way all that often and he was loathe to tell her to stop.

"What?"

"I just don't think it would be cool if some cadet walked in here and saw us making out."

"Oh," she said, biting his ear. "The poor little sexually frustrated things, they could stand a thrill now and then."

Lieutenant General Patrick Flynn stood on the wide veranda of Quarters 100, a short, taut figure in green against the whitewashed brick of the wall behind him. On the sidewalk just a few feet away, hundreds of seniors— firsties—streamed by, moving in loud clusters, in pairs, in groups big and small. They wore the summer dress uniform called "white over gray": white shirt, gray trousers with black stripe running down the side of each leg, white saucer caps. They were uniformly fit and, as far as Flynn could see, uniformly happy to be at the beginning of their last year. They had achieved the pinnacle of their short careers: the seniors were lords and masters over everything they surveyed at West Point. They had the most privileges and the most responsibility. But what animated them was the not-far-off scent of freedom, the promise of the change that would come when they pinned on the gold bars of second lieutenants in the spring. In between this night and that were months of hard work, academic projects, exams, and competitions, a dank winter in the barracks. Yet for tonight, at least, they were exuberant. Standing near them, Patrick Flynn felt their reflected enthusiasm.

The cadets were on their way from the evening meal to the cavernous auditorium in Eisenhower Hall. The occasion was the Dean's address to the first class, an annual event that, General Simon had told Flynn, was meant to help the seniors and soon-to-be Army officers get an historical perspective on the events shaping the world they were about to enter and on the challenges the Army would face in the next decade.

"The past," Simon had written Flynn in a pedantic note, "is the key to the future. Indeed, it's *the* key to their future."

The door to the house opened behind him and Flynn's aide, Major Darrell Carter, stuck his head out the door.

"Captain Timmer just called, sir," he said. "She's picked up Braintree and is on her way. ETA is twelve minutes."

Flynn nodded.

"She's good, right?" he asked Carter.

"The best, sir," Carter said, stepping out onto the planking. Major Carter had suggested to his boss that they send Timmer to the airport to meet the man Carter was already calling "the Inquisitor."

"Public Affairs is always asking her to represent the Academy. She's smart, funny, attractive, personable—I've never seen her fail to impress a visitor. She'll have Braintree on our side by the end of the evening, maybe even by the time she pulls up here."

"I hope so," Flynn said, tugging at the bottom of his green coat. The big silver stars—three on each shoulder—fairly glittered.

Claude Braintree was the point man for the Bruckner Commission at West Point, and he was a mystery. Senator Bruckner, knowing that the military would try to "G-2" his choice—that is, gain information that might help win over the Senator's designated hitter—had named Braintree at the last possible moment. His exact arrival time was also kept from Flynn until just hours earlier.

Flynn had made a half dozen calls that afternoon but was mostly still ignorant of Braintree's background. There was, however, one word that came up in conversations with several people who knew Braintree: ambition.

"I hope you're right about Timmer," Flynn said. "I hate dealing with an unknown quantity like this."

That's kind of how people around here feel about you, Carter thought.

"Yes, sir," he said.

Captain Jackie Timmer sat in the back seat of the plain military sedan, smiling and nodding as Claude Braintree talked, and remembering a bit of advice her mother gave her when she started dating.

"If there's ever a lull in the conversation," her mother had said, "and you're uncomfortable with it, just ask the boy about himself. Men can entertain themselves for hours that way."

Braintree, Jackie Timmer thought, hardly needed encouragement.

"I think this will be a wonderful opportunity for the Military Academy," Braintree said. "An objective review of how well West Point is meeting its goals, spending the taxpayers' dollars."

Timmer nodded agreement, recognizing a pet phrase of Braintree's boss, Senator Bruckner. Bruckner was always talking—whenever there was a microphone or a print journalist with a notebook around—about the taxpayers' dollars, as if he'd been the first to consider that such resources might need safeguarding.

"Now, why don't you tell me about yourself," Braintree said. "You mentioned that you teach, isn't that right?"

He had a trace of an accent from his native Georgia, but it was so slight that Timmer had to wonder if he deliberately kept that much for effect: the Yale-educated lawyer who could play the good ol' boy. Though he dressed beautifully—double breasted suit in a deep, rich blue, crisp shirt blindingly white—he was not conventionally handsome; his dark hair was thinning and there were startling tufts of hair in each ear. His bottom teeth crowded in on each other and his ears were too big. But his face was all strong lines—eyebrows, jaw, cheeks—and his dark eyes were lively. He seemed to have only one smile, a ridiculously wide one that consumed his whole face.

"This will be my second year teaching English, sir," Timmer said.

"Please," Braintree said, reaching across and touching the back of her hand, "call me Claude."

"OK. Claude. Please call me Jackie. This . . ."

He hadn't removed his hand. When she paused, he withdrew slowly, completely comfortable with himself.

"This is my second year teaching," she continued. "My husband and I managed to get assigned here at the same time."

"I take it he's in the Army, too," Braintree said, smiling widely.

"Yes. He teaches math."

"Is it difficult to get your assignments to work out like that? So that you aren't separated?"

"It can be, although the Army tries to accommodate people."

"And you and your husband are both graduates of West Point?"

Braintree posed the question as if he knew the answer. Timmer had a sharp picture of him as a litigator, throwing his exaggerated smile at the jury box as he skewered a witness.

"Yes, although we met in Germany when we were assigned there. He's a major, a couple of years senior to me."

Braintree glanced out the window as they passed through a five-point intersection that was an ugly jumble of loud, lighted signs and traffic lights.

"Well, I'm sure that it was in the best interest of the Army to keep you two happy, to make sure that you both were assigned here at the same time."

She was about to say that they didn't receive any special attention in their assignment, but then realized that wasn't strictly true. The heads of their respective academic departments had made a few calls, but that was nothing out of the ordinary. Braintree made it sound as if they got special treatment because they were West Pointers.

Jackie Timmer wouldn't realize until later, when she'd had a chance to consider this first conversation with Braintree, that his best trick had been planting that seed of doubt in her mind.

"We didn't really get any special attention," she said. "I mean, beyond what our assignments officers would have done for us anyway. Or done for anyone else coming here to teach."

Braintree looked back at her, smiled widely. "Of course," he said, finding her hand again, patting it with his own. Timmer looked out the window as they rolled over a steel bridge that spanned a postcard stream. This was not light conversation; the Inquisition had begun.

One of Jackie Timmer's strengths in representing West Point was that she put people at ease. Dignitaries, VIPs, journalists, visitors of all stripes relaxed in her company because she was unpretentious, forthright. Comfortable with her place in the great scheme, Jackie Timmer made others comfortable as well. That wasn't going to be the case with Claude Braintree, she realized. Claude Braintree made her nervous.

They drove south on Route 9, climbing Storm King Mountain, which shouldered the Hudson into another turn just before it reached West Point.

"There's a great view of West Point up here, sir . . . Claude," she said. "We're kind of pressed for time, but we could stop for a minute if you'd like to take a look. You can . . ."

"Not this time," Braintree interrupted.

Timmer wasn't used to being cut off. She smiled, paused, continued.

"At any rate, if you get to come back the view from up here is very instructive. You can see how the river makes two ninety-degree turns around West Point, which is what made it the perfect place for the American forts that kept British ships from using the Hudson. Sailing ships had to slow down to navigate the turns. Sometimes they even had to be pulled by longboats because the winds are so tricky down there; all that made them easy targets for American guns."

Braintree shined his wide smile her way, but his look said *So what?*

At the foot of the mountain, where the road doubled back toward Washington Gate, the car drew abreast of the golf course.

"Does this belong to West Point?" Braintree asked.

"Yes, sir," Timmer said. "It's part of recreational services here. Do you play golf?"

"And who may use the course?" Braintree went on as if he hadn't heard her question.

"Any active duty or retired military," Timmer said. "And their guests, of course."

Braintree was on the passenger side of the car, looking out the right window; his face was hidden from Timmer when he asked, "Is it hard for the common folk to get a tee time what with all the generals around here?"

She was back on the witness stand, Timmer thought. The implication was clear: there was a little too much privilege here to satisfy the guardians of the taxpayers' dollars.

"No, sir. The course is used by lots of people," she said.

Braintree turned to face her. Gave her the big smile.

"Do you play?"

"No, sir."

"Claude, please," he said. "Does your husband play?"

"No. . . ." she said, choking a little on "Claude."

"Have you ever tried to get a tee time for anyone? Ever been out on the course yourself?"

By way of an answer, Jackie Timmer simply smiled back. She wondered if General Flynn, who was waiting for them, presumably, at the Superintendent's Quarters, had any idea what was coming.

They drove in silence for the last few minutes, down past the gray mass of Keller Hospital, past the old brick quarters that dated back to the mid–nineteenth century, past the stately row of professors' homes, with the wide vista on the Hudson opening suddenly on the left.

"That's Eisenhower Hall," Timmer said at last as the big brick hulk came into view. Timmer could see streams of white-shirted cadets pouring down the stairs, headed for the auditorium.

"That's where tonight's lecture will be," she said. She was just filling up the quiet now.

When they were only a few hundred feet from Quarters 100, Claude Braintree pulled a slim phone from the breast pocket of his coat, pressed some numbers, and, after a pause, began issuing brisk instructions to someone named

David. When the car stopped, Jackie Timmer circled the rear of the sedan and opened Braintree's door, but the civilian made no move to get out. He sat comfortably in the back seat, chatting away as if he were in his own office, head back, smile in place, one hand resting lightly on the headrest of the front seat. General Flynn stepped off the veranda, then paused. Timmer held the door, looking from the General to Braintree and back again. Braintree dragged the scene out for a few more long seconds, keeping the Superintendent waiting. Then he slapped the phone shut and fairly sprang out of the open door.

"General Flynn," Braintree said, smoothing his coat, his hands pressed to his stomach. He walked quickly, purposefully toward the house, hand extended, too-wide smile in place, as Timmer tried to catch up to make an introduction.

"Very nice to meet you, Mister Braintree," General Flynn said without enthusiasm.

On a campus dominated by some of the finest examples of military gothic architecture in the country, the brick box of Eisenhower Hall was something of an anomaly: vast, unornamented save for enormous rectangular buttresses that marched away from the front of the building like sets of red wings. The south wall was dominated by a heroically scaled granite version of the SHAEF insignia: a two-story flaming sword of the Supreme Headquarters, Allied Expeditionary Forces, the command Eisenhower led on his crusade through Europe. The bulk of the building sat below the level of the Plain on a hill that fell sharply to the river's edge and the old north dock. The grand ballroom, a sterile expanse of wood floor and distant ceiling, was saved from resembling an airplane hangar or factory only by the magnificent picture of the river framed in its vast windows.

The giant auditorium in Eisenhower Hall—simply "Ike" to the cadets—was one of the largest on the east coast, its forty-seven hundred seats, on a main floor and two mezzanines, designed to accommodate the entire Corps of Cadets and a good part of the faculty. The dominant color was gray—seats, carpets, wall coverings—but the lighting was crisp, the architect's eye for clean lines unwavering, so instead of the unimaginative interior suggested by the outside of the building, the space inside remained surprisingly warm for its size.

Brigadier General David Simon stood behind one of the half dozen long curtains that faded back at stage left, shuffling his note cards and watching the cadets gather in their hundreds. On most of these occasions—this was the seventh time he'd given this kind of address in his eight years as Dean—he'd worried about whether or not he would reach the audience.

The cadets could be elusive; they were intelligent but easily distracted. Once he'd stopped speaking when a group of cadets, talking during his remarks, distracted him. They sat at the rear of the auditorium, feeling protected, no doubt, by the sheer scale of the place and the size of the group. But Simon squinted into the bright glare of stage lights until he saw the offenders, then leaned into the microphone and ordered the whole class to attention. When the thousands of little soldiers were all locked in place, Simon moved in his bird gait off the stage, down the wide aisle and the strained quiet to the offending cadets. He marched them, a little squad of miscreants, to the front of the big room, where he left them standing while he seated the rest of the class and continued his speech.

They might not listen and they might not learn, but they will be silent and respectful.

The annual lecture was a torture for him. Clear-headed and concise, in his own opinion, he nevertheless considered himself a poor public speaker, an opinion shared by the anonymous contributors to *Pointer,* the cadet humor magazine. He had a shrill voice that was too high and a nasal delivery that he hated. Any one of his faculty members could have told him—had he bothered to ask—that the talks were well organized and insightful, but laden with showy vocabulary and vague historical references.

But he believed in the message. For all that he became easily exasperated with the cadets, for all that they could act like children, finally it came down to this: their education was more important than his comfort. They would soon carry the future of the Army on their shoulders. Simon knew, as only an old man can know, that their years would fly like arrows; these men and women must be prepared for their burdens. His mission was to educate and train them to meet the measure of what the nation would ask of them. He would give them the long looking-glass of history; he would show them the truth behind the maxim that "what's past is prologue." Simon believed in this mission, lived it like a vocation.

But he didn't have to like them.

He was nearing the end of a decade as Dean; in another seven years he'd reach mandatory retirement. Although he would admit it to no one but himself, he knew the marks he'd made on the Academy were not major ones. He'd adjusted a few disciplines; he was proud of his record in opening up the curriculum to modern information technology—even though he did not understand it himself. But in dark evenings in his study, deep in his books, riding with Lee's staff or tracing Napoleon's brilliant path through the armies and cities of another century, David Simon was frightened by the thought that he was everything he was ever going to be.

Then Senator Bruckner, a man he had never met, had presented him with a gift.

Simon thought about George Marshall, the organizer of victory who, without the awful challenge presented by World War Two, would have retired as a colonel from some backwater Army post, his most impressive accomplishment the formation of the Depression-era Civilian Conservation Corps. But Marshall had been ready when the call to action came. As now Simon was ready. The Academy was at risk, but he was ready to take the helm and guide it through these troubled waters. History had seen fit to put David Simon in just this spot, at just this time.

The little man alone on the vast, garishly lit stage imagined himself a little like David, venturing into the frighteningly empty space between the warring hosts. The Bruckner Commission was the shadowy Goliath. Behind him, the Academy's two hundred years of history, his own army, depended on him. He shuffled his note cards, readied his sling. He would not fail.

* * *

114

Wayne Holder and Chris Dearborn were standing at the end of one of the long rows of seats, waiting for the show to start and talking about Kathleen Gates.

"So she brushed your leg with her foot," Dearborn said. "So what?"

"What do you mean, 'So what?' It wasn't like she accidentally bumped into me," Holder explained. "She did it on purpose."

"The Tac's wife was coming on to you?" Dearborn asked, his skepticism apparent.

"Looked like it to me," Holder said.

Wayne Holder did not, for a moment, suspect that Kathleen Gates's motives were as simple as lust. But he wasn't quite ready to admit to Dearborn that the woman frightened him; it was easier to joke about it.

"Be careful, Wayne."

"Oh, right. Like I'm really going to start messing around with the Tac's wife."

"That's not what I meant," Dearborn said. "I mean, it's pretty obvious that it wouldn't be healthy to cuckold our buddy Major Gates. I'm talking about being careful around her. She's a tricky one."

"Ah," Holder said, waving his hand. "She's probably just looking for a boy toy."

Holder put his hands in front of his waist, grasping, in his imagination, Kathleen Gates's hips; he moved his own in a small, slow circle. He was smiling lasciviously when Major Tom Gates charged up to them, shoulders thrown back, his big face scrubbed shiny, the awards and ribbons on his dress uniform seething color and reflected light.

"How're you men tonight?" Gates asked in his excessively friendly way.

"Fine, sir," Holder said, stiffening as if Gates could read his mind.

"What're you doing here, Dearborn?" Gates asked. "I thought this was for firsties."

"It's mandatory for the first class, sir," Dearborn said. "I'm here on my own."

While Gates was processing this bit of unexpected news, Dearborn said, "How's Mrs. Gates?"

Holder couldn't help himself; his head snapped around to

get a look at Dearborn. The junior was smiling at Major Gates; Holder dropped his gaze to the floor, suddenly interested in his shoes.

"She's fine," he heard Gates say. Holder knew that if he looked up, his eyes would give him away. He wondered if Gates could tell by the way he stood, by the way he was breathing, that something was amiss.

Gates turned to the back of the room, but he was hesitant. It was as if he was curious about the question, but not sure why. When he was gone, Holder punched Dearborn in the arm.

"What was that about?"

"Just being polite," Dearborn said, watching Gates's progress up the aisle.

"Apparently Major Mercury thought it an odd question," Dearborn continued. "Maybe he's used to having to keep an eye on the little lady." Then, turning to Holder, leaning toward him slightly, "Still, his reaction wasn't as obvious as yours."

"Fuck you, Chris, OK? Just fuck you."

"I did you a favor, Wayne," Dearborn said. "I figured if you're trying to impress me with your California-stud act, you might just try to do the same with Kathleen Gates. And you'll get crushed."

"I know that," Holder said sheepishly.

"Good."

Tom Gates was in a foul mood as he made his way to the back of the auditorium. He'd been snubbed by a couple of his colleagues that day. Apparently some people thought associating with him was not a good career move.

"Fucking smartass Dearborn," he muttered as he stood against the wall in the back of the room.

"Pardon?"

Gates turned to see Joanna Curry next to him.

"One of your cherubs causing you some anxiety, Major Gates?" she said sweetly.

"Nothing that a little ass-whupping wouldn't cure," he said, remembering to lower his voice.

"Same one . . ." She almost said *Same one you had trouble with,* but caught herself.

"My buddy from Friday night?" he finished for her. "Nah. This is some other kid who thinks he knows everything there is to know just because he gets good grades."

"You see that in some of the smart ones. It's probably just an extension of the attitude of most teenagers: my parents are so *stupid.*"

Gates chuckled and looked at Curry. Her uniform shirt was too tight; the buttons pulled at the buttonholes. Normally he had no time for people who let themselves get even a little out of shape. But Curry was smart and easy to talk to.

"I'm going to put him on the boxing team," Gates said. "Give him a chance to develop a little backbone."

"Is he a good athlete?" Curry asked.

"No. He's a tuna. Scrapes by his phys ed courses."

"Won't he get killed in the boxing ring?"

"He might," Gates said, a bit defensively.

"But it's not punishment."

Gates turned on her, ready to put Curry in her place. What right did she have to question his decisions?

She looked at him squarely, then smiled slowly.

And Tom Gates realized she was the first of his peers to talk to him—other than in an official capacity—since the incident Friday evening.

Maybe I could use someone else's opinion, he thought.

And the very fact that he was able to come up with such an idea—which seemed to him very forward thinking and open-minded—made him feel a little better. Maybe he wasn't a complete oaf after all.

"I guess I should be careful," he allowed.

"Let's find a seat," Joanna Curry said. Then gesturing to the nearest aisle, "After you, Major."

There was a stirring in the back of the room, and from his post behind the curtain General Simon saw Nicholas Hodges, the First Captain and highest ranking cadet in the Corps, striding down the long aisle. Simon, whose nickname as a cadet had been "Taxi" because of the way his ears stuck straight out from the side of his head—like a taxi with both doors open—had always been a little jealous of those whose looks helped pave the way for them. First Captains,

Simon had long suspected, were picked by the Commandant based at least as much on looks as on military or academic performance. The young man climbing the stage before Simon was no exception: six feet tall, clear-eyed, square-jawed, and intelligent-looking, Hodges would do well in every photo and public relations opportunity, in every limelight into which the Academy would thrust him. The young man took the stairs two at a time, smiling, straight, crisp, a catalog of every physical attribute on the wish-list for late twentieth-century American males.

He could be Jacqueline Timmer's brother, Simon thought.

Cadet Hodges took the microphone, asking his classmates to move to their seats. When the cadets were more or less in order, Hodges said, "Ladies and Gentlemen, the Superintendent, Lieutenant General Patrick Flynn, and Mister Claude Braintree, aide to U.S. Senator Bruckner."

The room grew instantly quiet as the cadets and officers came to attention. From the darkness below the first balcony Patrick Flynn appeared, walking his general's walk. Flynn was all of five seven, but his gait gave the impression of a much bigger man. Some combination of personality, confidence, and power conspired to make it seem as if he took up more space than that allowed other people his size. Flynn had been an All American wrestler for Lehigh University, and he still walked with the surety and intensity of an undefeated twenty-one year old athlete.

Claude Braintree, Esquire, was beside Flynn, matching him step for step, which was not hard, since Braintree was at least six feet tall. Braintree scanned the cadets on either side of the big aisle. Even from a distance Simon could see an oversized, strained smile spread across his face, as if he were trying very hard to look amused.

Simon looked down at his notes. He was beyond caring about reaching the cadets, the staff, and faculty; tonight he would be talking to one man: Claude Braintree. The cadets and the green-suiters in attendance would witness the beginning of the campaign that—Simon was sure—would see him installed as the next Superintendent. But they were window dressing, extras. Simon's sources told him that Claude Braintree was out to make a name for himself on behalf of a boss—Senator Bruckner—who stood a good chance of becoming the next President of the United States. Which made Claude Braintree the most important audience in the room.

Jacqueline Timmer followed General Flynn and Claude Braintree down the aisle to the front of the room, then walked across the first row to the right where Rob had promised to save her a seat. Faculty members, detailed by their departments, were scattered throughout the room to encourage the cadets to behave.

"At ease," Flynn called from down near the orchestra pit, releasing everyone from rigid attention.

"Mission accomplished, Jack," Rob said cheerfully as he turned to his wife.

"Just call me Jackie Timmer, escort to assholes," she grumbled.

"Uh-oh," Rob said, reaching over and touching her arm. It wasn't a particularly affectionate gesture; she'd seen him do the same with cadets.

"Is it that bad?"

"Yes," she said. "And the worst part of it is that I think he believes he's being subtle. But he came here with an attitude. Up at the Supe's quarters he kept General Flynn waiting while he made a phone call . . . and I'm not even sure there was anyone on the other end of the phone. I mean, he just pulled it out of his pocket at the last minute."

"What did Flynn do?" Rob asked.

"What could he do? He waited."

"Ah," Rob said, as if that were supposed to mean something. Then, "Uh-huh," and suddenly Jackie was thinking about moving toward the back of the room where she could see Jon Hillard and some of her other peers from the English department.

Jackie watched as Flynn began to introduce Braintree to the officers in the VIP seats, first row center, right in front of the speaker. Braintree shook hands with the Commandant, Brigadier General Tony Moro, seated next to him. On Moro's other side was Colonel Taylor Scotts, Head of the Department of Electrical Engineering. Scotts stretched across Tony Moro. Braintree did not extend his arm, but only held out his hand, so that Scotts was a bit off balance.

When Flynn motioned to the next officer in line, Braintree again made no move away from his seat, not even a meet-you-half-way lean. His feet stayed locked in place, so that the colonels were obliged to step away from their own seats and queue up like petitioners.

The officers, who had not witnessed the scene in front of Flynn's quarters, did not seem aware of what Braintree was doing to them.

You're probably imagining all this because he pissed you off, Timmer told herself.

She watched General Flynn, who had allowed himself an instant peevish expression back at his quarters but was now seemingly at ease with Braintree.

"We could be in trouble, then," Rob said.

"How's that?"

Rob was also watching the bowing and scraping going on in the front row.

"You think Flynn knows enough about West Point to make a good case for the Academy?" he asked. His tone left no doubt as to how he felt.

Jackie took the opposite position, something she'd been doing with Rob quite a bit lately. "I'm sure Flynn didn't get this job because he's a dummy," she said.

Rob turned toward her, a tiny smile—sarcasm?—playing at the corners of his mouth.

"Oh, so you think it's a good idea to have him here? You think he's the best person for the job?"

"What's your point?" she said. She hadn't yet put away her frustration with Braintree, and it was creeping into her voice now. She looked again at her friends in the back of the room. In an institution that never drifted very far from its identity as an engineering school, the humanists in the Department of English relished their roles as iconoclasts. Jon Hillard caught her eye and winked lasciviously; Jackie laughed.

"Don't you think it's a little suspicious that the very first Superintendent in almost two hundred years who isn't a West Point graduate comes along at exactly the same time as the most serious Congressional threat in this century."

He's doing that . . . thing with his voice, Jackie thought. Rob's lilting tone rose and fell like a series of low hills on a road that always made her carsick. She wondered if he did that in class.

"So now there's a conspiracy? An anti–West Point cabal in the Pentagon? Come on, Rob," she said. "You can't get six people in the Pentagon to show up at work in the same uniform unless you tell them two weeks in advance. And now they're in league with evil Congressmen, planning the demise of West Point?"

Rob smiled at her. It wasn't sarcasm. He was patronizing her.

One of her civilian friends had kidded with her about the fact that Rob outranked her; he was a major, she a captain.

"Does he order you around the bedroom?" the woman had joked.

It didn't matter, of course. But there were times when she wondered if Rob wasn't a little more aware than she of the difference in their rank.

He stuck his thumbs into the waistband of his trousers, running them to the sides to smooth out the front of his already-tight shirt.

"So you're saying Flynn can handle it?" he asked pointedly.

Jackie looked over to where Flynn sat next to Braintree. The general was small, powerfully built, with one of those no-nonsense Irish faces—not handsome, exactly, but attractive in a rugged sort of way. In another life, back in the old country, he might have been a soccer hooligan, or the kind of country priest who would fight young men rather than assigning them penance. He was that straightforward. And so, in spite of the fact that she resisted agreeing with Rob, Jackie Timmer wondered for a moment if Patrick Flynn was up to the job of handling the wily politicos who were sure to follow Braintree.

"Hey, sports fans," Jon Hillard said as he joined them in the row of seats.

"Hi, Jon," Jackie said, glad of the chance to talk to someone besides Rob, who didn't look at Hillard.

"Hello to you, too, Rob," Hillard said.

Rob Timmer turned to Jon, but before he could say anything, Hillard blew him a kiss.

"I hope you don't joke around like that in front of your

cadets," Rob said sharply. "Or someone will be 'asking and telling.'"

"Could you be a little more up-tight, Rob?" Hillard said. Then, to Jackie, he said, "Besides, rumors about my sexual orientation wouldn't stand a chance up against stories of my amorous prowess and my general allure to the ladies of the Empire State."

Rob was completely ignoring them now, which suited Jackie just fine.

"I take it this means you have a date with that woman, what's-his-name's sister," she said.

"Exactly," Hillard answered, swiping one hand over his bald pate. "Now the floodgates are really going to open. As a matter of fact, my social calendar will be so full from now on that I seriously doubt that I'll have time to speak to you, which is why I wanted to come down here and visit. Old times' sake, you know."

"And I do so appreciate it," Jackie said.

Hillard was in a joking mood, but Jackie knew that he was lonely at West Point. Most of the people they worked with were married; single people were often left out of all but the official social events. And Jon Hillard—confident, funny, smart, educated—was so homely that when he did screw up his courage to ask a woman out, often she would not even take him seriously. He faced rejection with humor.

"Actually," he said, "I'm thinking of leaving the Army to pursue a career as a gigolo."

Rob wasn't looking at them, but Jackie thought her husband was shaking his head at their sophomoric humor.

Jon leaned toward her and dropped his voice to a whisper.

"I'll specialize in blind women," he said.

Jackie put her hand to her mouth, then reached out and touched Jon on the arm. He was funny, but he was always laughing at himself. He grew uncomfortable with her watching him and crossed his eyes. Jackie turned to face the front. Rob was beside her with his arms folded across his chest and she wondered, not for the first time, how she'd wound up with someone who had no sense of humor.

Then she began to wonder if Layne Marshall had a sense of humor. She laughed when she was with him, she thought.

Or maybe she just smiled in the kind of light-headed giddiness his attention brought her.

Too bad I can't mix and match, she thought. *Jon's sense of humor, Layne's good looks, Rob's . . . what?*

"I should get back to my other seat before this thing starts in earnest," Jon said.

"No," Jackie said. "Stay right here."

Hillard jerked his head in Rob's direction.

"Nah, I think I'll go."

When he was gone, Rob looked around.

"He left, Mr. Personality," Jackie said.

Rob turned back to the stage, his arms still folded. "I'm sick with grief," he said.

"Did you see who was following the Supe and the civilian?" Holder asked Dearborn after the Superintendent's entourage walked by. "Quite a soldier, right there."

Dearborn followed Holder's gaze.

"You mean Captain Timmer, Poster Girl?" he said. "West Point personified. Duty, Honor, Country . . . Great Legs, Perfect Hair, Minty Breath."

Holder looked over at his friend.

"Minty *breath?*"

"You get the picture. The woman's a goddess. Ever get a look at her husband?"

Dearborn shot his hand up in a fascist salute. "The original advertisement for the master race."

"I heard he's a dope," Holder said as they took their seats. "I can't understand why someone like her would wind up with someone so dull. She's perfect."

"Perfect might be a little much," Dearborn said. "Of course, it's the middle of the week, which means you probably haven't gotten laid in the last seventy-two hours. At this point you think anything with a vulva is perfect."

"I just think she's got her shit together," Holder said. "I'll bet she was picked to escort this Congressman around. Timmer will have the guy licking her boots inside a week."

"Interesting image, Wayne, that boot-licking thing," Dearborn said, looking sideways at Holder. "No doubt something you've been dreaming of yourself."

"I could be talked into it," Holder said.

"By the way, Braintree isn't a member of Congress," Dearborn corrected. "He's an aide to a Senator, a hatchet man."

"Is he the guy who's going to do all the interviews?"

"He may do some of them," Dearborn said. "More likely he'll be overseeing what's going on here. There'll probably be a few other flunkies doing the nug work."

"You think the Academy's in any real danger from these people? I mean, you think they'd really want to shut it down?"

"Keep in mind that this whole study is just a publicity vehicle for Bruckner. That's how the guy operates. He goes somewhere, stirs up a nasty shitstorm, gets his face on the news and leaves. If he'll get the most publicity out of saying West Point should be closed, that'll be the message.

"Beyond that, people have been wanting to shut down West Point ever since it opened," Dearborn said. "They think we're a bunch of arrogant, elitist pigs."

Holder thought of his father, who had refused to follow the family tradition into West Point and had met Wayne's decision to attend the academy with an enthusiasm that seemed forced. Wayne had always believed his father had become a physician—a field with no shortage of arrogant practitioners—because of his love of medicine. Lately he wondered how much of his father's choice had been turning away from the military instead of turning toward medicine.

Holder's grandfather—his father's father—was a retired two star. The old man wore a tie and jacket to dinner in his physician son's California-casual home. Rail thin, a lifelong chain-smoker, he sat across the table from Wayne's father, who didn't wear a tie even for hospital rounds. They were like before and after pictures, the physical resemblance as remarkable as the spiritual differences. Wayne, passing his parents' room at night during one of the strained family visits, heard his father use the word "prig." He thought it meant the same thing as "prick"—a word he'd recently begun tossing about at Little League—but he'd looked it up anyway, thinking to use it in the schoolyard.

"What do you think?" Holder asked his friend.

"I think we're our own worst enemies. We want the country to love us, so we tell everyone that we've created this perfect world, with all these hard-working, unfailingly honest cadets. The public eats that shit up. And a few too many of our peers in gray even think that we live in some perfect other-world here. We're all plaster saints."

"So what are you saying? That we really don't work hard?" Holder asked.

"No." Dearborn shook his head, then began again patiently. "It's not that simple. It's just that we're constantly pumping ourselves up, telling ourselves how hard we have it all the time. It's a consolation prize: we don't get to have the freedom that other college students have—we get inspected, paraded, shuffled out for the public at every Saturday parade—so we crow our virtues all the time. Hey, we can't go out at night, can't sleep in, can't cut a single class. So what do we do? Tell ourselves we're tough, hard-working, virtuous, the hope of civilization."

Dearborn looked glumly around the room as he spoke, but there was no bitterness in what he said.

"I mean, it's fine—to a point. *Ad astra* and all that. But when somebody is a little human, makes a mistake, it gets blown out of proportion. And forget the big stuff—cheating, sexual harassment, hazing. Fail a course and people look at you as if you've come out against the Constitution."

Or freeze up in fear at jump school, Holder thought.

"So, yeah, I do think we're a little stuck on ourselves around here," Dearborn continued. "Still, it's nice to have a place where you can seriously talk about hokey things like duty and honor."

"And let's not forget all that West Point history you're always throwing around. Selfless service to the nation and all that," Holder said.

"That's all ancient history once the shooting stops," Dearborn said. He looked weary for a moment. Then he shook off that mantle and sat up straighter in his seat, one hand on a knee, the other in some mock Napoleonic pose on his chest. In a bad British accent he began to recite, " 'it's Tommy this, an' Tommy that, an' 'Chuck him out, brute!' But it's 'Savior of 'is country,' when the guns begin to shoot.' "

"Hey, Shakespeare."

Holder and Dearborn turned around. A massive cadet, a defensive tackle on the football squad, filled something more than one seat behind them.

"It's Kipling, actually," Dearborn said. He dragged out the last word, hitting the first syllable hard. *Ack-chew-elee.*

If the bigger cadet knew he was being mocked, he showed no sign.

"Yeah, whatever. Don't get the idea that I'm going to sit here all night and listen to you spout off like some goddamn faggot actor or something."

Holder smiled. His football-playing classmate was probably used to being able to intimidate people with his size; Dearborn brought other weapons to the fray.

"How thoughtless of me," Dearborn said, surprising the big cadet. "I shouldn't distract you while you're using all of your considerable powers of concentration fighting to master that tricky opposable thumbs business."

The football player shot Dearborn the finger. The junior smiled and faced the front again.

"And we won't *even* get into the intellectual climate here," Dearborn whispered to Holder.

"If you're looking for people to practice your boxing skills with, I recommend someone smaller," Holder said.

"Don't remind me of my fate," Dearborn said, squeezing his long legs against the seatback before him. "No, I'm here because that guy is here."

"Brainfreeze?"

"Joke all you want, Mister fourth generation West Pointer. The guy in the suit down there—or his boss—can make it so that there won't be any more Holder progeny coming through Hudson High," Dearborn said, settling further in his seat.

"A bunch of civilian straphangers poking around and asking dumb questions about cadet life and academics and whether the plebes are getting enough sleep?"

Holder, seated on the long aisle, looked down to the front of the room. He could see the civilian who'd followed General Flynn into the room sitting with the heads of the academic departments.

"I'll bet he's never been in the service."

"Good bet," Dearborn said. "But it hardly matters. One of the foundations of our republic, my dear boy: civilian control of the military. We get to make do with what they give us, get the job done and be happy about it."

"Sounds like a great life."

"Ours but to heave and sigh. . . ."

"Ladies and gentlemen," the First Captain said from behind the massive podium with the oversized West Point crest, "the Dean of the Academic Board, Brigadier General David K. Simon."

The cadets rose as one, coming again to stiff attention.

"Thank you, thank you. Take your seats, please," Simon said into the microphone. In the distance and the bright lights, dwarfed by the podium, Dearborn thought, he was a frail old man in a too-large uniform. And that bit of military formality—snapping to attention, kept them from having to render polite applause.

Claude Braintree's little power plays were not lost on Lieutenant General Patrick Flynn, but he kept his polite smile in place.

Tact was something that came late in life to Patrick Flynn. As a young officer, he'd received more than his share of unflattering attention from senior officers who told Flynn he said too much too quickly and too often. Bluntness, they explained, is not a military virtue. Fortunately, he'd grown smarter over the years. General Flynn was no courtier, but he was no fool either. He knew that civilians held the power—even the young, inexperienced, and apparently obnoxious ones like Braintree.

Braintree's show with the portable phone had been intended to knock him off guard. It had worked, apparently, on Captain Timmer, who'd been nonplussed by Braintree's rudeness. Yet if everything Flynn had heard was true, Braintree was a smart man—actually what Flynn's source had told him was the Braintree was "infinitely smarter than his boss, the Senator." If Braintree was so smart, he wouldn't expect Flynn to be disturbed by such a silly game; it couldn't be that simple. So Flynn was left with the question: What was the civilian trying to accomplish?

Flynn looked down the line of colonels, all of whom were looking at the stage. All except George Moffett, head of the English Department, who locked eyes with Flynn. Braintree, between the two men, was watching the stage when Moffett nodded toward the civilian, then drew his finger across his throat like a blade. Two rows back, a cadet who noticed sputtered a laugh.

Flynn looked back at the stage without smiling and considered what Braintree might be about.

After his initial interviews with the men beside him, with the heads of the academic departments and the Commandant, after he had met the Dean and these others and played his little games with them, kept them waiting or delivered some backhanded compliment about West Point, they would be seething. They would, as Moffett had already demonstrated, want Braintree's blood. Figuratively.

Flynn chanced another look at the visitor.

Why, if your job was to communicate with a group of people, would you want to start out by antagonizing all of them?

Simon was buzzing about Douglas MacArthur, Flynn's least favorite general in American military history. MacArthur had been adept at playing what a later generation would call head games: nepotism, intrigue, favoritism that broke staffs and headquarters into factions. Divide and conquer. Personal loyalty above all. During the Korean War, MacArthur ran his headquarters in Tokyo like a personal fiefdom. Harry Truman, the former Missouri National Guard captain who fired the General in 1951, either didn't know enough to be afraid of MacArthur's popularity, or he didn't care. The Superintendent thought he'd need to be more Truman than MacArthur in this job.

Flynn looked at Braintree, who returned the look and smiled but said nothing.

If Braintree had wanted input from the officers in the front row, he wouldn't have started out trying to piss them off. But he did exactly that. That left Flynn with only three possible explanations: Braintree was ignorant of the effect his actions would have, which didn't seem likely; he didn't care; or he *wanted* those reactions. And if he wanted those reactions, if he wanted to foster ill will, it was because communication was unnecessary; he had already made up his mind about what the commission was going to find.

Up on stage, Simon stood looking down at his notes, the terrific glare of the stage lights playing off his gnomish head. He looked up every half minute or so.

And if Bruckner arrives and finds a bunch of squabbling and backbiting, it'll be that much easier to give us the shaft.

Flynn looked over at Braintree again. The lawyer smiled back at him.

Got you, you bastard, Flynn thought.

When Douglas MacArthur stood before the Corps of Cadets in May 1962 to accept an award named for Colonel Sylvanus Thayer, the Father of the Military Academy, he was a legend on the wane. It had been ten years since his return from Korea, nine years since his speech to a packed joint session of Congress. His closing remark that "old soldiers never die, they just fade away," had sounded ironic at the time, like the promise of a run for the White House. But it had turned out to be simply true. MacArthur had faded away.

The eighty-two-year-old MacArthur made the trip from his apartment at New York's Waldorf Astoria because he wanted to leave something memorable at West Point, some peroration at the end of his dramatic fifty years in uniform. And he was the man to do it: in twenty-four hundred words, speaking without notes to the cadets assembled in the mess hall, he had captured it all, the drama of a half century of soldiering, the pity, the loss and the sorrow and whatever redeeming quality there was to the one thing he could hold up before even the most ardent critics, the most acerbic cynics—the pure nobility of sacrifice. He had evoked images of soldiers from all the nation's wars for the young men before him—many of whom were to die in a South East Asian country few of them would have been able to find on the map that day. He told them about sacrifice, about singlemindedness, about their focus and the importance of remaining true to that calling they had just begun to embrace.

He had been an old man then; cadets in the audience would later say that, had they known the speech was to become so famous, they would have paid closer attention.

But if his voice faltered, his mind did not. He was windy, and his language was more the language of the nineteenth century. But his vision was solidly forward.

David Simon was borrowing the words, of course. To his credit, he would never try to out-MacArthur the old showman. Coming from Simon, the words would have missed the mark. But MacArthur had known how to reach them, and looking out into the darkened recesses of the auditorium at the rows of young faces before him, Simon imagined the old soldier haranguing them.

You must prepare yourself, you must love what you do, you must love who you are. You must.

That is what the old soldier would have told them. That is what Simon wanted to make clear to them. He looked out beyond the yellow and white lights to the very promise of a generation.

"In the most famous speech of his long service to America, Douglas MacArthur advised the Corps of Cadets, and American soldiers everywhere, even soldiers not yet born, of their duty. In a phrase both elegant and simple, he told us what we are about—his generation, our generation, the next generation."

Simon looked down at his notes. He knew MacArthur's speech by rote, not because he had read it so many times, but because the phrases went together perfectly, fitted by a master joiner. In his imagination, before he even uttered them, the words floated above the audience, as pure and true as the ringing of the clearest bell.

"Duty—Honor—Country," Simon quoted, his voice pinched, rattling, nasal.

He heard a shuffling of feet. The cadets were required to memorize long parts of the speech as part of their indoctrination plebe year—drilling it over and over in their rooms, reciting at lunch formation daily before bored upperclass cadets. The surprise had gone out of the words; the speech had been bled dry.

No matter, Simon thought, his fingers working the edges of the pages before him on the podium. *I'm talking to Claude Braintree.*

"Those three hallowed words reverently dictate what you ought to be, what you can be, what you will be . . . Every pedant, every demagogue, every cynic, every hypocrite, every troublemaker, and, I am sorry to say, some others of an entirely different character, will try to down-grade them even to the extent of mockery and ridicule. . . ."

He resisted the temptation to imitate MacArthur's clipped diction, the near British enunciation that had distanced this most regal of American generals from his soldiers.

"And through all this welter of change and development, your mission remains fixed, determined, inviolable—it is to win our wars.

"Everything else in your professional career is but corollary to this vital dedication. All other public purposes, all other public projects, all other public needs, great or small, will find others for their accomplishment."

Finished quoting, Simon looked up from the page and removed his glasses, a gesture he had practiced in front of his bedroom mirror.

"MacArthur, you will note, says nothing about tradition. He did not say that we must hang on to the way things are now. In fact, it was the young Superintendent MacArthur who dragged the Academy, over the loud protests of my predecessors on the academic board, into the twentieth century. The Army he saw in Europe in the First World War was the most technologically advanced force the nation had ever fielded. Why, in some places the internal combustion engine had even replaced the horse. MacArthur came to West Point in 1919 and abolished the nineteenth-century practice of having the Corps encamped on the Plain for the summer . . . parading, riding, attending parties and teas, and hazing plebes. He did away with it—and how the old grads did howl—not because there was anything inherently wrong with the practice but because there were more important things to do. MacArthur sent the cadets to the field to learn their craft. It is hard for us to imagine that there was a time when people didn't think such training was important.

"It was MacArthur who saw that soldiers respected those officers who were physically able, and so Superintendent MacArthur made athletics mandatory. Every cadet an athlete.

"In twenty-four hundred words he never said 'hold on to traditions, because if anything changes, West Point and America are doomed.'

"Some components of how we accomplish our mission may change from one generation to the next. We must stand ready to accept change because if we did not, we'd still be practicing cavalry charges across the Plain."

A low murmur of laughter rippled across the room. *Maybe they are paying attention,* Simon thought.

"We embrace change carefully, thoughtfully. We cannot go rushing off after every whim, every untested new idea. But we must not be afraid to let go of the old ways."

Simon looked at General Flynn in the front row. The old man wasn't nodding, wasn't smiling; he was neither agreeing or disagreeing. There was in fact, nothing readable in his expression. Claude Braintree wore the same wide smile he'd carried down the aisle.

"It seems appropriate to ask why we have traditions," Simon said.

"We have rituals to remind us who we are, to help us remember what has come before. Traditions serve much the same purpose. They also inspire, they make us and the soldiers we lead *feel,* and we must never forget that we lead human beings, not machines. We stand at attention and salute when the bugle tells us the flag is coming down; when we do that we acknowledge that we are part of something that transcends just this one day, something that reaches back to those who have done this very thing before us. There is a place for continuity, for the traditions that remind us that we are part of something larger than ourselves. Think how much of your daily lives are caught up in this great thing that connects you to the past and to soldiers not yet born: the uniforms you wear, the martial music that punctuates your day, your ethos and tradition of selfless service. You are surrounded by reminders of what has preceded you and reminders of what you need to take forward. Douglas MacArthur took this whole welter of image and emotion and distilled it to its essence: Duty, Honor, Country."

In the front row, Claude Braintree was looking at the backs of his hands. Simon paused, breathed deeply. In the dark back of the auditorium, beyond the blaze of lights, someone coughed long and loudly. The cadets, of course, had no experience to help them make sense of all these things. It was all just theory to them now. Yet they would go out from this room, from this place above the river, to help guide the force that guarded the nation. The million small decisions they made would accrue, would light the path, hold it all together. They did not know this now, but David Simon knew it, and he wanted to make them understand.

"Our most important tradition is service. It is not the tradition of gray uniforms, of a place, of a way of doing things, of a specialized language. Guard those outward traditions too closely and we lose focus. If something gets in the way of Duty, Honor, Country, that tradition must go."

"What we cling to is the sure knowledge of our mission, stated so simply, so eloquently by this old man. 'Guard the nation. Win our wars.'"

This was his moment. Simon stepped from behind the podium, resisting the temptation to cup his hands in front of his groin in what a professor once referred to as the "fig leaf" position. He swallowed, his tongue moving in a dry mouth. He wanted to reach out into the audience, touch each of them on the shoulder like young knights, fire them with mission, with the love of what they were about. His chest seemed to fill.

"I bring the first class together to remind you to keep your focus. You will need to make hard calls; you will be surprised to find you are prepared. Do not become bitter in neglect or arrogant in power. Take care of your soldiers. Guard our nation. Win our wars."

David Simon drew himself up, savoring the silence, allowing himself to believe that it had worked. He hung on to the moment, let it rise up in front of him and watched as it quickly fell away.

"First Captain," he called.

The handsome cadet commander appeared before him.

"Dismiss the class."

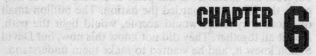

CHAPTER 6

ARVIN GYMNASIUM, A SPRAWLING COLLECTION OF STONE AND brick as big as a city block, crouches behind the Superintendent's quarters, a linebacker trying to hide behind a cheerleader. Because every cadet must take physical education courses throughout the four years, and because every young athlete must participate in sports at the intercollegiate, club, or intramural level, Arvin gymnasium is as central to the cadet experience as the academic buildings. And because of the storied difficulty of the instruction that goes on inside its fortress walls, it looms large in the lives of its charges and the memories of graduates.

The daily procession begins early—the first class is at seven fifteen—with plebes filing in the big doors like monks at matins. Here they do penance, here the flagellation that purifies and exhausts them. Boxing classes will make their arms quiver through note-taking in the rest of the morning's academics. Survival swimming will fill their bellies with water; they will show up in English or history or French class with red-rimmed eyes, ears leaking chlorinated water. Wrestling, gymnastics, self-defense; mats, bars, over-the-hip throws; threescore ways to exhaust them, to mold them.

The gymnasium is a cross between museum and cathedral. In the oldest parts—where the boxing rooms lie—polished stone floors bounce echoes to vaulted ceilings. The walls are lined with trophies and plaques that date back nearly a century. And it is clean: a platoon of maintenance workers moves about constantly, pushing mops and brooms and trailing behind them clouds of ammonia and disinfectants.

Tradition is revered here. Where the heads of other departments are professors, the chair of this department—who also holds a doctorate—is called the Master of the Sword, a throwback to a time when cadets took fencing because skill with a sword made a difference in combat. Every polished hallway, every ninety-year-old silver trophy and faded, century old plaque reminds cadets of what has gone before. Science is revered here as well. Just off the main foyer are the offices of the teaching staff, every desk equipped with a computer, every bookshelf lined with the latest scientific texts on cardiovascular endurance, optimum exercise heart rates, oxygen delivery, sports psychology. Legions of black binders embrace guidelines that spell out—in painstaking exactness—the standards for performance in any given area. Push-ups are done this way, sit-ups this way. Climb the rope in this manner only, ye Spartans.

Chris Dearborn stood outside the boxing room in the oak-paneled hallway that was a gift of the class of 1957. It had occurred to him more than once that many of the graduating classes were hard-pressed to come up with an original way to spend their gift money. The academy grounds were dense with stone benches, cluttered with ornate water fountains and inscribed tablets. Every little glen and wooded spot, every flat piece of landscape, it seemed, held some monument, so that the post looked to some visitors like a showcase for makers of gravestones. The Class of 1957, reaching for novelty, chose a long hallway in the oldest part of the gymnasium, paneled it in expensive oak and covered one wall with pictures from their days as cadets. On an arch at one end, oversized gold letters proclaimed "Class of 1957." Nothing else, just that. The passageway led to a locker room.

He stood with his headgear and gloves tucked under his

arm, studying a framed group photo of the Department of Physical Education staff that graced the wall just inside the entrance. In the photo, forty gray-shirts, arms folded behind their backs in identical poses, faces serious, bodies tightly fit, posed on the wide steps of the main entrance, like a phalanx of palace guards waiting to pounce on the weak. The photo was matted in gray, but some sign painter—no doubt ignorant of the department's draconian ways—had lettered it in bright colors and an advertiser's overly friendly tone: "The Department of Physical Education Welcomes You"—the "W" in "Welcome" done in a curled scroll that would have been more fitting on a music school sign.

"Chris, how you doing, man?"

Dearborn turned around to see his classmate, Miguel Viegas, advancing on him from the door. Viegas—a former Golden Gloves contender from New York and the coach of the company boxing team—carried his gloves and headgear slung casually over his shoulder; they looked like part of his anatomy. He walked up to Dearborn, dropped his gear in a pile on the floor, and faked a couple of jabs at the taller man's stomach.

"You look about as comfortable as a whore in church, man," Viegas said.

"Let's just say that this is not my favorite building on post," Dearborn said by way of answer.

"Now you know how I feel in all those classrooms," Viegas said.

At five seven and one hundred and forty-five pounds, Viegas was shorter and considerably lighter than Dearborn. Inside the ring he was a dancer, a dangerous, feral presence: quick, graceful, violent. Over the past two years of intramural boxing, Dearborn had seen Viegas knock down a dozen opponents. Were it not for the big padded headgear the cadets all wore in the ring, many of his fights would have ended in knockouts. His nickname was Kilo Mike. Kilo, the military's phonetic form for the letter "K," stood for "killer." Killer Mike.

Viegas was handsome in a gentle sort of way; with dark, lively eyes and fine features unmarred by his years in the ring. Dearborn had seen photographs of Viegas's family, including three sisters, all of whom were beauties, and all of whom looked just like their older brother. As far as Dearborn knew, no cadet had ever gotten up the nerve to tell Viegas he was pretty.

His walk telegraphed his personality, thrust it before him like a sign in bright neon: get out of my way. He rolled, he swaggered, he could signal menace or an almost childish innocence just by moving this leg in front of that. One of the women in Dearborn's class had watched Viegas walk into a dance, throwing his legs out in front of him, shoulders back, preening, smiling at all the young women. "He walks as if he's being led by his dick," she'd said.

"How's your course load this semester?" Dearborn asked. Viegas was a "goat," cadet slang for the bottom of the class, and a veteran of summer school.

Viegas had squared off in front of one of the glass-fronted trophy cases that lined one wall and was boxing his own image there.

"Me and the English department going at it this semester, baby."

"That'd be 'the English department and I are going at it,'" Dearborn said.

Viegas dropped his hands and looked at his classmate.

"You just can't help yourself, can you?" Viegas said clearly. The street language was gone. He was genuinely perplexed; he looked at Dearborn as if the big pale cadet were from another planet. Dearborn wondered that himself from time to time.

"Listen," Dearborn said. He shifted his gloves and head-gear to his other hand, holding them away from his body so that the smell—years of use by hundreds of cadets—that permeated the leather wouldn't be right under his nose. He handled the equipment as if it were diseased. "I can help you out in English."

"And you want me to help you out in boxing."

"Actually, my goals are more modest than that," Dearborn admitted, still affecting amused indifference. "I just want to survive this little game."

"That's part of your problem right there," Viegas said. "This ain't no game, pal."

The hallway suddenly filled with cadets as several boxing

teams, groups of a dozen or more cadets who'd marched from their company areas, came pouring through the huge double doors. They'd been cramped in classroom seats and laboratories all day; now, like young horses out of the paddock, they were ready to play. The stone floor and walls caught the noise and the excitement and upped the volume. This was the place where brains didn't count as much as muscle and coordination and courage. The Academy talked about developing the moral, the intellectual, and the physical: this was where the physical came to the fore. Viegas was in his element. Dearborn envied him and hated him all at once.

"Gates didn't put you on the boxing team as punishment, man," Viegas said.

"It's certainly going to look as if he did when I'm getting my lights punched out in the ring," Dearborn said. "You remember how I used to get kicked around plebe boxing all the time."

"It doesn't matter how the fight turns out," Viegas said. "It matters how you handle yourself."

"Aren't they the same things?" Dearborn asked.

"How could somebody so book-smart be so stupid?" Viegas said. "Gates put you on the boxing team so that you could learn something."

"How to bleed? I already know how to do that."

"How to rely on yourself."

"Sounds like the two of you had quite a little talk about me," Dearborn said.

"Your name came up."

Viegas looked around; the other teams, also preparing for practice, filled the hallway. Viegas shouted to a plebe from D Company.

"Oswood."

A giant fourth class cadet skittered through the crowd and appeared at Viegas's side. He was huge, with a neck like the base of a big tree and overly long arms that threatened to reach the floor. He looked down on Viegas; he was eight inches taller than and clearly in awe of the little junior.

"Get in that boxing room and make sure those lob-cocks from those other companies know that the first three practice bags belong to us."

"Yes, sir," the cadet managed. He didn't immediately turn away.

"Uh . . . sir, may I ask a question?"

"Ask your puny question, Oswood," Viegas said, scowling up at the plebe.

"Sir, I noticed that G Company has already taken over one of our bags, sir. And I was wondering . . . that is, I was wondering . . ."

"Wondering what you were going to say to them, Oswood? Or maybe you think you'd rather I went in and chased away the big scary upperclass cadets who are on our bag." Viegas's voice had changed to a mocking lilt. "Is that it, huh, Oswood?"

"No, sir," Oswood said unconvincingly.

"Get in there and tell any one of those motherfuckers touching our bag or taking up our practice space that they have three seconds to move before you tear their heads off and shit down their throats. You got that?"

"Yes, sir," Oswood said.

"Repeat it back to me."

Oswood swallowed hard. It was obvious to Dearborn that the plebe hadn't taken Viegas literally. But Viegas clearly wanted Oswood to do exactly as instructed.

"Sir, I'm to tell them that if they don't clear out, I'm going to tear their heads off and shit down their throats."

Viegas stepped up to the plebe, who tightened up.

Maybe he thought Mike was going to hit him, Dearborn thought.

Viegas sniffed three times quickly. "You smell something, Oswood?"

The plebe concentrated, trying hard to smell something. "No, sir."

"I think I smell pussy," Viegas said. "Are you a pussy, Oswood?" Viegas asked. He was still standing very close to the big plebe. "I mean, you don't sit down to take a leak, do you?"

"No, sir," Oswood answered firmly.

"Then I better be able to hear you out in the hallway. You copy?"

"Yes, sir," the big plebe said. It was clear to him that

crossing Viegas would be more dangerous than cursing out a bunch of upperclassmen.

"This oughta be good," Viegas said with a smile as his charge disappeared into the boxing room. The two juniors moved closer to the doorway. Oswood stood at rigid attention in front of a heavy bag that was being pummeled by two upperclass cadets and delivered his lines in a rigid staccato, like machinegun fire.

"Excuse me, *sir,* but if you don't clear away from the D company practice area I'm going to rip your heads off and shit down your necks, *sir!*"

The two upperclass cadets—juniors from another company in the same regiment, glanced over in surprise. A few other boxers whistled and cheered.

"Let me guess, Paul Bunyan," one of the cadets said. "Your coach put you up to that, am I right?"

"Yes, sir!" Oswood shouted, clearly relieved.

"Do you know he wanted you to do that because he's afraid of us?"

"No, sir," Oswood, still at attention, said.

"'No, sir' you didn't know that or 'no, sir' you don't believe it?"

"Just 'no, sir,'" Oswood said.

"Quit harassing my plebe," Viegas said, moving into the room, smiling now, walking on the balls of his feet. Then, in a tone that mocked every stuffy officer this kid from the streets had ever run across, "You're impugning his personhood and I, as a leader in the post-modern army, simply cannot have that."

The little show broke up into tiny knots of cadets pounding bags, dancing, skipping, jabbing, and feinting. Dearborn followed Viegas into the room. The coach gave instructions, splitting up his cadets into two-man buddy teams and putting them to work on the bags or shadow-boxing in front of the big mirrors.

"So what did Gates have to say?" Dearborn asked his classmate.

Viegas turned around. He paused for a few seconds before speaking.

"Why are you the only one in here who doesn't have his gloves on?" Viegas asked.

Dearborn tugged on one big glove, releasing a terrific stench where the sweaty palms of other boxers had stained the inside. Dearborn held this arm up and studied the red leather.

"Did you know that the Royal Navy used to paint the gun decks of their ships red so that the gunners wouldn't be panicked by all the blood scattered around during battle?"

"So some people should wear red shirts, right?" Viegas said.

"Very funny," Dearborn said. He pounded his hands together; the thick padding of the sixteen-ounce gloves did nothing to reassure him.

"Did Gates recruit you in this, too? Convince you what a great idea it would be for me to box?" Dearborn asked. He didn't like the feeling that his classmate—by definition an ally—was suddenly on the side of Gates, the "they" of the big "we-they" divide.

"He didn't have to," Viegas said. "I've always believed that boxing is for everybody. It teaches you things you can't learn anywhere else."

"So you think it's a good idea for me to get the shit kicked out of me?" Dearborn asked peevishly.

"I think it's a good idea for you to put your other fucking glove on, man, and quit whining."

So that was it, Dearborn thought. *Gates had gotten Viegas in on this, too. That wouldn't be hard, the boxing team was always in need of warm bodies.*

In spite of their instruction in the sweet science, in spite of the competitive and very physical nature of cadets, most of them had not been in a fight since the fourth or fifth grade. Dearborn remembered his plebe year instructor telling the class that the Academy wanted them to box "so that you'll know you're not going to die if someone punches you in the face."

Dearborn fastened his headgear, loosely, and pulled his gloves on tighter. He turned to the wall and studied his reflection in the big mirror there. The outsized headgear on top of his thin frame made him look out of balance, like a red basketball stuck on top of a pole. He began to swing his arms in large circles, loosening the muscles in his shoulders.

If I throw my shoulder out, I won't have to box, he thought.

How badly could that hurt, a little separated shoulder, maybe a torn rotator cuff?

He could not fake the injury, of course. He could not lie to the doctor about symptoms or pain. It would have to be the real thing or nothing. Of course, if the doctor asked him if he'd sustained the injury on purpose, he would tell the truth about that as well.

Yes, sir. I deliberately fell so that I could throw my shoulder out of whack, but I figured, hey, it's better than being a punching bag for the whole intramural season.

"Chris, c'mere."

He could see Viegas in the mirror, beckoning to him. When he turned around, Viegas was standing beside the big plebe, Oswood, who had chased the other teams away from D company's practice area.

"You and Oswood are about the same as far as experience goes. You both just have plebe boxing to go on in here," Viegas said. "I think I'll make you two sparring partners."

Dearborn looked up at the plebe. Oswood's red leather headgear was on tight, the chinstrap distorting his face, his lips bulging grotesquely where the plastic mouthguard pushed them out. His shoulders fell away from the big red bulb of his head in a long slope. Dearborn could see thick black hair visible above the collar of the shirt—*how old is this guy?*—and even at the back of his collar.

"He looks like he should be carrying a two-handed sword."

Viegas knotted his brows. "What?"

"He's got a good four or five inches of reach on me, Mike," Dearborn said.

"You're not going to be boxing," Viegas said. "Just take turns throwing punches. I think it'd be good if you two work together; you can help each other. OK, Chris?"

Viegas shot Dearborn a look that repeated—wordlessly—what he'd said earlier. *Stop whining.*

"OK, now all I want you to do is take turns throwing jabs, maybe a couple of combinations. Nothing fancy; don't try to hurt one another. One of you will punch, the other will protect. I want you to work on keeping your hands up and I want you to work on speedy jabs."

Dearborn fished in the waistband of his gym shorts for his mouthpiece. The plebe had already raised his hands in a textbook example of the boxer's stance. The gloves, also red leather, were enormous, two hams strapped to the ends of Oswood's arms.

Here we go, Dearborn thought.

"Uhll guhlldd fuhst," the big red tree said.

"What?" Dearborn asked.

Viegas, apparently fluent in around-the-mouthpiece talk, translated. "He said he'll guard first."

Dearborn put his hands up in his best imitation of the position he'd learned in plebe boxing. Left foot and hand forward, right shoulder and arm cocked back, knees flexed, chin tucked in just over the right fist. He caught a glimpse of himself in the big mirror beyond where Oswood stood. Something was wrong. This was the same pose he'd adopted two years ago and he remembered an instructor yelling at him to . . . what?

Viegas punched him in the stomach; his mouthpiece shot out, hitting Oswood in the chest.

"Get your elbows tucked in," Viegas said. He smiled at Dearborn and walked away, coaching them over his shoulder. "Take turns, one minute each, then switch. I'll be back."

Dearborn bent over to find his mouthpiece, tasted lunch again: chili and fruit punch, cookies and bile and humiliation. He pulled his hand from the glove and shoved the plastic in his mouth. Oswood had not moved but stood as he did before, hands up in a defensive posture.

"OK, let's try that again," Dearborn said around the guard. *K les shry aht gen.*

Dearborn put both hands up, remembered to tuck his elbows in, circled to the left, leading with his left foot.

Don't extend your leg too far or you'll be off balance. Elbows in, you don't want to get punched in the stomach again. Head down, hands up, look at your opponent.

A flood of instructions played on some tape in his mind. Dearborn circled, sliding his feet across the floor, bent forward slightly at the waist.

Hands up, that's it, hands up, looking good.

143

He stole a glance at himself in the mirror. The arms tucked in, no longer like chicken wings. His forearms protected his body, hands tight by his face. He circled cleanly, a predictable dance step, but the trick was to keep moving, keep moving, keep moving, and so the tape went on.

"Hey, Chris," Viegas called. "You going to throw a fucking punch or are you just gonna keep looking at yourself in the goddamn mirror?"

Dearborn felt a rush of hot blood and embarrassment, the eyes of the other boxers heavy on him. They expected him to fail. Viegas didn't know any better than to ridicule him in front of everyone because Viegas couldn't imagine not doing well in this room. Oswood stood before him, slowly circling; what Dearborn could see of his face was patient, bovine. Dearborn threw his left out in the general direction of the big figure in front of him. He got nothing but air.

"Again."

Viegas right beside him now. Dearborn threw another punch, thought he felt part of the big flat surface of his glove glance off Oswood's arm.

"Again."

Dearborn stuck his left hand out in front of him, connecting this time. Oswood's blocking arm did not move, and Dearborn felt a mild shock all the way back through his shoulder. For just a part of a second he thought about the big plebe in front of him punching back. But Viegas was right there.

"Punch, jab, jab," he repeated.

Dearborn wasn't sure, but it seemed that Viegas's accent was more pronounced in the gym, in the boxing room in particular. Maybe it was the excitement, maybe it was the smell.

He jabbed again and again, finding a point on Oswood's thick forearms, held like a shield in front of the plebe's face, where he could connect. He felt fine, there was a rhythm he picked up somewhere. Step, jab, step, jab.

"OK, switch," Viegas said.

Dearborn dropped his arms, which were beginning to feel a bit heavy, and Oswood landed a punch directly on his chin.

"Sorry, sir," the plebe said around his mouthpiece. But he still had his hands up.

Dearborn lifted his arms, trying to concentrate on where Oswood was moving, trying to focus in spite of the ringing in his head. But something was wrong, something seemed out of kilter. Before he could figure it out Oswood landed another blow that pushed Dearborn's hand back into his face, making his nose tingle sharply.

Oswood was circling . . . right.

That's it, Dearborn thought. *He's left-handed.*

Dearborn tried to remember if he was supposed to shift his own stance. But that didn't seem right.

It shouldn't be this hard to be a punching bag.

Jab.

The plebe's hands moved with surprising quickness. Something so big, Dearborn thought, should generate more wind resistance. Dearborn could see them coming, of course, but there was no time to do anything about them.

Jab, jab.

One of the blows glanced off Dearborn's glove and caught him on the side of the face, pushing his headgear out of line. He hadn't tightened it enough. Oswood had looked silly with his headgear pinching his face like some sort of torture device, but then Oswood's headgear was still facing forward. Dearborn's right eye squinted through an earhole. It threw his depth perception off, so that the next jab seemed to stop short of his face but in fact connected, hitting him high up on the forehead.

"OK, OK," Viegas said. "That's enough."

Dearborn tried to pull his headgear around to face front, but the big gloves were too unwieldy, the thumbs useless appendages, like sausages glued to mittens. His eyes teared from the blows to the head, his lips felt hot—Oswood had connected twice with his chin—and his arms were molten, as if suddenly filled with mercury.

"This is just great," Dearborn said. He spit the mouthpiece out, managing to keep it off the floor by pressing it to his body with a forearm. The big plebe stood just within arm's reach, his hands still up, glaring over the tops of his gloves.

"I'm so fucking glad to be here."

He was angry at Gates, angry at Viegas, angry at Oswood. He was angry at himself for not leaving West Point two years earlier, angry because he wanted it all so badly.

The smells of leather and sweat took him back to plebe year, to this very room, with the instructors shouting, "Ready, box," and his classmates aiming for his head and him wondering if he was going to make it through the next round. He hated the whole system then, but had managed to survive—gracelessly, in the estimate of the Department of Physical Education—but he had survived. Now that he had made it to junior year it seemed the system wanted to extract just a little more humiliation from him.

"Go get a drink of water, Oswood," Viegas said.

"You did that on purpose," Dearborn said to the coach when the plebe was gone.

"Did what?"

"You knew he was a good boxer," Dearborn said. His speech was slurred with sweat and snot and a tiny, sharp taste of blood.

Viegas shrugged.

"Did you tell him to pound the shit out of me, too?" Dearborn asked, his voice pitched too high. "Did you tell him I'd be an easy mark?"

"No," Viegas said. "I let you do that on your own."

"Fuck you, Mike," Dearborn said.

"No, fuck you, Chris. You want to keep your eyes closed, that's your business. But that doesn't make it my fault."

"What are you talking about? I didn't have my eyes closed."

"I'm not talking about when you're boxing, *cabron*. I'm talking 'bout you got your eyes closed because you don't want to see that this is part of it." He raised his hands, gesturing to the room around them. There were dozens of boxers, a score of little wars going on, men in red and black leather breathing sharply, straining, dodging, sweating in single combat.

"This is part of getting through this place, man."

"How many times in four years do I need to be reminded that I'm not a great athlete?"

"It's got nothing to do with being a great athlete, Chris."

"That's easy for you to say. You don't have DPE on your ass all the time."

Viegas leaned closer to him. "No, I have the Dean on my ass all the time. The difference between you and me is that I've figured out that I have to be good at more than just a few things. It's not enough that I can box. I have to be book-smart too."

Dearborn wiped his nose with the back of his glove. He tasted blood on his lip, but it was hard to see on the red leather. Oswood reappeared beside them, dancing on his toes.

Incredible, Dearborn thought. *The guy is as big as a house and he moves like Fred Fucking Astaire.*

"You gotta figure out for yourself that it's not enough to be smart," Viegas said. "You gotta be able to do more than that."

"What? What do I have to do?"

"You gotta be able to reach down inside and find more of whatever it is that keeps you going, man."

Viegas stepped back, slipped into his coach voice.

"Put your gloves back on, Chris," he said.

Chris Dearborn felt no closer to understanding whatever physical-courage-mumbo-jumbo Viegas was spouting on behalf of DPE and the Tac and all their classmates who breezed through physical education.

But he put his gloves back on.

"Look here, Oswood," Dearborn said to the plebe in front of him. "Don't be trying to rattle the finest brain in the Corps of Cadets now, hear?"

"Yes, sir," Oswood said as he raised his fists.

The visitors were framed in the doorway. The young man—dressed unimaginatively in a blazer, tan pants, rep tie—held a notebook. Peering through perfectly round glasses at the chaotic scene in the boxing room, his expression was of mild surprise, as if he were looking at interesting animals in a second-rate zoo.

"And every cadet must box like this?" he asked.

His escort, a young captain from DPE, standing with his arms folded in the go-to-hell stance favored by the gray shirts, sighed before explaining again.

"No, these are intramural teams. Each of the thirty-six companies in the Corps fields a boxing squad for the fall intramural season."

"So these are volunteers?"

The captain laughed. "Not all of them," he said.

"You mean someone could be *drafted* onto the boxing team?" the rep tie asked, blinking behind his glasses.

"Sure," the captain answered. "It builds character."

"Yes, I imagine it does. May I speak to a few of the cadets?"

"Yes, *sir,*" the captain said, trying to be ironic. "We'll come back in . . ." The captain looked at the black watch strapped tightly to his wrist. "We'll come back in twenty minutes, when practice is over."

"That'll be splendid," the rep tie said, smiling.

The captain willed his lips to move, but it was a poor imitation of a smile.

Splendid, he thought. *Now there's a word you don't hear around the boxing room all that much.*

Wayne Holder missed the beginning of the soccer match on Target Hill field; fortunately for the teams scheduled to play, he was only half of the officiating contingent.

"Nice when the officials can get here on time," he heard a woman's voice say as he jogged on to the field. He turned away from the play and saw a classmate, Elizabeth Wrenson, also wearing vertical stripes; she was the other referee.

"Sorry, Liz," Holder said.

He smiled at her, but she made a funny face and shouted "Heads up!" just as the soccer ball caromed into the back of his head.

"Out of the way, ref," a cadet in a green shirt yelled at him as he recovered the ball from where it landed near Holder.

"God*damn,*" Holder said, rubbing the back of his head and scurrying over to where Wrenson was calmly watching the scrimmage.

"You're off to a great start," she said without taking her eyes off the play.

Liz Wrenson had been in a couple of Holder's classes over

the previous three years, and it was hard to miss her. She was as tall as Holder, maybe a little taller, and a gifted gymnast who'd had her years of intercollegiate competition cut short by a bad knee—a memento from a night jump at Airborne School. She was smart; she wore on the collar of her dress uniform the gold stars of a Distinguished Cadet, an honor reserved for the top five percent in order of merit. (In a throwback to the days before women came to the Academy, the top cadets were still called "star men.") She was attractive—ivory skin, dark brown hair tightly curled, almond eyes just as dark.

"Obviously some Spaniard snuck ashore in England way back when and did a little doggie paddle around the old gene pool," Holder had once heard her comment about her dark looks.

Holder was a little intimidated by Wrenson, who seemed serious and adult, while Holder was content to extend his adolescence just as far as West Point would let him. Now, in their senior year, she was a "striper dog"; she wore the six stripes of Deputy Brigade Commander. Out of the eight hundred plus cadets in Holder's class, only the First Captain outranked her. And if all that wasn't enough to make Holder keep his distance, she was engaged to a guy who'd graduated a few months earlier; they'd been inseparable as cadets: people called them the "velcro couple."

"Yeah, I'm having a great day."

"I was talking about your *year,*" Liz said. "Your year is off to a great start."

Bold, too, Holder thought.

"Word gets around, I guess," he said.

The ball dribbled toward the sideline and two cadets, one from each team, slid to save it. One of them wound up on the bottom of a tangle of muddy legs, and he got a little belligerent in his attempts to push the other cadet away. There were a few muttered curses, but in a moment the two were back on the field.

"Did you really get into a fight with your Tac?" Liz asked.

"Hey, Liz, just come right out and ask, OK?" Holder said, as if she'd brought up something very personal. "I mean, don't beat around the bush or anything."

"Sorry, Mister Touchy," she said. "I never figured you'd be sensitive about something the whole Corps is talking about."

By way of an answer, Holder jogged across to the other side of the field. When he turned back, whistle in hand, Liz was smiling at him. He nursed his small anger—embarrassment, really—through the game. It didn't grow, but it didn't go away completely.

The two cadets who'd tangled on the sidelines were at it again, this time in front of one of the goals. Arms down, cheeks puffed up, they were pushing each other, chest to chest, neither one of them willing to back down, but neither one of them willing to risk getting written up, on a disciplinary report, for throwing a punch.

Holder stood on the sideline, twirling his whistle around his finger by the long cord, just the way he used to do on the lifeguard stand. When he saw Liz move toward the fracas, he thought he'd get closer to hear what she had to say.

"Let's hear how the striper-dog handles the big leadership crisis here," Holder said to himself.

Liz walked directly up to the bellicose pair, unhurried, relaxed, everything about her body language signaling calm. "You two heroes need a little time to cool off somewhere?" she asked the two players.

The one in the green shirt turned away from Liz and toward Holder, who was still ten yards away.

"Bitch," the green shirt said, loud enough for Holder to hear.

Holder turned back to the sideline, pretending not to notice.

"Hey, coaches," Liz called out. "You think you can control your people?"

When play was joined again, Liz saw Holder watching her and winked at him.

Holder didn't smile back.

Three or four minutes later the two cadets who'd been fighting were at it again, this time shoving one another. Liz was closer than any of their teammates, and she stepped in between them.

"Knock it off," she said, arms out, one hand on each of

the combatants. She was taller than one of the men, and gave up only an inch or so to the other.

The field was muddy, and there was little purchase even with cleats; the two soccer players were sliding, which made them angrier still. The tallest of the fighters, the one who'd called Liz a bitch, fell to his knees, got halfway up, fell again. When he finally did get his footing he was livid, red in the face.

He took a swing.

For a tiny part of a second Holder thought Liz, who was squarely between the two men, was going to catch a shot to the face.

Instead, she leaned back as the other cadet lurched forward, and with a quick move of her foot to his instep she shoved his leg out from under him. Instead of striking Liz or the other soccer player, he ate a mouthful of dirt. By the time he scrambled to his feet, his teammates and coach had him firmly in hand.

Liz leaned toward her would-be assailant. "Slippery here, isn't it?" she said. There were a few muffled laughs, then someone laughed out loud, and in a moment even the cadet she'd tripped was chuckling at himself.

An official on a nearby field blew an air horn, signaling the end of the intramural period. Liz made the two cadets who'd been fighting shake hands before they left the field.

"You handled that pretty well," Holder said, falling into step beside her as they began the long walk up the hill toward the barracks from the riverside playing fields.

"Thanks, Wayne," Wrenson said.

"So how's what's-his-name? Your fiancé," Holder said.

"Oh, that's over," she said.

Holder had no clever comeback.

"Speaking of personal," Liz said.

Holder was beginning to think he'd made a mistake in starting to walk with her, but when he looked up she was smiling at him. It was not the same smile she had for the embarrassed cadet she'd knocked down, this one had a trace of fragility.

"So how are you doing with it?"

"I'm OK," she said. "Thanks for asking."

They took their time on the way back to the barracks. All about them hundreds of men and women were leaving the fields and courts that lay like satellites around the cadet area. Football players and lacrosse teams, runners and cyclists, swimmers and boxers, carrying their various gear, all converging on their barracks.

This was Holder's favorite time of day. He carried with him the pleasant release that exercise brought, the sure relaxation that followed exertion. In the late afternoon even the sprawling cadet barracks—seven different buildings, thousands of rooms—got a short reprieve from the omni-present clock that ruled everything. The rituals for the hundred-plus family members of D Company were simple: banter in the hallways, hang the dirty athletic gear up to dry, hot shower, clean uniform for dinner. In the drab confines of the barracks, this was an aesthetic he could enjoy. In a world run by clocks, this was the time of the day that came closest to being relieved of that constraint. This was when it felt like home.

"How's your roommate?"

"They put his fingers back together and there's no perma-nent damage," Holder said.

"So they haven't taken any action on this little thing with Gates?" Liz asked.

"I got chewed out by the Commandant. That wasn't any fun, but it looks like that's all for me."

"Unless Gates kills you in the middle of the night. I hear you guys call him Major Mercury."

Holder laughed. "Yeah, but for all his problems, he's actually a stand-up guy. I mean, if he was going to kill me, he'd do it right out in the open. But I don't think he's holding a grudge because he knows he was wrong."

"What will happen to him?"

"Well, they didn't relieve him, but I doubt if he got off completely clear."

"Maybe they're sitting on action against him until the Bruckner Commission thing goes away," she offered.

"This Bruckner Commission thing really has people going crazy, talking about West Point being closed."

They entered a sally port in Eisenhower Barracks and the

hallway where the Brigade Staff lived. Once she stepped into the door, Wrenson stopped and pulled the band off her ponytail, shaking her hair out. It hung past her shoulders in rich, dark waves. Holder caught a scent of shampoo.

"I think Senator Bruckner is trying to ride this Champion of the Taxpayers thing right into the White House. If closing the service academies can move him in that direction, I don't think he'll hesitate. He likes finding these juicy little scandals to get himself in the news. And he's been trailing in the primary polls; he's liable to do anything."

Wrenson leaned against the wall, playing absentmindedly with the whistle that was still on a cord around her neck. With her hair down and her long legs glowing cleanly beneath the black shorts, she could have been a college cheerleader, an advertiser's dream who could draw flocks of young men to any school that dressed her up in a letter sweater. Holding forth on Presidential politics, she was even more attractive.

Holder realized that Wrenson had always intimidated him: with her looks, with her brains, with her athletic ability. It wasn't the same as with Kathleen Gates, who made him nervous because she was dangerous.

"Have you met with any of the Inquisitors?" Holder asked.

"Not yet. Some of the women are supposed to meet with the head guy, Braintree, sometime later this week."

"He wants to talk about women's issues?" Holder asked.

"I gather," Liz answered.

"Women's issues" had become a synonym, among many of the cadet men, for "political correctness" and, more insidiously, "mind control." Anything that smacked of liberalism was suspect; anything that seemed to give preferential treatment to some small group—and women were the most instantly recognizable minority—was bound to come under attack by barracks philosophers.

"I know you guys think that every time the women get together all we do is bad-mouth the guys," Wrenson said.

A tiny smile passed over her face; she was having fun with him. Holder was enjoying her company.

"And of course that's true," she said.

"Well, what do you talk about?"

"The weird sexual proclivities of the cadet men," she said, straight-faced.

Holder blinked.

"Kidding," she said. "Sometimes it's just nice to talk to other women, to hear that other women have the same kinds of problems here that I do."

"Are you saying it's harder here for you than for me?"

"No, Wayne," Liz said. She pressed her back to the wall and let her feet slide out in front of her so that her back was flat, her hands under her buttocks. Part of Holder's brain knew that this was an intellectual conversation with a smart woman; another part wanted to do nothing more than admire the long symmetry of her flexed quadriceps.

"Mostly, our experiences are very similar. That's one of the things that makes West Point unique. We all go through just about the same ordeals. That's where the bond comes from, I think."

She turned her face toward him. With one finger she pushed a tendril of hair behind her ear.

"But your experience is different from mine in some fundamental ways."

Wayne Holder tried to concentrate on what Liz was saying, but his eyes kept going back to the way her hair shined, to how dark it was against her porcelain skin. She sounded like a professor; she looked like a goddess.

"How . . . uh . . . how's that?" Holder asked.

A couple of cadets came through the door from the sally port and walked by. Holder was a bit self-conscious, and in fact this was why he had never dated any of his women classmates. There was some sort of stigma attached, as if they weren't "real" women.

"Well, for me," Liz said, "I came here when I was seventeen, just a little high school girl, really. And although I was used to sports and not at all afraid of boys, I wasn't used to competing against them. And then I didn't know if I was supposed to try to be one of the guys or I was supposed to be different.

"I can remember a time during our first summer, we were out on the land navigation course, groups of three. And my two partners were guys. So we're running through the woods, trying to figure out how to use a compass and a map and not get lost, and we're drinking from our little canteens like we'd been told to do.

"Anyway, we stop to take a break and I have to go to the bathroom. Well, my two partners just stood up against a tree, I mean, they went a little distance away out of decency, but they didn't wander off. When it was my turn I had to think, 'OK, do I just say to hell with all that training my mother gave me about modesty, just move a few yards away and squat. Or do I try to hang on to some of that decorum?' I had no idea what those guys would think."

She paused in her story.

"So?"

"So when it came my turn I did exactly what they had done."

"Except you didn't stand," Holder said.

"Funny. Except I didn't stand. I went a few yards away and leaned my back up against a tree and pulled my pants down. And I could hear one of the guys say, 'Gross.'"

Liz paused here; she wore the slightly bemused look he'd seen her turn on the cadet she knocked down. But something told Holder she hadn't been so cavalier about the little incident at the time.

Holder didn't see the big deal. The guy was some stupid plebe who'd been tired and worn out and who wasn't used to being out in the woods and was probably frustrated by the whole land navigation problem. Holder accepted that immature young men made stupid jokes, that they could be unfeeling. He didn't think she had a Federal case, though.

"So when I came back to the two of them, I asked the guy who made the comment, 'What was I supposed to do? Find a ladies room?'

"See, some of the guys will only be happy if we do everything they do. And other guys think we should be prom queens in uniform. It took me a while to figure out what to do."

"What did you come up with?" Holder asked, genuinely curious about a problem West Point had never given him.

"Finally I decided, 'The hell with 'em. I'll do what I think is right.' And I've stuck to that pretty much the whole time."

"But it's gotten better, right?"

"Yes and no," she said. "See, if you show up someplace with your shoes unshined, people say, 'That dirtbag Holder needs to learn how to shine his shoes.' If I show up with my shoes unshined, people say, 'Those goddamn women are dirtbags.'"

"I don't say stuff like that," Holder said.

"That's because your shoes are always unshined and you think of that as a virtue," Wrenson joked.

Holder laughed, but the point was well made. He was trying to think of a graceful exit when she got his attention again.

"Look, Wayne, I don't want to be a guy. Never have. Being a woman here shouldn't make things any easier or any harder for me."

"Is it that way?"

Wrenson pushed off the wall, stretched her arms over her head. Holder found himself standing a little straighter to look her directly in the eye.

"Tell me something, Wayne—I'm just curious—why didn't you say anything to that guy who called me a 'bitch' out on the soccer field?"

Holder, a bit embarrassed at his complicity, recovered quickly.

"Ah, he was just pissed off, that's all. You saw what a moron he turned out to be. Besides, you fixed him good when you knocked him down." Holder spoke quickly, something he did when he was nervous, or on the spot.

"But why didn't you say anything?"

"I thought it was no big deal," Holder said. "It's just a word."

"OK," Liz said. She smiled broadly. "Maybe I'm making too much out of it. And you're right, I did get the last laugh on that guy."

Wrenson moved toward her room; Holder, checking the clock again, figured he had less than fifteen minutes to shower and dress for dinner, but he wasn't ready to leave yet. He wanted to see Wrenson again, but he was—uncharacteristically—hesitant to ask her out on a date. And the objections played in his head like a tape.

Maybe she's already seeing someone else or maybe I'm supposed to leave some amount of time after the breakup of her engagement because maybe there's a grace period or a mourning period and besides that who wants to take the razzing that goes with dating a woman cadet even though she's a knockout and besides she's so freakin' smart. . . .

And just as he was about to give up, she spoke first.

"Wayne, you're friends with Dwight Andre, aren't you?" Liz asked.

Andre was one of only seven black cadets in Holder's company of one hundred and ten.

"Suppose Dwight had been officiating that game with you and had made the same call and that bonehead had called him a 'nigger' and you heard it. Would you have said something to him?"

"I'd have jacked him up good," Wayne said. "But don't you think there's a difference between that word, which is pretty vile, and 'bitch'?"

"No, actually, I don't," Wrenson said. "If that guy was looking for some generic put-down, if he'd been talking about you, for instance, he would have called you an 'asshole' or something about that original. He picked 'bitch' only because I'm a woman. *He* was making a big deal out of it."

"There are always going to be people like that, Liz. You just can't get upset about it," Holder said, repeating a justification he'd heard so many times that it had taken on the ring of truth.

"Do I look upset?" she asked, smiling. It was clear that it would take a little more than name-calling to rattle her composure.

"But I'm not about to tolerate it, either. That kid isn't ready to function in the Army with that attitude."

"So now West Point is supposed to teach people social graces and political correctness?" Holder said. He sounded a little too much like one of the petulant, whining sophomores.

Wrenson reached back with both hands and pulled her hair into a pony tail, then twisted the thick cord around in a knot.

"I don't know about West Point," she said. "There is no West Point beyond you and me. We were the ones on the field; it's our responsibility. A *personal* responsibility. Yours and mine."

Holder felt as if he were being dressed down; and he only felt that way, he knew, because he deserved it.

"You didn't say anything to him, either," he said defensively.

"Not there, but I am going to talk to him in a few minutes. I asked him to stop by on his way to dinner."

Wrenson opened the door to her room.

"You know, it's funny," she said. "I was thinking about this when I talked to those people from the Bruckner Commission. They're going to come around and look at classrooms and sports events and the barracks, but none of that is really what this place is about. It's about all those little decisions we make. That commission would have to hang out for a long time to see all that and really get an appreciation for what goes on here."

"I've been here three years," Holder said, "and apparently I don't even have a clue as to what's really going on."

Wrenson smiled at him.

"I'll probably figure it out the day before Major Gates gets me tossed out."

"Gotta shower before dinner," Wrenson said, her hand on the doorknob.

"OK," Holder said. He felt glued in place, wanting to ask if he could see her again. Wrenson was inside her room with the door half-closed when Holder finally spoke.

"I was going to ask if maybe we could do something together one night this week, or this weekend," Holder managed. "But now I'm afraid you think I'm some kind of misogynist, some kind of idiot."

"I'd like to spend some time with you, Wayne. That would be fun. And, no, I don't think you're a misogynist."

"Great," he said, smiling widely, backing up, eager to clear the hallway before he committed any more gaffes.

"I'll talk to you later, then."

"Sure thing . . . asshole." She shut the door quickly; Holder froze, then heard laughing on the other side of the door. It swung open a crack.

"Just kidding, Wayne. You guys are so *sensitive* sometimes."

After twenty minutes of sparring with Oswood, the oversized plebe, Chris Dearborn felt as if he'd been the victim of a hit and run. His hands, clenched inside the sweaty gloves, were sore from his white-knuckled grip. His arms seemed to have been filled with something heavy, inert, like sawdust or rock shavings. His shoulders ached and his chin was sore and there was the beginning of a ferocious headache lurking at the base of his neck. Blood spiced the inside of his lip and the front of his shirt was covered with sweat and snot. On top of all that he had to endure Viegas's excessive enthusiasm.

"How you feeling, man?" Viegas said as he clapped him on the shoulder after signaling the end of practice. "You stood toe to toe with the big man, the best plebe boxer in the company, and you're still here."

"Oswood is the best plebe boxer?"

"In our company, yeah," Viegas said, smiling.

"You put me in there with the best boxer? You asshole," Dearborn said.

"Ahh, don't get your fucking panties in a wad," Viegas said. "You came out just fine."

"I came out alive," Dearborn said. "And that's no guarantee of a trend."

"You know, we could come over here after supper, practice a little shadow boxing," Viegas said. He was still grinning. Dearborn was incredulous.

"Are you nuts?"

"Hey, you said yourself that you need some work," Viegas said. "I'm just agreeing with you." He was backpedaling now, throwing jabs into the air. Dearborn shuffled along, head down, following his classmate. "I can help you, Chris. This is what I'm good at, you know? Just like you help all those other people who are flunking this course and that course. You just gotta admit you need a little help."

Viegas tucked his body in tight, threw lightning punches. "Come on, Chris. I know it's killing you to admit you need something from a dummy like me, but you gotta say the magic word. Just admit it, baby."

"No, what I need is to get off this team. I have no business in the boxing ring, Mike."

"This is the perfect place for you, man," Viegas said, dropping his hands. He stood just inside the boxing room; other cadets streamed past, on their way out the big front doors of the gym to the barracks, the showers, dinner. "As a matter of fact, there's no place you need to be more than here."

"I passed plebe boxing, Mike. I don't have to go through it again to graduate. I don't care what you or Gates thinks."

"Because you know all the answers, right, Chris?" Viegas said. He had lost his smile and it seemed to Dearborn that his accent was more pronounced. "No one can tell you anything."

Something seemed to have broken loose in Dearborn's head and was rolling around painfully. He could feel his heartbeat all up and down the back of his neck, across his scalp. A giant hand had taken hold of the crown of his head and was squeezing to see what might come out.

They were just inside the boxing room doors when one of the company plebes appeared just outside in the hallway, came to attention, and addressed Viegas.

"Excuse me, sir," the plebe said.

"Get the hell out of here, douchebag," Viegas snarled.

The plebe disappeared as if vaporized.

"No . . . one . . . can . . . convince me," Dearborn said with exaggerated slowness, "that the ability to punch someone in the nose is a critical skill in the modern Army. No one can convince me that I need to be on the intramural boxing team in order to graduate."

Dearborn tried to step around Viegas, but the smaller man reached out, laying his hands on Dearborn's arms.

"That's because you don't *listen*, man," Viegas said. "You only hear what you want to hear."

"What the fuck does that mean?" Dearborn snapped. He dropped his gloves. Bending down to pick them up, he kicked them. He straightened, suddenly dizzy, suddenly out of patience for this lecture he was being given.

"You sit in that fucking room and talk about West Point like it's some sort of . . . some sort of . . . I don't know,"

Viegas struggled, as if dropping his hands made him inarticulate.

"But you think it's all parades and history and all that shit. All the paintings in the mess hall and the stuff piled up in the museum."

Dearborn wanted to ask what was wrong with that, but his head seemed to be moving independently of his body and he had to concentrate to keep from falling over. He managed a quizzical look.

"All that romantic shit can only take you so far, Chris," Viegas said.

Dearborn put his hand to his cheek, afraid that his eyes would betray him, afraid he would squirt hot tears at the absolute truth of what Viegas was saying.

"Well, book smarts will take me to graduation, Mike. Of course, you might not be there to see it."

Viegas paused, his eyes going flat and cold. The big room behind them was empty, an echo chamber for the loud migration of cadets in the hallway outside.

"I'll see you at the next practice," Viegas said.

He turned and joined the throng leaving the gym.

Way to go, you ass, Dearborn thought. *Just what you need, more enemies.*

Feeling suddenly nauseous, he stepped out into the hall and sat on one of the padded benches that lined the near wall. He had his head in his hands and his eyes on the floor when he saw two pair of shoes appear in his field of vision.

"You feel all right, cadet?"

Dearborn looked up. The black sports shoes belonged to a narrow-faced DPE instructor whose monogrammed waistband announced him as Captain Dillard.

Dearborn stood slowly.

"I'll be OK, yes, sir," he said.

The other pair of shoes belonged to a civilian.

"I'm Sandy Van Grouw," the civilian said, holding out his hand. Dearborn took it.

"Cadet Dearborn." In spite of his nausea, Dearborn thought, *Not a DPE-approved grip there, buddy.*

"I'm with the Bruckner Commission," Van Grouw said.

"Yes, sir," Dearborn said, somewhat surprised. The

Bruckner Commission had been talked about and demonized for so long that Dearborn had half expected its members to have cloven hooves.

"Please, sit down," Van Grouw said. "Captain Dillard was just telling me about the boxing teams."

Van Grouw sat next to Dearborn on the bench but did not make room for Dillard. He crossed his legs—suspending a scuffed shoe just in front of Dearborn—and propped a leather-bound notebook on his knee. He was thin—his shoulders seemed hardly wider than his head—about five nine, light brown hair sprayed back in an aerodynamic sweep. The glasses made him look bookish; he wore too much cologne.

"Are you one of the volunteers for your company's team?"

"Uh . . . not exactly," Dearborn said. He looked up at Captain Dillard.

Van Grouw followed Dearborn's eyes and said, "Would you excuse us, please, Captain?"

Dearborn was surprised when the instructor said, "I'll be in my office when you finish, Mister Van Grouw." Dillard turned and walked away down the hall.

Dearborn and the civilian were alone in the big hallway, which had finally emptied of cadets. Dearborn looked around.

"Afraid someone will see you consorting with the enemy?" Van Grouw asked. He was smiling when he said it.

"Something like that," Dearborn admitted. He leaned back against the wall and closed his eyes for a moment.

"Looks like you had a helluva match," Van Grouw said.

When Dearborn opened his eyes, Van Grouw nodded at Dearborn's stained shirt. The look said "I've heard such things exist, but I've never seen them myself."

"How long have you been a boxer?"

Dearborn snorted through his nose; more blood and snot landed on his shirt. Van Grouw jumped back a little.

"Sorry," Dearborn said, wiping his face with his sleeve. "That's just the last term anyone would use to describe me."

"Yet you're on the boxing team."

"My Tac—and apparently some of my classmates—think it will be a good experience for me," Dearborn said.

"And you don't agree."

It was not so much of a question as a statement, as if Van Grouw already understood what was going on. Dearborn studied the other man for a moment.

His face was unlined, not just youthful, but unstressed.

Not much chance that you've ever been in a boxing ring, I'll bet, Dearborn thought.

He recognized his natural reaction—he wanted to defend West Point, or more precisely, defend what he'd been through, the various tests and hurdles he'd passed to get to this point in his career. Because if he let someone denigrate them, if he let someone—an outsider, a goddamn civilian, for chrissakes—if he let someone say it was all so stupid, then he was a fool for submitting to those tortures.

But it would be so easy, Dearborn thought. *I could finally let someone know what I think about all this bullshit that takes place in the name of physical development, and nobody is going to say "your ideas don't count because you got a C minus in swimming or because you almost flunked gymnastics or because you can't box."* Dearborn let his eyes wander. Where the vaulted ceiling met the opposite wall, a colorful mosaic showed an early version of the Academy crest; in it Athena's helmet faced right, opposite its depiction on the modern crest.

Athena, the warrior goddess who preferred peaceful ways of settling quarrels.

Van Grouw must have recognized his hesitancy. "Anything you tell me is strictly confidential," Van Grouw said.

I could get Gates off my back, Dearborn thought. *All I have to do is tell this guy what a nut case Gates is. Hell, I might even get off the boxing team.*

"Oh, I'm not worried about that, Mister Van Grouw," Dearborn said. "West Point has no bigger fan than me. I'm a believer . . . a regular acolyte . . . it's just that. . . ."

Alex Trainor was sitting at his desk, Bible open before him, his clublike, bandaged hand propped up on a plastic milk crate, when Holder came into the room.

"Hey, welcome back! How's it going?"

"Looks like I'll survive," Trainor said. He looked up and saw Holder staring at the plastic crate.

"I have to keep it elevated while I'm sitting down," Trainor said.

"We'll get a plebe to stand next to you during formations so he can hold your hand up. Like a retainer," Holder said.

"I'm thinking more on the lines of a squire," Trainor said without smiling.

"You OK?" Holder asked again.

"Yeah," Trainor said unconvincingly. "I guess my arm just hurts."

Alex wiggled the fingers of his mangled hand. "I've been trying to do the Christian thing, forgive Gates," he said. "Truth is, I was hoping he'd been fired."

"Looks like he's going to be around."

"I thought maybe he'd get shipped out before this Bruckner thing got rolling. It'd serve him right."

Holder wanted to say something about Gates being a stand-up guy, about the fact that Gates had treated him fairly since the incident. But Alex, still in pain, probably didn't want to hear it.

There was a moment of quiet, then Alex said, "Chris Dearborn stopped by."

"He say what he wanted?"

"No, but he looked a little weirded out, you know?" Trainor said. "I mean, more than usual, even. He said he'd talk to you after dinner."

Holder walked across the hall to the combination latrine and locker room. He hung his athletic gear on a hanger on the drying rack and stepped into a room cloudy with steam and populated by five or six other cadets—naked, loud—showering and talking about their sports adventures.

"What's this, a sword fight?" he joked.

"Right here," one of the juniors said, gesturing obscenely. "It's my dick and it's my soap and I'll wash it as fast and as hard as I want."

"Ooo, baby," another said as he swished out of the shower room, arm up, wrist limp. "I'm askin' and I'm tellin'."

Holder finished quickly, toweled off. Listening to the

others, he remembered his amazement during plebe year at the obscenity that peppered the everyday language of cadets. For the most part they were men and women from conservative backgrounds—clean-cut, All American—but their language could peel paint. Holder carefully cleaned up his speech outside the barracks, on leave, on dates. But he had once startled a blind date, a young woman he had just met, when he nonchalantly referred to another cadet as a douche bag.

He slipped on his bathrobe and stepped back across the hall.

"You know Elizabeth Wrenson?" he asked his roommate as he dressed.

Trainor now had a textbook in front of him and was using a yellow marker to highlight sentences in a textbook. He'd missed three days of classes and had a lot of catching up to do.

"Sure," he said without looking up. "Kind of hard to miss her right out there in the middle of the parade field with all those stripes on her arm."

"I know you know *who* she is," Holder said. "I meant, do you know her?"

Trainor looked up, curious now.

"I guess we've been in a couple of classes together," Trainor said. "Smart lady. Pretty serious, seems to me."

"I'm going to ask her out."

"That's rich," Trainor laughed, shaking his head and going back to his book.

"What's that supposed to mean?"

Trainor put his marker down and used his good hand to lift the bandaged limb gingerly off the milk crate. He lowered it to his side, then stood up slowly. Since returning from Walter Reed in Washington after his surgery and four days there, he moved as if he were sixty years old.

"Remember that Rutgers University cheerleader you dated last year? Big hair, big boobs, big blue eyes?"

"How could I forget?" Holder asked. "We did the wild thing right out there in the Supe's garden." He pointed out the window as if Trainor might have temporarily forgotten the important geographic details of Holder's sexual escapades.

"I'm sure her mother was very proud," Trainor said without inflection. "My point is: that's the kind of girl—and I do mean girl—you should be dating. Stick to the sporty models."

Holder had his dress white shirt on; he checked the alignment of his pin-on nametag in the mirror. "You don't think I can handle Liz Wrenson?"

"Thank you, you just made my point," Trainor said. He had picked up his white saucer cap and was waiting for Holder so the two of them could walk to the Mess Hall for dinner, the only meal for which there was no formation. Cadets could choose to skip the evening meal if they needed the uninterrupted study time between the end of the class day and lights out at midnight. Some of them slept.

"Elizabeth Wrenson isn't the type to be 'handled,'" Trainor said.

"So I'm not good enough to go out with her, just because I like to have some fun every once in a while?"

Trainor put his hat on, studied himself in the mirror, took the hat off again.

"How do you feel when you're around Miss Rutgers University Boob Extravaganza?"

"Horny."

"Exactly. A five-foot-ten-inch raging blue veiner. How do you feel when you're around Liz Wrenson, or, as you should probably start calling her, Doctor Wrenson."

"Doctor?"

"She's on her way to medical school right after graduation. So? How do you feel?"

"She's . . . exciting," Holder said. He pulled his white cap from its appointed place on his closet shelf and opened the door for Trainor. Neither one of them stepped into the hallway. "And interesting. And she has a sense of humor."

"Perfect. She'll make someone a great wife, a lifelong partner. Do you feel intimidated by her?"

"No way," Holder said.

Trainor paused, smiled an almost imperceptible smile. "My mistake, then," he said, stepping past Holder and into the hallway.

"Why should I feel intimidated?" Holder asked before he

even admitted to himself that it was true. "I may not be a star man, and I'll never be a cardiologist, but I'm in the fast reading group."

"I didn't say you *should* be intimidated," Trainor said as the two headed for the stairwell. "I thought you would be. Look, Wayne, you're certainly smart enough to hang out with her, date her, all that. But ask yourself why you're doing it. That's all."

"Thank you, Reverend Trainor," Holder said. Alex raised his hand in a mock blessing.

Holder was entering the stairwell, thinking about a Rutgers University letter sweater nicely filled out, when someone called him.

"Wayne."

The charge of quarters held the orderly room phone out to him.

"Who is it?" Holder asked, his hand over the mouthpiece.

The yearling shrugged. "Some woman."

"Cadet Holder," he said into the phone.

"Hello, Wayne."

Soft, hard to hear over the noise of a hallway full of cadets migrating to chow.

For a moment, he hoped it was Liz Wrenson.

"I hope you don't mind my calling you at the barracks. . . ."

It was Kathleen Gates.

"Er . . . no, that's OK. What can I do for you?"

Holder looked over his shoulder. The CQ was just a few feet away with his head buried in the newspaper.

"I have a big favor to ask of you, Wayne, and I hope you'll feel free to say no if it's too much."

No, Holder said to himself.

"Sure," he said out loud. "What is it?"

"I wonder if you could meet me tonight—I thought the library might be a good place. I have something I want to talk to you about. It concerns . . . well, is it all right to speak freely on this phone?"

As if it weren't bad enough that he was talking to the Tac's wife again, the extra bit of intrigue had Holder feeling suddenly warm.

"You want to meet me in the library?"

"It'll only take a few minutes," Kathleen Gates said.

Now here's a woman who intimidates me, Holder thought. Every self-preservation instinct he'd developed in three years of living at West Point told him to say "No."

"Please say yes, Wayne," Gates said again in a cooing, girl's voice. "I promise not to keep you out too late . . . I wouldn't want to get you into trouble."

He had an image of himself in the Tac's office, with Alex Trainor standing beside him saying, "I told you to stay away from these women. Stick to the big-hair girls."

What the hell am I afraid of? he thought. *I can handle Liz Wrenson and I can certainly handle Kathleen Gates.*

"I guess I can get away for a little while," Holder said. *She called me, right?*

"I have a meeting with a group for a design project. Can I meet you late? I can be in the main reading room—you know that one, first floor?—at twenty-two hundred. Sound good to you?"

"Ten o'clock," Kathleen Gates said. "I'll be there."

Alex Trainor wandered slowly down the staircase after Holder turned back to answer the phone. His hand was throbbing beneath its heavy bandage and he felt nauseous. The doctor had told him to eat, but he wasn't looking forward to the meal and thought a little fresh air might help clear his head.

Who am I kidding? he thought as he stepped outside the door—the one in which Gates had smashed his hand—to wait for Holder in the cool sally port.

The hand is the least of my worries.

Wayne had called Alex's parents after the accident to let them know what had happened. They had wanted to fly east to West Point immediately, but didn't make the trip because Alex got on the phone the next morning and assured them that he was fine. They were worried about him, but at least they knew where he was. Holder didn't know there was anyone else to call because Alex had a secret, and her name was Ruth.

Trainor's painful shyness around women was legend in the Corps. One of Holder's girlfriends had set Trainor up and the two couples double dated. Alex barely spoke the entire evening, and Holder had called him Autistic Alex for weeks. But Trainor found he could talk to Ruth, whom he'd met in a pastry shop in Manhattan. He visited the shop three times in one afternoon and asked her for a date on the last visit.

Not an especially pretty girl, Ruth could never stand beside the flashy women Holder sported around with. She was a bit overweight, with rounded legs and buttocks that stuck out too far, like a sofa table. She had shoulder-length dark hair and thick eyebrows and although she had grown up in the exclusive horse country of northwestern New Jersey, her speech often slipped into the near-comic accent of Newark and Hoboken. Her vowels rolled about like beer barrels and she kept her mouth open too long when she spoke, so that there was a sort of nasal follow-through to whatever she said.

Alex had not told his parents about the relationship. Ruth was a little too brash for their conservative tastes, and Alex couldn't help thinking his parents wouldn't find her smart enough for their son. Besides that, she came from the worst kind of money—money she had not worked for—and she didn't hesitate to let that fact be known.

But Alex liked her liveliness. Where he was quiet, she was gregarious. Where he dressed conservatively, she dressed in bright colors that matched her personality. He liked the way she laughed with every part of her; liked the way she wore her clothes, which managed to be both expensive and showy.

And she had kissed him on that first date. Close-mouthed, brief, but with a tiny electric shock that seemed to promise something more. Alex, who had not kissed a girl since high school, was a twenty-one-year-old virgin when he met Ruth.

He knew all about the hazards—corporeal and spiritual—of sleeping with a woman he didn't love, much less wanted to marry. He had lectured Wayne Holder on that catalog of sins for years. Holder, of course, was blissfully unaffected by the sermons; in fact, he seemed to enjoy Alex's monologues. When Alex started sleeping with Ruth in her little Brooklyn apartment, he managed to convince himself that he could marry this woman. She was sweet and lively and funny, and if she wasn't so smart, so what?

But she had changed when she became pregnant.

She was two months along, had quit her job and was not interested in working, and—without an engagement ring— unwilling to tell her parents that she was pregnant. She wanted money to bring back the cleaning lady, more money to buy maternity clothes. And because she had no under- standing of how much money was a great deal, she thought Alex should provide for her as her father did.

Alex's allowance out of his cadet pay was only a few hundred dollars a month. From that he was supposed to make car payments and pay for the occasional privileges allowed senior cadets. There weren't many nights out, but the tab added up quickly. By July he had spent most of his savings, foolishly allowing Ruth to use his credit cards. She had filled the tiny apartment with baby things, clothes and a bassinet and a crib and playpen and a changing table. When Alex had protested she cried and said he didn't love her. Which he knew, in his heart of hearts, was true. Alex wasn't going to cut her loose; but all the good intentions couldn't change a few immutable facts: he was nine months away from commissioning and his first real paychecks. And he had no idea what to do.

Alex Trainor paced in the sally port, waiting for Wayne Holder, cradling his smashed hand and wishing he could ask for help. He was embarrassed because he had violated his own rules. He had let people down; he was ashamed. There had even been a few moments when he thought that he deserved what had happened to his hand, although he wouldn't go so far as to say that Major Gates was an agent of God's punishment.

CHAPTER 7

THE HOTEL THAYER IS A BRICK AND STONE TOWER THAT SITS like a trifold picture frame on a bluff above the river just inside the south gate. From street level, guests climb stairs to the lobby, so that the size of the room is exaggerated. A huge fireplace sits across from the entrance. Its mantle is topped with an oil painting of the old Hotel West Point, a modest block that housed Douglas MacArthur's mother during that future general's entire cadet career. The floors are dun-colored marble, the ceiling a showy display of wood, gilded flourishes, and shields bearing the insignia of the various branches within the United States Army: crossed rifles on blue for the infantry, crossed cannons on red for the artillery, and so on around the top of the room.

Like many old buildings in the government inventory, the Hotel Thayer was built in a generous time; but its upkeep was entrusted to ever-more vigilant budget watchers. The result: cheap furnishings in a sumptuous, if small-scale, setting. The hotel bar, located just off the lobby on the river side, offers a spectacular north- and east-facing view of the Hudson through tall windows that march around two sides of the room. Inside, it's all lowest-bidder government issue:

vinyl and plastic, formica and paneling and thin carpet. A gray metal folding chair would not be out of place here. There is a self-serve popcorn dispenser at one end of the bar; that end of the room is carpeted in dark synthetic and ground popcorn that leads from the machine like the fabled yellow brick road. The drinks are more expensive than at the Officer's Club, but cheaper than elsewhere in the Empire State. In contrast to the dining room, which retains much of its early century glitter, the bar's decor is all VFW Hall, bus station, late twentieth-century government-functional.

And so it was that Claude Braintree sneered when he entered the room to join the staffers so far assembled at West Point.

"Ladies, gentlemen," he said, gliding into the room and waving as the men at the table found their feet. "Please, keep your seats," he said, smiling widely.

"I declare," he continued, letting a little bit of Georgia creep into his voice for effect, "I believe that all this military decorum is starting to affect you positively."

The chuckling that followed was no more than polite acknowledgment that Braintree was the boss.

There were four men and three women at the table, all of them young, ambitious, poorly paid and individually convinced, to varying degrees, that Claude Braintree was going to bring them along on Senator Bruckner's triumphal ride to the White House. They were smart—Phi Beta Kappa and Magna Cum Laude in political science, history, journalism—articulate and, to a surprising degree for their tender age and inexperience, keenly aware of even the most subtle nuances of inside-the-beltway politics. Any one of them could recite the box scores of the power struggles constantly being waged on Capitol Hill: who was in, who was out.

Someone watching from the next table might have guessed them a management training team, maybe a bevy of young lawyers or business consultants. With their conservative suits and haircuts and cheap shoes, they might even have been missionaries.

In reality they were anything but a team. They were climbers, and they had already made it off the bottom steps of the dizzying pyramid that, each of them hoped, would lead to a Bruckner White House. The other people sitting around the table were the competition; so the camaraderie was artificial, if not forced. Claude Braintree had enticed each of them with talk about "blue passes"—the badges that gave access to the first floor of the West Wing where the Oval Office is located. The blue badge was the Holy Grail of the political appointee, the climbers who wanted to be able to attend their fifteen-year college reunion and hand out the ultimate business card: plain white with black lettering that said "The White House."

Braintree ordered a Scotch and sat down carefully, unbuttoning his coat, smoothing the legs of his trousers. It was eight o'clock in the evening, and not only was he still wearing a suit, but he looked as if he just stepped out of a fashion photo spread; his jacket and pants were still flawlessly pressed, his collar stiff, his shirt barely creased. He chose a seat that faced the door—so he could see the comings and goings and be seen himself—and next to Dorothy Sayer, arguably the prettiest member of the team assembled so far.

Sandy Van Grouw suddenly felt a little rumpled. He had loosened the knot on his tie, affecting a weary-journalist look that he thought put him one up on the other men around the table. Now that Braintree was seated and looking as if he were on his way to a state dinner, Van Grouw felt he needed a little straightening. He also needed to go to the bathroom, having downed two beers and worked his way through most of a third—all on an empty stomach—while waiting for the boss to make his appearance. But he did not dare get up from the table. There was no telling how long Braintree would stay around, and Van Grouw's colleagues, all of them rabid for attention, would be only too happy to push his empty chair away from the table and forget to mention him. Besides, Van Grouw wanted to hear what the others had done.

They'd been assembled to do the advance work for the commission, to learn the academy's systems, to put faces with the names in all the written reports. Their inquiries had a scholarly look about them: they carried briefcases and notebooks and sharp pencils. But they knew that the balanced approach was a facade. Senator Bruckner was a slash-and-burn man, and he wanted the biggest, most sensational stories.

Sandy Van Grouw wasn't surprised to find that the people here hadn't done a lot of homework before arriving. There was no glamour in careful preparation. The glory was in finding the dark secrets that would get Lamar Bruckner on the news.

Van Grouw was reasonably sure that he had accomplished something, but because of the competition, they were all operating in isolation, and so he had nothing by which to judge his work. The others at the table were not about to share what they had done until the boss came, and even then it was not to be trusted. To say that each person would polish what he or she had done to put it in the best light for Braintree would be a gross understatement. Van Grouw wasn't sure there'd be any outright lying at the table, but there might be a few long noses by the end of the night.

He crossed his legs, determined that he wouldn't miss his chance with an ill-timed trip to the rest room.

It comes down to this, he thought. *All this work, all those years of school, and the big test turns out to be: can I hold my bladder?*

The bartender, working the room alone, put Braintree's Scotch on the bar. The Washington lawyer pretended not to see it, obliging the bartender to come around from behind the bar, pick up the glass and carry it the five or six feet to the table.

"Here's your drink."

Braintree, deep in a story about the Superintendent's Quarters, looked at the glass as if he expected to see a roach floating in it.

"Sometimes you even see people serve these things on a tray," he said as he took the glass. Big smile.

When the bartender turned away, he said to his audience, "Charmingly provincial, don't you think?"

After the obligatory chuckle from the disciples gathered round, Braintree said, "Well, let's hear what we did for the taxpayer today." Another big smile.

Four or five people began to speak at once. Dorothy Sayer was not the loudest, and so might have been expected to concede the floor. But she was next to Braintree, and she put her hand on his arm as she spoke, slowly, evenly, as if she knew all along that everyone else at the table would become quiet.

"I've decided to go after the women's stories," Sayer said.

Very original, Van Grouw thought. *Who'd have thought that a woman would want to beat that dead horse?*

"I made some very interesting classroom visits this morning and again this afternoon," Sayer said.

Her tone was businesslike, barely a trace of inflection. It was even noticeably deeper than her normal speaking voice. Van Grouw had an image of her attending seminars with titles like "Sound Like a Leader."

But if she'd pushed her femininity out of her voice, her body language more than made up for it. She leaned toward Braintree, and, using one hand, swept her hair—parted in the middle—along the top of her head so that it fell immediately back into place with a little hint of wildness to it. Van Grouw looked around the table at the other women, who were smirking.

"I took note of how often the instructor called on the women in the class versus how often he called on the men. There seemed to be a decided tilt toward the men."

She sat back in her seat, apparently satisfied that this observation alone was enough to make her point.

"And what did you conclude from this?" Braintree asked. He picked an invisible piece of lint off of his trouser leg.

"That this is still very much a male institution," Sayer answered confidently.

Braintree smiled widely, then turned his attention to the rest of the table.

Feeding time, Van Grouw thought.

"Did you talk to the women cadets after class?" one of the other women asked. Diane Clementon, a wide-shouldered former speech writer who favored blue suits, looked over the top of her glasses at Sayer.

"Yes, I did," Sayer said. She still had a hint of smugness in her voice. Van Grouw wondered if Braintree was screwing her yet.

"And what did they say?" Clementon asked sweetly.

"They said they hadn't noticed that the instructor called on men more often," Sayer said with some finality. But she was trying to tie up a bundle that wasn't complete.

"I meant, what did they say about their class preparation. Maybe they hadn't read the lesson."

The others around the table swiveled their heads as if watching a tennis match: advantage Clementon.

"It could be that the instructor didn't assign much point value to class participation," Clementon added.

Sayer hesitated.

Bad move, Van Grouw thought. *There's blood in the water now.*

One of the other men, a cerebral Texan named Holly, jumped in.

"If you want to do empirical work," he said, his emphasis on "empirical" leaving no doubt that he was talking about a low level of difficulty, "I think you would have to attend a number of classes to get a big sample before you could draw conclusions." He smiled at Sayer. "Unless of course the women had told you that this was a fairly common occurrence."

Van Grouw was doodling on a legal pad before him: a dorsal fin cut through the blue line at the top of the page.

"I think we're after anecdotal evidence," Holly said jovially, "rather than scientific evidence. What you may have in your classroom experience is the beginning of a scientific inquiry."

"I think I read a study like that a few years ago, as a matter of fact," Clementon added.

Ooo . . . there's the kill, Van Grouw said to himself. He held his legs pressed tightly together and felt sure that if he laughed, he'd lose control of his bladder.

Sayer put her hand out again to touch Braintree's arm, a connection she hoped would save her. It looked to Van Grouw like the move of someone who'd fallen overboard. Braintree didn't budge.

"Well, I was looking for a direction today, someplace to go with the rest of my inquiries," Sayer said. The hand went up for the hair sweep. "And I did accomplish that."

Right, Van Grouw thought, leaning back in his chair. Sayer had not removed her hand from Braintree's arm.

Why don't you just get down on your knees under the table?

"Sandy, you're smiling like the cat who ate the canary," Braintree said. "Why don't you tell us what you have."

Van Grouw looked up; Braintree was wearing his wide smile. With the exception of Sayer, who was rubbing her eyes with thumb and forefinger, everyone was looking now at Van Grouw. He turned the legal pad over.

"Well," he said, swallowing. "I spent some time at the gym today. . . ."

"I could tell," Clementon interrupted, drawing a laugh.

Van Grouw smiled; it wasn't the first joke he'd endured about his physique.

"I'd be happy to show you where the gym is, Diane," Van Grouw said to his stocky colleague.

His joke fell flat. It was perfectly acceptable to tear someone to shreds, as they had just done with Sayer, as long as the tone was "drawing room civil." It was not cricket to show one's claws in the open.

"Now, now, children," Braintree said, though he clearly loved these exchanges. "Let's hear what Sandy learned over in that torture chamber. I understand the cadets have a special name for the Department of Physical Education."

"They call it the Department with a Heart," Van Grouw said. "Facetiously, of course."

"And what tortures did you witness today?" Braintree asked. The boss was smiling again. Van Grouw felt that if he could stay in conversation with Braintree, the others might not jump on him as they had Sayer. He squirmed in his seat; it felt as if someone were dripping cold water into his groin.

"The most interesting thing I saw was intramural boxing," Van Grouw said. "Each of the thirty-six companies fields a boxing team. It is not the most popular sport they have to choose from, although there are a few zealots."

"They *have to* box?" Clementon asked.

Van Grouw turned to her. Her big arms in their big blue sleeves were resting on the table; she leaned forward, looking at Van Grouw as if she didn't quite believe what she'd heard.

"All the men take boxing as part of their plebe year instruction; it's one of the four courses during their first year. Twenty lessons. Theoretically, all the male cadets are at least familiar with the sport. . . ."

"I can't believe they have to take *boxing*," Clementon said, incredulous, as if she were talking about foot-binding.

Van Grouw folded his hands on the table, ready for her.

"I mean, what if you're morally opposed to boxing?"

"If you're morally opposed to boxing, then I suggest maybe you'd selected the wrong college," Van Grouw said coolly. "I mean, if you won't punch some guy, you're sure as hell not going to shoot anybody."

Braintree laughed out loud, and, on cue, so did everyone else around the table, save Clementon.

Emboldened, Van Grouw continued.

He flipped over the legal pad on which he'd made a few notes while waiting for Braintree. Putting his hand over the dorsal fin drawing, he told the story of Chris Dearborn.

"I talked to one cadet who's in the top of his class academically but has always had trouble with physical education," Van Grouw said. "He's passed all the required courses and tests."

Van Grouw felt he was rambling a bit. He looked around at the circle of faces. Braintree's laughing at his joke—at Clementon's expense—held the sharks at bay for the moment, but he couldn't expect that to last long. The predators were looking for a way in.

"But his tactical officer ordered him on the boxing team," Van Grouw said.

He heard a sigh—it was Holly—and he expected at any second to hear someone say, *So what?*

And he didn't have an answer for that.

He remembered that he felt a little sorry for the cadet—his name, written on the margin of the page, was Dearborn. But now Van Grouw wondered if that was because he identified with Dearborn as an underdog. It wouldn't help to portray the cadet as some sort of wimp complaining about having to struggle through physical education. It had to be more than that. Someone would make the connection—probably Clementon, once she got her nerve back—the connection between Dearborn the wimp and Van Grouw the wimp. He'd pissed Clementon off, embarrassed her in front of Braintree; now he had to be on his guard.

Dearborn's story had to be more dramatic than what Van Grouw had so far or the sharks would close in.

"This is in retaliation for something that happened over summer training," Van Grouw said.

Two of the people at the table leaned forward. Even Clementon looked mildly interested.

"He ran into some trouble down at Airborne School. . . ."

"What kind of trouble?" Holly wanted to know. "Discipline problems?"

"No," Van Grouw said. He flipped over to the second page of his notes, but the sheet was mostly covered in doodles.

It's here somewhere, he thought. He could feel the others at the table watching him. Out of the corner of his eye he saw Braintree begin to pick more imaginary lint from his dark blue suit. This seemed to be some sort of signal to the pack.

"Did he say what it was?"

This—clean and precise as a stiletto—from Clementon. Van Grouw didn't have to look up to know she was back in the ring. He could feel the attention begin to pass from him; any second now and Braintree would dismiss him with some caustic remark and move on to the next eager staffer.

This was what brought them to the lowest common denominator—this competition, this clamoring to be noticed. It was what made the sensational so important.

There, on the top corner of the page, the number "34" was circled.

Van Grouw looked up. *Shit! What does the number mean?*

Clementon was drawing a breath, preparing to speak.

"He was supposed to jump off a thirty-four foot tower," Van Grouw said quickly.

"He was supposed to jump thirty-four feet?" Holly asked. "To the ground? No wonder he froze."

"There was some sort of suspension apparatus," Van Grouw said as if that were not important. He moved quickly past that part of the story he hadn't written down.

"The point was that he didn't go immediately when he was supposed to, and there was a bottleneck of sorts and the cadets behind him started taunting him. . . ."

Come to think of it, he didn't actually say they taunted him, Van Grouw thought. But they did say things to him. Van Grouw was familiar with taunts. The stupid people always resorted to such things. They had tortured him in just such a way on countless occasions. Van Grouw could almost hear the catcalls and jeers. Probably in a voice very much like Clementon's.

"Then the instructors told jokes on him. At any rate, when the story got back to West Point, this cadet's tactical officer—who is a paratrooper himself," Van Grouw said, confident that he'd nailed that detail. "This kid's tactical officer was angry."

Dearborn hadn't said that, exactly, Van Grouw thought. *I'm inferring. But that would be the natural reaction for a paratrooper, right?*

Van Grouw looked down the table at Clementon.

She's probably paratrooper material herself.

"And?" Braintree asked.

He had stopped picking lint from his suit, but there was very little patience left in his voice.

"And the tactical officer put him on the boxing team as a punishment. The cadet is not a good boxer and he expects to be beaten pretty regularly."

"They might as well just have a blanket party for him," Holly said.

Thank you, Van Grouw thought. He wondered if Holly even realized that he'd come down on Van Grouw's side. More likely, Holly was watching Braintree, whose interest was piqued, and had decided to go with the winning team.

"That might be interesting," Braintree said. "A tactical officer who's using his position and power to punish cadets who don't meet his personal standards, over and above what the regulations call for. Maybe we should find out more about this man. Do you have his name, Sandy?"

"His name is Gates, sir. Major Thomas Gates," Van Grouw answered.

"Gates," Braintree said. "I wonder if there's more we

should know about Major Gates. There might be something there. Good work, Sandy."

Jacqueline Timmer lay propped up in bed in a neat circle of light from her reading lamp and a ragged circle of as-yet-ungraded cadet papers strewn on the bedspread. She held a paper in one hand, a green pen poised above the page in the other. She had read the same paragraph at least three times but was unable to think about anything but Layne Marshall.

"This essay will juxtapose a comparison and contrast of . . ."

She groaned, underlined the word "juxtapose," then looked over at the bedside table where the phone sat quietly. The clock there said nine-oh-nine.

Timmer had mentioned to Layne Marshall—or rather, in front of Marshall—that Rob was not going to be home until ten or eleven that night. Now it was after nine, and she wondered if she should have come right out and asked Marshall to call her.

Don't be silly, she told herself. *He could be out also.*

Then she had a sudden image of Marshall on a date, not with some known quantity from the West Point community, but some glittering professional woman from New York City, a woman who wore expensive business suits instead of green polyester, a woman who could take a few days off to visit New England, do Martha's Vineyard. . . .

"Jesus," she said out loud. "You're jealous. How pathetic is that?"

She underscored "juxtapose" again. Timmer used green because she thought students were conditioned by years of seeing teachers' marks in red. She wanted her students to focus on the comments, on what could be improved, not on the negative aspects of grading.

She looked at the clock again, it was nine ten.

Rob said he'd be home "around" ten or eleven. He had a meeting with the Cadet Marathon Club and then he and a few of the other instructors, men he'd served with in the Gulf War, were going out for a few beers. She supposed he could come home early.

And so what if I'm talking to someone on the phone? a

petulant little voice inside her said. *Can't I talk to whomever I want?*

In the next instant she pictured Rob answering the phone. And Layne Marshall on the other end, cool as he could be, would probably just say "This is Layne Marshall calling for Jacqueline Timmer."

But maybe Layne would think that might cause her problems, and he'd just hang up. Of course, that could cause her more problems.

You're making yourself crazy, she decided.

The clock said nine eleven.

She put her pen on the paper, thought of a comment.

You like big words? How about malapropism?

"A littly bitchy tonight, aren't we?" she said to the empty room.

She wrote "WC" under the green line, for "word choice."

The clock now said nine twelve.

There were thirty-seven papers left on the bed and on the floor beside her. In thirty minutes she had graded exactly two.

"At this rate I'll be finished in . . ."

The phone's electronic bleating startled her, but she snatched it up before it stopped the first ring. She put her hand over the mouthpiece and took a deep breath, then smiled, because she'd read somewhere that if you smiled when you talked, the person on the other end could tell.

"Hello," she said.

"Hey, Jack." It was Rob.

"Hi."

"Nichols and Berndt want to go down to Highland Falls to get a beer. We're just leaving now, so make it an hour and a half, at least. That OK with you?"

"Sure, Rob." Jackie said, looking at the clock—nine thirteen.

"Good," Rob said. "What are you doing?"

"Just sitting here in bed surrounded by cadet papers," she answered.

There was another voice besides Rob's; then she heard Rob repeat what she'd said.

"Jeff Berndt says too bad you're not in bed surrounded by cadets," Rob repeated, laughing.

"Yeah," Jackie said. Jeff Berndt was one of those people whose humor always concerned sex; his wife was another. Mary Berndt was always talking about hiring a few cadets to be pool boys.

"Forget that I don't have a pool," she'd said once at a party. "I just want them around to handle the hoses."

Jackie Timmer kept her counsel, but she had always looked down on that kind of humor.

And look at me now, she thought.

"You there, Jack?"

"Yeah, I'm here," she said. "I'll probably be right here when you get home, too. I mean, right in this spot. You have a good time."

"Thanks," Rob said. "Oh, by the way, could you empty out my gym bag? Just throw the stuff into the laundry room? I left my sweaty gear in there and I'm afraid it'll mildew."

"I'd be delighted," she said, "to pick through your dirty workout clothes."

Rob, deaf to sarcasm, said, "Thanks."

There was more muffled conversation. It sounded to Jackie that Jeff Berndt had already had a few beers. She put the receiver back in its cradle and stood up next to the bed.

The phone rang almost immediately. Sure that it was Rob again, she answered brusquely. "Hello."

"Hello, Jacqueline."

It was Layne Marshall.

"Hi, Layne," she said sweetly. She sat straight up on the bed, pulling her legs up and crossing them under her. A couple of cadet papers fell to the floor, landing in a tangle.

"This is a nice surprise," she said.

"Is it?"

"Of course it's nice," she insisted.

"No, I mean, is it a surprise?"

Where she'd been feeling a little giddy a moment before when she'd heard his voice, Jackie now felt a shudder, a tiny electric thrill. It was out in the open now. They had crossed an imaginary threshold before which propriety demanded that they pretend the flirtation was only make-believe. This phone call at home was the equivalent of the note in fifth grade math class that said, "I *really* do like you *lots.*"

"Yes, it's a surprise," Jackie said. "It's not a surprise that I wanted you to call. But it's a nice surprise that you did."

"What are you doing?"

She was tempted to say, *Lying here thinking of you.*

Instead, she answered, "Grading papers. Same thing I'm always doing when I'm not actually teaching."

"And how are those papers?"

"Uniformly dull, so far," she said.

"What are you wearing?"

The question was so unexpected that she wasn't sure she heard him correctly.

"Pardon?"

"I said, 'What are you wearing?' Isn't that the customary question to ask before the heavy breathing starts?"

Jackie Timmer laughed out loud, a sudden snorting sound that embarrassed her; she slapped her hand across her mouth.

She didn't think she'd be any good at flirting. Whenever Rob called her, it was generally because there was something newsworthy.

Maybe I just need to practice.

"I have on a pair of black stretch pants, exercise tights," she said. "And a big, oversized tee shirt."

She almost added, "and no bra," but she wasn't quite ready to go that far yet.

"I expected you to say you were wearing some sexy lingerie," Marshall said. "And then I would have accused you of making it up, embellishing a little bit."

"I don't need to embellish," she said, warming to the game. "I look good enough in what I'm wearing."

Now it was Marshall's turn to laugh. "I'll bet you do."

"So what have you done for your country today?" Timmer asked, shifting to safer ground.

"Actually, I spent part of the day talking to one of those Bruckner Commission people," he said. "I understand you met the big boss. Braintree."

"I picked him up at the airport and brought him here. Quite a show, that one."

"His minions are in awe of him," Marshall said. "I gather it has something to do with the fact that they all think that

Braintree is going to the White House with Senator Bruckner."

"Is that what you think?" Timmer said. She had kicked more of the cadet papers to the floor and was now stretched out on top of the bed, absentmindedly running her hand across her stomach beneath her shirt.

"I find modern politics tedious. Give me prerevolutionary America any time," Marshall said. "However, I have to say that Senator Bruckner is out to make a big splash over this look at the Academy."

"Do you think he's really got it in for West Point?"

"I'm not sure that makes a difference," Marshall said. His voice was like warm liquid; Timmer thought she could listen to him all night. More than that, he talked to her like she had a brain.

"His objective is to get a lot of exposure. If he can get more by recommending the Academy be shut down, he'll jump on that. If he can do better in the polls by rescuing this venerable American institution, then you can expect to see him standing next to the Superintendent at some press conference, talking about Patton and Lee and Grant and Jackie Timmer and the other famous graduates with just as much sentimentality as your basic maudlin admissions officer.

"But however it turns out, this can be a great opportunity for West Point," Marshall finished.

Jackie thought about how Claude Braintree had quizzed her on the ride from the airport, as if he'd already decided what he'd find and just had to go through the motions of shining a light on the corruption.

"How's that?" Timmer encouraged him.

"It's good to shake things up every once in a while; challenge your basic assumptions about what's going on, what should be going on."

"I agree with you there," she said.

Marshall didn't answer right away; when he did, he said, "That goes for individuals, too. People need to shake things up once in a while. Challenge their assumptions."

"But that's the exact opposite of what most people want," Timmer said. "Most people want the same old thing, the predictable, the comfort zone, the rut."

"Most people lead lives of quiet desperation," Marshall said, "to put a politically correct spin on a familiar quotation."

"Is that true for you, too?" Timmer asked. She had her eyes closed now, remembering what he smelled like. "Do you challenge your assumptions?"

"Sure," he said. "That's probably why I'm not married any more."

"You got divorced because you wanted out of the comfort zone?"

"No, I got married because I thought that's what I was supposed to do. And I stayed in an unhappy marriage for a long time because I thought *that's* what I was supposed to do.

"Despite my home state's reputation for the gothic, I was raised amid some very conventional expectations. Go to school. Get a job. Get married. Have kids. Stay married."

"That all sounds familiar," Jackie said. She was completely prone now; she had pulled her tee shirt up just below her breasts and was languidly brushing her fingernails across the taut skin of her abdomen.

"Then one day you wake up and you think, 'How did I get here? Whose idea was all this, anyway?' And you feel a little trapped."

"That's how I've felt lately," Jackie said.

There was a pause on the other end that stretched into a few seconds, then four, five. Jackie wondered if she'd said too much, if she'd said the wrong thing. She paused with the fingertips—just the very pads—of her right hand lightly brushing the prominent ridge of her bottom rib.

"I sensed that," Marshall said.

She wanted to come right out and say she'd been questioning more than her career, that she'd been questioning her marriage. But that wasn't exactly true. Although her marriage did not excite her, she couldn't point to any specific complaint. Or was it enough that it didn't excite her? Was that in itself something wrong with it?

"I mean, the Army is changing daily, it seems," she said, trying to steer the conversation back to careers. "Some of the people I went to school with who were determined to make this a career have left the service. There seem to be no rules, no predictability."

She could hear him breathing on the other end; there was no question as to whether or not he was listening. He was quiet precisely because he was a good listener. Another luxury.

"So what does one do?" Jackie asked.

"Well, there's a risk involved, certainly, when you start questioning things," Marshall said. "But that risk is only to your peace of mind. It's when you start acting on your impulses that you really take risks."

They were circling something neither of them would name. Not yet.

"But without doing that, without taking those risks, how will you know what it is you really want?" she said.

Her hand was up under her shirt again, the fingertips playing over one breast. She felt the nipple harden beneath her touch. Her voice dropped, became slower, as if the words were something she could taste, tiny, sweet morsels.

"And it's risk taking that lets us know we're alive," she said.

"Yet we live a very sedate life here in academia," Marshall said. "I mean, where do we take risks?"

Timmer rolled over onto her side and pulled her knees up.

"I'm taking a risk right here," Timmer said, "talking to you."

She held the receiver in one hand; the cord stretched over the back of her neck and threatened to tug the phone off the bedside table. She put her free hand between her knees, pushed her thighs farther apart so that her legs were splayed, and caressed herself with two fingers.

"It was no accident that I met you, Jacqueline," Marshall said.

"Perhaps not," Timmer said, her voice muffled by the pillow.

There was a heft to the silence now.

"I would like to see you," he said.

There. It was out in the open now, or at least his end of it was.

Jackie Timmer rolled onto her back, knees up, feet flat on the covers, hand still between her legs. She faced Rob's side of the bed; her twenty-one-year-old face stared back at her from a frame on Rob's bedside table. His favorite picture of her, taken on graduation leave. She wore a white crew neck shirt; her hair was longer then, pulled back in a long ponytail, the ribbon just visible above her shoulder.

"I'm afraid, Layne," she said.

"I understand," he replied. But she wasn't sure he did.

"I'm afraid because of what I'm risking, afraid of what I might do to Rob, afraid of what I might find out about me."

"It's OK, really," he said. "Really, it's OK."

And she suddenly felt bad for him; she had let him take her to this point, and then she had turned away.

"We could still have lunch," she said, surprised at how anxious she was that he might stop paying attention to her. "I mean, I think that would be OK, don't you?"

"That would be great," he said. "Just great. I'd also like to invite you—and Rob, if he wants to come—to a little show we're putting on down at the Old Cadet Chapel."

Jackie sat upright on the edge of the bed and started recovering cadet papers from the floor. She pinched the phone between her shoulder and ear and used both hands to smooth out the edges of the sheets she'd rumpled. "Really? What's that?"

"Well, I'm talking about the Puritans in two of my courses; talking about the tremendous influence religion had on the daily lives of the people. I told my class that modern American society, cynical as it is about nearly everything, cannot begin to imagine how much control the church exerted on the lives of the people. Not surprisingly, the cadets are having a little trouble seeing it. I mean, some of these kids don't even go to a church; how can they fathom what it was like to live in a community where the church exercised absolute power and religion suffused everything?"

He was talking fast, as if to relieve his nervousness.

"And some of the kids said they thought the early settlers came here to escape all that—religious persecution—when in reality the community was anything but tolerant."

"Witness *The Scarlet Letter*," Timmer said, glad to be back on the mundane.

"Exactly. So what we're going to do is take them down to the Old Cadet Chapel one night and we're going to have an actor deliver a fire-and-brimstone sermon, Jonathan Edwards's 'Sinners in the Hands of an Angry God.' Do you know it?"

"No," Jackie said. She spoke out of politeness when she said, "Sounds great."

"Well, it probably doesn't sound like much, but we've got a lot planned for the evening. I don't want to ruin the surprise. I hope you'll come," he said. He didn't mention Rob again.

"Sure, I'd love to see that," she said. And then, more boldly, "And I'd like to see you, too."

"Good," Marshall said. "Good. I'll let you know the time and date."

"Thanks, Layne," she said.

When she'd hung up the phone she sat quietly for a few minutes on the edge of her bed. She picked up the remainder of the scattered papers and put them all in her briefcase, then fell asleep with the light on, still wearing the tee shirt and tights. Rob came in late, slightly drunk; he climbed into bed noisily and put his hand up under her shirt. Jackie lay still and quiet while he pushed at her clothing and put his mouth on her belly, then she gave up all pretense of sleeping and began to stroke his hair while he kissed and licked her breasts and his hand sought her, roughly. She was surprised that she became aroused, and she helped him pull her tights off; but she turned her face to the side as he moved atop her, as he pressed himself inside her. She put her arms around him in a familiar embrace, but kept her eyes closed for the short time it took him to climax. When he fell asleep, open-mouthed and snoring as he did when he'd been drinking, she moved to the far edge of the bed, where she quietly, very quietly, masturbated and thought about making love to Layne Marshall.

Kathleen Gates walked around the perimeter of the Periodicals Room on the first floor of the cadet library, scanning the cover photos of the hundred or so magazines and journals arrayed neatly on forward-tilted shelves. Most of the space was taken up by scholarly works: foreign affairs, engineering journals, literary reviews.

She reached up and ran her finger over the cover of one of the news magazines.

This is what Bruckner is after, she told herself. *A little coverage, a little scandal, perhaps.*

At ten minutes to ten she walked through the stairwell into the first floor reference room and sat at one of the big wooden tables. There were six or seven cadets in the big room, most of them working individually. One young woman sat just at the next table surrounded by piles of oversized texts, writing frantically in a spiral-ring notebook. Directly across from Kathleen hung an almost life-sized portrait of Robert E. Lee. Although the U.S. Senate had declared him a traitor and stripped him of his citizenship for leading the army that came closer than any in history to destroying the United States of America, Lee was pictured in Confederate gray.

On the other side of the room, directly behind Kathleen so that his portrait faced his opponent's, was Ulysses S. Grant. To her left, through the diamond-paned glass of the big windows, she could see the bronze of George Patton silhouetted against the lights ringing Washington Road.

Such a place of heroes and myths, she thought. *And what was it that made fortune smile on one man and not another?*

Kathleen Gates's brother had been her hero, but the Navy had broken him. After he left the service, he got a respectable job as a midlevel manager of a manufacturing company on Long Island. But his spirit was constantly at sea somewhere.

Kathleen didn't think her husband had any more resilience than did her brother. Lately Tom Gates had been running scared of the letter that was coming from the Commandant's office. In the modern Army, the smaller Army, such a letter would be a signal to promotion boards: here's one we can get rid of. If Brian couldn't bounce back, she couldn't imagine Tom doing so. And in the meantime, they had two kids to raise. She had invested a lot of effort in Tom's career; the reprimand would end it only if she gave up. The Bruckner Commission gave her a way of continuing the fight.

Kathleen Gates knew that such study groups were given to seeing bogeymen behind every tree, in every shadow. All of that would work to her advantage. Her theory was that the military feared negative publicity, and now the publicity devil was lurking right here amid the ranks, amid the stone buildings and the bronze monuments and oil paintings. There was a lot of potential power and a lot of potential trouble, but Kathleen Gates thought she could stand close to the fire without getting burned. All she had to do, she thought as she contemplated Robert E. Lee's dark eyes, was remember to step out of the way when the shrapnel started flying.

At night, in the barracks, cadets in the three upper classes are allowed some leeway in what they wear. While they have to be in some uniform—and there were dozens, depending on the activity—to leave the barracks, inside the buildings during evening study period, they could pretty much wear what they wanted. Long athletic shorts were popular, and legible clothing in general seemed to be the order of the day. Some cadets favored tee shirts from other colleges in a sort of "This is what I might have done" display. Others liked to show off the odd collection of military tee shirts they'd collected during their summer duties at various Army posts around the country. Wayne Holder's favorite was an old one from the First Infantry Division, known as the Big Red One. The shirt showed a representation of the simple unit crest, a red numeral one on a shield-shaped olive patch. The legend on the back of the shirt said, "If you're gonna be one, be a Big Red One."

Wayne Holder, who usually studied in the barracks dressed in black soccer shorts and a tee shirt from one of the schools in the California University system, felt conspicuous when he changed into class uniform to go to the library. But no one asked where he was going.

Holder left the barracks and walked out onto the apron, the concrete pad that fronted MacArthur and Eisenhower barracks. The two great wings, facing the Plain and comprising nearly one third of all the barracks space it took to house the Corps, were lit up. Long rows of bright rectangles, six floors of cadet rooms. This was where the yeoman's work went on, the daily grind through studies, readings, problems, and labs.

I won't miss the schoolwork, Holder thought.

Yet he was a prisoner of his training. Like a good engineer, he thought about Kathleen Gates in terms of problem solving. Here are the known quantities, here are the possible solutions. Take your best—your most educated—guess. She'd told him she had something to discuss with him. Assuming that she was telling the truth, that could only mean the little showdown he'd had with her husband.

Holder checked his watch in the vestibule of the library. Two minutes until ten.

Where Wayne Holder just wanted to do his duties and graduate on time, Kathleen Gates always seemed to have a few agendas going at once. Her biggest concern, he reminded himself as he held the library door for another cadet who was coming out laden with books, had to be her husband's career.

There was no telling what she'd do to protect that.

Just remember to stay on guard with her, he told himself.

Holder had decided not to tell anyone that he was meeting Kathleen Gates in the library. If someone saw him there, that was fine, but he didn't volunteer the information. Alex would have tried to talk him out of it, and he was pretty sure Dearborn would too. They would remind him that there was nothing to be gained and quite a lot to lose in dealing with the Tac's wife. All of which left Wayne Holder wondering why he was entering the library at all.

She asked me for help, he told himself as he passed the main circulation desk.

But the shining knight image didn't exactly fit; he was, after all, just a cadet. Eager for some rationalization, he tried another tack.

How much trouble can I get into in the library? he reassured himself. *She just wants to talk.*

He stepped past a glass case filled with some of the published works of faculty members and into the main reference room of the library. Kathleen Gates sat near one of the great windows. There was a closed book on the table;

her hands were folded over it. She looked right at him, and when she smiled in greeting, Wayne Holder knew why he'd agreed to come. She was a beautiful woman and there was something exciting about standing near the edge.

"Hello, Wayne," she said as he sat down next to her.

"Hello," he said, scanning the room. He saw no cadet from his company and only one other senior in the room.

"Thanks for coming to talk to me," she said.

"No problem."

She had her hair pulled back and tied loosely with a black velvet ribbon. Her dress, another long summery thing with flowers in blues and greens, set off her pale skin; and Wayne Holder thought he'd never seen her in anything but a dress.

Gates leaned closer to him, and for a moment Holder was sure that she was going to kiss him, but she merely whispered, "Maybe we should go someplace where we could talk without disturbing these other people."

She stood, and he followed her to the stairway, which she climbed to the third floor. There, above the reference room, they entered a reading room decorated with military paintings and statuary. Kathleen Gates chose one of two couches that formed a little seating area. She patted the cushion next to her, but Holder sat on the other couch.

What had seemed to Wayne Holder like a good idea when he was in the barracks suddenly didn't look so great. He glanced around the room, wishing there were some other cadets present. Here he was in the library, the very arena for staid, controlled behavior, with a woman who'd legitimately asked to see him, and yet his stomach felt as if he'd just finished his third espresso.

"Thanks for taking time away from your studies," she said, smoothing her dress.

"No problem," Holder responded. "You said there was something you wanted to talk to me about?"

"Well, you can probably figure out what it is," Kathleen said. "It's about that awful incident over there by Mac-Arthur's statue. Tom has just been so worried about it lately, and I have, too."

Wayne Holder couldn't imagine Major Tom Gates sending his wife on a little peace delegation to talk to his subordinates. If nothing else, Major Mercury would handle any problems he'd caused head on. Probably head down, like a bull. No, this little meeting was all Kathleen Gates.

"Tom doesn't know I'm here, of course. But it's so important that he keep a good working relationship with the cadets in the company, and you're the key to that. Which is why I wanted to talk to you: what you say or don't say will go a long way to undercutting his credibility, or to helping him."

Holder nodded, trying to be helpful. The last thing in the world he expected was that Kathleen Gates would be asking him to look out for Major Mercury's reputation.

"I just hope that you'll take into consideration that it's not just *popularity* we're talking about, we're talking his career and my family's livelihood as well. Please remember that."

Holder, unsure of what he might say, what assurances he might give her, merely nodded.

"The good thing is: you don't strike me as the gossipy type," she said.

"Thank you," he said, glad to finally know the correct response.

"As a matter of fact, I feel that you and I could probably be good friends, Wayne," she said. She dabbed at a corner of one eye, although Holder hadn't seen a tear, with the back of her hand. Then she smiled widely at him.

"You know, we'll be seeing each other again," she said.

"We will?"

"I mean in the Army." She laughed, and Holder knew it was at his surprise.

"The Army isn't all that big, really, and we'll keep running into each other at different assignments and when you guys travel around for training or conferences or schooling. Why, there will probably come a time when you'll bring some pretty young wife around to see Colonel Gates and his wife, ol' what's her name."

Holder couldn't imagine any of that: wife, dinner with the Gates—or forgetting Kathleen's name.

"That would be very nice," he said with as much sincerity as he could muster.

He was feeling a bit more relaxed. Apparently Kathleen

had bared as much of her soul as she needed to. He'd read somewhere that women just liked to talk about problems, even if they didn't solve anything, it made them feel better somehow.

He had just started thinking about stopping by Liz Wrenson's room on his way back to his own barracks when Kathleen surprised him by reaching across the small gap between the couches and putting her hand on his knee.

"I suppose I seem rather silly to you," she said. "What with all this worrying."

"Not at all," Holder said. That was a bald-faced lie, but even the rigid Cadet Honor Code didn't expect you to tell your dinner hostess that you hated the meal.

"Can I impose on you for just a few moments longer?" she asked. "Walk me to my car, will you, please, Wayne?"

"Sure," he said, and although he was not at all sure, he followed.

As she walked down the library steps, Kathleen Gates realized she wasn't as nervous as she thought she'd be, and certainly not as nervous as Holder. The heels of her flats made little clopping noises, and the ten or twelve cadets at the terminals in the big catalog room below her looked up. She was, as ever, conscious of the way the male cadets stared.

The young men made it all too easy. Eighteen, nineteen, twenty years old, they were at the peak of their sexual power. Yet most of them were denied, sex-starved, frustrated. Vulnerable.

And all that gave Kathleen Gates just the leverage she needed. She remained focused on the outcome she wanted. She did not allow herself to think about how all this might blow up in her face, how it might hurt Tom, or even what it said about her that she could come up with such a plan. She thought instead about the letter, about how much she wanted to help her husband.

This will work, she told herself as she glided down the stairs. *This will work.*

Holder followed her down the main stairway, conscious once again of her perfume, of the way she moved on the stairs. She was talking about how they kept running into the same people at various assignments, how they had so many dear friends, and she really did sound enthused about the Army.

"It's so nice to see your old friends from time to time. I mean, I grew up an Army brat, so I have as many connections as Tom does . . . more, I sometimes think."

Holder put his garrison hat on with one hand and used the other to open the door for Kathleen Gates. A second class cadet he recognized from one of his elective courses stood aside to let them pass. Holder nodded hello.

"My car is just up the road here on the other side of the baseball field," Kathleen said.

They crossed the street to the sidewalk that passed in front of the Officers' Club, then in front of Lincoln Hall, where the Department of English shared office space with the Social Science department. The sidewalk was lighted, but not powerfully.

"There's enough light to find your way without tripping," Kathleen Gates said.

"Just enough," Holder agreed.

"Better to be on the safe side," she said, slipping her hand under his arm to lean on him. "Besides, there's not so much light that anyone is really going to see us."

Her hand was the touch of an electric current, hot, dangerous, it unsettled him all over. He wanted to pull away, he wanted to bend his arm and take her hand as well.

What the hell are you doing, Holder? he thought.

He looked over his shoulder, as if Trainor might be there, or Dearborn, or Liz Wrenson.

Or Major Gates.

"Does this make you nervous, Wayne?" she asked.

"Yes, it does," Holder said honestly.

She laughed, and even beyond his shallow breathing, he could hear the musical quality there.

"Don't worry about it," she said. "You're just escorting me to my car and being a perfect gentleman. Besides, I'm not old enough to be your Mrs. Robinson."

"Who?" Holder asked.

She laughed again, and this time Holder knew for certain

it was at him rather than with him. "Never mind," she said. "Maybe I am that much older than you."

Once past Lincoln Hall they recrossed the street and entered the parking lot nearest the baseball stadium. It was darker here, and Wayne Holder felt Kathleen's grip tighten on his arm.

"Back there I just wanted to hold your arm," she said. "Now I really might trip."

In one instant Holder was thinking that Trainor and Dearborn would never believe the things she was saying tonight. In the next instant he knew he could never tell them.

"Here it is," she said, facing him and putting her back up against the quarter panel of a small car. "Thanks for walking me."

"Sure," Holder said. "I . . . uh . . . that is, I'm not sure what you wanted to accomplish tonight, I mean, seeing me and talking to me and all."

"Maybe I just wanted to see you, Wayne," she said, as if it were the most obvious thing—as if it weren't totally outrageous that this married woman, this wife of a man who probably had it in for Holder, this woman who was nearly ten years older than he—as if it were not outlandish that she'd be flirting with him.

Wayne Holder wanted to break and run. He willed his foot to step backward, but just at that moment she reached out with both her hands and took his.

"I'll be jealous of her, you know," she said. That sweet voice again.

"Of who . . . whom?" Holder said.

"That pretty young wife you'll bring around someday."

"Oh," Holder said, feeling ridiculous. Then, "Ah."

Lurid pictures flashed through his consciousness: Kathleen Gates naked, her feet up in the air; her husband bearing down on him with an M16, bayonet fixed. At the other end of the lot, at least a hundred yards away, someone was getting into a car.

"You'll be surprised at how quickly the years will pass."

Holder wanted to pull away from Kathleen's hands.

"We have so little time, Wayne," she said. Then she put

her hands on his shoulders and pulled him to her, and then her hot mouth was on him, her fingers on the back of his head, in his hair, knocking his cap off.

She dropped her hands to his waist and pulled again, and there was her body, matching his in curves, testing his with hard and soft places, and incredibly, she had forced her thigh between his legs, pressing it up to his crotch.

And all Holder's thoughts of who she was and what he had to lose melted away in that feverish coupling of lips and mouth. She was back on the car now, pulling him, one leg hooked around his. Holder could feel himself instantly erect, which was uncomfortable in the tight uniform pants. His excitement was something apart from him, because there was still an insistent message flashing through his brain—*this woman is dangerous*—but it was being overridden, pushed away by her hands on the back of his neck, in his hair.

Kathleen Gates kissed him deeply, her mouth open, wet. She nipped his tongue, hard, and then Holder had his arms around her and felt the compact life there, the cool cotton tight across her back, her breasts pressing his chest, her hips moving already up against him, hard, insistent, determined.

Kathleen moaned and turned her head; Holder's open mouth cupped her throat. Then her hands pushed at the front of his pants, fingers kneading his penis, pulling it upright, stroking through the tight cloth and he was moaning *Oh Jesus, oh God, oh, oh* and Kathleen Gates was making little growling sounds, hungry little growling sounds in the back of her throat.

Wayne Holder heard the familiar tinkling of his brass belt buckle as Kathleen Gates slipped it loose. She held him squarely by the hips and dropped to her knees, pressing her face to him, biting at the gray cloth there.

Oh God, oh don't, oh man, oh hell, oh, oh, oh.

And then she had freed him and she was ravenous and his hands were in her hair his fingers tight on the back of her skull as she sunk him deeply into her mouth and everything seemed to turn as if on some swivel point some giant propeller that centered on this blood-thickened pole that he had in his hand and in her mouth and the sweet wave started somewhere in his brain and told him he would climax like that, yes, just like that, yes, oh, yes and yes again. . . .

But she pulled off of him, standing abruptly and leaving him bent slightly forward at the waist.

"I want you in me, Wayne. I want you to give it to me," she said, and she rustled the cloth of that dress, or maybe he did, and his hands were on the tops of her legs, one hand caught against the fender of the car.

"Oh, Jesus," he said aloud.

We're right outside and now his eyes were open and there were headlights on the road so close by.

"In the car," she said and she opened the door and slid in backward, beckoning to him, demanding him, one foot on the seat so that her legs were hiked up and he could see a white flash of her panties there.

Wayne Holder hesitated and Kathleen Gates grabbed him by this erect handle she had made of him and pulled him toward her.

Holder was standing, looking over the top of the car.

"In here," she said. "Hurry."

"We can't," he said, but he did not pull away.

And in that instant she knew she would lose him, that he would back off, run. And because she had not come this far to be denied, to have her plan—her only hope—smashed, Kathleen Gates slid to the edge of the seat and made fast work with mouth and tongue, breathing high and hard around him. And she knew, as she felt his body tense, as she tasted the surprising salty-sweetness of him in the back of her throat, that she had won this first round.

CHAPTER 8

GENTLEMEN, GENTLEMEN." CLAUDE BRAINTREE BREEZED INTO the Commandant's office, dripping conviviality and saccharine good cheer, his excessively friendly politician's persona already in place at seven thirty in the morning.

"I hope you don't mind the early start to our meeting," Brigadier General David Simon said as he took Braintree's hand.

"Not at all, not at all," Braintree answered. He turned to Tony Moro and shook hands with the second officer. "As the Senator is fond of saying, 'The Republic's business knows no schedule.'"

Simon and Moro smiled thin, polite smiles.

"Of course, the Senator doesn't come in until ten, so that's a little easier to swallow down on the Hill."

Simon laughed out loud, trying a little too hard. Moro's smile never gained a foothold on the serious mask of his face.

"As you know, we've just begun our interviews with people in each of your respective areas," Braintree said as he sat in the leather armchair directly across from the fireplace. Moro and Simon flanked him, one on each of the two couches that made up the rest of the sitting area.

"And I wanted to chat for a moment with you about how we're going about that and what we think we'll learn."

Braintree smiled widely at them, and Tony Moro thought, *Here's a man made for the public eye.*

Braintree wore a dark gray suit, double breasted, of beautiful light wool. Whenever Tony Moro met civilian businessmen, he checked their shoes. It always amazed him that a man would spend a thousand dollars on a suit but wouldn't use a dime's worth of shoe polish.

Claude Braintree's shoes, clean and well shined, could have stood inspection at any cadet formation.

"First of all, General Simon, let me say how much I enjoyed your speech the other night. I think your message was timely: we can't afford to hang on to tradition just for the sake of tradition."

Big smile at Simon, who smiled back, and big smile at Moro, who did not.

"Now, having said that, I realize that traditions are very important to the military; the historical context is part of the ethos, and tradition is a part of the historical context."

"Well," Simon said, "the commission's visit has caused some . . . concern. I don't want the cadets to develop a siege mentality, because that kind of defensiveness would get in the way of work that has to be done. I want them to see that change is not inherently evil, that there can be good aspects of change."

"And I appreciate your saying all that," Braintree said.

Moro watched the two men, their polite little dance, ingratiating, complimenting, bowing, and scraping. David Simon—a little too eager to please—was doing everything but roll on the carpet like the star graduate of a dog obedience school. It was one thing to acknowledge civilian control of the military and to accept that changes were probably inevitable; it was quite another to lap up every stupid joke and say, "Whatever you want, sir."

And it seemed to Moro that Claude Braintree was just the man to put his foot on someone's throat.

"We're not strangers to change, Mister Braintree," Moro said. "Many civilian observers would have trouble accepting that. Look around and you see uniforms that haven't changed substantially in half a century. We observe military customs and courtesies that are older than the republic—I mean, we still signal the end of the day with a bugle call. But don't forget that in the tenure of most of the officers on the staff and faculty, the Army has undergone tremendous change.

"When I came on active duty we were still recovering from the shock of Vietnam and the mess that the Army was in at that time. In the eighties we built the force that eventually convinced the Soviets that they could not win a land war in Europe, the same Army that made short work of the Iraqis. Then we dismantled that Army, piece by piece, all the while taking on more missions—peacekeeping, humanitarian missions. We had to reinvent our trade after the Gulf War. So we've seen some changes."

"Yes, you certainly have," Braintree said. He pressed the sharp seam of his trousers between thumb and forefinger, then looked up. "And you're bound to see more.

"Senator Bruckner believes that the American Defense establishment might be in line for a major overhaul during the next decade, not unlike the significant change in direction taken in the decade before the end of the Cold War. We're here—my people and I—to get a glimpse as to how things are going now. From that will come recommendations for further study.

"I'm sure each of you has experience working with a short-handed organization. Many of my staff are quite junior people. They go a long way toward making up in intelligence and enthusiasm what they lack in experience. Frankly, though, I'd rather have the experience, but that's beyond my control.

"Two things of interest have come up," Braintree said. "One has to do with the climate for women—and I suspect, for other minorities. The second has to do with what I'll call 'cowboy' interpretations of the rules. These are two areas we'll be concerned with as we proceed."

"Can you be more specific?" Simon asked.

Braintree smiled, that wide smile again.

He likes playing the cat in this game, Moro thought. *And Simon is too willing to play the mouse.*

"One of my staffers has decided to talk with women about their role here, about how well they're accepted, how well they fit in. She got the idea from sitting in a classroom and watching an instructor who seemed to call on men more often than women."

Oh, that's fucking great, Tony Moro thought. *Now we'll get some government mandated limit on how many times we can talk to the male cadets versus number of times we talk to the women. It's hard to imagine who'll hate that more—the men or the women.*

"We've come a long way in the integration of women in the Army and at West Point," Simon intoned. "Because we're dealing with human beings, there will always be areas for improvement. And we must keep in mind that we're dealing with a changing population here. Obviously one fourth of the cadets are new every year; in addition, one fourth to one third of the faculty changes as well."

"I had the opportunity to meet one of your women graduates now serving on the faculty," Braintree said. "Captain Timmer. I don't recall her first name."

"Captain Jacqueline Timmer," the Dean said helpfully.

"Yes. A most impressive young woman."

"We think so," Simon added.

"I'm sure she'll be able to tell us a great deal about the role of women here," Braintree said. "And I'm just as sure that you selected one of your most talented officers to be my escort. In our efforts to get beyond the authorized version of the West Point story, I'm sure that you can see we'll go a bit beyond the hand-picked spokespersons."

"Naturally," Simon said.

"And it's important to me that we get to talk to people honestly, openly, without command influence."

The word is 'secret,' Tony Moro thought.

Claude Braintree was bluffing. He was speaking as if his staff were a competent bunch of analysts, investigators, and interrogators instead of a collection of overly ambitious, bright young zealots whose sole agenda was self-advancement.

He was also fishing. The little alarmist Van Grouw had presented him with nothing spectacular that would get Bruckner in the news. Braintree wanted to see what Simon and Moro were concerned about. They had not reacted visibly to his comment about women in the classroom, which meant they either were confident that it was not a problem or that they believed the lovely Captain Timmer would convince him that everything was fine.

He had one more piece of bait to throw out.

"The other thing that has come up in my preliminary discussions with my staff is the liberties some people in authority may take in pursuing what they think West Point should be, or should provide cadets."

Braintree saw something curious in Moro's face: some loss of animation. One second he was right there, listening, attentive, if a bit bored. The next minute he had withdrawn, pulled back somewhere. Braintree looked at Simon, whose face registered nothing. Simon was either a better actor or didn't know what Moro knew.

"What do you mean?" Moro asked.

This is the bold one, here, Braintree thought. This was the part he liked best, sparring with someone who was willing to come out and fight with him, mix it up a little.

"Well," Braintree said, smiling and leaning far back in the chair. "I'm just speaking hypothetically, of course. But say an officer, for instance, thought a cadet needed some additional training, some extra development. And he chose to pursue this extra training within the bounds of what the Academy is already doing . . . I mean he's not having them skip class to go to the rifle range, or having them do push-ups in math class, but he's taking liberties. Isn't it possible that an overzealous officer, or cadet for that matter, could interfere with what the Academy is actually trying to accomplish?"

Simon blanched.

They're hiding something, Braintree thought. *That little twerp Van Grouw turned up the first piece of useful information.*

"Are you talking about a specific situation, sir?" Moro asked.

The Commandant had shifted in his chair, uncrossed his legs, moved forward on the cushion of the couch. His body language signaled alarm, or aggressiveness, or both.

Braintree kept quiet, his eyes on Moro, holding his smile for one beat, two.

"Well, as I said," Braintree continued, "we're speaking

hypothetically. And even if we weren't, remember that I want to preserve the confidentiality of the people who talk to us."

He moved forward in his chair, placing his hands carefully on the armrests, his feet flat on the floor. He was leaning into Tony Moro.

"I want to reiterate that I think that confidentiality is essential."

Essential is a bit strong, actually, Braintree thought. But he had merely picked this point to challenge Tony Moro. It could have been anything.

"My concern goes to safeguards," Braintree said.

Simon lifted his hand from his knee, like a student.

"It comes down to trusting subordinates," the Dean said. "At some point we have to trust our people, their understanding of the system and how it's supposed to work. In addition, no one here works in a vacuum, Mister Braintree. If someone is stepping out of bounds, someone else is going to notice. We live in a small world."

"And the command climate is such that a subordinate could feel secure in reporting things that are out of line?"

"Yes, sir, I believe it is," Moro said.

His voice still had an aggressive edge, something that Simon must have noticed. Braintree saw the older officer smile at Moro, a smile that looked suspiciously like a signal to shut up.

"You *believe* it is, General?" Braintree asked. There was no more trace of friendly banter in his voice. He was facing a clever witness. There was a jury box in his imagination.

"I bet my rank on it every day, sir," Moro said.

Braintree laughed and sat back in his chair.

"Did I say something funny?" Moro wanted to know.

"No, General, no. It's just that I so like dealing with soldiers, with anyone, for that matter, who isn't afraid to come out and say what he thinks. You must understand what a refreshing change that is from my experience in Washington."

"I'm so glad I could provide you some comic relief," Moro said, looking not at all pleased.

"Well, I must run along," Braintree said, standing, buttoning his coat. "It will be a pleasure working with you gentlemen."

Simon and Moro found their feet and shook hands with the civilian.

"Thank you for filling us in," Simon said.

Moro was quiet.

"Certainly," Braintree said as he moved out the door. "And I'll keep you apprised as we go along. I think we all have the best interests of the Academy in mind here."

"That's rich," Moro said to the closed door as soon as Braintree was gone. "He has his own best interests in mind."

"So what does he know?" Simon asked. He dropped back on the couch and put his feet up on the coffee table.

"Hard to say," Moro said, taking a seat on the other couch. "Sounded like he was talking about our friend Major Gates and the little spirit run."

"It's only a matter of time before he hears about that," Simon said. "He and his staff would have to be blind to miss that little piece of gossip."

"What about the issue of women in the classroom?"

"I'm not worrying about that," Simon said. "I'll mention it to the department heads and let them figure out what to do about it—if anything. Braintree's flunky could have been sitting in on a class where one or two women just weren't prepared. Just because they're in the minority doesn't mean they're not entitled to bad days. No, this Gates thing has the potential to come up and bite us on the ass.

"Did he get a letter of reprimand?"

"No," Moro said. "Not yet."

"What are you waiting for?" Simon asked, exasperated.

"I've drafted it; I just haven't given it to him. He knows it's coming."

"You didn't relieve him?" Simon asked. "Are you waiting to see if he screws up again?"

Moro, conscious of his turf, was sharp in his answer.

"Last time I looked, the man worked for me," he said.

"OK, OK, I didn't mean to tell you your job," Simon said. He rubbed his eyes with thumb and forefinger. "I'm just saying that we need to be careful."

"Look," Moro said. "The climate here has everybody a little juiced up. If we were inclined to make a mistake, it would probably be on the side of overreacting."

Moro knew that Gates had been wrong to come to the barracks after drinking beer, but he resented being told how to handle the problem. Simon recognized that and decided to back off; he needed Moro on his side in the coming weeks.

"Look, Tony, you're going to handle this the way you think is best, and I respect that," Simon said. "But this isn't the biggest problem we face."

"What is?"

"It's Flynn. I've been thinking a lot about his comment that we just need to do our jobs and not worry about what's going on with the Bruckner Commission. I think he's caving in."

Moro looked doubtful. "I don't think it's gone quite that far yet," he said.

"He doesn't even have a strategy for dealing with this," Simon responded.

There was something in the way Simon was sitting, the way he was talking, that made Moro suspect there was more to this little speech.

"And you have a strategy?" Moro asked.

Simon almost smiled; maybe Moro wasn't going to be hard to convince after all.

"I've been thinking a great deal about the possibilities, about some contingencies," Simon admitted.

"And?"

There was something in Moro's eyes that told the Dean not to push too hard.

"Nothing definite yet," he said. He took his feet off the table and pulled himself upright, then walked to the big windows with their beautiful view of the Plain.

"But I've been talking with Foster down at Navy and kicking around some ideas. They have a plan on the shelf that they can whip out if the word comes to downsize. Admiral Chichester's thinking is that if they have a plan ready—their plan—it'll be more likely to be adopted. And they're the ones with the best ideas of what the Academy and the Navy need."

Moro had turned around in his seat to watch the Dean. "Makes sense to me," he said quietly.

Simon was encouraged; he wondered if he should spring his Two Star plan on Moro now. It was early in the game, and he had already seen how Moro did not like to be pressured. But this wasn't the time to be timid.

"This downsizing wouldn't happen to include getting rid of General Flynn, would it?" Moro asked.

Simon shrugged.

"I haven't thought about it in that detail," he lied. There was a noticeable pause, a silence marked only by the ticking of the mantle clock. "But a downsizing would have to include restructuring the command."

Moro felt his patience slough off like a dirty coat. "With you as Supe," he said.

Simon remained silent. There was no point in denying it; Moro would find out sooner or later.

"You did everything but bend over backward to show Braintree that you're on his side, that you understand that some changes have to be made. Now you're saying Flynn is the real threat."

Moro was talking rapidly now; he was on a roll and didn't want to be interrupted.

"I wouldn't be surprised to find that you've been planning this for a while."

"That's the most incredible accusation . . ." Simon began. "I'm simply trying to develop a vision for this place, Anthony," Simon said. "In the absence of real leadership."

He paused. He hadn't wanted to skewer Flynn, and he wasn't doing a very smooth job setting his plan in motion.

Simon looked at the younger man. Moro was accusing him of recklessness, but he was not being reckless; he had thought it all out. There had to be change, and it had to ride in on the shoulders of men who saw its necessity.

Moro, Simon saw clearly now, was not one of those men.

"We can talk about this later," Simon said.

Moro didn't answer, and as he made his way to the door, Simon knew that the two men would not talk of this again in private.

Moro was out of the picture.

When he was outside in the hallway, waiting for the

elevator, Simon studied a large photo of an early twentieth-century Army football squad that decorated the wall. The young men in the photo, unnamed, a hundred years dead, looked back at him serenely.

David Simon was determined to make his mark.

Chris Dearborn took three laps around the small indoor track in the second floor gymnasium to warm up, then bounced down the wide stairs to the ground floor and the boxing rooms. Classes were over for the day, and the gymnasium was full of cadets: scores of volleyball players, packs of wrestlers, squadrons of swimmers—all heading in different directions. They were intent, laughing, jovial, and indifferent to what waited for Dearborn in the ring.

Maybe I'm making too much out of this, Dearborn thought as he pushed his way into the crowded boxing room. *It's only three rounds—or until the referee calls it off. A couple of minutes out of a four-year career of sucking wind here.*

He worked his way to the front of the crowd, down to the ring that pushed up against the wall at one end of the long, narrow room. As he moved, the noise grew louder; a murmur of voices at first, then distinct shouts, names and company designations called out as the two sides prepared to back their favorite gladiators. He could see only one of the men in the ring: on the lighter side, but tall, maybe one fifty seven class. The cadet was facing Dearborn and the rest of the room, banging the fronts of his fists against each other. Another cadet, this one wearing a coach's shirt, was standing behind the boxer, rubbing the fighter's shoulders.

Dearborn strained to look into the near corner, but his view was blocked by cadets surging toward the ring. All he could see was the back of a head, the red leather and elastic, the hammerhead effect of the protective gear. Now the cadet on the far side was shifting his weight from foot to foot, still banging his hands together. It was hard to read his face, but he looked calm enough, Dearborn thought.

I can look calm, too, he thought. *At least part of it has to be an act,* he told himself, trying to intellectualize. *If I can't psych the other guy out, I can at least convince him that I'm not particularly nervous, not scared. He's bound to be worked up, too.*

Three judges took their seats around the ring, more senior cadets in striped shirts.

That's what I could do next year, Dearborn thought. *Run the show, officiate. Probably not even break a sweat.*

The room was picking up the noise, making it louder still as it caromed off the steel rafters, the brick and stone and packed bodies. More cadets were pressing in the door behind them, the room was full, and Dearborn recognized the hot smell of perspiration and excitement and something else: anticipation, bloodlust.

"C'mon, c'mon, Jantorno," a cadet in front of Dearborn was yelling. "Knock his head off."

Dearborn couldn't tell if Jantorno was the cadet facing him or the one he couldn't see, the one still on his stool in the near corner. And why wasn't that guy standing up. What was going on there?

Another cadet, this one a yearling in class uniform with his arm suspended dramatically in cast and sling, held a cupped hand beside his mouth as he hollered into the square of open space.

"Ahh—*ooo*-gah, ahh—*ooo*-gah, ahh—*ooo*-gah. . . ."

Dearborn looked around at the faces surrounding the ring. All the men in the room had been inside, and most of them had probably lost at one point or another.

Maybe it won't be so bad, he tried. *Maybe I can feed off the excitement. It's not killing that guy.*

He remembered a fistfight in the sixth grade; a boy much smaller than Dearborn had been making fun of the taller boy's glasses. Egged on by his friends, the smaller boy had come up behind Dearborn and pushed him, hard. Dearborn was ready to run—his preferred defense—when he saw that the smaller boy was scared, that he had pushed only because his friends had put him up to it, that he didn't want to fight Dearborn any more than Dearborn wanted to fight him. But they had been hemmed in, their choices taken away from them by the crowd. And the little boy had come after him then, arms pinwheeling, head down. Dearborn, trying to back away, had thrust his hands out to ward the boy off and had gotten in a lucky punch, a solid connection to his opponent's downturned chin. The little boy's head snapped up, and then there'd been yelling and cheering and Dearborn had gotten as carried away as the rest of them until he found himself exhausted, blowing hard, and circling in the tiny space allowed them, the smaller boy crying and wanting to hide it.

It had been the crowd, Dearborn remembered. He looked around the boxing room. The crowd was older here, but really not much more sophisticated, still looking for excitement in someone else's pain.

We are primitives. Then, in the next instant, *But if I don't make it work for me, the other guy will.*

Now the referee had stepped into the ring. This was not the first fight of the afternoon, but the one before had apparently been exciting, and the crowd wanted more.

Two or three yearlings had picked up a chant that Dearborn remembered from bayonet drill in basic training, a relentless, heavy-bass beat.

"Blood, blood, blood makes the grass grow . . . blood, blood, blood makes the grass grow. . . ."

It wasn't even clear which boxer they were cheering for. They were cheering for the fight itself.

Dearborn was on the balls of his feet now; he could feel the blood moving through him, through his legs. He wanted to stay warmed up, not grow cold.

I should go back out into the big gym and do some more stretching, more warm-ups.

But, like so many people here, he was unable to tear himself away.

Across the ring, the cadet named Jantorno looked grimly determined, his eyebrows pressed down by the face guard, his hands still fluttering, faster now, in front of him. It looked to Dearborn like Jantorno couldn't wait to fight.

Dearborn thought he would watch, wargame the fight with Jantorno, a little dry run, prepare himself mentally.

This is what it will feel like, he said to himself: the noise, the crowd. *But I have to stay focused on my opponent, I have to be there with the other boxer.*

"Blood, blood, blood makes the grass grow . . . blood, blood, blood makes the grass grow."

It was no louder than the inside of the plane down at

jump school. Once he'd gotten out of the tower, the rest had been surprisingly easy. Dearborn had told himself that it wasn't the tower, it was just that he had hesitated, a stutter step at the wrong time.

As long as you don't hesitate, as long as you go when the man says go, you'll be all right. And it would be that way in the ring, too. The bell—a big showy thing right out of television fights—would clang and he'd step in and he'd punch the other guy and the other guy would punch him and no one was going to die and it was only a few minutes anyway and if it got bad the ref would stop it. All he had to do, he was sure as he watched the room, was tune into the noise, the yelling, let it come over him and carry him up, invade his body like the crashing of the slipstream in that first airplane, when they opened the door and he not only was not afraid, he was pulled to the door, compelled to it, by something that he didn't quite understand.

And I can do the same thing here, he thought. *It's just as freakin loud, for one thing, and it won't last much longer than floating down to the ground.*

And now the boxer named Jantorno, the one with his eyebrows crushed down on his eyes, swung his arms in big circles, and then the bell rang and there was the back of the other cadet, the hidden opponent who had not gotten off his stool for the warm-up. The other cadet was wearing a black shirt, and Dearborn couldn't see his face, just the beer-barrel shape of the headgear from the back, and he went to the center of the ring to touch gloves, the ref right there, no doubt saying something about fair play and no hitting below the belt and every cadet an athlete and all that shit. And then the bell and the cadet in black, the one Dearborn could see only from behind, steps up to Jantorno and his right rockets away from his shoulder like a goddamn missile and Jantorno—just like that—is in the air, his toes trying to stay in touch with the floor but it's doing him no good, it's as if he's been pushed by a giant, godlike hand. And he disappears beyond the ring of cadets in front of Dearborn, who cannot see the mat. But the other boxer, the kid in black, now turns to the neutral corner, and the crowd is screaming and Dearborn can hear the ref, just barely, counting, "One, two, three . . ."

Dearborn turned and walked out of the boxing room, two quick turns and up into the men's latrine. He closed himself in one of the tiny stalls, bent over at the waist, and vomited up lunch and his black fear and almost everything he hated about this, about West Point.

Wayne Holder pushed his way to the front of the crowd watching the boxing and tapped Mike Viegas on the shoulder.

"Where's Chris?"

"Good fucking question, man," Viegas said as he tightened the strap on the headgear of one of his other boxers.

Dearborn said that Viegas's accent became more pronounced when he was near the ring. "Something to do with the smell of leather and blood, I believe," Dearborn had quipped. Holder thought it was true.

Goo' fuckin' queshun, mahn.

"When is he supposed to box?" Holder asked. He was wearing his striped referee shirt; he had run to the gym from the soccer field in time to catch his company's team, and Dearborn in particular, at their first match.

"We got Glenn here, then Yearwood, then it's Dearborn's turn," Viegas said. He turned and looked at Holder, made no attempt to lower his voice when he said, "Unless he ran away."

"He didn't run away," Holder said, smiling, pretending that he and the coach were joking, pretending for the benefit of the other cadets on the team, the others from the company who'd gathered to watch the boxing.

Holder turned back and moved upstream toward the door, determined to find Dearborn. The room was packed with noisy cadets, some of whom had run down from other floors, from the various gyms and pools when they heard about the ten-second fight and the first knockout of the intramural season.

Blood, blood, blood makes the grass grow.

He entered the crowd, arms out in front of him like a diver, pushing through cadets standing shoulder to shoulder as if they'd been glued together. When he looked up, Holder saw Major Gates just beyond the doorway of the boxing room. Standing on his toes, Gates could see all the way into the room. Gates in his green shirt, his big face bobbing above the crowd like a Roman standard. Holder ducked to the side, hoping Gates had not seen him, because the officer would ask where he was going, and Holder, bound as always by the Honor Code, would have to answer that he was looking for Dearborn, who appeared to be missing in action—or missing before the action. Even more frightening, Holder was afraid that Gates could somehow look at him and tell what had happened last night.

Gates came into the room, a little bubble of space opening around him as the cadets made way. There was another tactical officer with him, a Captain Carothers, also come to watch his charges in single combat. Like parents with children on several sports teams, the Tacs spent afternoons going from one field to another, cheering on their company in soccer or football or volleyball. Boxing, even more bellicose than football—that other all-American substitute for war—attracted all of them at some point.

Holder waited off to one side as Gates entered the room. When the officer passed, Holder went out into the hallway and looked around. No Dearborn.

The cadet who'd been knocked out in the previous fight was sitting on one of the padded benches, his coach on one side, a DPE trainer on the other looking into his eyes with a flashlight. Holder had heard stories of a cadet—and this was going back some—dying after boxing, slipping into a coma down in the locker room and never coming out again.

He turned down the long, narrow hallway that passed in between the two boxing rooms like an alley. He saw a group of plebes from his company, asked if they'd seen Cadet Dearborn. No, sir, they hadn't.

He paused at the bottom of a big stone staircase decorated with more heraldic art: bas-reliefs of wrestlers, nude runners, all muscle-bound on stone shields way up in the corners.

"You seen Cadet Dearborn?" he asked another D Company plebe who ran to catch up with his classmates.

"Yes, sir," the plebe said, coming to a dead stop, to attention, arms slapping his sides. "He's in the latrine, sir."

"Carry on," Holder said, releasing the plebe.

Of course he's in the latrine, Holder told himself. *He's just taking a leak, and Mike was ready to write him off as a no show, as a runaway, a combat refusal.*

I was, too.

Before he had time to chastise himself, he was in the door. Dearborn was there, bent over one of the old ceramic sinks that stood like miniature bathtubs along one long wall.

"You OK?" Holder asked.

"Sure," Dearborn said, not looking up, recognizing his friend by the sound of his voice. "I just like to come in and throw my guts up in solitude so that I don't do it in the ring, in front of everybody."

"Good plan," Holder said, trying to keep it light. Dearborn was sick, but he didn't mention anything about not going into the ring. That's what Holder wanted to avoid.

"Soon as you're ready, we can go back into the other room," Holder encouraged him.

Dearborn surprised him by laughing, but it was a hard-edged cackle.

"You make it sound like we're going back inside to a dinner party," Dearborn said. He had loosened his head-gear and pushed it back. His gloves lay on the floor, one at his feet, one clear across the room, as if he'd thrown them.

"Something like that," Holder said, still smiling. "Gates just showed up."

"Sure. Come to watch the hanging," Dearborn said.

He wiped his chin with the back of his hand and looked into the mirror.

"Maybe I can just breathe vomit breath on my opponent and he'll concede defeat."

"You could try it," Holder said. Then, over the sound of running water as Dearborn washed his face, "I know you don't agree with this boxing thing."

"That's an understatement."

"But maybe Gates is on to something. I mean, it's not like he's out to punish you."

"What about that little incident at jump school? You don't think this is punishment?"

"Maybe this will be good for you, buddy," Holder said. "I don't think Gates is out to get you."

He might try to settle a score with me, though, Holder thought. *One quick bullet to the head, most likely.*

"Kilo Mike got to you, too?" Dearborn asked. He had finished at the sink and was putting his headgear back on.

"Whaddya mean?"

"Viegas has bought into the Tac's whole thing about building character and all that," Dearborn said.

"Don't you think that's a much more plausible explanation than Gates is out to get you?"

"From *your* position, I'm sure it is," Dearborn said sharply. He watched Holder's reflection, his eyes narrowed into sharp slits. There was no missing the animosity in his voice.

"From your position, too," Holder countered.

And suddenly the little mantle of control Dearborn had managed fell away. Holder could smell the sharp tang on his breath as Dearborn shouted at him.

"You have no idea what it looks like from my position," Dearborn raged, the sound amplified in the big room. "You fucking waltz through this place with everything handed to you."

"Right, Chris," Holder said. "You're the one sits up on the bunk all night reading paperback novels instead of studying."

"Big deal, classes come easily to me," Dearborn said, struggling to find control again. "But all this other shit . . ." he waved his arms in a small arc, taking in the whole gym, Holder supposed. "These assholes over here and those other assholes in the Tactical Department are always trying some new way of getting rid of me and people like me. We're not fucking *macho* enough."

"You love it here, Chris, in spite of all that," Holder said. "Boxing is part of the whole experience."

"No, plebe year boxing was part of that. This is harassment, pure and simple."

"Extra training," Holder said. "This is what it's gonna take to get you to graduation. Gates's job is to see that you're as well prepared as you can be."

"You believe they're right, don't you?" Dearborn said. "Putting me in here."

"I don't think it's going to kill you," Holder said.

"What the hell would you know?" Dearborn said. "Hell,

you get into it with the Tac—you defy him—and nothing happens. *You* should be on the boxing team."

Dearborn was on a tear.

"You've never had to work this hard to get anything; that's your whole fucking problem, Wayne. You don't get excited about anything because nothing is that important to you. Every fucking thing is given to you, so it's no big deal one way or the other. Hell, Mike Viegas is more like me than you are. He hates the Dean, I hate DPE, but at least we both know what it feels like to generate a little passion about something. There's no passion in it for you, one way or the other."

Holder wanted to reach out and smack Dearborn, give him one good pop that would somehow push away what Dearborn was saying.

The best he could manage was, "Oh, so I should try to be like you?" Holder said. "Always fucking whining about something or other."

"At least I notice what's going on around me," Dearborn said.

He had his headgear on now, had picked up his gloves, found his mouthpiece.

"I can't believe I'm about to go in there and get my lunch handed to me and I'm spending the time counseling you.

"You know something, Wayne? You're right. I love it here, and I must be one sick motherfucker. I hate it, too, all at the same time."

He looked at himself in the mirror again, tapped his gloves on the front of his headpiece as if trying to clear his head.

"You don't love it or hate it because you always keep your distance from everything. So now I'm going to go in here and get my ass kicked—even though I don't think it's going to do me a bit of good. And I'll hate every freakin' second of it, and if Gates is in there, I'll hate him too."

He walked up to Holder and touched the senior on the chest with one overstuffed glove.

"But at least I have enough in me to muster up a good, healthy loathing."

Chris Dearborn left the latrine, his athletic shoes making

a lonely scuffling sound as he turned on the polished floor at the bottom of the stairs. Wayne Holder leaned over the sink and looked at himself in the mirror; he didn't like what he saw there.

He had been about to say something cutting to Dearborn, something about how Dearborn was jealous because Holder was content, content to be in the middle of the class, even the lower half of the class. And he told himself—had been telling himself for years, that that was perfectly fine, that was who he was. Laid back. Too cool to care. Ain't nothing but a thing.

But maybe Dearborn was right. Maybe all that hadn't been a decision at all, maybe it had been backing away from a decision, from a heart-and-soul commitment to what he was doing. Wayne Holder always thought of such people— the ones with focus, with a mission—as so adult. Alex Trainor was like that. And Liz Wrenson. Chris Dearborn would have been like that if he didn't have to spend all his time running in fear from the DPE.

Wayne Holder wondered if he'd ever be like that.

He thought about Kathleen Gates out in the parking lot, wondering why he wasn't able to stop. Maybe he was an anomaly, an undisciplined soul in an institution that lived and breathed discipline.

Wayne Holder stood in the long latrine off the pool and the main hallway of the gym and thought about his father, out in California, making hospital rounds in his golf shirt, his big California Smile in place. His father had made a world for them that didn't want to admit stress. Be cool. Take it easy. Wayne Holder, for all the hard work he'd done as a cadet, wasn't sure he'd learned how to act in a crisis. Oh, he'd gotten into it with Major Gates, but he didn't think he should make a habit of defying his superiors.

And he thought about his grandfather, the veteran of two wars, sitting in his blazer and his starched white shirt amid the uncomfortable stillnesses of the family dinner table, smoking one cigarette after another, content to keep his stories to himself because his son did not want to hear them and his grandson did not know how to ask.

The comfortable little world Wayne Holder had erected about himself was coming apart; there were great breaches in the walls: Major Tom Gates, Kathleen Gates, all of that had rattled him. He wondered if he wanted West Point enough to fight his way into the Long Gray Line, as Chris Dearborn was doing in the next room.

It wasn't a match so much as an exposition, a chance for Dearborn's opponent, a plebe in a yellow C Company shirt, to show off the textbook punches he'd learned in boxing class.

The plebe threw two quick jabs before the sound of the opening bell had even cleared the ring. Dearborn reached for the jabs with both of his own hands, which prompted a fit of heavily accented advice from Kilo Mike.

"Keep your hands in, keep your hands in," Viegas yelled. "Circle, circle!"

Another jab; magically, Dearborn's hands both went out again to meet the threat, even as part of his brain told him that such a move left him uncovered. He had figured it out before the yellow shirt did, but it didn't help any. The plebe threw another jab and Dearborn's hands went out instantly, as if of their own volition, as if they were all part of the same mechanical contraption.

Bam!

The plebe found his jaw with a straight right, hard from the shoulder, a beautiful punch.

"Now keep your hands in," Viegas yelled.

Dearborn felt his breath like shallow fire in his lungs. He was vaguely aware of the faces around the ring, some people hanging on the corner posts, the judges in their chairs.

Bam!

The kid landed another right, didn't even bother to lead off with a jab this time. Dearborn pulled his elbows in tight, determined to protect himself.

"You gotta throw a punch sometime, Chris," Viegas said. Not quite as loudly this time, but some people around the ring smiled. Viegas saw a few backs as spectators turned away, bored, leaving.

Dearborn reached out tentatively with his left, an ineffectual jab, almost in slow motion. The plebe stepped inside Dearborn's outstretched hand and answered with a hard jab to the chin, then a second one before backing away. The punches hurt, sharp stabs that left behind a residue of pain, like the tiny ringing after a bell has stilled.

Dearborn pulled his elbows tight, kept his left in front of his face. Another jab. Dearborn straightened, heard Viegas yell something unintelligible, then saw, before he felt, the yellow shirt hunch down, the kid's right dropping low, coming up, right into Dearborn's belly.

The effect this time was dramatic. Dearborn's hands popped away from his face as if his opponent had found a linchpin. And even as he did it, even as he knew he must gasp for air and protect himself and throw punches all at once instead of in some slow motion sequence, Dearborn knew it wasn't going to happen.

The plebe, who had lost any look of uncertainty, stepped in close. Jab to the chin, straight right that caught him on the jaw, snapping his head to the right, then a roundhouse that connected somewhere just in front of his ear.

Then the mat came up and jammed into his knees and Dearborn was looking at the yellow shirt's waist and the referee was sending the kid to a neutral corner, and then he was on all fours, and there were groans from his company corner and an exasperated Viegas yelling at him to get up, get up, just get to your feet. But even as his coach went through the motions of cheering him on—no longer giving unheeded advice, just doing his duty—Dearborn was both hurt and vindicated.

I told them this would happen. I knew it would be this way.

Because he had seen it all before, tasted public ridicule in a dozen schoolyards, on athletic fields, in the cadet gym, everywhere but in the classroom. He was the butt of the joke. It was what he did, what he knew best.

"Get up, man," Viegas said now, but with nothing to the voice. He was just saying it, not believing for a moment that Dearborn would get up.

The referee pulled him up by the shoulders and looked into his eyes.

Dearborn let his eyes go unfocused for just a second. It was deliberate, an act. Later he might even wonder if it was a lie, a violation of his Honor Code. But for right now all he wanted to do was to get out of the ring.

The referee, charged with the safety of the boxers, said,

"This fight's over." He helped Dearborn back into his corner.

Kilo Mike pulled the ropes apart so that Dearborn could climb through to the outside of the ring. Viegas was already talking to the next D Company fighter, giving him instructions.

Dearborn made his way to the nearest wall and leaned there, facing away from the crowd as he pulled off his gloves.

"You OK?"

Dearborn turned to the familiar voice. It was Major Gates.

"I'll be all right, sir," Dearborn said, his breath still coming in jagged sweeps.

"I'm not so sure about that," Gates said.

Dearborn straightened, took his weight off the wall, studied the officer's face. Gates was smiling, but there was no mirth there, and Dearborn began to worry.

Gates looked around the room once, then pushed off the ropes and headed for the door.

"Follow me," he said to Dearborn over his shoulder. As he walked, he said over his shoulder, "You should have gotten on your feet in there."

Dearborn did not respond, just followed dumbly back out into the hallway, out of the gym and onto the street. When they were out in the hazy sunshine, Gates turned on him.

"That was pathetic in there," Gates said. He was leaning forward at the waist, his face only inches from Dearborn's, his teeth clenched tightly, the muscles in his jaw clearly straining.

Dearborn didn't answer; he was along to listen.

"Do you fucking hear me?" Gates seethed.

"Yes, sir," Dearborn said calmly.

"I don't even think you were hurt in there," Gates said. "You just didn't want to box anymore."

That's right, Major, Dearborn thought.

"I think you're just a pussy."

Right again, sir.

"I put you on the boxing team so that you'd develop a little backbone," Gates said. "But I can see you didn't take the hint. And now you think you're just going to lie down in the middle of every match. Is that how you're planning to defy me, you gutless little shit?"

Gates had squared off with him, hands on his hips, off the side of the street fronting the gymnasium. Just a few feet away dozens of cadets came and went through the big gym doors; Dearborn could almost feel their eyes burning the back of his neck. He concentrated on a tiny clump of white spittle that had collected at the corner of Gates's mouth; that kept him from having to think about his humiliation.

"What the hell am I gonna do with you, Dearborn?" Gates said. The question clearly did not call for an answer; Gates was not looking for a dialogue.

"You could let me off the boxing team, sir."

Dearborn regretted speaking the second it was out of his mouth.

Gates eyes grew wider still. He brought his hand up quickly and Dearborn flinched. Gates poked his index finger into Dearborn's chest hard enough to make the skinny cadet step backward.

"That's just what you're *not* going to get, little girl."

Gates straightened; he was breathing fast.

"I want you to meet me tomorrow morning at five fifteen, right over there," Gates said, pointing with his thumb at the sally port beneath D Company's barracks.

"Wear running gear."

Dearborn groaned inwardly. "Yes, sir," he said.

Gates straightened, looked about as if noticing for the first time that there were other people within earshot. He looked at Dearborn through lidded eyes. There was some sort of grim amusement there.

"And don't fuckin' be late."

Dearborn straightened to attention as Gates pushed past him and headed back to the gym. He held the pose for a ridiculously long time, standing in the middle of the street, staring off into space and pretending that he was somewhere else. Finally, he turned back to the gym.

"Tomorrow should be a lot of fun," he said to himself.

He went back into the boxing room, where he could hear Mike Viegas shouting at the D Company plebe. Box, box, box.

Dearborn waited until the round was over before approaching Viegas.

"I'm going to go wash this out," Dearborn said, fingering the cut above his eye.

Viegas did not look up. "Sure," he said.

Dearborn had just cleared the doorway to the boxing room and was turning left when he heard his name.

"Cadet Dearborn."

It was the civilian from the Bruckner Commission, Van Grouw, looking all out of place again in a blazer and gray pants amid all the athletic gear.

"I didn't get here in time for your match," Van Grouw said.

"It didn't last long," Dearborn said. "And you didn't miss much."

"Did it . . . uh . . . did it turn out the way you expected?"

"You mean did I get my ass kicked?" Dearborn snapped. He turned on the civilian, who was a good six inches shorter, and unleashed the anger he'd held in check with Gates.

He wanted to say that it had turned out exactly as he'd predicted, that Gates and Viegas and all the others had their laughs, that the other fighter got a little practice in at no cost and the only possible disappointment was that the match didn't last longer. But his head hurt badly and nausea spun inside like an off-balance cam.

"Are you hurt badly?" Van Grouw asked solicitously, sounding just a little too concerned, a little too mothering. He actually reached up to touch the cut above Dearborn's eye.

"I'm fine," Dearborn said, his arm shooting up as if to defend himself from another blow, but it was only Van Grouw's soft touch he was afraid of.

"And was Major Gates there, too?" Van Grouw asked. But before Dearborn could answer, Van Grouw had already started talking again. "I've found out some interesting things about Major Gates."

He leaned forward, a coconspirator, one investigator to another.

"Major Gates is something of a loose cannon, isn't he?"

"Yeah, you could say that," Dearborn said.

"I gather this isn't the first time that Gates has made up his own rules, his own way of doing things as he went along."

Dearborn stared at the civilian before him and knew instantly that Van Grouw offered him more than a way out. He could actually do some damage to Gates.

"That's what he's best at," Dearborn said.

"What do you mean?" Van Grouw asked. "Specifically."

"I . . . uh . . . I'm not sure I should be having this conversation with you," Dearborn said. Some part of him was afraid that this would get back to Gates. Another, smaller voice told him that it was wrong.

Fuck that, Dearborn thought. *Gates is the one with all the power here. He's the one who wants to make this a fight.*

Van Grouw smiled, a patronizing little smirk.

"Of course I understand that you can't take on the whole establishment by yourself, Mister Dearborn," he said. "May I call you Chris?"

He continued without pause. "And I assure you that you won't have to."

Van Grouw closed his little pocket notebook and inched closer to Dearborn.

"That's why we're here."

Van Grouw took Dearborn by the arm and led him down a narrow hallway; they stepped out of the traffic there into the partial shelter of a stone alcove. Dearborn felt as if someone had clapped him on the forehead with a wide board. His neck hurt; he recognized the injury from plebe boxing, the strain that came after you'd had your head snapped back a few times by quick, hard shots.

"I saw you two outside," Van Grouw said. "Major Gates looked pretty upset. What did he do to you?"

Dearborn put his hand on one of the cool walls to steady himself. He concentrated on Van Grouw's words, watching the man's mouth move as if in slow motion.

"I assure you that none of what you tell me will get back to you, will cause you any problem," the civilian was saying now. "Major Gates isn't going to find out you raised these issues. . . ."

"Extra training," Dearborn said.

"What's that?"

"He's going to take me on a little run tomorrow morning at five fifteen. I suspect it has something to do with my poor performance today."

"Can he do that? Order you to get up at that ungodly hour?"

Dearborn laughed, then used his sleeve to blot the blood above his eye. He could barely feel the cut anymore, the hammering at the back of his skull and through his neck was too insistent.

"That's hardly the big problem here," Dearborn said. "But yes, he can."

"What's the big problem?"

"I think Major Mercury would like to beat the hell out of me himself."

Van Grouw was clearly surprised.

"You really think he'd try something like that?"

Dearborn thought of Trainor's hand and the stories about the Holder-Gates showdown.

"I guess I'll find out," Dearborn said. "But, yeah, I think he would."

He watched Van Grouw's reaction. He'd made a pretty bold statement, but the toughest decision was still ahead of him. Could he provoke Gates to the point where the officer would hit him? And if he did, would he have the guts to tell Van Grouw about it? He hadn't done anything irrevocable, and right now his head hurt too much for him to plan that far ahead. He'd let Van Grouw take it from here.

"Where are you going to meet him for this run?"

"At the sally port by MacArthur's statue," Dearborn said, standing a little too quickly. The motion made him think he might throw up again.

"Are you all right?"

"I'll be fine," Dearborn said. *Especially if you can get Gates off my back.*

"I'll be in touch, Chris," Van Grouw said, tucking his little notebook under his arm. "Don't worry about a thing."

Dearborn didn't answer, but instead turned and hurried into the latrine, his hand over his mouth.

This is too good to be true, Van Grouw thought.

Braintree had been genuinely interested in what he had

turned up. In fact, the boss had asked him about it again at the lunch meeting they'd had. More importantly, Braintree hadn't asked anyone else specifically about their ongoing talks with the community. Just Van Grouw.

"You're just the little scandal I need," Van Grouw said to the empty doorway into which Dearborn had disappeared.

When the cadet had gone, Van Grouw walked out to the gym's main entrance. A big man in a green officer's uniform came to the wide doors at the same moment, then stood aside politely to let Van Grouw go through first. Van Grouw came up to the man's shoulder and so had a good look at the nametag.

Gates.

"Thank you," he said, and hurried through into the humid afternoon.

It was hard to be alone in the barracks at West Point, with their very military lack of privacy, with their crowded rooms and boisterous camaraderie. The cadet experience made roommates like twins, made brothers and sisters of classmates. But a secret could change all that, and Wayne Holder had a secret.

He went back to the barracks early. The floor was mostly empty; the other cadets were still scattered around the athletic fields and the gym. Holder pulled his chair out from the desk and turned it toward the window, sat and put his feet up on the wide sill.

What the hell am I gonna do now?

When he returned to the barracks the night before from his tryst in the parking lot, Holder's room had been filled with a half dozen cadets, some of them helping Alex Trainor with the classes he'd missed, others waiting for Holder with company business. That kept him busy until Taps, the end of the day, and lights out. After that he had gone into the latrine—where the lights were allowed to stay on—to finish some reading for class. He gave up after fifteen fruitless minutes of reading the same page, and he slept fitfully, afraid that he was going to dream about Major Gates. All day in class he wondered what Kathleen was going to do next.

Holder told himself that Kathleen Gates had acted for the

same reason he had, out of impulse, sexual desire. By mid-afternoon he had managed to convince himself that no one had discovered them, no one had seen them in the dimly lit parking lot. He had no evidence that this was the case, but hope fielded a powerful—if flawed—argument. Kathleen Gates had as much to lose as he did—more, perhaps—and so he wasn't in danger from her.

At lunch formation he'd looked around at all the familiar faces, all the sounds and sights that had been there the day before, and the day before that. Everything was the same.

Then Chris Dearborn told him he'd been fooling himself for a long time about many things.

Holder picked up a framed picture from his desk, the one decoration allotted him by the achingly precise Barracks Arrangement Guide. It was a five-by-seven of the Rutgers cheerleader, a glamor shot staged on the sidelines. He'd put it there, he realized now, not so much because he was emotionally attached to the woman in the picture—her name was Marianne—but because it was a trophy. And it was a standing joke among his classmates that Marianne's photo was only the top one in the frame. Pull her out and there was Jessica, and beneath her Anna, then Cheryl and one whose name he forgot at the moment and on the back of the frame was taped a small piece of red lace, a souvenir from another woman who wasn't even represented by a photo. Holder held the frame on his lap, on his outstretched legs, chuckled to himself and said out loud, "I wonder where Chris gets the idea that I don't take things too seriously."

Dearborn was right, he knew. During his first three years at West Point, he'd thought of that approach as a kind of philosophy, the Zen of getting through it all. He had always thought of his attitude as a choice. Like his father. California Cool. Now he wondered if that attitude was just the lack of a choice, simple disinterest.

Mike Viegas was fighting every time he set foot in a classroom; Chris Dearborn battled every time he faced one of the gray-clad instructors from DPE. On paper, Wayne Holder had outperformed both of those men, but they'd done things he hadn't.

What do I have that I would fight for?

Kathleen Gates had something to fight for, too; her fortunes were riding with her husband's. Holder didn't know if Major Gates had received a letter of reprimand, and he wouldn't be privy to that. But it was certainly a possibility.

"It's not just his popularity with the cadets that's involved," she'd told him in the library. "We're talking his career and my family's livelihood as well."

That's something worth fighting for.

"Shit," Wayne Holder said out loud, pulling his feet off the sill and letting the chair drop sharply to the floor.

"You weirdin' out on me, Wayne?"

Alex Trainor was in the room before Holder heard him.

"Sitting in here all alone and cursing at . . . what . . . the window?"

"Shit. *Fuck,*" Holder said.

"Sounds pretty serious," Trainor said, folding his arms across his narrow chest as if to protect himself from the vulgarity.

"I can't believe how fucking stupid I was," Holder said. He stood abruptly, pushing the chair back with his legs and sending it careening into the desk.

"Hey, hey, hey," Trainor said, raising his bandaged hand to protect it and sidestepping the flying furniture. "You wanna watch that, huh?"

"Oh, man, Alex, I think I really screwed the pooch this time," Holder said. He dropped to the edge of his bunk and put his head in his hands.

"You mean literally," Trainor joked. "You got caught with someone's dog? How many times have I said you think with the wrong head?"

When Holder didn't look up, Trainor changed his tone and pulled the desk chair around to face his roommate.

"Hey, really, is everything all right?"

"I don't know," Holder said. "I just had a scary thought and I'm not sure if I'm just being paranoid or if I really did mess things up . . . beyond fixing this time."

"Vell," Trainor said in a mock Austrian accent. "It's just your luck that Herr Doctor is in and, this being Vest Point, you have a whole"—he looked at his watch—"nine minutes to tell me all about your life."

Holder ran his fingers through his hair, the blond locks a little too long. He pressed the heels of his hands into his eye sockets. When he looked up, Trainor saw something there he often saw around West Point, but couldn't remember seeing in Wayne Holder. Fear.

"Why do you think Ryder picked me to be CO?" Holder asked. "And no bullshit."

"Because he thought you'd do a good job," Trainor tried.

Wayne Holder's expression didn't change.

"Because he knew that you had some natural leadership qualities. . . ."

Still no response. Wayne Holder was waiting for something else, but Trainor wasn't sure what that was.

"Do you think I'm a fuck-up, Alex?"

Trainor paused, wondering what had launched Holder into this reverie. One thing was clear: his roommate wanted straight answers.

"Not in the conventional sense," Trainor said.

"What the hell does that mean?"

"It means you don't get written up for sloppy uniform or being late returning from leave or any of that stuff."

"But what?"

"But you don't take things very seriously, Wayne. I mean . . . anything."

"Well, for chrissakes, Alex, it's not like we're fighting a war here," Holder protested.

"Yeah, but you don't take anything seriously enough even to get the best experience from it. I mean, it's not that it's important that you're the best student or the best athlete or any of that. But *something* should be important to you."

"I'm not sure that's the case," Holder said. "Where does it say that you have to go after something, after anything?"

"Nowhere, Wayne," Trainor said, already exasperated with Holder's overused argument. "You're right. But if you don't have a single passion, if there's nothing worth working hard for . . . then what's the point?"

Holder stood and walked to the window just to be doing something. He faced the center of the room, arms folded across his chest.

"Look," Trainor said. "My old man drives a delivery truck. Spends all day dropping off potato chips and pretzels and cheese doodles to these little mom and pop stores and gas stations in the middle of nowhere. He's got about a ninth-grade education. And when he's working, he's always smiling, always chatting up the customers, always asking them about their arthritis or their sister's son who's in the Navy. And it's not because he loves the work, let me tell you.

"But every Sunday he sings in the choir. Lead tenor. He stands up there with other men—most of whom are better educated, make more money, have been to more places, and he sings his heart out. That's his passion. That's what he lives for. And it lights up everything else in his life.

"You gotta figure out what you love, Wayne." Trainor stood and walked to where the framed picture of Marianne the cheerleader lay on Holder's chair. Trainor picked it up off the seat as he sat down. "I mean, it's great to date pretty women and all that—and I'll certainly admit to being jealous—but it wouldn't kill you to have a grown-up thought now and then."

Holder turned away from his roommate and rested his palms flat on the window sill.

"I messed up big time last night, Alex."

Trainor sat perfectly still.

"Kathleen Gates asked me to meet her in the library, and I did. She told me how concerned she was about what might happen to her husband and to his career—I suppose she was talking about if he got a letter of reprimand or something like that."

"I hope he gets at least that," Trainor said, his voice hinting at the anger he held in spite of his Christian zeal to turn the other cheek.

Holder paused, waited until Alex was with him again.

"Then she asked me to walk her out to her car, out by the baseball stadium."

Holder had been looking at the floor as he talked; he lifted his eyes, shifted them left and right, dropped them again, hoping that Trainor would guess what had happened and that he wouldn't have to admit, out loud, just how stupid he'd been. But his roommate responded only by gingerly lifting his cast with the opposite hand, tilting it so the blood would flow back down from his still-sensitive wounds.

"We . . . uh . . . we had sex in the parking lot," Holder said.

Trainor drew a long breath, then let it out.

"You're kidding," he said delicately.

"I wish," Holder said.

Trainor stood up, cradling his bad arm across his chest.

"Did anyone see you?"

"Not that I know of."

"Has she called you or tried to contact you?"

"No."

"Do you think she will? I mean, I can guess what you were thinking, or what you were thinking with, but what was she up to?"

"That's what just occurred to me," Wayne Holder said. "She was up to something."

"Protecting her old man," Trainor said. He seemed somehow pleased, vindicated in his harsh judgments of Major and Mrs. Gates.

Holder chuckled, the sound like disgust. "Wish I'd figured it out that fast," he said. "I might not be sweating things so much."

"But it's not like she can blackmail you or anything, even if she accuses you of forcing yourself on her . . . by the way, you didn't, did you?"

"Didn't what?"

"Force yourself on her."

"No, Alex," he said sharply. "I'm just your run of the mill fool. I'm not a rapist."

"OK," Trainor said, embarrassed at having asked. "So it's not like she can tell you to keep quiet about the fight with her old man. I mean, you've already talked to the Comm about it."

"So there must be another angle," Holder said.

The two men sat quietly for a moment. Outside the room, someone walked down the hall singing.

"Why don't you confront her?" Trainor asked.

Holder looked at him without speaking, so he continued.

"Just go talk to her, tell that you're on to what she's doing, that you know she's setting you up. Maybe if you call her out early she won't go forward with whatever she has in mind."

"Because all she'd have to say is that she let herself go, that it really was about sexual attraction. Then I'd really look like an ass."

Holder began pacing between the windows and the door.

"Shit, Gates will kill me for sure this time."

"Gates isn't going to find out," Trainor said, although he didn't believe that was true. "His wife isn't going to tell him, you can bet on that.

"Now, suppose I go talk to her," Trainor said.

"What would you say to her?" Holder asked. He was looking at Trainor as if his roommate had proposed murdering Kathleen Gates. But there was a bit of hope in his voice.

The trouble was, Trainor wasn't sure what he would say to Kathleen Gates. But Holder was in trouble and needed help; that was good enough for now.

"OK, I'm just thinking out loud here . . . suppose I go and tell her that you confessed to me and that you're completely upset about all this. But then I let on that I'm the suspicious one. I could even just imply that I know what she's really about—protecting her husband. Maybe that will get her to keep her mouth shut."

"It could work," Holder said. In truth, he thought it a desperate plan. "I guess it depends on what she's up to."

"I suspect we won't have to wait long to find out," Trainor said.

CHAPTER 9

TOM GATES SHOWED UP OUTSIDE THE D COMPANY BARRACKS AT
five ten the next morning. Chris Dearborn was already
standing by, waiting in the still-dark sally port.

"Good sign, so far," Gates said to himself.

Dearborn straightened up when he saw Gates approach;
the officer motioned to him—*follow me*—and Dearborn
jogged over. Gates turned and began running even before
the cadet caught up.

"Don't fall behind," was the only thing Gates said.

They wound back on the small road that ran between the
gym and the Superintendent's quarters, turning the corner
past the big block that housed the Olympic-sized pool. A
long stairway led away from the parking lot and up to the
hill behind the Catholic Chapel; Gates heaved his large
frame up the steps three at a time. He could hear Dearborn
behind him, already winded.

Gates had left his quarters with no clear plan as to what
he was going to do with Dearborn. He wanted to punish the
cadet, push him to the point of exhaustion, to the point
where he didn't have the wind for one of his clever come-
backs. But even as he listened to Dearborn's ragged footfalls
and uneven breathing, Tom Gates knew that a run—even

on the killer hill that led to the football stadium—was not going to be enough. He wouldn't get through to Dearborn that way alone.

He hadn't been able to come up with a plan; he'd been too concerned about everything else that was going on.

Kathleen had been moody and distracted all week, barely talking to him one moment, lecturing him at length the next. Then there was the Commandant's letter, which would fall on his head any day. Finally, the cadets were treating him differently. They still met all the basic obligations of military courtesy, but there was some cool distance between them, as if they knew he was a marked man and so didn't want to get too close to him.

Gates kept up a fast pace all the way out into the housing areas, a mile and a half out to the big white gates on Lee road, then a mile and a half back to the gym.

And all those things were out of his control, just like Dearborn in the boxing ring. All the kid had to do was get up after he'd been knocked down. Gates wasn't interested in seeing him win; Gates didn't even care that the fight lasted such a short time. Gates wanted the bout to last just long enough for Dearborn to show he had something in him besides a talent for quitting. But, of course, standing outside the ring, there was nothing the officer could do about that either. The circle of what he could control seemed to be getting smaller. And if it wasn't large enough to contain Chris Dearborn the boxer, it was large enough to contain Chris Dearborn, winded and perhaps a little frightened, running beside him.

"Get right up here even with me," Gates directed, pointing to a spot beside him.

Dearborn responded by picking up his pace a bit. Gates looked over: there was nothing smooth about the way the cadet ran. His bony knees pointed out to the sides as they came forward. He held his arms high and his shoulders tight, as if holding them above waist-deep water. Dearborn's face—unlovely in repose—was contorted; his breath came in jagged spikes.

Gates knew that Dearborn was probably giving all he had because the gym was so close, and the cadet would think they were going to stop where they'd started. But at the last moment Gates turned up the sharp hill that led to the football stadium.

The road climbed steeply for a quarter mile, and Gates poured on the speed while Dearborn fell behind. When he reached the top, Gates turned around and looked downhill.

"C'mon, c'mon, c'mon," he said.

Just before Dearborn caught up with him, the cadet began to slow, anticipating the pause at the top as Gates did. Gates turned and ran again as soon as Dearborn reached him.

"Don't stop, hero," Gates said.

He was running backward now, backpedaling in front of Dearborn, who was leaning forward at the waist, all pretense of good running form dropped.

Gates taunted him. There was some weakness in the younger man that Gates hated, and he tried to drive it out of the cadet with cruelty.

"Don't be a fucking quitter, Dearborn. Only losers quit. Are you a loser? Do you want to be a pussy all your life?"

Gates kept up the patter all the way around Lusk Reservoir, alongside the empty mass of the football stadium. He turned to the front and ran faster; Dearborn fell farther behind.

"C'mon, Dearborn, you little girl. We haven't gone five miles yet and you're pussing out on me. What the fuck is wrong with you?"

Dearborn was some twenty yards behind Gates when they started downhill. The cadet's feet slapped the pavement in an awkward rhythm on the down-slope; he had no control.

"Pick your feet up, you goddamned loser. You think I'm gonna feel sorry for you?"

But Dearborn wasn't listening. His face was a mask of pain and his eyes seemed focused on something far away. He was trying to shut Gates out, to ignore the officer's advice, just as he had when he was in the ring. Beyond Gates's control.

Gates stopped beside the entrance to a wooded area on the left. When Dearborn caught up to him—still not looking at the officer—Gates grabbed him hard by the arms.

"Why do you think I brought you out here, Dearborn?" Gates said. His own chest heaved, but the edge in his voice was anger.

"Don't . . . know . . . sir," Dearborn breathed.

"Don't give me that shit," Gates said, angry that Dearborn still resisted him.

"Because you want to develop my leadership qualities, sir," Dearborn managed. The sarcasm was evident, even though Dearborn seemed ready to collapse.

"Because you don't listen, Dearborn," Gates said. He had raised his voice; he was practically yelling, but he didn't care.

"Because you think you know more than everyone else. Because you think you're so fucking smart. Because you're a fucking quitter and I'm not gonna let you slide through this place and into *my* Army."

Dearborn bent over, his hands on his knees, and dribbled spit to the ground. When he'd caught his breath somewhat, he said, "I think you're just taking out your problems on me. Sir."

Gates' eyes went wide with rage, his arms were suddenly tight as wires. He wanted to hit someone.

"Why you little shithead," he said. "Stand up."

Dearborn raised his head, looked at Gates from under his eyebrows, took his time straightening. He seemed just about to say something more when Gates said, "Put your hands up."

Dearborn took his fighter's stance, probably not because he thought sparring was a good idea, but because he was afraid, Gates saw.

Gates reached out and tagged Dearborn in the mouth with a stiff jab.

Both of them were clearly stunned. Dearborn, Gates noted with some glee, finally seemed at a loss for words. That passed quickly, and instead Gates imagined himself in the Commandant's office, trying to explain why he shouldn't be court-martialed for striking a subordinate.

He said the first thing that came to mind. "A little sparring might do you good."

Dearborn still had his hands up, unsure of what to do next.

"All I want you to do, Dearborn, is have the guts to get up after you take a shot," Gates said. He snapped his left out again, a quick jab. Dearborn managed to block it.

"Good," Gates said. "And every time you do that, every time you get up when you'd rather just stay on the mat and give up, it gets easier the next time."

Dearborn's eyes, just visible over the tops of his closed fists, were wide.

"You pissed off at me, Dearborn?"

By way of an answer the cadet stepped up to Gates and threw a jab, which the bigger man easily parried.

Gates hit him in the chest. Dearborn stumbled, but immediately gained his footing and lunged at Gates, faking a jab and throwing a straight right at the officer's face.

Gates reached up with one big hand and caught Dearborn's fist. He held on and squeezed, a trick he used to play on his kid brother. Dearborn stopped trying to pull away when he saw that it was hopeless. He dropped his other arm in a gesture of surrender.

Gates laughed, squeezing harder.

"Goddamn, boy," Gates said. "You might grow some balls yet."

Kathleen Gates, two-year-old daughter on her hip, picked up the phone on the first ring. She stood in the doorway between the kitchen and the living room and watched her four-year-old, who was sitting in front of the television, methodically grind small pieces of cereal into the carpet.

"Alexander," she said sharply. And then into the receiver, "Oops, I'm sorry. This is Kathleen Gates."

"Hello, Ms. Gates. This is Matthew Holly calling. I'm with. . . ."

The Bruckner Commission, Kathleen thought.

"Oh," she interrupted. "Just a moment, please."

She set the baby on the floor at her feet, put her hand over the mouthpiece, and leaned into the living room.

"Alexander."

The little boy turned around and smiled at her. There were bits of cereal between the knees of his jeans and the carpet.

"Mommy is going to be on the phone for a bit. You behave, now."

Alexander Gates turned back to the television, seemingly content to limit his destruction to the small circle of crushed cereal.

"Sorry, Mister . . . Holly," she said into the phone in her best sweet-Mom voice. "I'm juggling two babies here as I'm talking to you. I hope you'll forgive the interruptions. What can I do for you?"

"Yes, of course. I'm with the Bruckner Commission, Ms. Gates. I know it's early; I hope I'm not disturbing you."

"No, the little ones get started early around here," Kathleen said.

"You responded to our call for members of the community who would be willing to be interviewed."

"Oh," Kathleen said. She could see her reflection in the glass fronted cabinet behind the kitchen table; she watched her performance there.

"Yes, yes, I did do that."

She ran her fingers through her hair, then checked the glass to see if she looked nervous enough.

"We'd like to set up a time for you to come in," Holly said. "We're just down at the Hotel Thayer."

For all she knew Holly was just a telephone receptionist, although it seemed likely they'd find someone to man the phones who didn't have such a marked accent. But Kathleen had practiced and planned and decided that it would be best to play things to the hilt. Turn it on right from the start.

"Oh . . . I, uh . . ." Kathleen paused, looked in the glass again. Her two-year-old, Melissa, was rocking back and forth on all fours in front of the kitchen trash can, butting the plastic with her head.

"I suppose that's still a good idea," she said.

No reaction from Holly.

"The notice said that people who wanted to remain anonymous could do so, is that right?"

"Yes, that's right," Holly said. The only change in his tone signaled impatience; there was some rustling of papers on the other end.

"Would it be possible for me to talk to a woman?" Gates asked.

"Certainly," Holly said. "If that's significant to you, we could arrange that." Crisp, all business.

"That would make it easier," Kathleen said, lowering her voice. "There are just certain things around here . . . well, certain things that would be easier to talk with a woman about. No offense, Mister Holly."

"None taken," Holly chirped. "I'll have someone, one of the women on our staff, give you a call this morning."

"Thank you," Kathleen said.

When she was off the phone, Kathleen picked up Melissa and sat at one of the kitchen chairs, the baby on her lap.

"Well, I'm not sure if I got through to that guy or not," she said to the child, running her fingers through her daughter's strawberry blond curls.

"Men just aren't tuned in. If that had been a woman on the phone, she would have known immediately that something was up, just by the tone in my voice."

The baby smiled up at her, clapping chubby hands on each of Kathleen's cheeks in a tiny embrace.

"Yes, yes, yes," Kathleen said. She took the little hands in her own, leaned forward until her forehead was pressed to Melissa's, and continued in the cooing baby talk that made her daughter smile.

"And *that's* why we can *always* get them to do what *we* want, sweetums," she said. "Because they're just out to lunch all the time. Yes, they are. Yes, they are."

The baby giggled and Kathleen Gates laughed out loud.

Matthew Holly was walking down the hotel hallway toward Diane Clementon's room, fingering the message slip with Kathleen Gates's home number, when he saw Dorothy Sayer letting herself into her own room.

"Good morning, Dorothy," he said cheerfully.

He had helped savage her in the meeting the other day, so Holly thought it might not be a bad idea to tilt the scales in the other direction. A little peace offering.

"Oh, good morning, Matt," Sayer said, startled.

As he drew closer he noticed that Sayer's makeup, always

impeccable, looked a little worn. There was a single crease that cut diagonally across her skirt, a line that could not have come from sitting but might mean the skirt had been thrown across a chair. All night.

"Ready to do battle for the forces of right and justice this morning?" Holly said. He smiled as he spoke and maneuvered so that he could catch a glimpse of the room through the open door behind her. The bed was still made, and since it was too early for the maids to have come through, that meant she hadn't slept in it last night.

"Not just yet," she said, pushing her pretty hair away from her face in that theatrical sweep—fingers splayed, hand straight back along the center-line part, hair falling down playfully.

"Well, then," Holly said. He looked down and noticed that her legs were bare.

I'll bet I can find some balled up pantyhose in your purse, he thought. *Or maybe you tore them and they're in the wastebasket in Braintree's room.*

He made no move to leave, just stood before her enjoying that he'd caught her tomcatting around.

"I won't keep you any longer," he said finally.

She looked relieved as he turned to go.

"Oh," he said. She turned in the doorway.

"I remember you said you wanted to deal with women's issues," he said sweetly. "I have a name here, the wife of an officer, who wants to talk to a woman from the Commission. Something about 'women will understand better.'"

He held out the paper with Gates's number.

"She sounded a little nervous, but maybe it's just what you're looking for."

"Thank you," Sayer said, grabbing the note without looking at it, eager to get inside the room and away from Holly's stare.

"Have a good lay . . . *day,*" he corrected quickly.

Sayer slipped inside and closed the door. Holly heard the bolt slide over, then laughed to himself as he turned for his own room.

"If you don't want people to know you're sleeping with the boss," he said to the empty hall, "don't walk around with that JBF look. On the other hand, if you have the boss by the ear, and not just by the dick, it won't hurt me to cozy up a little bit."

A little paper sign on the Gates's door said, "Shhh, Baby Napping," so Dorothy Sayer knocked very lightly.

"Mrs. Gates?" Sayer said when the door opened. "I'm Dorothy Sayer."

"Come in, come in," Kathleen Gates said just above a whisper as she held the door open. Sayer was a bit uncomfortable; she felt as if she'd just entered the intensive care unit and had to be quiet around all the really sick people.

"If this isn't a good time . . ." Sayer began.

"No, this is the best time," Kathleen insisted. "We shouldn't be interrupted for a while, as long as you don't mind the spy stuff—whispering and all that."

"Not at all," Sayer said.

Truth was Sayer was uncomfortable. She didn't know the rules around children, what to do, what to say to them or their moms. In her experience in Washington in the few years since she'd been out of college, she didn't think she'd met one stay-at-home mother. She thought of them as a breed apart, and she expected that the woman answering the door would look like a cross between Betty Crocker and June Cleaver.

"Why don't we go into the kitchen. Can I get you a glass of iced tea?" Kathleen asked.

"That would be nice." Sayer stepped over some bright plastic toys as she followed Kathleen Gates through the tiny dining room—just big enough for a table—and into a brightly lit kitchen. There were more toys underfoot, and there were so many cows decorating the room that there seemed to have been an explosion in black and brown and white.

"How have your interviews been going so far?" Kathleen Gates asked.

"Well, we're just getting started, really," Sayer answered. She put her leather portfolio down on the table; it stuck when she tried to slide it.

"You know what, I'd better wipe up a bit before we sit here," Kathleen said, getting up for a sponge, then swiping at the table.

Sayer thought about her skirt—the only clean one she had thanks to last night's fireworks—and wondered if she should have wiped off the chair in which she sat.

"I understand you wanted to speak to a woman for the interview," Sayer ventured. "May I ask why?"

Kathleen Gates wiped the table again, then threw the sponge into the sink, and dried her hands on a dishtowel. She gave Sayer a weak smile, then examined her hands again as if looking for some clue as to what to say next.

It was clear to Dorothy Sayer that this woman was nervous. She closed the portfolio and sat serenely, her hands folded primly in front of her. Psychology was one of the six majors Sayer dabbled in as an undergrad; she took no small pride in what she imagined was a great ability to read people. The main thing was patience.

Kathleen Gates looked to be about thirty years old, maybe thirty-one. She was a pretty woman, but she wore no makeup and was dressed in a pair of long shorts in an unfortunate aquamarine color and a loose fitting top, white cotton with short sleeves. There seemed to be some sort of stain on one shoulder that had resisted the washing machine.

God, I'm glad I'm not in her shoes, Sayer thought.

"I just thought it would be easier," Kathleen said. "The things I wanted to talk about, I mean. I thought it would be easier talking to a woman."

She was clearly unsure of herself, so Sayer tried to encourage her.

"I'll be concentrating on issues that concern women as I work here at West Point," Sayer said. Pleased with the official sound in her voice, she carried the exaggeration a bit further.

It's not like this lady is going to go checking on me in between diaper changes, she thought.

"I've already done some work in the classroom with cadets. I'm glad of the opportunity to talk to some people who aren't in uniform."

"I'm sure you find it easy to get people to open up to you," Kathleen said. "I mean, you're very pretty and seem so . . . I don't know . . . self-confident, I guess."

"Well, thank you," Sayer said, running her hand over the top of her head, right down the part, hair falling in practiced disarray.

"You probably don't even find it hard to work with men all the time."

Sayer had a sudden image of the night before, a mental picture she saw in the mirror above the desk in Braintree's room.

"Well, you just have to know how to handle them," Sayer said coyly. Girl to girl.

"That's a skill I wish I had," Kathleen Gates sighed. "I don't know, sometimes, if I just don't have the experience, or maybe I'm too naive . . . I'm not sure what my problem is."

"What makes you think you have a problem?"

"Oh, I have a problem, all right," Kathleen said. "I just don't know what to do about it."

"Well, if you think talking would help, I'm a good listener," Sayer said. She tried a different smile, a "trust me" look.

There was a clock on the wall behind Kathleen, a cow-figure clock with a pendulum shaped like a tail. When the tail clicked back and forth, so did the cow's eyes. Sayer turned in her seat so that she wouldn't have to see the clock in her peripheral vision.

"Well, I have to tell you that the things I wanted to talk about, when I first agreed to be interviewed, those things have changed a bit," Kathleen said. She picked at the skin alongside her thumbnail.

"Well, would you like to start with what you originally wanted to talk about, and then, if you're comfortable, we can continue. How does that sound?"

Kathleen nodded, and Sayer reached across the table to touch her arm lightly. It seemed a bit melodramatic, but this woman needed some basic encouragement.

"My husband isn't a graduate of West Point," Kathleen said. "And I feel, more than he does, that he isn't treated the same. It's like he's somehow less of an Army officer because he was commissioned through ROTC."

Sayer nodded, opened her notebook.

243

"OK with you if I make some notes?" Sayer asked.

"Confidential, right?"

"Absolutely."

Kathleen pulled at the bottom of her shirt, tucked one leg under her on the chair, moved her iced tea glass from one spot to another, then wiped at the condensation ring with the flat of her palm.

"People around here call West Point graduates 'grads,'" Kathleen said.

Sayer wrote "grads" on the blank page before her.

"Which makes sense, I guess. But every one else is a 'non-grad,' as if these other officers didn't go to college."

Sayer wrote "non-grad" in her book. When she looked up, Gates was watching her. There were a few empty seconds while Sayer waited for more.

"Doesn't sound like much, I guess. But I think it's part of a pattern. We're . . . like . . . second-class citizens around here."

Sayer wrote "2d-class citizens" under "non-grad" and wished the woman would get to the point, if she had one. Sayer was sore and uncomfortable in the hard chair; Braintree, it had turned out, was a pounder.

"That's why I've been quiet about the other thing," Gates said.

Sayer was still looking at the tablet, about to write something else when she heard a sniffling. She looked up; Kathleen Gates was crying.

"That's why I've been afraid to tell anyone about the cadet who forced himself on me."

Sayer watched Kathleen Gates's face, wet with tears now.

"Forced himself on you how?" Sayer asked, in part because she had to—it was the obvious question—and in part because she was intrigued, titillated.

"Sexually."

"You were raped by a cadet?"

"NO," Kathleen said quickly, her voice surprising both of them. "I never said that. I didn't use that word . . . oh, God. I didn't say he raped me."

"He forced you to have sex with him . . . that means he raped you," Sayer said. She was keenly aware of the details of her surroundings now; she had stumbled onto something big, something none of the other investigators would be able to match. Dorothy Sayer could already picture the news conferences, she and Bruckner sharing the dais.

But first she had to get this woman to call it what it was.

"No," Kathleen insisted. "I was scared. I shouldn't have been there with him, I shouldn't have let him walk me to my car, and . . . and . . . oh, *damn!*"

"It's OK," Sayer said, leaning forward and touching Kathleen Gates on the arm. She had seen a movie like this once, or maybe it was a television show, where the female cop just took her time and reassured the victim.

"There, there. It's all going to be OK, now."

"Not when my husband finds out," Kathleen said, shaking now, just at the edge of sobbing.

"Have you reported this to anyone?"

"No, no, no. I can't do that. Don't you understand? I wasn't even going to tell you except that you promised to keep my secret. If I report this my husband will be the one who suffers. They'll protect the cadet and they'll drag my name in the mud and my husband will be humiliated."

"What makes you think they'd protect the cadet?" Sayer asked. "I mean, doesn't the Army have a lot more invested in your husband?"

"Because the cadet has already been involved in something else," Kathleen said. "It's already happening."

Sayer scooted her chair closer to this little domestic figure. Apparently Kathleen's world of baby bottles and plastic toys didn't prepare her to deal with the establishment.

That's where we come in, Sayer thought, feeling very much the champion.

"Don't worry, now," she said, "Don't worry now."

"I can't believe how small these showers are," Dorothy Sayer called from the bathroom.

"That's because it's an old hotel," Braintree answered over the sound of running water. "Things weren't built as big back then."

He sat on the edge of the big bed, telephone cradled between his shoulder and ear. Annoying elevator music drifted over the wire; he had been on hold for four minutes.

"You on with the man yet?"

Braintree turned to face the bathroom. Dorothy Sayer stood in the doorway, a towel wrapped around her. When he shook his head "no" she pulled the towel open, giggling and flashing him for a second or two, before turning back into the bathroom.

"Just a little something to entertain you while you're on hold," she called as she climbed into the running shower.

"Mister Braintree?" a voice on the phone said. "Please hold for Senator Bruckner."

"Claude?"

"Right here, Senator," Braintree said.

"Looks like you've been doing some digging up there," Bruckner said. Braintree had sent a fax outlining the most interesting details he'd uncovered so far at West Point, a list that included the allegation made by one Kathleen Gates.

"This thing with the Gates woman sounds like a bomb-shell," Bruckner said.

"I'm not convinced of that, yet, Senator. Although it certainly has the potential to be . . . interesting."

It seemed to Braintree too much of a coincidence that Major and Mrs. Thomas Gates could be involved in so much at once. Those people were having a *bad* week.

"Give me the run down," Bruckner said. Which meant, as his long-time aide well knew, "just a few facts, don't bore me with anything in-depth."

"One of my associates up here, a young woman named Dorothy Sayer, talked to this woman today. Mrs. Gates's husband is on the staff here. She said that a cadet forced himself on her. . . ."

"He raped her?" Bruckner interrupted.

"No, sir. When Sayer used that word, Gates reacted strongly, saying it wasn't rape. It was somewhere shy of consensual sex, though."

"What do you make of it?"

"Sayer seems to think that the woman is just scared. She's a frumpy little thing, from what I hear, out of her league. Her husband is not a graduate of West Point, and Mrs. Gates made the point that they feel a little like second-class citizens up here. She let on that she didn't feel the Academy would treat the allegation fairly, that the cadet would be protected and it would cost her husband his career if she made an issue out of it."

"Did you talk to this woman?"

"No," Braintree said. He used his foot to pick Sayer's panties off the floor. "My associate did. To tell you the truth, Senator, I'm a little concerned about exaggeration, here."

"On whose part, Claude?"

"Well, Mrs. Gates, for one. She hasn't reported this to anyone, chose to talk to us instead of filing a complaint. And her husband already has some sort of discipline action against him—I haven't had time to sort that out yet.

"Apparently he got into some sort of very public argument with one of his cadets. The same cadet she's accusing."

"Sounds odd."

Braintree looked over his shoulder at the bathroom door, which was ajar. He could hear Dorothy splashing in the shower.

"And our Ms. Sayer has a tendency to get a little overzealous, become the feminist standard bearer and all that."

There was a pause on the other end of the line, and Braintree wondered which of his other aides was vying for the Senator's attention. It wouldn't do to stay isolated in New York too long.

"Well, let's be careful not to treat this too lightly, Claude. You know how the press can go after these allegations of sexual misconduct. I wouldn't want it to look as if we turned our heads."

As Braintree had expected, his boss was distracted by the possibilities for publicity. He didn't consider how complicated the affair might be, or that there might be a down side to rushing in.

"Right, sir."

"And if West Point is trying to ignore this, I expect you to get to the bottom of that, as well."

"Certainly, Senator," Braintree said.

When his boss let him off the phone, Claude Braintree

stood in front of the windows that looked out on yet another athletic field, this one called Buffalo Soldiers' Field after the cavalry regiment of black soldiers once stationed there.

"You still out there, sweety?" Sayer called from the bathroom; the water was off now.

"Still here," Braintree said.

"Waiting for me?" she trilled.

"Yes, indeed," Braintree said.

As his lover made small talk from the steamy little bathroom, Claude Braintree thought about the power wielded so rashly in the velvet glove that was sex.

That's how this cadet got in trouble with frumpy little Mrs. Gates, and it's going to be what really pisses off Mister Major Gates.

"I'm ready," Sayer said.

Braintree turned. She was naked, backlit in the bathroom door.

And it's the little tool Dorothy will try to use to find out what's really going on with Bruckner.

"What did the boss have to say?" Sayer asked.

"Silly girl," Braintree said, walking to her and putting his hands on her waist. "Let's not talk shop, shall we?"

As he walked toward his quarters from the parade field, Lieutenant General Patrick Flynn could see two figures in green on the porch of the house. He had sent word with his aide to the Dean, David Simon, and the Commandant, Tony Moro, that he wanted to see them at his quarters right after the parade.

Flynn had no doubt that he was interfering with what were probably already tight schedules. The three men had just participated in the Awards Review, the parade in which cadets received recognition for academic and military excellence. Simon, Moro, Flynn, and the head of each academic department stood for nearly an hour on the hot expanse of a windless parade ground while the names of the honored cadets from two of the four regiments in the Corps were read. And they had done it the previous day for cadets of the other two regiments. Flynn knew that some department heads wanted to send subordinates, but he had vetoed that. He wanted to send a signal to the Corps: it's important to recognize the good performance of your subordinates. And if that meant dragging a couple of dozen old men out of their air-conditioned offices to swelter in the humidity of an end-of-summer day, so be it.

Flynn had his glasses on, and he could see that Simon and Moro were both watching him, no doubt wondering why he had interrupted their afternoons yet again. They would be impatient, he knew. Tony Moro wouldn't show it, but David Simon would.

In his short time at West Point, Flynn had found that those officers who had been at the Academy for some time tended to forget about military protocol. The members of the academic board, in particular, thought of themselves as a college of fellows—and most of them were the same rank and about the same age.

Flynn had been injected into that. He was a lieutenant general, most of them were colonels. Patrick Flynn was not above reminding a few colonels, even those who'd been in the Army longer than he had, that three stars outranked a colonel's eagle, no matter how long you'd been in your job.

But because he was a good leader, Flynn was not cavalier about his interaction. He had called these two busy men to his quarters because he wanted to talk with them privately, and because it was a serious matter, and because he didn't want to do it in his office.

"Good afternoon, sir," Moro said as Flynn drew closer. Both men saluted; Flynn smiled as he returned their salutes.

"Good afternoon," he said. "Thanks for coming. I know you guys are busy this afternoon, so I won't keep you long. Why don't we grab a seat in here," Flynn said, leading the way to a screened section of the wrap-around porch.

"Darrell," Flynn called to his aide, "do you think you could have someone send out a pitcher of iced tea?"

The aide went to find the houseman.

Flynn unbuttoned the heavy green uniform coat and draped it over the back of a chair, prompting Moro to follow his lead. David Simon sat on one of the chairs and kept his blouse on.

"Hot as blazes out there," Flynn said. His shirt was dark with sweat stains.

"I was looking at some old pictures of the Academy in an

album in my office," he went on. "The cadets used to wear those dress gray coats all year round," he said, referring to the heavy wool uniforms, the tight, high-collared tunics the cadets called "the iron lung."

"Must have been a killer when it was hot."

There were a few seconds of silence. Moro said nothing; Simon looked out over the adjacent parade field.

Flynn guessed that Simon was sending him a signal: "I've got more important things to do."

It did not occur to the Superintendent that the two men had not been talking to each other in the moments before he joined them on the porch.

The houseman brought out a tray with three glasses, a bowl of lemon slices, and a sweating pitcher of iced tea.

"Thank you," Flynn said as the man withdrew.

David Simon twisted in his sweat-soaked uniform coat, hot, uncomfortable, and more than a little bit worried about what might happen here on the Superintendent's porch. Simon and Moro had done nothing to recover their civility in the wake of the little flare-up in Moro's office. Now he wondered if Moro had run to the Superintendent with tales that he, Simon, wanted to oust Flynn and become Superintendent of a smaller academy.

Or maybe Flynn would talk about the need for a united front, would ask Simon his opinions on contingency plans such as the Naval Academy was preparing. He would also have to court Simon's support. Yes, all of that made perfect sense to the Dean, since the other two men were really just transients at West Point, in and out for the short haul. Flynn would probably retire after this assignment—that was the normal course for outgoing Superintendents. Moro would soon be on his way to another star and an assignment back to the field Army. Only Simon would be around when the dust had cleared, and Simon was convinced that the West Point left at the end of all this had to be West Point as he envisioned it.

As he reached for the iced tea Flynn offered him, Simon relished his role: the true visionary, the seer, the defender of the faith.

* * *

"The name Gates has come up again," Flynn said without preamble as he sank into one of the padded chairs.

"Where was that, sir?" Moro asked.

"I got a call from a friend of mine who is doing some legal work for the Bruckner Commission," Flynn said. "He thought I needed a warning."

"They're talking about Gates and this cadet?"

"No, this time it was Mrs. Gates," Flynn said. "Kathleen, I think her name is. Have you met her?"

"Yes, sir," Moro answered. "My wife and I had a reception for the new Tactical Officers and their spouses. I met her there."

"And what was your impression?"

Moro used his thumb and forefinger to pull his wet shirt away from his chest.

"I only spoke to her for a moment. Seemed nice enough. Articulate, smart, not the kind to wait around for her husband's permission to speak."

David Simon watched this little exchange, wondering why he'd been brought along. He was about to say that he had other, more important things to do when Flynn dropped the grenade.

"She told a Bruckner Commission interviewer that a cadet forced himself on her—sexually."

"Holy shit," Moro said.

"Exactly," Flynn agreed.

"I haven't heard anything about this," Simon said peevishly. "She didn't report it to the Military Police."

"That's right," Flynn said. "Nor, apparently, did she tell her husband or anyone else. Until she started talking to one of the women on Braintree's staff."

"Why, she was probably frightened to tell her husband," Simon said. He noticed that his voice had risen slightly, as it did when he was agitated. This could be the kind of thing that prejudiced the commission, just the kind of thing that could be avoided by judicious handling of Braintree and his staff.

"We should talk to this woman," Simon said. "We have to get to the bottom of this."

Flynn refilled his iced tea glass, then took a long, slow sip.

"Well, there are a couple of problems with that," he said.

"The first is that there has been no official report. Mrs. Gates has chosen to confide in only one person. . . ."

"You mean we're not supposed to know about this," Simon interrupted.

"Obviously not. This friend put me in a tough spot. I told him I appreciated his concern, but that the interviews were confidential. I can't undo the fact that I've learned, but I can't act on the information."

"But it would be irresponsible to ignore it," Simon said.

"All we know, David," Flynn said calmly, "is that Mrs. Gates reported this to a woman on the Bruckner Commission. I think that raises some other important questions."

"It raises the question of why we haven't done anything about Major Gates in the first place," Simon said sharply.

Moro did not even look at him.

"Tony has handled that incident," Flynn said. "And that's not what I was thinking of."

"Now, it may be that Mrs. Gates did choose to keep quiet about this to spare her husband, or out of fear of her husband, if we want to take a less generous reading. But there are certainly other possibilities. She may be going on the offensive."

Simon flopped back in his chair. His tee shirt, dress shirt, and jacket clung to him like a thick, wet towel sliding across his back. He had heard about men who were unwilling to believe accusations of sexual misconduct, men who were all too ready to blame the woman. But he had never seen it firsthand.

Flynn had recklessly exposed West Point by failing to handle the Gates fiasco firmly; now he was going to compound that problem with his reading of these allegations.

Moro was wearing that same knowing, self-satisfied expression that Flynn wore.

"The cadet wouldn't be Wayne Holder, would he, General?" Moro asked.

"None other," Flynn said.

"Who's Wayne Holder?" Simon demanded. It seemed to him that Moro and Flynn were in another discussion, one that he wasn't following.

Flynn and Moro ignored him.

"Did she happen to say if this alleged incident was before

or after her husband's little run-in with our notorious Cadet Holder?"

"No indication," Flynn said.

"Who's Cadet Holder?" Simon asked again.

Moro turned to face the Dean, speaking slowly, as if to a student who was having a particularly difficult time understanding a concept. "That's the cadet Major Gates tangled with out by MacArthur's monument," he said.

Simon digested this information for a moment.

"Quite a coincidence, wouldn't you say?" Moro said.

"So . . . what?" Simon stumbled. "Now you're saying that this Mrs. Gates is making this up? That she's trying to blackmail this cadet?"

"No," Flynn said. "It's not quite that simple. First of all, she may have told the truth to this investigator. But let's say, hypothetically, that something odd is going on here. It couldn't be as simple as blackmail—the cadet has already told his side of things. He's not going to go back and change that. Besides, Gates's letter of reprimand is based on what he told us about his actions, not based on what the cadet had to say. But it is possible that she is issuing herself a little insurance here."

"She thinks that the threat of a scandal of some sort will be enough to keep her husband from getting canned," Moro said, thinking out loud.

"That is one possibility," Flynn said. "What do you think, David?"

Simon had slumped in his chair so that his uniform coat rode up on his shoulders, making him look like an old man in a too-big suit of armor.

"I don't know what to make of it," Simon said. "I guess if she wants to set up a trade, she has to show a little bit of her hand. I mean, none of this does any good if we're unaware of the threat."

"She's already told the story to an investigator, so it's all but out in the open," Flynn said. "She's either telling the truth, or she hasn't thought this all the way through, or she has something else in mind."

"So the next move is hers," Moro said.

"Or Braintree's," Flynn added. "Maybe Braintree will want to run with this. You might talk to this Holder kid again. You can't mention Kathleen Gates, since we're not supposed to know. But maybe he'll offer something. At the very least a little more attention from the Commandant may put the fear of God into him. Maybe he'll keep his dick in his pants."

Moro nodded agreement; Simon watched the two of them, so obviously on the same wavelength, so obviously wrong.

"It looks like the next move is Braintree's," Flynn said.

Not necessarily, Simon told himself. *Not necessarily.*

Kathleen Gates brought the children along for effect.

Alex Trainor had called her just before ten that Saturday morning. She suspected that he'd first gone by Tom's office to make sure that her husband was at work. He had been unfailingly polite—that was how she remembered him from their first meeting at the picnic, a shy, corn-fed Bible thumper from the Midwest. She suspected she knew what he wanted: Alex Trainor was going to tell her that Wayne Holder—his roommate and friend—was sorry about what happened in the parking lot, and then Trainor would beg her to be quiet.

It's working, she thought. *I'm in control.*

Then it occurred to Kathleen that Trainor might confront her. Perhaps Holder was smart enough to realize she'd set him up. She hadn't approached this casually, but she did enjoy the sex, and it was fun to discover she still had that kind of power. Still, Holder had to see the coincidence of this happening within a few nights of the showdown with Tom.

But that didn't matter to Kathleen Gates. All she needed from Holder, when the time came, was an admission that they'd had sex in the parking lot. And Holder wouldn't lie about it. If anything, he'd brag about it to his friends down in the barracks. For now she wanted Holder quiet, compliant. She decided to take an easygoing approach; she could always play hardball later. For now it would be better to play the role she'd shown Dorothy Sayer: the little lost wifey.

She couldn't dress down, as she'd done for Sayer, because she had to meet Trainor out in public. But she'd found a shapeless summer shift, then put a round-necked tee shirt on beneath that. The dress reached well past her knees, the shirt had half sleeves. She put on only a tiny bit of makeup, just enough to make her eyes show against her pale complexion.

Gates pushed the stroller along Merritt Road toward the Jewish Chapel. To her left was a stone wall and a magnificent view of the river over the tops of the professors' homes. To her right the hill climbed steeply through thick brambles for another few hundred feet. The morning was sunny, with a welcome hint of cool air.

She spotted Alex Trainor at some distance. His hand was wrapped hugely and resting in a sling around his neck.

"Good morning, ma'am," Trainor said as he drew closer, looking at her from under the shiny black brim of his dress cap.

"Good morning, Cadet Trainor," Gates said sweetly. "How is your hand?"

"It hurts quite a bit, but it's getting better. And there's no permanent damage, praise the Lord," he said.

Trainor looked down at his hand, and Kathleen wondered what he'd really like to say about what her husband had done.

"I'll have this on for a few weeks," he said, touching the sling with his good hand.

Trainor was polite but stiff; Kathleen could handle this one.

"Thank you for agreeing to meet me," he said.

A car drove by, one of Kathleen's neighbors on the way back home from the commissary with a car full of groceries. Kathleen waved, then smiled at Trainor as she began to rock the stroller back and forth in place. Both children were ready for their morning nap and were quiet; the rocking lulled them further. Kathleen looked at Trainor with a blank expression; she would give him nothing.

"This is very . . . ah . . . very awkward," he said.

Kathleen turned and faced upriver and began to work herself up for a little cry. Trainor turned also and stood beside her, some six or seven feet away, and put his good hand on the wall. He was mustering his courage to speak, and Kathleen Gates was enjoying watching him squirm. Kathleen figured the more he hesitated, the less sure of himself he was.

"Wayne told me what happened the other night, ma'am," Trainor said, his voice very low, as if he had done something wrong. "He feels terrible about it."

Alex Trainor had been sure of what he was going to say to Kathleen Gates right up until the moment he spotted her pushing the stroller.

He had assumed that Wayne Holder was partly at fault for what had happened—the boy was always getting into trouble when women were involved. But he did not think Holder was stupid enough to initiate the scene he'd described: Kathleen Gates, her skirt pushed up around her waist, beckoning him from the back seat of the car. Back in the barracks Trainor had no trouble believing that Kathleen Gates had staged the whole scene, although he still hadn't figured out what her angle was going to be.

She probably knew Holder's vulnerability—he shared it with most of the men in the Corps. She certainly seemed cunning enough: everything Wayne Holder told him about their meetings confirmed Trainor's belief that she was dangerous, a force to be reckoned with. The roommates thought they had her figured out. Trainor was sure of all that right up until he met her.

Yet the Kathleen Gates standing before him was a pale representation of the vibrant woman who had caught the attention of so many of the men at the Gates's picnic. She looked tired. Her clothes were rumpled and unflattering; she stood with her shoulders slumped forward and stared into the space above the river. She had two babies in the stroller at her feet, and yet Trainor was going to accuse her of seducing his roommate—who was, after all, known as "Holder the Horn Dog" in the company. Seducing him, then lying about it.

How did I get myself in this mess? he asked himself.

Kathleen Gates let her eyes brim with tears. She dabbed at her face with one hand and sniffed noisily.

"I'm sorry, ma'am," Trainor said. "I know this must be

terribly upsetting for you. It's very upsetting for Wayne, too."

"I should think so," Kathleen said weakly, unable to resist pushing him back against the ropes.

"I can't sleep, can't eat, and my husband knows that something is wrong with me."

She turned to face him, blinking her eyes widely as if fighting off the tears.

"You know, it's really amazing," Trainor said. "I mean, the coincidence. What with the little problem that Wayne had with Major Gates and all."

"I should have known he was trouble," Kathleen said. "I should have stayed away from him."

"Excuse me, ma'am, but Wayne said you called him."

"I did call him. And I asked if he would come and talk to me because I was so worried. I was trying to help the company and my husband. I guess he figured I was vulnerable."

Trainor stared at her, trying hard to see, in her startling blue eyes, if she was telling the truth.

"So you're saying that what happened was Wayne's fault."

Kathleen waited a long count before answering. When she spoke, she spoke precisely. "That's exactly what I'm saying."

She rocked the stroller back and forth, gently, while she let Trainor collect himself. He had come out here ready to play the wronged party; he had expected her to give in. But she had just begun.

Trainor wished her good day and turned back to the barracks, walking away with his head down. Kathleen Gates turned her stroller around and headed back to her quarters.

When she had the children in bed, she phoned her brother and explained the barest details of her plan to protect Tom's career, leaving out the part about having sex with a college boy.

"Well, I don't know if it has any bearings on what you're thinking about up there," he said, "but I talked to my buddy at Navy again yesterday. Seems like this guy Simon—what's he? The Dean up there?"

"Yes," Kathleen said.

"Simon was talking to the Dean at Annapolis about this plan to downsize. So anyway, Navy's Dean—who thinks Simon is a prick—makes a joke about how General Simon is going to stage a coup at West Point, see himself promoted to two star, and installed as the new Supe of a smaller West Point."

"How could he do that?" Kathleen wanted to know.

"Get in good with the civilians," Brian answered. "That's just for starters. Then they'd have to see a reason to get rid of the Supe you have now."

"Now *that's* an interesting little piece of news," Kathleen said.

"It was a bust, Wayne," Trainor said. "She all but accused you of raping her."

Holder sat on his bunk, dressed in civilian clothes. He'd made Saturday night plans with Liz Wrenson, now he wasn't so sure he could go through with them.

"Now what do we do?"

"We'll have to wait to see what she does next," Trainor said. "Unless you want to go to Major Gates now, we're going to be playing this by her rules."

"Great," Holder said. "That's just great."

When Alex Trainor walked into Ruth's apartment a little after two o'clock on Saturday afternoon, the first thing he noticed was her hair. There was very little left on the sides of her head, a fair approximation of his own military haircut. And what was left on top seemed desperate to call attention to itself by sticking almost straight up. She wore an expensive pink bathrobe and cotton slippers, but from the neck up she was ready to join a biker gang.

"Hi, there," Alex said, making an effort to look her in the eye.

"You're late," she answered.

Ruth was sitting on the couch, flanked by empty ice cream containers that stood in pools of congealed goo on the end tables. She fished the remote control out of the seat cushion and turned off the television, then stood. She was short, only a hint over five feet, with large doughy limbs and curves. It seemed unlikely that she could have gotten heavier in the week since he last saw her, but the evidence was there. Trainor, in an unkind moment, wondered if she cut off her hair in an effort to keep her total body weight a constant.

"I can't stay as late as last time," he said. "I've got a group project due and we're meeting tonight."

Ruth harrumphed, a snort that was a combination of "I don't believe you" and "I don't care."

Alex thought about ignoring the haircut, but it screamed for attention. Not mentioning it would be too obvious.

"You got your hair cut," he said as tonelessly as possible.

"Yeah. I hate it," she said, nervously running her fingers over the blonde bristles above her ears.

Alex, feeling some test of his loyalty, said, "No, I think it looks pretty sharp."

"What did you bring me?" Ruth asked, eyeing the grocery bag Alex had tucked under his arm. She sidled toward him, one big white leg slipping out of the front of her robe.

"The milk you asked for," he said. "Also some apples and tangerines I saw at the market."

Ruth was unimpressed; she liked gifts. Small ones, big ones, surprises of all kinds. The favored daughter of wealthy parents, she was used to lovely things appearing as if out of thin air. She sidled up to him, offering her cheek to be kissed. They hadn't had sex in Trainor's last four weekend visits.

"How are you feeling?" he asked, handing her the bag.

She dug inside and he stepped behind her, putting his good hand on her waist, then sliding it up to her breasts, which had been heavy and generously round to start with and seemed to be getting larger. He was instantly aroused.

"Stop that," she said, pushing him away. "They're very tender and I certainly don't want you groping them and making them hurt."

Alex slumped into one of the two mismatched kitchen chairs and felt himself deflate. The visit wasn't getting off to a good start.

Maybe she can't have sex while she's pregnant, Alex thought. Which left . . . seven more months.

The apartment was a wreck. Three or four paper grocery bags of trash slumped like body bags in a corner of the kitchen. A haphazard pile of magazines fanned out on the floor beside the couch, and a long tail of some piece of dirty laundry stuck out from under the cushion where she'd been sitting.

"I fired the cleaning lady," she said, following his eyes around the room.

"Why?"

"Daddy cut my allowance. He said I was perfectly capable of doing my own cleaning."

"Uh-huh."

"But it's *his* fault that I was used to having someone come in twice a week," she said. "We always had cleaning ladies when I was growing up."

Ruth had grown up in the lovely horse farms of northwestern New Jersey, a spoiled little girl with too few friends. She had confessed to Alex that she hadn't dated all that much; there was not a lot of opportunity at the all-girls' schools she attended. And the boys her parents introduced her to at the clubs were dreadfully boring, and all they wanted to do was drink.

Ruth had taken the apartment last year, just before Alex met her. It was exciting to know a girl who had her own apartment, although he had often thought that if she lived with her parents they wouldn't have had sex, wouldn't have had what his Sunday School teacher used to call "the occasion of sin."

But her parents lived half the year in Boca Raton and sent checks regularly. On their fourth date, Alex had found himself here, in the company of this slightly overweight and—he now realized—self-conscious girl who was thrilled with the attention he paid her. And although he often told Wayne Holder that sex before marriage was nothing but trouble and damnation, Alex Trainor had given in to temptation.

And once he had fallen, he fell regularly. Right up until she became pregnant.

Once Alex had gotten over the shock and had learned to live with the threat of eternal damnation, he had been genuinely happy about the baby. He wanted a big family with lots of kids running around and crowded, noisy dinners and holiday gatherings. The timing was terrible, but

Alex was determined to take care of Ruth and the child. Yet the woman he'd slept with bore very little resemblance to the woman before him now. There were two Ruths, it seemed. In the middle of the night, tossing on his lonely cadet bunk, Alex wasn't thrilled about the prospect of marrying either of them.

"I've been sick," she said to him. "Throwing up every morning."

Alex had a mental picture of Ruth's expanding backside bent over the toilet in the booth-sized bathroom.

"Isn't that normal?" he asked.

"I don't care if it's normal or not," she said, stomping her foot. Her discomfort was clearly his fault. "I don't like it."

"How's school?" he asked, trying a different tack.

Ruth was attending classes at the Brooklyn School of Design where she was studying, haphazardly, to become a fashion designer. Alex wondered if you could get thrown out of such a place for an aesthetic sin—such as a bad haircut.

"I quit," she said.

"What?"

"I quit, I said. I was sick of going there, I was getting sick while I was there. I don't want to do that anymore. Besides, when the baby comes I want to stay home."

"Have you told your parents that you quit school . . . or that you're pregnant?"

"Don't be stupid," she said. "They'll be furious."

And they'll cut off your allowance for good.

Ruth had been in and out of four different colleges in the last three years. The pattern was always the same. She quit, her parents became angry and cut her allowance until she enrolled in some other school. But her comment about wanting to stay home made him think that she had no plans to repeat the scenario.

"How are you going to support yourself?" Alex asked.

"I thought maybe the baby's father would support me," she said.

It was a vicious thing to say, and she knew it. Alex Trainor was sick with guilt over all he could not do to help Ruth. He had slept with a woman who wasn't his wife, and now he was failing her when she needed him. They had been over this ground before, dozens of times, and she had agreed to stay in school until he graduated and was commissioned.

"I can't support you on my allowance," Alex said.

"You're supposed to be an officer in the Army . . ." she began.

"That's nine months away," he said.

Ruth made a face and sat down heavily on the other chair.

"We could get married now. Then at least I'd be able to tell my parents. What do you think this feels like, carrying a child of a man who won't marry me."

She hit him hardest where it hurt the most.

"If I marry you they won't let me graduate," he said. "Cadets can't be married."

"Who has to know?" she demanded. "The only people I want to tell are my parents. My dad would be glad to help us out, to pick up the *slack*," she jabbed again, "if he knew we were at least being respectable about this."

"I'd know we were married. I can't lie about it."

"You wouldn't have to lie. Just don't tell a soul."

"I'd be living a lie," he said.

"That's just great," she said, leaning toward him, hands on her hips. "So you get your precious Honor Code and I'm stuck in this apartment all week. I'm just *so* sick of your self-righteousness, Alex."

She stormed into the bedroom and slammed the door.

Alex Trainor put his face in his hands and took a deep breath. Just a few months before, at the end of the spring semester, everything had been going so well for him. He was at the threshold of his last year at West Point, at the beginning of a new adventure and a responsible—adult—life. Then he had met Ruth and he imagined them married, settled in a cozy set of Army quarters someplace. With his class rank he could draw just about any first assignment he wanted. Then they would have a child, and Ruth would learn about the Army and how things worked and she would become more understanding and they would be happy. He couldn't believe what a mess he'd made of his life in just a few short months.

It seemed to him that he spent a great deal of his time pleading—often through a locked door—for her to try to see more than one side of a problem. And the worst part of it was that he wasn't convinced she was wrong. He did feel as if he was letting her down, shirking his responsibilities, and maybe it was out of self-righteousness. And who was he to talk about the Honor Code when he was living a lie, when he wouldn't marry the woman who was carrying his child?

Oh, God, he prayed, *the child.*

That's what it all came down to, he realized. He had to take care of this child. Ruth may or may not ever understand what he was talking about when he said he couldn't live a lie. She might never be happy with what he could give her, but his first duty was to the child. That did not mean he had to marry Ruth right away, but he did have to support the baby, take care of Ruth as best he could.

And if he couldn't do that while wearing cadet gray, then maybe it was time that he gave up that dream.

"Ruth," he said as he stood and walked to the bedroom door and tapped lightly on the wood. "I'm sorry. We'll work this out, honey, I promise. And I'll take care of you."

CHAPTER 10

Captain Jackie Timmer walked quickly along Thayer Road, past the stone towers of Pershing Barracks, snapping salutes at cadets who greeted her, answering them with curt, mumbled responses.

Timmer was angry at the Dean, who had called her that Monday morning and told her to be at Grant Hall reception area at eleven hundred hours; she was angry at Claude Braintree, the boor she had to meet; she was angry at Layne Marshall, who had unsettled her life and sent her another long letter which she carried in her pocket.

She desperately wanted to finish reading the letter, which began with a story of how he'd lain in his bed after they'd hung up the other night, watching the moon and thinking about how it was also shining on her. But the letter, which she'd found in her distribution box that morning, had done nothing but remind her that she had no privacy; that made her angry as well. Jon Hillard, her officemate, was at his desk when she'd returned from the Department mail room. There were two people in the lunch room, students in the hallway sitting areas, another instructor in the fourth floor library. The only place she could read it was in the latrine, and she'd only been in there a minute or so when a woman cadet rapped insistently on the door.

Timmer was also trying to be angry at her husband, whom she'd just left in a confused state in the hallway outside his office after a short, surprisingly heated spat. The problem with getting mad at Rob was that she knew she'd started the fight, that there was nothing, really, to fight about in the first place. And she was angry at herself for not being able to come up with something better.

It started when she asked Rob if he wanted to go with her to the presentation at the Old Cadet chapel.

"What's it for, again?"

"Some of the instructors have hired an actor to do this fire and brimstone sermon from the eighteenth century. They're trying to impress on the cadets how much power the clergy had in colonial America."

"Gosh, Jack, sounds tempting," Rob had said sarcastically. "I mean, I like to get threatened with everlasting hellfire as much as the next guy and all . . ."

"You don't have to be a smartass about it, Rob," she'd cut him off.

"Sorry," he'd said, surprised at her sharp tone. "It's just that, I don't know, it just doesn't sound all that interesting to me."

And it was then, looking at his honest face, that Jackie Timmer knew why she wanted her husband to come along. She needed a chaperone.

But even without him, she would be unable to stay away. And the fact that Rob was completely trusting of her made it worse.

"You go, if you want to, honey," he'd said. "If it interests you."

She'd stood there for a few seconds longer, without speaking, wanting him to say something else, some remark about her romantic streak, or something about the uselessness of the humanities, something from his logical, engineering, mathematical mind. But instead of giving her the ammunition to attack him, he said, "Of course, if you really want me to go . . . I mean, if it's important to you, I'll go. And I'll even behave myself and won't keep getting up to go to the bathroom."

He had seen something in her eyes, and he was ready to make the sacrifice. All he wanted was a little acknowledgment that it wasn't for him, that it was for her.

But she couldn't give it to him. She didn't have it in her to give anything to him.

"Fine then," she'd said. "I'll go by myself."

"Are you sure?" he said, though he was obviously relieved. "I mean, I'll go if it's important to you, sweetheart."

"No, that's OK, *sweetheart,*" she'd said, deliberately skewing the word he'd meant sincerely. "It's not like I need you to hold my hand or anything. I'll be better off by myself."

And she'd turned quickly away, angry at him because he couldn't read her mind, couldn't see what she needed even though she could not have articulated it herself. She'd turned away from him in the hallway outside his office, and she started walking quickly. She was still walking fast a half mile later when she reached the doors to Grant Hall, an ornate room that functioned like a hotel lobby—but without the hotel. It was here that cadets could meet their families, could sit and talk in civil surroundings to the people who were not allowed to come into the barracks.

The room was a long rectangle: more arched windows, oak paneling, and clusters of chairs. The air-conditioning barely made a dent in the heat, and Jackie Timmer paused just inside the door, giving her eyes a moment to adjust to the relative darkness. She brushed at her short hair and wiped her forehead where her hat had left a ring of perspiration.

Claude Braintree was sitting on one of the leather couches, half-glasses on the end of his nose, paging quickly through the contents of a manila folder. A nervous young man sat next to Braintree, fingering the edges of a half dozen other folders.

"Ah, Captain Timmer," Braintree said pleasantly, looking over the tops of the little glasses. He did not make a move to get up.

"This is Sandy Van Grouw. Sandy, this is Captain Jacqueline Timmer."

Van Grouw stood. He was shorter than Timmer, with a

pale complexion and a privileged look about him. He did not speak but offered Jackie a limp grip.

Nice handshake, she thought as she withdrew her hand.

"Won't you have a seat?" Braintree offered.

Timmer selected a chair at right angles to the couch, sat down and opened the leather-bound planning calendar she carried everywhere. Braintree went back to his reading.

"I'll be with you in a moment," he said.

Timmer smiled at Van Grouw, who was still watching her.

"Are you on the faculty or staff?" Van Grouw asked.

"Faculty. I'm in the English department."

"Oh," Van Grouw said, smiling as if they'd just discovered they had a mutual friend. "That was my major as an undergrad. What courses do you teach?"

"Sandy," Braintree said as he closed a folder and pushed it into Van Grouw's chest. "I brought Captain Timmer away from a very busy schedule, and while I'm sure she'd love to chat, she does have pressing business."

Van Grouw's smile faded instantly. He nodded and began collecting his papers.

"Certainly," he said, fumbling as he tried to gather himself.

Timmer saw immediately that Van Grouw was flustered by her presence, and in the next instant she realized that such a presumption was something new for her. Lately she had become much more aware of her sexuality—as if it had been lying dormant and was just waking.

Van Grouw gathered the folders awkwardly in his arms, then tried to wrestle his briefcase open with one hand.

"Perhaps you could do that over there," Braintree said, waving regally at one of the empty tables in the big room.

"Certainly," Van Grouw said, his face flooding red. He scooped up the briefcase and walked through the big room bent over, arms and folders clutched to his chest.

"Thank you for coming by, Captain Timmer," Braintree said. He was completely self-assured; she wondered if it even registered that he had just embarrassed his subordinate.

Braintree gave her the big smile.

"How are things with you?" he asked.

"Fine," she said. And that quickly her head filled with treasured pictures of Layne Marshall. She conjured up what he looked like, what he sounded like; she could see the firm lines of his handwriting in his letters. She rehearsed the way he said her name.

And then she came back to the room with Braintree, who was looking at her. She had no idea how long she'd been gone.

"Thanks for asking," she added.

"Well," he said, uncrossing his legs and placing both feet on the floor. He wore a khaki suit, chestnut wingtips, a conservative navy blue and yellow tie. No wrinkle dared come near him; there wasn't a trace of perspiration on him. Jackie Timmer wondered if he wore a suit to bed.

"We've been moving right along with our little study," he said. "It really isn't all that difficult to gather information. The hard part will be sorting through it all to determine what is significant."

Timmer sat back in the chair and crossed her legs, pressing her thighs together and feeling—imagining?—the heat there. And just before she let herself think about Marshall again, she drew a sharp little breath and dragged herself to the present. The Dean had harped on her that she needed to develop close relationships with Braintree and his staff, stressing the point and repeating himself annoyingly. It was obviously important. Fortunately, Braintree was taking the lead; maybe he hadn't noticed that she was daydreaming.

"I was thinking about taking some of what we've gleaned and going to a few groups with it, to see if these concerns are widespread," he said.

He looked at her earnestly, and Timmer paused before speaking, as much out of politeness—to see if he were finished—as out of suspicion. Maybe she had missed something and he was waiting for an answer. She watched his mouth, his eyes. Every silent second underscored her inattention.

"I wonder if you could help me ask for some volunteers," he continued, leading her, trying to be helpful. "If we could get ten or twelve women from the faculty, for instance, all of them military, that might be a more efficient way of addressing some of these issues."

He stopped talking again, a question in his tone. Jackie Timmer had lost the trail of his inquiry again; she was picturing Layne Marshall's face across a candlelit expanse of dinner table.

"Are you all right, Captain Timmer?" Braintree asked.

"Oh . . . yes, I'm sorry, sir," she said, looking down at the blank sheet in her book. "I was just . . . my mind wandered a bit, I'm afraid."

"Would you like to discuss this at another time?"

"No. No, sir. I'm ready," she said, stumbling along, eager to redeem herself, to find a place to begin. "The Dean . . . General Simon talked to me this morning about some of your concerns. Sexual harassment, the integration of women and minorities."

For just a moment, Braintree looked mildly surprised. *This must be,* she thought, *what he wanted to talk about.*

"Yes," he said. "Tell me about the command climate. In your opinion, if a woman had been sexually harassed, or even sexually assaulted, would she feel comfortable reporting it? Would she assume the command here would give her a fair shake?"

"I feel that the command climate is such that anyone with a legitimate complaint should feel comfortable raising the issue," Timmer said. She felt somewhat more in control now. She was in a familiar role, talking about constants, things she believed in. Yes, of course the Academy would investigate, and the authorities would help, and justice would be served. She was on solid ground. Yet part of her couldn't get past the feeling that Braintree had something specific in mind.

Timmer had pulled the sleek steel pen from the tiny leather strap that bound it to the side of her book. She tapped the point against the clean sheet in her lap.

"Suppose a woman, a civilian, was assaulted by a cadet. We're speaking hypothetically, of course. But suppose it happened. Would the woman have to worry that the academy might cover that up?"

"This is all just speculation?"

Braintree smiled. "We'll make a politician out of you yet," he said. *"Of course* it's speculation. I'm asking you to think hypothetically.

"You've heard of or seen these Trojan Horse cartoons? You're aware, are you not, that some people think that General Flynn was sent here to make it easier for West Point's critics to dismantle the academy?"

"Yes, sir," Timmer said. "I've heard all of that. I don't put a lot of stock in it."

He had leaned forward, closer to her, and Timmer noticed a light in his eyes that had not been there before. If she'd been having this conversation with Layne Marshall, she might have responded in kind.

"So you think a woman with a serious complaint would come forward?"

"Most women, the ones with any experience with the command, know that their complaints would be taken seriously," Timmer said.

"That's what I thought you'd say," Braintree said, smiling. He stood, looked down at the plumb line crease of his trousers, touched the knot on his tie.

"Let's put this idea about a discussion group on hold, shall we?" Braintree asked. "I'd like to think more about it."

"Yes, sir," Timmer said, following his lead and standing. She made the day's first entry in her notebook.

"If you want to call me 'sir' in front of the group," Braintree said. "Fine. But call me Claude here, OK? 'Sir' reminds me of how old I am."

"Right," Timmer answered.

"Thanks for coming by," Braintree said, smiling widely again. "I must hurry off now. I've been invited to sit in on a history class."

"I hope you enjoy it," Timmer said, shaking Braintree's extended hand.

"There is one more thing," Braintree said. "You said the Dean mentioned that I'd be interested in hearing about sexual harassment and the assimilation of women, is that right?"

"Yes."

"Did he say what made him think that?"

"No, sir . . . Claude. He didn't. I assumed it was from some conversation you two had."

"OK," Braintree said. "Thanks again. You've been most helpful."

Braintree left Grant Hall and crossed the street, joining a throng of cadets that snaked over a stone bridge and into the maw of the big academic building, Thayer Hall. Braintree found himself walking faster, the pace set by the crowd around him. He paused inside the rotunda, watching the cadets hurry by and wondering what Brigadier General David Simon was up to.

Simon had gone out of his way, Braintree thought, to convey that he—and maybe he alone—understood that some changes might need to be made. Perhaps this latest move was another clumsy effort on Simon's part to ingratiate himself with the civilian visitor. Maybe he thought he'd send a signal that he was a forward-thinking guy.

"Or maybe he has something else in mind," Braintree said aloud.

If he did, Braintree figured, it wouldn't be long before Simon contacted him.

Jackie Timmer hurried into the cadet library to read Marshall's letter, which she had stuffed in her date book. By the time she reached the front doors of that building, any concern she had over Braintree and the Bruckner Commission had faded.

Most of the cadets were in class at this hour; a few of the librarians were about, pushing book-heavy carts back and forth to the elevators. Timmer walked back into the Moore Wing, with its quiet cabinets full of microfilm. She was the only one in the room.

She pulled a chair up in front of one of the microfilm readers and tugged the envelope from its hiding place. Holding it greedily in both hands, she read the salutation twice.

"Dear Jacqueline."

She looked up and around the room once more, and when she saw that she was still alone, she leaned far back in her chair and held the letter over her chest.

I went for a drive after I spoke to you the other night, trying to leave behind, I suppose, a little of my embarrassment. I am not ashamed at the way I feel about you, but I should not impose on you. It is one thing for me to think about you constantly, to watch for you in the hallways, to leave you notes, to dream up pretenses to talk with you. It is quite another to ask you to reciprocate, something else entirely when I ask how you feel about me.

I do not mean to cause you any harm, any worry about your life. I am just so thrilled that we've met that I sometimes don't know what I'm saying when I'm around you. That probably sounds funny to you, since I have made a life out of speaking and knowing what I'm talking about. Around you I feel more like a clueless adolescent than I felt when I was a clueless adolescent. Back then I had at least convinced myself that I knew all the answers.

Here are a couple of things I've learned at West Point:

Just because all the people dress alike doesn't mean they think alike. Underneath the green uniforms are poets and athletes and scientists and at least one goddess with a lover's soul.

I've learned this about myself: I am capable of feeling a sweet, frightening helplessness I thought only existed in novels. I feel that way near you, all tongue-tied and bumbling, and I've enjoyed every goofy minute.

I hope you're not angry at me for letting you know my feelings for you. I'm tremendously attracted to you. That much is OK. It may or may not be OK that I let you know that. Depends on your reaction. Everything, from this point, depends on your reaction.

Timmer read the last sentence again, then held the paper up to her face and breathed in his imagined scent.

"Everything depends on my reaction," she said aloud. "Nothing like putting the ball squarely in my court."

She pushed her chair back from the console, put her feet up on the little workspace, studied her shoes. Ugly little black things. She had grown so used to uniformity that she wondered if she were even capable of having a reaction.

When has it ever been about choice, she asked herself. *When has it ever been about how I feel?*

"Who the hell has ever cared about what I think," she said aloud, "about what I want?"

"Pardon?"

Timmer dropped her feet to the floor. There was a librarian behind her, a woman in her mid-fifties, leaning on a book cart and watching Timmer through thick glasses.

"Just thinking out loud," Timmer said. "Sorry."

Jackie watched as the woman pushed her wheeled cart up and down the aisles formed by the big metal cabinets.

That's me, she thought. *Going through the motions.*

Timmer held the letter up again. At the bottom, a postscript read, "The sermon is at the Old Cadet Chapel, Monday at eight thirty P.M. Please wear something approximating period costume."

Jackie Timmer smiled and put the folded letter back in her planner.

"That's twenty thirty around here, Layne," she said as she turned and walked to the brightly lit hallway.

It was the big photograph of Richard Nixon that first caught his eye.

Patrick Flynn saw the poster-sized image as he hurried down the main staircase of the library. It was part of a display in the second floor lobby, put together by the library staff to showcase some of the materials in the collection. A series of panels, each about seven feet tall and five feet wide, stood in the room-sized space, connected to each other with hinges and set at right angles in a sort of maze effect. The matted surfaces displayed dozens of photographs, artwork, headlines, and blocks of text. A banner over the big photo of the President was a reproduction of the headline: Nixon Resigns.

Flynn paused in front of the display. He was too old to be

amused that events he had lived through were now considered history, and not quite old enough to resign himself to that inevitable development.

The photos were familiar: a shot of Nixon's televised farewell and attempt at self-exculpation; the former President waving good-bye just before he entered the helicopter that would carry him into history—but not, as it turned out, oblivion. And in the bottom corner of the display, a small aerial view of the White House that triggered a memory for Patrick Flynn.

He had been serving in Korea at the time, getting news about the political crisis in pieces through Armed Forces Network, Korean sources, and patchy telephone calls home. But even on the other side of the globe, there was the sense that momentous things were happening on the American stage. A South Korean officer Flynn worked closely with had asked him, as the two men stood in the chow line at a hot field site, what the expected resignation would mean to the Army.

"What do you mean?" Flynn had asked the younger man.

"Do you think there will be a coup?" the Korean had asked.

Flynn had almost laughed, but his Korean friend was serious. As they sat cross-legged on the ground and ate their meal, Flynn's boss delivered his opinion.

"In many other countries in the world—maybe even in most—the prospect of a coup would be real. A paranoid President who doesn't want to go, who thinks he's being railroaded; no precedent for the resignation of the Chief Executive; a vice president who was never elected to that office . . . yeah, there are lots of governments that couldn't pull it off peacefully."

The Korean officer sat politely, his plate of food in his lap, as the American lieutenant colonel tried to explain why the U.S. Army was taking things so calmly.

"In lots of other countries, you'd wind up with Army tanks parked on the White House lawn," he'd said around a mouthful of runny, reconstituted eggs.

"But it ain't gonna happen in Washington. The U.S. Army doesn't play that game," he announced.

Satisfied that he had explained his country and his Army

sufficiently, the colonel went back to his breakfast. The Korean officer began to eat as well, although he did not look at all satisfied. Flynn tried to explain things a little better when he and the Korean were alone again.

"We have a long history of civilian control of the military," Flynn told the man. "It's so ingrained that I can't think of a single American soldier I've ever met who would say, 'Now's the time to take over the government.' We have a long tradition of following the rules."

His Korean friend had nodded, and Flynn knew that the man had thought him naive. Any student of history could give a dozen examples of such rules falling apart in crisis. Flynn had not been satisfied with his answer either.

As he left the library, Flynn considered that for all his years of service, he understood it only a little better now. If his Korean friend were with him as he pushed through the big bronze doors of West Point's library, Patrick Flynn would say that no tanks appeared in Washington in the summer of 1974 because two centuries of following the rules had built that mindset. Two centuries of soldiers swearing to support and defend the Constitution. Two centuries of steady—sometimes plodding—service. It didn't happen in a day; it didn't happen with one great general or one momentous decision; it didn't happen exclusively at West Point. But all those things contributed.

And as he walked through the steamy morning, returning the salutes of the cadets who would help guard that ethos when he had long since retired, Patrick Flynn knew that part of his job was to make sure that the young people around him learned to make all those tiny right decisions, day after day, constant as duty.

CHAPTER 11

KATHLEEN GATES SAT IN THE WAITING AREA OUTSIDE THE
Dean's office and went over, once more, what cards she
held.

Because of what her brother told her about the Dean's
plans to see himself as Superintendent, she hadn't been
surprised that the first call came from Simon.

If Braintree had officially told West Point of her accusation, the response would have come from General Moro,
who was in Tom's chain of command, or Flynn. And Tom
would have known. She was betting that Simon's call meant
he knew about the accusation she was going to level against
Holder. He knew, and he wanted to make that work for him
as well.

The Dean had called her at home and asked to meet her.
There was no place on post where they could meet without
being seen, so he suggested she come by the administration
building and his office. Kathleen, still playing the innocent
victim with nothing to hide, had agreed. His calling her had
already put him at a disadvantage. It would look, to any
observer, as if Simon had set out to influence her. This
belief gave Kathleen a sense of security. There would be two
meetings: the one that took place in Simon's office and the

one she reported. If it came down to it, she could lie about what was said, confident that she'd be believed.

If she had stopped to think about it, she might have been worried that lying was becoming easier for her, that she was digging herself deeper in. But whenever her conscience threatened, she told herself she was doing it for Tom.

She had tried to reach her brother at work because she wanted to ask him more about the Naval Academy's plan to downsize, but Brian was in meetings all day. As she moved about her house and considered the possibilities for this meeting, she became more convinced it had something to do with Simon's ambition to become Supe.

"Mrs. Gates," the secretary called to her. She was a hugely fat woman in a black dress that looked like a poncho. "You may go in now."

Kathleen passed through double oak doors and into an office that was much smaller than she'd expected. There were books and papers and file folders on every horizontal surface in the room, and even the magnificent view of the river through the windows behind the desk seemed diminished by the clutter.

"Mrs. Gates," the Dean said, entering the room after her. "Thank you so much for coming."

"Not at all, General," she said.

Simon offered her a chair; she sat down and watched his birdlike movements as he settled behind his desk.

She had seen him only from a distance at the parade field. He was smaller than she expected, and there was a nervous hesitancy in his movements, as if he expected to be told, at any moment, to sit still.

"Mrs. Gates," he began.

"Please call me Kathleen," she interrupted.

"Yes, of course," Simon said, looking even more nervous. Kathleen tried not to smile.

"I know that you've been going through some difficulties lately," he began. "That is, I know that the past week or so has been tough on you and your husband."

He paused, waiting for her to give him some encouragement, a little direction. Kathleen Gates just stared at him. He was making this up as he went along; his hesitancy convinced her that he was not acting on behalf of Flynn.

"I wanted to meet with you to open up a channel of communication," he continued.

"Between?" she asked.

"Pardon?"

"Between me and the Academy? Between me and the Dean's office?" she asked.

Simon shifted uncomfortably in his seat.

Kathleen had long ago ceased to be surprised at how indecisive and tenuous some men were, even men in responsible and allegedly powerful positions. There was a moment of quiet as she reveled in what was happening in the room: the power was shifting to her. She had to use it or let it slip away. Left on his own, Simon would dawdle and consider and move slowly, maybe for months. But the Bruckner Commission would lose interest in her story quickly, so Kathleen had to act fast. She had to force the issue.

"Or between you and me?" she asked.

Simon looked up, still unsure of how far he should go.

Kathleen Gates stood, stepped behind her chair and closed the door.

"Funny how no one wanted to talk to me when I was the one doing all the worrying," she said. "When it looked like my husband might get relieved over that ridiculous little incident with that cadet, nobody gave a damn."

Simon sat with his mouth open. Kathleen Gates hadn't meant to lecture him; she was surprised at how much anger was in her.

"No one cared what was going to happen to my family."

"I assure you, Mrs. Gates," Simon stuttered, "General Moro did not take his responsibility lightly."

"Yeah, whatever," she said, waving her hand. "Now because this same cadet screwed up and your precious West Point is at risk, everyone is suddenly concerned about me."

Simon moved his lips, but no sound came out. Kathleen Gates was sure of it now: Simon knew about her accusation.

"I knew they'd never be able to keep all that stuff secret, in spite of their talk about confidentiality," she said, stepping in front of the chair. She took a deep, calming breath, then sat down slowly in the big leather chair. Simon began to speak; Kathleen cut him off.

"Does Flynn know?"

The Dean was still for a long moment, then he nodded.

"Good. The Bruckner Commission is very interested in what I have to say about the command climate and why I didn't feel comfortable reporting this incident of sexual harassment."

Simon was still nodding, an annoying little tic. Kathleen leaned forward until she was almost touching his desk.

"I want the letter of reprimand pulled from my husband's records. . . ."

"Mrs. Gates," Simon said, still trying to resist. "I have no authority here. That decision rests with the Commandant."

"The Superintendent could override the Commandant," she said.

"I don't think General Flynn is inclined. . . ."

"I'm not talking about General Flynn as Superintendent," she said bluntly. "I'm talking about you as Superintendent."

Simon remained quiet.

"If they cut West Point in half," Kathleen said, "you'd be the logical choice for Super."

She wasn't convinced that this fact was true; she was hoping that Simon's ambition would make him a little less rational.

"What makes you so sure the Bruckner Commission is considering a downsizing?" Simon asked.

"It's one of the logical choices," she said. "Besides, isn't that what they're planning at the Naval Academy? And they can't help but consider that option if you propose it."

Simon looked around the room. Kathleen pictured a fish swimming around the bait.

"Make it one of a set of proposals," she went on. "Make it the most attractive one."

"That might not be enough," Simon said.

"Suppose General Flynn made some egregious error in handling this little drama," she said.

Simon thought of Flynn's reaction to the story; he hadn't believed Kathleen. Now it was clear that Flynn was right. The woman was a shark.

"Then he might leave the Academy to save it from bad publicity at such a critical time. You could serve as the interim Superintendent. From that position, anything is possible."

"I don't think General Flynn is so careless as to make a mistake significant enough to merit his resigning," Simon said. "And the actions of one cadet, no matter how bad, are not going to get him relieved."

"Of course not. It's how he handles things after he learns of the accusation," she said. Then, calmly, "I'm not finished playing hardball."

"What does that mean?"

"It means what it means. I want that letter taken out of my husband's file. That'll be your end of the deal."

"Mrs. Gates . . ."

"Stop jerking me around, General," Kathleen Gates said sharply. "This is what you want, so have the guts to go after it. Have the balls to admit it."

Simon was struck with a sense of how surreal this all was. When he called Kathleen Gates, he thought he might find some information that would help him. Now she was claiming she could bring down Flynn. It was too easy. In spite of his feeling that entering into a pact with this woman would turn out to be a bad idea, she was making it hard to resist.

"And if I refuse? If I take your story to General Flynn?"

"Then we're all going to be on the news, courtesy of Lamar Bruckner. And I'm sure you don't want that for West Point. Or for yourself."

Simon nodded.

Kathleen Gates gave him a most charming smile.

"You'll be hearing from me," she said. Then she stood and let herself out the office door.

Jackie Timmer parked her car in the lot at the Post Exchange and walked through the high, dark evergreens and into the cemetery proper. The light from nearby Washington Road did not reach this back part of the cemetery; she found a footpath, by the sound of her feet on the gravel, before her eyes adjusted to the gloom. Timmer walked slowly, enjoying a cool breeze that had come down the Hudson with a promise of a summer thunderstorm. To the left she could see part of the river, framed by branches still thick with leaves. She could not see very far in either direction; from this angle the river looked like a lake.

To her right were the ranks of stones, markers of many different shapes. Less than half, it seemed, were the standard government-issue white headstone. Nor was the cemetery arranged in the neat ranks and files of most American military cemeteries. This one was a series of concentric circles, with the oldest graves in the center, forming the smallest circles. Timmer had remarked, on one visit, how many of those plots from the nineteenth century belonged to the children of instructors and soldiers assigned to West Point, struck down by childhood illnesses that were no longer so deadly.

The wind picked up all at once, a short, strong blow that pulled at Timmer's skirt. She turned north, upriver, planting her feet apart and holding her arms away from her sides to let the air wash over her. It was heavy with the scent of rain and the tangy metallic smell she thought of as coming from the flat silver plate of water below the bluff.

She wore a long black dress, the only thing in her closet that was near eighteenth-century costume. It was close fitting, with a row of small black buttons running in a tight line down the center front, and a high, squared-off collar of black velvet. On a hanger, it looked like a priest's cassock, though that image disappeared when she put it on and it fell to the contours of her body. She had covered her shoulders with a muted scarf, dark purple, tied across her bosom. The modesty, she smiled to herself, would serve her well in a room full of cadets. She had left the house before she thought of wearing a hat, and so went back and found one: black felt, round, unornamented, flat brimmed.

I look like a little Amish girl, she'd thought as she studied herself in the mirror. But she was finding the costume fun, and so she wore the hat now, holding it on her head against the unpredictable wind.

She approached the Old Cadet Chapel from the rear, past the odd football-shaped headstone of Earl Blaik, coach of Army's national championship teams. Voices came to her from the front of the building; she turned the corner and stepped into the tiny circular drive filled with cadets. There was no sign of Layne Marshall.

"Evening, ma'am," one of the cadets said. Timmer recognized the young man; she'd taught him when he was a plebe.

"Hello, Mr. Pruitt."

The cadets with Pruitt straightened up a bit, not quite coming to attention—the setting was informal and Jackie was not in uniform. There were four men and a woman.

"Why are you all wearing that uniform?" Jackie asked.

The cadets wore their full dress coats, the famous high-collared gray tunic with the bullet buttons that West Pointers had worn since the early nineteenth century. Their starched white pants shone in the dull light from a streetlamp. The coats were form fitting, flattering on these athletic young men and women; they were also, Timmer knew from personal experience, excruciatingly uncomfortable.

"Part of the costume thing, I think, ma'am," one of the other cadets volunteered. She didn't recognize this one, but he looked like the others: young, healthy, scrubbed. Standing in the poor light, wrapped in their wasp-waisted uniforms and flat-front starched pants, even the homeliest among them looked good. Nubile.

"Well, there was no such thing as an eighteenth-century woman's uniform, so I had to go for a different look," Timmer said. She stood on her toes and twisted her hips a tiny bit, just enough to make her skirt swing. When she looked up, all four of the young men standing directly in front of her were staring at Jackie Timmer's body. She imagined she could feel the heat from their gaze on her sheathed legs. The young woman met her eyes.

The wind, hot on the back of her neck, tilted her hat forward. Timmer removed the cover, letting her thick hair whip her face. She had perfume on—something she never wore when in uniform—and she imagined the cadets, standing downwind, getting the scent of her.

Timmer rocked back, landing flat-footed so that the dress stopped moving. She was feeling dangerous.

"I hope it's not raining when we come out," the woman cadet said, bringing everyone back.

"Tell me about the lesson tonight," Timmer said.

"It's Jonathan Edwards's 'Sinners in the Hands of an

Angry God,' ma'am," Cadet Pruitt offered. "He delivered it in Massachusetts, I think. . . ."

"Enfield, Massachusetts, 1741," another cadet interrupted.

"Right," Pruitt said. He nodded as if this were something he would need to remember, something for a quiz.

"Anyway, he scared the dickens out of his congregation, really got the people going and all that. It was part of The Great Awakening, a religious revival."

"An upheaval," the woman cadet said. "That's what Professor Marshall called it. An 'upheaval.'"

They turned when they heard the tall doors of the chapel creak open. Timmer looked up, expecting to see someone framed in the light from the doorway, but the little building was dark inside. The figure on the small porch was dressed in dark clothing, his face just a pale smudge.

"Hear ye," the dark man called.

A few of the cadets in front of Timmer giggled.

"SILENCE!" the dark man commanded, and the young people became instantly quiet.

He stepped down among the cadets, and now Jackie could see that he had long hair, past his shoulders, that flew about in the wind swirling against the chapel wall. She stood perfectly still among the gray statues.

"You will march to the front pews," the man told them. "You will be silent."

She could see him more clearly now. He was in his sixties, his hair white, thin, unruly. He had a long face, as if some sculptor had stretched it too far. Just below the pointed chin, a white collar wrapped his thin neck. The light from the streetlamp, filtered through windblown trees, jumped and splattered across his sallow complexion. For all his unhealthy appearance, his voice was strong.

"As you sit in the darkness, think on your sins," he said. *"God knows your every straying step."*

He walked up to several cadets in turn, standing so close that Timmer thought he might plant an awful kiss on their cheeks.

The cadets dared not move.

The old man withdrew and the cadets, still silent as commanded, began to file into the narrow doors and into the dark chapel. Jackie Timmer was almost alone on the drive when the old man appeared beside her.

"Captain Timmer," he said.

The accent was odd, Timmer thought, or maybe it was the voice, which seemed to well up from a body bigger than this one. Timmer turned to face the old man and smiled.

"That was quite a performance," she said. "You've got them going already."

There was no flicker of acknowledgment; it was as if she were speaking a different language, as if she had not spoken at all. Above her, she could hear the wind push through twisting leaves.

"You will sit in the rear of the sanctuary on the right hand side," the old man said.

Timmer merely nodded; the old man followed the cadets into the chapel.

"Guess I'd better be careful not to step out of character," she said as she gathered her skirts and headed for the door.

At first the inside of the building looked black; it took a moment for Jackie's eyes to adjust to the dim light of candles burning on four overhead chandeliers, with another brace on a table beside the tiny pulpit. From the rear of the chapel, which measured only sixty feet from back to front, she could see the cadets sitting stiffly in their seats. The only sound was the reeling of the wind just beyond the windows. The reason for the late meeting became instantly clear: the darkness, the candlelight, the stiff uniforms, the unfamiliar surroundings (the Old Cadet Chapel was used only for memorial services), the imposed silence, and the actor all took the cadets away from the familiar, made them that much more vulnerable. And the thunderstorm brewing outside was the perfect stage accompaniment.

The setting was perfect, but was saved from being mere theater by what the cadets brought to the chapel.

This will work because we're so used to being told exactly what to do, Timmer thought to herself. The cadets would sit perfectly still, not talking, not looking about, for no other reason than they had been told to do so.

We're such sheep, sometimes, she thought.

Timmer felt her way into the rear pew on the right so that she could see the pulpit between the cadets before her. She sat quietly, hands in her lap; and when someone moved into the pew beside her, she resisted looking for a few long seconds. When she did look, Layne Marshall was sitting beside her. He wore a dark suit, like the actor's, with just a tiny patch of white showing at his throat, the collar high on his neck.

"Reverend Dimmesdale, I presume," she whispered.

Marshall brought his hand quickly to his mouth; Jackie stifled a laugh. She sat back serenely, hands primly folded, as her mind raced wildly and her pulse tried to keep up. The back of the chapel, far from the uncertain light of the candles, was dark as a cave; she could reach out and touch him, hold his hand, slip her arm in his. A door opened at the front of the sacristy and the wind, given an opening, bulled in, killing the flames on three or four candles near the pulpit. There was a sharp, eerie wind-whistle up high near the ceiling, and a river sound closer by that Timmer knew was her rushing blood. Then all in an instant the room lit up in bleached white relief, and there was a sharp crack like stone splitting as lightning licked down to the surface of the river and Jackie Timmer and half the cadets jumped straight up in their seats.

"Oh!" she cried and when she came down the hair on her neck buzzed with the sudden electric charge. Layne Marshall had his hand on top of hers, the effect was anything but calming.

"GOD KNOWS YOUR SINS!"

In the moment of the lightning's flash the old man with the long white hair had climbed the pulpit. Jackie Timmer could see it in the way he walked: the dark-suited actor *was* Jonathan Edwards. He raised both arms high above his head, black scarecrow limbs that ended in frilly cuffs and hands like long bones. Another man in black arranged several candelabra at the front of the chapel; the yellow light painted moving shadows on the wall above the minister. He was remarkably thin; in spite of his age, his skin was stretched tight over his skull, a *memento mori.*

"There is *nothing* that keeps wicked men at any one moment out of hell," Edwards thundered at them, "but the mere *pleasure* of God."

The cadets in front of her could have been mannequins

for all they moved. Edwards leaned on the edge of the pulpit, hands and face glowing like tallow, and his voice rattled and rolled until the tapers seemed to quake at his words.

"We find it easy to tread on and crush a worm that we see crawling on the earth; it is easy for us to cut or singe a single thread that any thing hangs by: thus it is easy for God, when he pleases, to cast his enemies down to hell. What are we, that we should think to stand before him, at whose rebuke the earth trembles, and before whom the rocks are thrown down?"

There was another flash and crack, and Jackie Timmer reached for Marshall, entwined her fingers in his, pressed their hands on his hard thigh. Outside, now, there was thunder, like great barrels set loose to roll down the mountain-sided valley.

"The sword of divine justice is every moment brandished over your heads, and it is nothing but the hand of arbitrary mercy, and God's mere will, that holds it back."

Jackie Timmer thought they would talk when it came to this, their first touch, because it was Marshall's voice, his words that had first pulled her toward him. But all her longing came to an inarticulate point that for the moment was centered in the hot flesh of her palm.

At the front of the room, the figure in black beat his hands sharply on the pulpit and the lightning cracked again, as if on cue.

"The wrath of God burns against you!" he cried.

In the back, in the dark, and hidden by the pew, Layne Marshall had grabbed her arm with his free hand; his fingers in the muscle above her elbow. He leaned close to her. They were face to face when he spoke, but his words were lost in the deep bass of thunder.

"Your damnation does not slumber," Jonathan Edwards assailed them. "The pit is prepared, the fire is made ready, the furnace is now hot, ready to receive you."

Timmer looked up at the ghost-figure in black. His eyes were wide; he flung spittle and rage with every word.

Layne Marshall still leaned close, but she could not hear him over the threats from the pulpit, over the sound of the wind pulsing at the windows, above the stampeding sound of her own heart.

". . . outside . . ." Marshall was saying.

"The flames do now rage and glow. . . ."

". . . whatever you want . . ." Marshall said.

She missed the words, but his breath was hot on her ear now; he pulled her arm to his chest. Their clasped hands were between his legs; under the cloak he was hugely erect.

Another crack as the door just behind the last seats blew open, then crashed shut. Edwards's voice had grown louder, closer still.

"The glittering sword is whet and held over you and the pit hath opened its mouth under you. . . ."

In the rows before them the cadets sat transfixed, eyes straight ahead, while in the back of the room Jackie Timmer tried not to think of her husband. When she turned again to Marshall, he was so close that his lips brushed her eyebrow.

"I want. . . ." she breathed. Her voice faltered but the wind did not, and then Layne Marshall was on his feet, holding her by the hand, pulling her to the door and she was following him, not looking back. He yanked the door open; the wind blasted them and danced up the aisle underfoot and they stepped out into the storm.

"There is the dreadful pit and the glowing flames of the wrath of God," Edwards called out.

Jackie looked back. No one was watching them, save the preacher.

"There is hell's wide, gaping mouth open; and you have nothing to stand upon, nor anything to take hold of; there is nothing between you and hell but the air. . . ."

And they were out the door, Edwards's voice fading in her ears as the wind bellowed and bent the big trees above them. Marshall did not look at her, only led her by the hand back the way she had come, down the gravel path as the wind spun loose leaves at them and blown gravel stung her ankles. Timmer was hurrying, almost running, her mouth dry.

They passed the little building that had once been a caretaker's cottage. To her right she could see the Anderson family monument, a low wall that looked like a fountain. Marshall darted between sheltering trees and shrubs, stepped among the markers; he knew what he was looking for. He stopped suddenly at a tiny stone bench, and she nearly tripped into him in the dark. He caught her in both arms, pulling her tight to him, chest to chest.

Jackie Timmer could not remember making a single conscious decision that had brought her here, nor did she stop to wonder. She had forgotten about her promises, she had forgotten about the cadets nearby and her role as a model, as an officer. She had pushed out of her mind everything except the moment and the exquisite burning that seemed to come up alongside her throat, that was in her lips, in her loins as she pushed herself into this man.

Layne Marshall hooked her in his arms, pressed his splayed fingers into the small of her back, brought his open mouth to hers. He kissed her hard, and Jackie Timmer was startled by the electric taste of his tongue in her mouth, the sharp stab of his beard on her lips; she was shocked even more by the feeling that she could not draw close enough. Her hands were on the back of his head, pulling him to her, raking his long hair forward; she willed him closer even than two bodies could be, wanting to occupy the same space.

She bit his lower lip, hard, then darted her tongue across his teeth. When he responded she caught his tongue in her lips and sucked it hard enough to hurt. They stumbled, locked together, heads twisting, all mouths and jagged breaths. Marshall put his hands under the cheeks of her ass and she leaped up, a little hop that landed her with legs wrapped around his middle, her hips bent forward so that she could feel his hard swell against her. She leaned her head back and his mouth found her throat, tongue pressed hard under the ridge of her jaw, along the column of her neck. And then his hands were under her dress, inside her panties, and she squeezed with her legs and lifted higher still so that his fingers could find her, and it wasn't until he probed and stroked her that she found that she was tremendously, deliciously wet, wet as she had not been for a long time, as she had never been.

"On the bench," she breathed, and he sat her down gently.

But she was having nothing of gentle, not tonight, and she

raked her nails across the back of his neck as he bent over her, pulling at her panties.

And then the rain.

It did not simply begin; it did not test the earth or measure gravity with a few drops. It came all at once, in a solid sheet of water, warmer than the air, and Jackie Timmer leaned back on her elbows as her lover explored her and she moaned up the hot river of falling rain. She quickly undid the buttons on the front of her dress, unfastened the center snap of her bra, and let the rain find her breasts. She imagined she could feel steam rising there, like water thrown on hot coals, and Layne was with her, hulking down there and all but blotted out by the torrent and the darkness, all but for the stiff, insistent invasion of his hands.

And then he stood before her, the rain drawing long vertical lines in the liquid dark, and she knew that he was opening his pants and although he was going as fast as he could she could not wait. She slid her hips to the edge of the stone bench, now a flat panel of black water. The lightning cracked again over the river and the sound shook them. The rain was tremendous, sharp pinpricks stinging her bare chest, forcing her to shut her eyes, to hang on to the rounded stone of her perch. The storm was massive, impossibly scaled, and in all its power it only served to remind her of her need to be filled. She wanted it all, Layne, the water, the lightning and thunder and flashing light—she wanted it all inside her, but only Layne obliged her.

Thirty feet away, inside the chapel, the actor portraying Jonathan Edwards reached his climax, drawing out his words, singing his tale of sure damnation to a roomful of cadets made believers by the cracking storm.

"The God that holds you *over the pit of hell,* much as one holds a spider or some *loathsome* insect, *abhors* you, and is *dreadfully* provoked: his wrath toward you burns like fire; he looks upon you as worthy of nothing else, but to be cast into the fire."

Marshall had his arms beside her now, and he entered her quickly. Timmer moved so that she had all of him, her legs wrapped around his back, her strong thighs pulling him toward her, demanding a rhythm. She tore at his shirt, watched the water shine on his chest in waves.

She put her hand between her legs and stroked herself with the pads of two circling fingers while he was inside her—something she had never done before but had often thought about.

Jackie climaxed first, awash in rain and alight in the storm, wind and water beating against her cheeks, into her open mouth. And when Layne reached the precipice she pulled his face to hers, pressed her open mouth on his even as he cried out, catching his groan and his breath and some vital part of him as she swallowed his come-cry.

Inside the chapel, the preacher went on.

"Let every one that is out of Christ now awake and fly from the wrath to come. The wrath of Almighty God is now undoubtedly hanging over a great part of this congregation: let every one fly out of Sodom: Haste and escape for your lives, look not behind you, escape to the mountain, lest you be consumed."

His voice was still strong, but there was no hearing him out in the storm.

CHAPTER 12

ALEX TRAINOR WAS SITTING ON A FOOTLOCKER, HIS INJURED arm propped up on the metal and wood frame of his bed, when Holder came in the room. A single desklamp that shone in the corner provided the only light.

"What's up, Lefty?" Holder asked.

Trainor looked up at his roommate, but said nothing.

"Somebody in history asked me if you were sick or in the hospital again. Said you weren't in your econ class this morning."

"I cut."

Holder laughed. "That's rich," he said. There was no way to get away with missing a class at West Point. Cadets showed up where they were supposed to be or faced severe consequences. Wayne Holder had never even heard of a cadet deliberately missing class.

"I skipped this afternoon, too. Four classes total. I'm finished going to class," Trainor said, his voice flat. "I'm going to resign."

"What the hell are you talking about?" Holder asked.

"I've decided to resign, Wayne. . . ."

"In your senior year? Are you nuts? You can't do that."

291

"Of course I can," Trainor said.

Holder found his roommate's calmness unnerving. It was as if he'd already gone through with it.

"You'll have to go into the Army and they'll send you to East Jesus, Idaho, or some other godforsaken place as punishment. . . ."

Trainor stared at Holder. He was practically sitting on the floor, stuck in the corner between the bed and the sink. He looked like a little boy.

"All right," Holder said, dropping his books on the desk and turning to face his friend. "Let's take this from the top. What makes you think you want to resign?"

"My girlfriend. . . ." Trainor began.

"You have a girlfriend?" Holder interrupted. He couldn't believe Trainor had kept such a thing from him.

". . . is pregnant."

"Holy shit," Holder said. He dropped onto the trunk at the foot of his own bed; they were separated by a few feet of cool floor. "This is the first I've heard about you even having a girlfriend, Alex," he said.

"I know, and I'm sorry I've been so secretive. But this is all very new to me, Wayne. And then when we started . . . you know, I was embarrassed."

Before coming to West Point, Wayne Holder had no experience with the kind of religious conservatives who often made their way onto the covers of the news magazines, demanding legislated morality, prayer in school, and end to abortion. He didn't doubt that these people were real, he just hadn't met any of them until he met Alex Trainor. He'd been suspicious of Trainor at first, but once he got past the point where he wanted to save Wayne, Trainor was a good guy. He was still capable of an amazing degree of denial, Wayne thought. But it turned out he was human after all.

Wayne watched his roommate, who was so obviously tortured with guilt. He wanted to gloat a little bit, but that wasn't possible in the face of such obvious pain.

"Her name?"

"Ruth."

"And now she's pregnant?" Holder asked.

Trainor nodded, pushed the heel of his good hand into his eye. He was crying.

"And she wants to have the baby?"

Trainor's head snapped up.

"Of course," he said sharply. "We'd never consider harming our own child. That would be. . . ." he shuddered rather than finish the sentence.

"I didn't mean to imply anything," Holder said. "It's not an unreasonable question. What about adoption?"

Trainor shook his head. "I need to take care of her and the baby."

"So you plan on marrying this woman. Is that why you need to resign?"

"She quit school and her parents cut her allowance. She needs me to take care of her."

"Did you tell her that you'd marry her after graduation?"

"She doesn't want to wait."

"She wants you to throw away three years of preparation because she's in a hurry?"

"She doesn't want the baby born without a father, born out of wedlock."

Even as he said it, Alex Trainor wondered if that were true. Ruth had never actually said anything like that to him. Maybe he was putting his concerns on her.

"Wed*lock*," Holder said. "Now there's a word for you."

"C'mon, Wayne."

"OK," Holder said. "Doesn't she realize how much better off the two—three—of you will be if you can just wait a few months? Maybe her parents would be willing to help out if you explained things to them."

"She's afraid to tell them."

"She's afraid to tell them, so she wants to take the *easy* way out and get married?" he asked sarcastically. "For such a smart guy, Alex, you can be a real dummy sometimes."

"She wants to be able to tell them that we're married, or are about to get married, when she tells them she's pregnant."

"It's not going to do either of you any good, Alex, if you throw away all that you've worked for these last three years. You're so close, man. There are other ways to do this."

"We're taking some time to think," Trainor said. "We agreed not to talk for a few days."

"Maybe I can talk some sense into her."

There was a bit of hopefulness in Trainor's eyes when he looked at Holder.

"Would you try?" he asked.

"Sure thing, buddy. But you've got to get your ass in gear and go to class. And we'd better go to Major Gates."

Trainor looked at Holder.

"He'll have the attendance reports," Trainor said.

"And he'll want to know why you weren't in class," Holder said, finishing the thought. "Better we should tell him instead of making him contact you first."

"Will you go in with me?"

"Sure. It'll make me look good in comparison," Holder said. "I can say, 'Hey, sir, your wife gave me a blowjob, but at least I didn't cut class.'"

Trainor almost smiled. "This won't be fun," he said.

"You can just offer up your good hand as a sacrifice. Maybe he'll just smash it in a drawer or something and you can call it even."

Kathleen Gates found the Superintendent with the help of the post newspaper. Flynn was scheduled to attend a small ceremony at the alumni center on Tuesday morning; he was there to accept a sizable gift from the widow of a member of the Class of 1948. Kathleen Gates installed herself in the Association of Graduates gift shop and watched for the end of the ceremony, which was attended by Flynn, his aide, a representative from the Association of Graduates, West Point's alumni organization, the widow and her two grown sons.

She had planned this "accidental" meeting for days; her whole scheme for rescuing Tom's career was riding on this meeting with Flynn, and she was feeling the pressure. But she hadn't come this far to turn back. She walked through the little shop, fingering all the little West Point trinkets: etched wine glasses and beer mugs, lap blankets and cufflinks and tie clasps and scores of framed prints.

You could turn your home into a shrine, she thought.

Kathleen saw the Superintendent's car parked on the

street outside, so she knew which door he would use. She positioned herself in the rotunda and watched the little party come down from the upstairs office of the President of the AOG; she wiped her sweaty palms on the light fabric of her dress.

Patrick Flynn was talking to his aide, a handsome black major, as he came down the wide stairway. The general was shorter than she expected, but he had a serious air about him, and as he turned to look at her—she stood in his path—she knew that he was the polar opposite of the tentative, quivering General Simon.

I'll have to be careful with this one, she told herself.

"Hello, General," Kathleen Gates said. She resisted the temptation to flash her most winning smile, the one that rarely failed to make men notice her, or even stop to talk when she wanted them to. She was playing the victim here, and she made an effort to look upset.

"Hello," Flynn said, pausing.

As she expected, he was too much of a gentleman to walk by a woman who was upset.

"Is something wrong?" Flynn asked gently.

"Oh, no," she fluttered, leaving no doubt that something was wrong. She took a step as if she wanted to leave, hoping Flynn wouldn't let her get away. It was important that the talk, which she had planned completely in her head, look like his idea.

The aide, whose nametag said Carter, seemed impatient. He held up a notebook and began to speak. Flynn said, "I'll meet you in the car, Darrell," and the major disappeared.

"I hope I'm not being too forward," Flynn said, "but you look upset."

Kathleen looked at Flynn and let the tears come. Flynn, as she expected, was disconcerted. He couldn't just stand there, but he could hardly take her in his arms and comfort her, either.

"Can I get you a glass of water?" he asked.

Kathleen wondered if men always offered water to crying women because they thought of it as fluid loss.

"I just wasn't expecting to see you here, sir," she said. "I'm Kathleen Gates."

Something passed over Flynn's eyes, and for a moment

she thought he might walk away. She had to control the situation.

"Maybe we could find a place to sit for a moment," she said.

Flynn was clearly uncomfortable at the prospect of talking to her, but Kathleen took his arm and leaned on it a bit. Flynn responded as if programmed and led her to a small sitting area just off what looked like a ballroom.

Flynn sat stiffly in his chair across from her. She experienced the same little thrill of danger she'd felt in Simon's office.

"I've been so upset these past few days," she said. "I've even met with a representative of the Bruckner Commission."

Flynn clearly did not want to be here, having this conversation with her, and any junior lawyer could have told him he should keep his mouth shut. Kathleen was positive that he knew about the accusation she'd leveled against Holder, but he couldn't admit to that. The interviews were supposed to be confidential. Still, some part of him looked intrigued, and some part of him, Kathleen Gates knew, was too proud to admit that he should run. That's not how soldiers act.

"You're free to meet with the commission's representatives," Flynn said. "They need to hear about West Point from all quarters."

"I'm just so worried," Kathleen said vaguely. "I mean, everything seems to be happening at once."

She watched for some reaction from Flynn to that comment. He kept a poker face.

"I mean, I was worried over this awful letter of reprimand that is going to end my husband's career."

Flynn looked as if he wanted to speak, but he held his counsel.

No matter, Kathleen thought. *It might be easier if you brought up Cadet Holder, but finally it won't make a difference.*

"Oh, and I know you must be so worried, too," she said as sweetly as possible. She reached out and touched Flynn's knee; he discreetly pulled it out of her reach.

"I mean, you have the whole Academy to think about."

She snuffled mightily, reached into her purse for a tissue,

and blew her nose. A man in a suit came into the room, saw them sitting side by side, then left.

"In fact," she said, "we're kind of in the same situation."

"How's that?" Flynn asked.

"You need to protect West Point," she began. Her heart banged away inside her chest; there was no predicting what his reaction would be when she spoke the next words. But she had done what she could to cover herself, and this was no time to be timid.

"And I want to protect my family and my husband's career."

Unlike Simon, General Flynn did not seem at all surprised at what he was hearing. Yet Kathleen Gates had no doubt that he knew exactly what she was proposing. The accusation against Holder sat between them, like some ugly pet in the middle of a party that none of the guests would acknowledge.

"Mrs. Gates," he said, speaking carefully. "I appreciate that you're concerned about your husband's career. As for the letter—and this is West Point's position—it is in no way connected to any discussion you might have with representatives from the Bruckner Commission.

"What you say to those people is entirely up to you."

He leaned forward and lowered his voice. He could have been assuring her; he could have been challenging her.

"I'm sure you'll be guided by your conscience," he said.

Kathleen Gates wanted to scream. Her husband had served faithfully for over a decade; she had dragged her family from one Army post to another, had spent months alone wondering if Tom was safe. And the thanks they got was a letter—a single sheet of paper!—that would cut Tom off from the life he loved. They wanted to do that to her husband, and still this man across from her had the nerve to talk about conscience.

But Kathleen Gates didn't scream; she smiled.

"Thank you so much, General, for your time. We are all facing tough choices, I suppose."

She stood and Flynn followed suit. She offered her hand; when he took it she squeezed his fingers.

"Let's hope we all make the right decisions," she said.

* * * *

"You know, if I let Trainor get away with this kind of crap, people will say it's because I feel bad about his hand," Tom Gates said.

He was sitting behind his desk, chair tilted back, hands on top of his big head, while Wayne Holder stood before him, feet shoulder width apart, hands joined in the small of his back. The position was called "at ease," but Wayne Holder wasn't.

"I understand, sir, but this is no ordinary screwup. Cadet Trainor skipped class yesterday because he had decided to resign."

"Get the hell out of here," Gates said. "At the beginning of his last year? What is he thinking?"

"He thought that was the only solution to his problems," Holder said. "But I talked him into trying, at least, another way."

Gates let the chair come forward so that all legs were on the floor. "I'm listening," he said.

Holder went through a quick explanation of Trainor's dilemma, half-expecting Gates to interrupt with comments about how stupidly Alex was behaving. But Gates listened closely, nodding almost imperceptibly from time to time.

"And there's something else you should know about Alex, sir, something that makes this all the more sensitive. He's from a very religious, very conservative Christian family. I'm sure he's convinced that he's going to hell for this. At any rate, he'll want to do what he thinks is the right thing and marry this girl."

Gates ran his hand over the stubble on his chin. Holder braced himself for an explosion, something along the lines of "you people could screw up a wet dream." But Gates just looked thoughtful.

"So what's your plan?" Gates asked.

It was not a question Holder had expected; fortunately he had an answer. As he spoke, he wondered where Major Mercury had gone and who this imposter was.

"I thought I'd try to talk to her, try to convince her that they'd all be better off if Alex got his commission. All we need to do is get her to agree to wait."

"That sounds like an approach," Gates said. "Maybe you do have some leadership ability somewhere, Holder.

"All right, I'll tell you what," the officer continued. "I'm going to put Trainor on room confinement for missing class. He loses his weekends, but maybe that'll do him some good. If he spends time apart from this girl, he might have a clearer head as to what he needs to do."

"Thank you, sir," Holder said.

"Don't thank me, Holder," Gates snapped. "I'm doing my job. And besides, he isn't out of the woods yet. You tell him if he screws up again—and I'm talking a speck of dust on his uniform—I'll hammer him.

"Now you get your ass in gear and talk to this girl, but don't screw it up. If she chooses not to buy the part about their being better off, that's her business. Let me know what she says, you read me?"

"Yes, sir," Holder answered.

"Good. Now shove off."

Holder snapped to attention, did an about face, and walked quickly out of the office. He hustled up the stairs and found Alex Trainor sitting in their room.

"How did it go?" he asked.

"That wasn't our Tac," Holder said. "Someone kidnapped Major Mercury and replaced him with an android. I mean, he listened and was downright understanding. Maybe we had him pegged wrong.

"I think," Holder continued, "that Major Gates is getting in touch with his sensitive side, his feminine side."

Gates turned around and looked out the window. He could see plebes entering and leaving the gym, hurrying to change so they could rush to their next class so they could sprint back to the barracks for intramurals and then race through dinner to hustle to study barracks. It never stopped.

Gates had been prepared to rip into Holder if the cadet had come by with some lame story about why Trainor missed four classes, but Holder had used his head. The Tactical Officer was pleased and glad he had declared a truce about what happened out by MacArthur's statue. Holder was showing promise. But something else had come up.

Tom Gates had gotten wind of something between Kathleen and Holder. Gates heard, fourth or fifth hand, that

Kathleen had called Holder at the barracks. Nothing more than that, really, but it had given Tom Gates pause. Just for a moment.

It wasn't that he didn't trust Kathleen around other men. Or in this case, boys. It was more that he was never quite sure what she was thinking. Her mind worked at a different level, at a different speed. She'd told him time and again since that first incident that she loved him and wanted to protect him, his career, and their life. Tom Gates had given up when he got the letter; Kathleen only seemed to become more determined. Tom Gates didn't know her plans and was fairly certain she wouldn't tell him if he asked.

Gates sat back down, picked up the phone and tried his home number again. Kathleen had been out earlier; this time she answered on the first ring.

"Hey, it's me," he said. "I called earlier."

"I was at the alumni center gift shop," she said. "I thought maybe your parents would enjoy something from there. Their anniversary is coming up."

"Did you get them anything?"

"No. Not because I couldn't find anything cheesy enough to fit in with your parents' decor. Once I got up there I didn't feel like shopping."

"I just finished talking with your buddy, Wayne Holder."

Kathleen Gates was caught off guard. The expression was one Tom often used, mostly when he was being ironic. He might say something like, "That was back when your buddy, Mussolini, had the trains running on time," or "When your buddy, Ted Bundy, got fried." Still, the mention of Wayne Holder's name gave her pause.

"He was in here to plead for his roommate, Trainor. That little asshole skipped four classes yesterday."

Kathleen breathed again. "You're kidding me," she said.

"Yeah, he was all set to resign because his girlfriend is knocked up and he thinks he needs to marry her right away. Holder is going to try to talk some sense into the girl, convince her that it would be better to wait until after graduation."

Kathleen pictured Alex Trainor, nervous and a bit smug, trying to muster the courage to challenge her version of what had happened with Holder. She had backed him off handily.

"Holder is going to do that?"

"He's going to try. I put Trainor on room confinement, so he won't be making any trips to the city."

Kathleen's mouth was dry. She didn't like talking to Tom about these cadets. They knew too much that could get her in trouble, and they were in and out of Tom's office several times a day. Now Tom would be watching Trainor even more closely, and he'd be talking to Holder more often. It was only a matter of time until something slipped out. Tom would hear about her accusations eventually, but if it was after things had played out, she thought she could control him. She didn't need much time to get things where she wanted them with Flynn and Simon, but she saw now that she wasn't going to be able to let the plot unfold by itself. She was going to have to push things along.

Kathleen was reasonably sure that Holder wouldn't talk; the consequences for him would be devastating. She wasn't so sure about Trainor, who had always been so holier-than-thou. He could blow things wide open.

"You still there, honey?" Tom said.

"Yeah," she answered. "Tell me, did Trainor's girlfriend consider an abortion?"

"No, I don't think so. Trainor is a serious Bible-thumper. Wouldn't dream of it."

"Yeah, but what about the girlfriend?"

"I don't know for sure, but I imagine she's thinking along the same lines if she wants to get married."

"That's good," Kathleen said. "They don't need to compound their problems with something that would haunt them for years."

She licked her lips.

"Maybe I could talk to this girlfriend. You know, woman to woman. She'd probably like an explanation about all this military stuff from someone other than one of you guys."

"Hey, that'd be great, Kathleen," Tom said enthusiastically. "You wouldn't mind doing that?"

"Not at all."

"Good, wonderful. I'll get her number from Holder. I'd hate to see Trainor and his girlfriend screw things up without at least considering all the options available to them.

"By the way, did you talk to Holder on the orderly room phone the other night?"

"Sure," Kathleen said. Her pulse took off; she suddenly felt hot. What had Holder said?

"About what?"

"I called to ask about his roommate," she lied. "You know, a little compassion."

She made herself pause, took a breath so as not to seem too anxious.

"Why do you ask? What did Holder say?"

"Oh, he didn't mention it. I heard it from someone else," Tom said.

"Oh," Kathleen Gates said. But she didn't trust her voice, so she said her goodbyes and hung up the phone.

She had lied to her husband. And that was going to happen again, no doubt, before this was all over.

Kathleen Gates stood at the kitchen counter, stared out the window above the sink, and told herself—again—that this was for Tom. It was all for Tom and her family.

After he hung up, Tom Gates lifted the framed photo of his family from the windowsill. As often happened, just when he'd been ready to question Kathleen's motives, just when he began to wonder about what made her tick, she surprised him. Now she was willing to reach out and help a young woman she'd never met.

A few of the men in Tom's company were engaged to young women with little knowledge of what they were getting themselves into. Being newly married was hard enough, being an Army wife, Kathleen had often told him, presented a different set of difficulties. Whatever happened between Trainor and this young woman, it would be good to have friendly advice from someone like Kathleen.

"Another crisis handled well, Major Gates," he said aloud as he reached for the pile of papers in his in-box. "These cadets don't know how lucky they are."

Dorothy Sayer came into the meeting late and made, Van Grouw thought, as much noise as she possibly could.

"Sorry I'm late," she said, looking not at all bothered.

They were sitting around one large, round table. Sayer pulled a chair from another table nearby and pushed it in beside Claude Braintree. Van Grouw thought of baby pigs pushing at each other to get to the biggest teats.

"Well, well, well," Braintree said. "and what news do you bring us from the front, Dorothy?"

Sayer swept her blond hair back and gave an insincere smile to the others at the table. She clearly loved being the center of attention, Van Grouw thought. She could have accomplished that much based on her looks.

"I just had a very interesting meeting with a woman who had quite a story to tell about General Flynn, the Superintendent."

Braintree, Van Grouw noticed, was staring at Sayer's breasts. His eyes clicked upward as she spoke and he seemed on the verge of saying something when Sayer bulled on.

"It seems that the Superintendent offered to remove an unfavorable action against her husband in exchange for her silence on this sexual harassment issue."

Braintree held up a hand; Sayer stopped talking.

"Hold on just a minute," he said sharply, clearly unhappy that Sayer had spoken in front of the whole group. "Let's you and I discuss this in private first, shall we?"

"Certainly," Sayer said. She folded her hands in front of her. There was a tiny smile at the corners of her pretty mouth, Van Grouw saw. She had gotten everyone's attention, and if that meant incurring a little of Braintree's displeasure, well, she could fix that later in the boss's hotel room.

That bitch, Van Grouw thought.

He looked down at his notes. He had been prepared to brief Braintree on his plans to investigate the entire Tactical Department; he wanted to see if Gates's abuses of Cadet Dearborn were part of a larger pattern. In his own mind, he believed that Gates was probably an aberration, but if he wanted to capture Braintree's attention—and, more importantly, the attention of Senator Bruckner himself—he needed something a little more dramatic.

One man's misconduct wasn't going to be enough to

attract notice from Braintree for very long, or from Bruckner at any point. Unless that one man was the Superintendent.

And it sounded like that slut Sayer had stumbled into just that situation.

Van Grouw listened as the other staff members briefed. All of them, it seemed to Van Grouw, had the same reaction he did: they felt suddenly upstaged by Sayer.

"Sandy, what do you have?" Braintree asked.

Nothing on the Superintendent, Van Grouw thought.

"I'm continuing my look at the Tactical Department," he answered. "I'm curious as to whether the methods being used to train cadets—such as forcing them to box—are in line with what the academy professes."

"Oh," Braintree said. "You're still on that?"

Out of the corner of his eye, Van Grouw thought he saw Dorothy Sayer hide a smile behind her hand.

I'll fix you, you witch, Van Grouw thought.

There were two ways out of this. He would continue his own work—maybe drag something out of Dearborn that was sensational enough to attract Braintree's attention.

And if there isn't anything good enough, we'll stage something.

The other way, clearly, was to discredit Sayer. Braintree had seemed a bit skeptical; maybe it wouldn't be so difficult.

For that, I need the name of the mystery woman.

Braintree listened to a few other status reports, most of which had to do with money. West Point was expensive, no one would deny that. But with the ever-tightening budgets following the end of the Cold War came ever-stricter money management. The dollars were spent wisely. It was as if West Point operated on the assumption that any day would see some hostile Member of Congress descending to poke into the account books. The books were that clean.

And for the Bruckner Commission, that meant boring. In spite of all the public talk about the Senator's concern about taxpayer dollars, there simply wasn't much there.

Which is why, Sandy Van Grouw mused, *we're all looking for dirty laundry.*

"Very well," Braintree went on. "Let's not forget, people,

that we need to keep our eyes open. Don't let yourself become too narrowly focused."

Braintree stood up.

"I think that's it, then," he said. He turned to the door, then back to Sayer.

"I'd like to speak with you, Dorothy."

"Certainly," she said.

Van Grouw stepped behind his chair and headed for the door.

"Sandy."

It was Sayer. She was standing beside her chair, savoring the moment, it seemed to him. She smiled at him, swept her hair back.

"You don't look like you're enjoying yourself very much."

"Well," Van Grouw said, forcing his own smile. "Things are really only beginning to get interesting."

He turned and walked away. There were still three or four people in the room when he reached the doorway and turned back to Sayer.

"Don't forget, Dorothy. Claude wants to see you in his room."

"My dear Dorothy," Braintree said when Dorothy Sayer let herself in with her own key.

"You must be careful about what you let the others know. Loose lips sink ships and all that."

"I'm sorry, Claude," she said. She walked over to him and kissed him on the forehead, then sat down on the edge of the bed.

"I guess I got a little excited in there. I should have told you everything first."

"Tell me now," he said, reaching over and patting her pretty knee.

Sayer told him about that morning's follow-up call to Kathleen Gates.

"I went there to get more details on what happened between her and this cadet. She's been very vague and I was starting to wonder if she was going to come through for us. When I got there the poor woman started crying, sobbing. She's so upset and she's completely out of her element.

She's a bit unsophisticated and hasn't a clue how to handle all this."

"All what, dear?" Braintree asked patiently.

"Mrs. Gates ran into the Superintendent this morning, I forget where, exactly."

You would, Braintree thought.

"Anyway, the Superintendent remarked about how difficult things have been for her lately. Kathleen said something about the letter killing her husband's career, and General Flynn said they had similar concerns. He wants to protect the academy from bad publicity, and she wants to protect her husband's career.

"And then he said to her, 'Maybe we can make a trade.'"

"Trade what?"

"Kathleen Gates claims that General Flynn knew about the assault—the alleged assault—and that he offered to pull the letter in exchange for her silence."

Braintree thought it highly unlikely that Flynn would know about Kathleen Gates's story of sexual assault. Unlikely, but not impossible.

"I don't suppose anyone else heard this exchange," Braintree asked.

"No," Sayer said. "Flynn was very careful that no one else was around."

Or Kathleen was very careful, he thought.

Braintree sat back in the chair and looked out the window. He considered reminding Sayer that they were not at West Point to conduct criminal investigations. He thought about warning her against allowing herself to be manipulated by people with other agendas. He might also have told her that it was clear she was competing with the rest of the staff.

If Flynn did know about the accusations, from some leak in the Senator's office, or even from a leak started by the talkative Dorothy Sayer, he might act on it. It was possible that Flynn, eager to protect West Point at a time of intense scrutiny, would want Mrs. Gates's accusations to go away. But it seemed unlikely that Flynn would be so ham-handed.

Which left Kathleen Gates, whose name was coming up too often for mere coincidence.

It could be that the woman had dreamed up this entire

scenario. The timing was that unbelievable. Maybe she had seduced the cadet—although Sayer had described her as frumpy. She could have made that part up, or she might have actually played it through with the cadet. Locked up in the barracks all the time, the little soldiers were probably horny enough to screw mud.

Kathleen Gates might have made up the entire story about meeting Flynn. Or she might have met him and then lied about what was said. Then it would simply be a matter of finding someone to believe her.

And that someone was Dorothy Sayer.

But there was something missing.

If Kathleen Gates had staged the whole incident to protect her husband's career, she had left General Flynn with no room to maneuver. She couldn't accuse him of blackmail one day and then go along with him on the next. Yet her story was tough to believe; there had to be some other angle. And Claude Braintree, survivor of many Washington battles, was confident that he'd discover what that angle was.

In the meantime, he figured it served his purposes well to let Sayer go on digging, to let his staff go on worrying that she was getting an advantage.

"So what do you think?" Sayer asked.

"I think you've been doing an excellent job," he said. "But now that we're talking about the Superintendent, you should leave some of these concerns to me. I'll want you to keep in contact with Mrs. Gates, in case she has anything to add."

"What should I tell her about how we're handling this?"

"Tell her the truth," Braintree said. "That you've handed this over to your superior and you'll have to wait to see what happens."

"OK," Sayer said. She put her hands behind her on the bed and leaned back, tossing her hair again.

"So I did a good job," she said in her purring voice that meant she wanted sex.

But Claude Braintree was somewhere else, thinking about how Kathleen Gates might help him move into the spotlight himself.

He had thought that this assignment to West Point would

be dull. In fact, the place had enough intrigue to keep Versailles going. Yet everyone he'd met at West Point, as well as the people on his own staff, had the wrong perspective. Even Kathleen Gates, if she turned out to be as manipulative as he suspected, was after small game. The cadets functioned on a day-to-day level, and the officers weren't much better. Even the long-term faculty saw the preservation of their jobs as their main responsibility. Even Simon saw his own advancement as the ultimate prize.

They were all so shortsighted. The cadets, he could understand. They didn't even have the luxury of living day-to-day. They lived hour to hour in a whirlwind of activity, with little time to slow down and figure out what was really going on. The Bruckner Commission might just decide on the fate of a national institution.

Yet the most shortsighted of all was Lamar Bruckner, who would become rabid at the prospect of such a high level scandal. Bruckner would refuse to see the dangers of playing along with Kathleen Gates; he would be blind to the damage he could cause his presidential hopes. He would not just *allow* Kathleen Gates to use the Bruckner Commission, he would probably insist on it.

Unless Claude Braintree took control.

❦

WASHINGTON, DC—Senator Lamar Bruckner's office today announced a series of investigative hearings at the United States Military Academy.

"We're going to be looking at the role of all the service academies in the twenty-first century defense establishment," a Bruckner spokesperson said, "beginning with West Point. Senator Bruckner wants to ensure that the taxpayers are being well served by these institutions."

The flamboyant and media-conscious Texan has been accused of recklessness in some of his efforts to root out what he calls "thieves who are robbing the taxpayers."

When asked if there was a possibility that the academies might be closed, Bruckner's office replied, "We have not ruled out any courses of action at this point."

The announcement sparked comments from several

members of Congress and the administration. Senator Henry Turner II (R-OR) said that "Senator Bruckner wants to throw everything away and start from scratch, without determining what works and what doesn't, just to get his face on the news. These institutions—all the service academies—have served the nation well in war and peace for two hundred years, and now they're under attack by the worst kind of opportunist."

When told of his colleague's remarks, Senator Bruckner said, "My esteemed colleague is a West Point graduate. Naturally he wants to protect his alma mater. But that does not answer the question: Does the country need these expensive—and some would say elitist—institutions?"

The United States Military Academy is the nation's oldest federally funded school for military officers. Recent studies by Senator Bruckner's staff have found that a "West Point education may be the least economical way to train Army officers. Why are we funding this institution, at the cost of two hundred thousand dollars per graduate? So that we can have parades and little toy soldiers and statues of old generals?"

The committee, chaired by Senator Bruckner and directed by Claude Braintree, the Senator's longtime aide, will hear testimony from members of the military community. "We want to make sure that West Point is doing a good job with all the money they're spending."

Senator Bruckner's office announced that Mr. Braintree has been at West Point for nearly two weeks, doing preliminary work and organizing the investigation.

Some sources in the military community have expressed fear that Senator Bruckner will sacrifice the service academies in the interest of getting air time.

"This is free campaign advertising," remarked House member Diana Mailer (D-CA) who was a member of one of the first classes that included women. "Bruckner will stop at nothing to gain notoriety. If that means doing a disservice to the nation's armed forces, he'll be glad to trade that in for a little air time."

Told of this criticism, Senator Bruckner remarked, "What do you expect? Of course they're going to start circling the wagons. That just makes me think that maybe they're hiding something.

"But that's OK," the Senator said, lifting his trademark Stetson. "I love a good brawl."

CHAPTER 13

WAYNE HOLDER SAT AT TOM GATES'S DESK AND TRIED THE number again. He got the machine; he'd already left one message, so he hung up.

"Any luck?" Gates asked as he entered the office.

"No, sir," Holder said, standing. "She must be out for the morning."

"When Kathleen was pregnant she stayed home every morning puking her guts up," Gates said. He grinned, threw his garrison cap onto a table. "Maybe this girl . . . what's her name? Ruth? . . . maybe this girl is in the bathroom."

Holder walked around from behind the desk. Gates had given him permission to use the office phone to make the call, but Holder had a moment of doubt when he entered the room. There were papers piled in uneven stacks on the desk, a sweat-stained uniform shirt hung over the back of the chair, newspaper towers on the floor. This was not like Major Tom Gates at all, and Holder wondered if Gates had intended for him to see the office in this state of disarray.

"Did you write the number in the log?" Gates asked. He was required to keep a record of official calls.

"Yes, sir."

Holder was in front of the desk now; Gates fell into the

311

chair, which squeaked loudly. He rubbed his face hard with both hands and let out a long sigh. It wasn't yet noon, but Gates looked as if he'd been up for days. His handsome face seemed longer.

"You hear of a guy named Van Grouw, one of these assholes from the Bruckner Commission?" Gates made the question sound like a challenge.

"No, sir," Holder said, smiling, unsure what Van Grouw's sin was.

"What's so funny?"

"Nothing, really sir. It's just that . . ."

"What? You think that maybe there's a chance that he isn't an asshole?" Gates said. He looked mildly amused himself. "You think I should give everybody a chance? Think the best of everyone until they show me differently? Is that it, Holder?"

"Something like that, I guess, sir," Holder answered.

"Well, I'm an equal opportunity motherfucker," Gates said, stabbing the air with an extended index finger. "I antagonize people without regard to race, religion, skin color, or country of origin. I hate everybody until they give me a reason to think I shouldn't."

"I understand, sir," Holder said. The man was one of a kind, a genuine character. Holder hadn't seen anything like him at West Point. He doubted that West Point—sanitized, self-conscious, and politically correct—had seen anything like him in quite some time.

"I'll bet you do, you little twerp."

"Anyway," Gates went on, animated now. "This little queer Van Grouw is all hot to talk to your buddy Dearborn. I guess this guy left a bunch of messages with the CQ, but Dearborn hasn't called him back. Van Grouw's boss called my boss and so on. So tell Dearborn to get in touch with this douche bag so they'll stop bothering me. Got it?"

"Roger that, sir," Holder answered. Then, after a pause, "I guess you heard the announcement this morning about the hearings."

"Yeah," Gates said. "This place is gonna be a fuckin' zoo."

"How do you mean, sir?"

Gates looked down at the newspapers piled beside his

chair as if noticing them for the first time. He kicked at the stack, which made it fall over. Newsprint lay like a thick carpet between the desk and the credenza. Gates rolled his chair right over the mess.

"This guy, Bruckner, is a publicity hound. Every time he goes on one of these witch hunts, his main purpose is to get more publicity for Senator Bruckner. These people will be doing everything they can to be in the spotlight."

"I would think there are lots of better places to get into the spotlight than here, sir," Holder said.

Gates, who'd been delivering his opinions rapid-fire, paused.

"Not if there's a scandal," he said.

Holder wondered if Gates could be talking about Kathleen's adventures.

"Has anyone contacted you?" Gates asked.

Gates and Holder had not talked about what had happened between them at MacArthur's statue; by mutual agreement and without specifying anything, the subject had simply wound up being off limits. Since then, of course, a few other things had developed that gave Wayne Holder more to worry about. And although it looked as if Tom Gates was doing enough worrying for both of them, Holder was the one with something to hide. He decided to keep his mouth shut and say as little as possible. He even tried not to think about Kathleen Gates, in the unreasonable fear that Gates would be able to read his mind.

"No, sir."

"They will, you know," Gates said.

Holder didn't answer, and Gates said, "A lot of people have been giving me advice, lately. Some of them have said that I should change my whole way of operating, just keep a low profile from now on, especially considering what happened between you and me."

He leaned his big forearms on the desk; the room seemed suddenly very quiet.

"What would you do, Holder?" Gates asked.

"Sir?"

"What would you do if you thought you were under a microscope? Maybe you'd done something that you wish you hadn't done, and suddenly a whole bunch of people might find out about it, and that's going to change every-thing for you. What would you do?"

Holder's guilty conscience had him on the ropes. He was suddenly very much afraid that Gates was going to say, "I know about you and Kathleen."

Here it comes, Holder thought. He pictured himself bolting through the door behind him, Gates on his heels, murder in the air. A crime of passion.

"I don't know, sir."

"Not good enough, Holder."

"Sir?"

"I want more of an answer than that. Jesus, Holder, you're going to be a lieutenant in a few months. You could be taking guys to war in a year. You get asked a hard question, you think you can give a dipshit answer like that?"

"I . . . uh . . . I don't know, sir."

"Well, you can't," Gates said. He relaxed, leaned back in his chair. "So what are you gonna do?"

"I guess it would depend on the circumstances, sir."

Gates shot forward and pounded his big fist on the desk top, making the telephone jump.

"You goddamned guardhouse lawyer," he said. "It doesn't depend on the situation. You just do your job. If you fucked up, you take your licks like a soldier. In the mean-time, you do your job, and you don't worry about what other people might think. The taxpayer isn't paying you to cover your ass. You're getting paid to soldier."

"Right, sir," Holder said.

Gates looked somewhat mollified. "So I say, fuck 'em," he said.

He was looking out the window now, and Holder won-dered which of his tormentors Gates was thinking about.

"Fuck 'em. Right, sir," Holder said.

"Don't you patronize me, Holder," Gates said, spinning around quickly in his chair. "Or I'll jump across this desk and kick your ass. Do you know what the hell I'm talking about here?"

I hope it's not the fact that your wife blew me, Holder thought.

"The incident out by MacArthur's statue, sir?"

"That's part of it, Holder. But it ain't because I give a shit

314

about what these civilians are going to say. I'm a big boy. I'll take what's coming to me. I want you to learn something from this, Holder, you little turd. What do you think that would be?"

Holder had moved his hands to the small of his back, his feet shoulder-width apart. He thought he could feel his pulse alongside his throat.

"That one has to do one's . . ."

"Plain English, hero," Gates demanded.

Holder swallowed.

"Do your duty. . . ."

"Stop right there," Gates said, raising a hand. "That's it. That's all there is. Do your duty."

Gates stood and walked around to the front of the desk. Holder tried to keep from tensing visibly.

"The problem with you college boys is that you're always outsmarting yourself. You're always trying to make that harder than it is," Gates said. "It's right there on the side of that ring that you all wear. Duty. First word of your motto. Right?"

"Yes, sir. It's the first word of the motto."

"I *know* that, numbnuts. I meant, 'do you see what I'm talking about?' Do your duty."

"Right, sir."

Gates leaned closer to Holder. The cadet could smell coffee strong on Gates's breath.

"You know something, Holder. If I thought I could make that point better by punching the shit out of each of you, beating it into your head . . . I wouldn't hesitate."

"I believe that, sir," Holder said.

"Now get the hell out of my office. And tell Dearborn that if I get another call from this limp-dick civilian I'm going to come upstairs and throw his non-boxing ass right out a third floor window. You read me?"

"Loud and clear, sir."

Dearborn's room was empty, but Holder checked the class schedule taped to the blotter. Dearborn had a free period. Holder left him a note and then went to his own room, only to find Dearborn sitting in Holder's chair.

"I was just looking for you in your room," the senior said.

"I'm hiding," Dearborn said.

"From Van Grouw?"

Dearborn put down the book he'd been reading and turned to face Holder.

"How did you know that?"

"I'm psychic," Holder said. "I'm psychic and Gates told me to pass along a little message. This guy's boss called Gates—apparently he doesn't like the silent treatment—and Gates doesn't want any more calls from civilians. Bottom line: call Van Grouw."

"Shit," Dearborn said, standing abruptly and slamming his book closed. "Gates wouldn't be so eager if he knew what this guy wanted."

"Oh, and what's that?"

"He wants Gates's head on a platter, I think."

"What are you talking about?"

Dearborn told Holder about the training run with Gates.

"He hit you?" Holder asked. "Are you sure he wasn't just sparring?"

"Of course that's what he said to cover it up," Dearborn said.

"And you gave this to the Bruckner Commission? What the hell did you do that for?"

"Hey, don't start in with me. It's true."

"Yeah, but how did you say it? I mean, did you make it sound like sparring—this is all about boxing, after all. Or did you make it sound like he assaulted you?"

"He did assault me," Dearborn said.

Holder pulled Trainor's chair from under the desk and sat. "I guess that answers my question," he said. "Why was Van Grouw bothering you in the first place?"

"He was at the gym one day, and he started to ask me a bunch of questions about boxing. Then he tried to come see a fight, but I didn't last long enough."

"So he just has an academic interest in you?" Holder asked.

Dearborn leaned against the opposite desk.

"I know what you're thinking," he said. "You're thinking that I'm trying to use this guy to get Gates off my back."

"And are you?"

"Gates is overstepping his bounds, Wayne, and you know

it. He isn't supposed to take cadets out on extra runs at five in the morning. And he sure as hell isn't supposed to be giving boxing instruction up by Lusk Reservoir."

"Gates is trying to do his job. He may have unusual methods, and he definitely gets carried away pretty easily. But I think the guy is just trying to do his best by us. I don't think he has a vendetta against you. He believes that this boxing experience is going to make you a better leader, and so that's what he's trying to do."

"That's rich," Dearborn interrupted. "Since when did you become his defender?"

Holder laughed, a sad little snort.

"Maybe I'm trying to make up for what else has been going on," he said.

"What's that?"

Holder looked at his friend, considered telling him everything that had happened with Kathleen Gates.

"Never mind," he said. "I just want you to consider this: there's a good chance that Van Grouw is using you to grab some headlines for his boss."

"I didn't sic Van Grouw on anybody, Wayne. But to tell you the truth, I wouldn't exactly be heartbroken if Gates had other things to worry about."

"It won't stop him," Holder said. "He said he's going to keep doing his job, every day. And fuck anybody who thinks he should be covering his ass."

"You and he have become pretty chummy, then," Dearborn said.

"No, I just think I've opened my eyes a little bit," Holder answered.

Dearborn smirked at him, then turned to leave the room.

"Did you hear the announcement about the hearings?" Holder asked his friend's back.

Dearborn, pausing by the door, sounded tired when he spoke. "How could you not hear it? It's all anyone is talking about. The fucking Inquisition arrives shortly."

"Has Van Grouw asked you about testifying?"

"No," Dearborn said. The idea had occurred to him, but he had managed, so far, to push it aside.

"Look, Chris. Ask yourself if this guy is using you. If the answer is no, then OK. But if you think the answer might be yes; or even if the answer is that you're using each other, then you gotta be careful, my friend."

"Thanks for the advice," Dearborn said. He left the room without looking back.

"Death to all imbeciles," Jon Hillard announced as he picked up the cadet paper he was grading and flung it out the open door of his office and into the hallway. "Shooting's too good for 'em."

The fluttering white mass just missed the face of a civilian who ducked out of the way at the last second.

"Sorry," Hillard said.

"I'm Sandy Van Grouw," the man said, fingering his tie and checking the name tags on the office door. "Is this Captain Timmer's office?"

"The very one," Hillard said. "But you can't see the Wizard now."

Van Grouw blinked behind his round glasses. "Pardon?" he said.

Hillard gestured, palm up, to the empty room. "We await her royal highness."

"I . . . ah . . . I see," Van Grouw said, trying a tentative smile. "I'm supposed to meet her here in a few minutes. I wonder if I might come in and wait."

"Certainly," Hillard said. He held out his hand as the man passed in front of his desk.

"Jon Hillard."

"Pleased to meet you," Van Grouw said, offering his hand palm down, like a bishop.

"You're with the Bruckner Commission," Hillard said.

"That's right. How did you know?"

"Your black hood is sticking out of your pocket."

Van Grouw actually looked down to the pocket of his jacket before catching himself and forcing a laugh.

"Do you know when Captain Timmer will return?"

Hillard checked his watch.

"She was supposed to be here ten minutes ago," he said, leaning sideways and looking out in the hall. "She's got some students coming by as well.

"Why don't you grab a chair?"

Van Grouw looked around the office, studied the drawing

of the tank on the wall across from Hillard's desk. He had a strange look on his face—halfway between amusement and disgust. It was all the invitation Hillard needed.

"That's the Abrams Main Battle Tank," Hillard explained. "Sent a lot of martyrs to Allah with that thing."

Van Grouw turned slowly, studying Hillard for another hint of a joke. Hillard gave him the war face.

"I see," the civilian said.

Two sharp raps on the door turned their attention that way. A frightened looking plebe stood in the doorway, books clasped in his left hand, eyes blinking rapidly behind ugly government-issue glasses. There was a sheen of sweat on his forehead.

"Sir, Cadet Newcombe to see Captain Timmer," he reported.

"Stop talking about yourself in the third person, Mister Newcombe," Hillard said. "This ain't the friggin' Navy."

"Yes, sir," the cadet blurted out.

"You here for AI?"

"Yes, sir," the cadet parroted again. AI was additional instruction.

"Captain Timmer isn't here yet. Why don't you go out in the hallway and jog in place until she gets here."

"Yes, sir," the plebe said. He turned sharply on his heel, posted himself with his back to the wall opposite Hillard's office, and began to run in place, lifting his knees almost to waist level.

"At ease, Mister Newcombe," Hillard said, leaning out into the hallway. "It was a joke."

Newcombe came to attention immediately. "Yes, sir," he said.

Hillard turned back into the office; Van Grouw looked confused.

"They're so *literal*," Hillard said.

Van Grouw fidgeted and shuffled his feet and cleared his throat and drummed his fingers in the chair beside Timmer's desk for nearly ten minutes. It wasn't long before Hillard was sorry he'd invited the civilian in. Another cadet showed up to wait for Timmer; Hillard was starting to feel crowded.

Jon Hillard wondered if something had gone wrong. He

couldn't imagine Jackie Timmer being late for anything, much less forgetting an appointment. He dialed her home number; when he got the machine he hung up.

Timmer was twenty-five minutes late when the phone rang.

"Major Hillard."

"Jon, it's Jackie. I'm running a little late," she said.

"I noticed. You've quite a crowd here."

"Oh, shit," she said. "I forgot to tell the cadets. . . ."

Her voice faded into static.

"I didn't hear you," Hillard said. "Are you on a car phone or something?"

"Or something," Timmer answered. "Tell the cadets that I'll have to reschedule their appointments. Is Van Grouw there?"

"Yep. Is something wrong?"

"I . . . I can't talk now," Timmer said. "Will you bail me out, please? Tell Van Grouw I'm on my way in. I'll be there in ten minutes."

"What about these cadets and their papers?" Hillard said. "You're just going to . . . ?"

There must have been a tone of accusation in his voice, he noted, because Timmer responded with an attitude of her own.

"I can't help them if I'm not there, Jon," she said.

Hillard heard another voice, a man's voice, indistinct over the line.

"I'll be there as soon as I can, OK?"

"Right," Hillard said. He put the phone back in its cradle, stood, and made his way around the front of his desk.

"Ten minutes," he said to Van Grouw.

Van Grouw dropped his shoulders and sighed, looking a little too much like a disappointed schoolgirl.

"I don't have . . ."

"Take it or leave it, buddy," Hillard said. "I don't care either way."

Hillard went out into the hallway; he caught one of the cadets nervously looking at his watch.

"Something came up, men. Captain Timmer had to cancel. Let's see if I can help you."

* * *

"Shit," Jackie Timmer said, snapping the phone shut.

"What is it?" Layne Marshall didn't take his eyes off the road, but he reached over and caressed her thigh.

"Jon Hillard is pissed at me," she said. She slipped the phone into the console and took Marshall's hand in hers, playing with his fingers.

"I had two cadets come by for help . . . I forgot all about them."

"I'm sure you'll torture yourself with guilt to the point where it won't happen again," he said.

He was talking about her missed appointments, but Timmer thought about their morning tryst.

"I know what I *would* like to do again," she said. She brought his hand to her mouth and licked the backs of his knuckles. His fingers smelled like her sex.

"You have to give me a few minutes between rounds," he said. "I'm an old man."

"Could have fooled me, Mr. Triple Play," she said.

They rode in silence for a while, still several miles from West Point on the way back from a Newburgh motel. The "No-Tell Mo-Tell" Layne had called it. Jackie had parked her car at a shopping center. It would not do for them to ride back on the post together.

"Did Jon send the cadets away?" Marshall asked as he pulled behind her car in the parking lot.

"I asked him to, but this guy from the Bruckner Commission is there. Van Grouw."

"What does he want?"

"Don't know yet," she said. "He called and asked to see me."

"And you stood him up, too? All for me?"

"Yes. And if I'm going to see you again, I'll have to make sure I don't pull that kind of stunt anymore."

"It's not your fault," he said. "All the blood rushed away from your brain for an hour back there."

Jackie Timmer kissed him on the lips, her mouth closed. She was thinking about Jon Hillard being angry with her.

"When can I see you again?" Marshall asked.

"Day after tomorrow," she said. "I'll have the same class periods free in the morning."

"I have to wait two days? I'll be frantic."

"Consider it foreplay," she said. She opened the car door and got out, then waved as Marshall drove away. There was a woman loading groceries into a car a few spaces away; she watched Jackie unabashedly.

Timmer got in her car and checked herself in the mirror.

"She's watching you because you look like you just had sex," she told her reflection. She pushed at her hair with two hands, started the car and drove away.

For the rest of the trip back to West Point, she thought about what she would say to the cadets whose appointments she'd missed, and she thought about her image in the big mirror on the wall across from the bed, and she thought about what she should say if Jon Hillard asked where she'd been, and she thought about Layne Marshall's kisses on her back. She did not think about her husband, or the long-standing promise—*forsaking all others*—she'd broken this morning.

Seventeen minutes after she'd spoken to Hillard from Marshall's car phone, she hurried into her office in Lincoln Hall. She was dressed in workout gear.

"I'm so sorry I'm late, Mister Van Grouw," she said. Closing the door as she entered, she fumbled a hanger from a hook behind the door—a clean uniform—then pulled a pair of black shoes from under her desk.

"I just have to run to the ladies room to change, I won't be but a second," she said, fleeing the office before Van Grouw had a chance to protest.

Five minutes later she was back, her hair brushed, her uniform crisp. Her cheeks had a ruddy blush, which Van Grouw took to be a sign of her rushing about.

"I can't tell you how sorry I am to keep you waiting," Timmer said when she came back into the room.

Van Grouw got up and closed the door behind her. Jon Hillard was not there.

"There's been a very interesting development in the commission's work," he said when he sat down again. "Very unusual. Unexpected, unorthodox, even. And I wanted your opinion."

"Go ahead," Jackie Timmer said.

Sandy Van Grouw studied her for a few seconds. Something about her—the way she held herself, something in her eyes—reminded him of Dorothy Sayer, but he couldn't identify just what it was.

"Actually," Van Grouw said, sitting down and dropping his voice. "I'm probably way out of line here. But I think someone should know what's happening, and you came to mind.

"I have a colleague named Dorothy Sayer who interviewed a woman last week—the wife of an officer. This woman said that a cadet had forced himself on her—sexually."

"That's pretty serious stuff, something for the Military Police, Mister Van Grouw," Timmer said.

"It is if she makes the accusation publicly," Van Grouw said. "And please, call me Sandy.

"Anyway, that's not the news. This woman's husband is apparently facing some sort of letter of reprimand for something he did. Now the wife is saying that the Superintendent, General Flynn, approached her and offered to protect her husband from the letter of reprimand if she keeps quiet about the sexual assault—excuse me, the alleged sexual assault."

Timmer raised her eyebrows. "That sounds a little farfetched."

"That's exactly what I thought," Van Grouw said, sounding very pleased with himself. "Which is why I thought someone on your side of the fence should get a heads-up about this."

"Do you know the names of any of the people involved?"

"Yes," Van Grouw said. He had the names; for twenty dollars the maid had brought him the trash from Dorothy Sayer's room, and a crumbled piece of paper had revealed the names Gates and Wayne Holder. Quick checks of the post phone book and the cadet directory told him that Holder was the cadet, Tom Gates the officer, Kathleen Gates the wife.

Van Grouw had briefly considered calling Kathleen Gates directly, trying to throw her off her quest. But then he thought it might be wiser to remove himself and have someone else do that work for him. Jackie Timmer came to mind. But now, confronted with the reality of what he was doing, he wasn't so sure he wanted to reveal everything. It was one thing to try to cut the legs out from under Dorothy Sayer, it was quite another to accuse the Superintendent of something so terrible. Besides, someone might be able to trace the information back to him—and that would not sit well with Claude Braintree. In spite of his love of intrigue, Claude Braintree did not appreciate being left out of the juiciest schemes.

"Well, I'm not sure what you want me to do with this," Timmer said.

"I'm a little anxious about exposing myself here," Van Grouw said.

So you thought you'd get me to walk point, Timmer thought.

Timmer leaned back in her chair. "My first inclination is to go to the Superintendent."

"For purely selfish reasons, I'd hoped that wouldn't be necessary," Van Grouw said, smiling weakly. "General Flynn would no doubt confront my boss, and then it would only be a matter of time until Mr. Braintree traced the information leak back to me."

"So you'd rather I approached the principals? Kept it away from the Supe for now?"

Van Grouw smiled at her. "That would be better. Yes. That way, I could keep feeding you information as it becomes available."

There were all sorts of reasons Jackie Timmer should not become involved. She didn't want to be in the way when the Bruckner Commission steamrolled across West Point. Nor did she want to step in front of a bullet for General Flynn.

But Van Grouw had selected her, and he could continue to feed her information that might help the academy avoid a public relations disaster. That she was willing to try might be enough to save her if Flynn found out about her investigation and became angry.

No matter that in almost every other aspect of her life she was acting out of character, Jackie Timmer was not one to run away from a fight.

She pushed a tablet of paper across the desk to Van Grouw, then slapped a pen down on the pad.

"I'll see what I can do to keep your name out of the spotlight."

Van Grouw was gone by the time Hillard came back.

"So," he said with his usual bluntness. "Where the hell were you when you were supposed to be here tutoring your students?"

"I . . . uh," Timmer began, but the lie caught in her throat. "Something came up."

Hillard didn't comment. He was standing behind his desk, hands on the back of his chair, watching her.

"What's wrong with you?" he asked.

"Nothing."

Hillard walked closer to her. "You feel OK?"

"I feel fine, Jon," she snapped. She immediately regretted her tone. If there were anyone who was genuinely interested in her well-being—and that alone—it was Jon Hillard.

"Well, you don't look fine."

He turned back to his desk, ran both hands over the shiny cue ball of his head. "You look like you got caught with your hand in the cookie jar."

"Give it a rest, will you?" she said. She knew what she must look like: her minister father used to call it the indignation of the rightly accused.

Hillard raised both hands in a gesture of surrender.

"I talked to those kids who showed up for help with their papers," he said.

Timmer melted. "Thanks, Jon. I owe you one."

"Yeah, well," he said, sitting down without looking at her. "Make it up to your students."

"Ah, the circus is in town," Liz Wrenson said as she and Holder emerged into the sunlight from Thayer Hall and their afternoon class.

Two television vans squatted by the library; the steel mast of the remote truck stuck up like a silver missile. A small knot of gray gathered in front of Patton's statue; Holder could see the ring of cadets focused on something inside the circle.

"Let's see what's going on," Liz said, stepping off the curb in the direction of the crowd.

"Let's not," Holder said.

"Are you in a hurry?" she asked without looking at him.

"No, I just don't want to be anywhere near those people." Liz turned to him.

"The TV people?"

"The TV people, the Bruckner Commission, the print media. I want to stay away from them like they have the plague."

"Are you afraid they're going to find out about the little blowup between you and Gates?"

"Something like that," Holder said.

Over the past week he and Liz had spent a fair amount of time together, walking to class, at intramurals, in the library. Last night they'd slipped out for dinner at a local pizzeria. Holder had expected that he would relax after he got used to Liz's company. And he did, in a manner of speaking. But it was not the way he relaxed with other women. When he had returned to his room last night, lying in his bunk, thinking of the way she laughed, he had been surprised to realize he had not even tried to kiss her. Nor had he used the banter that was so familiar to him that it had become a memorized—and effective—spiel designed to talk young women out of their panties.

He wanted Liz to think well of him, and he wanted to deserve it. And the more he thought about Liz Wrenson, the more he knew that he did not want her to find out about Kathleen Gates.

"I'm sorry that you're so worried, Wayne. But they're much more likely to hear about it from the rumor mill. Your standing around when they're filming an interview isn't going to tip them off."

She took him by the arm and pulled him playfully.

"You can be one of those people you always see in the back of the crowd in street interviews. Wave to the camera and mouth 'Hi, Mom.'

"Besides, did you really do anything so wrong?"

Did I ever, Holder thought.

The crowd was a mix of civilians—tourists, most likely—and cadets. A few faculty members stood off to one side. Liz mumbled "excuse me" a few times and shouldered her way into the crowd. The Academy's public affairs officer, a fat lieutenant colonel named Grath, was sweating dark rings through his green uniform shirt. He crooked his finger at Liz, who made her way to his side.

Holder stood on his tiptoes in the back rank.

"It's that Shanya chick from New York," he heard one of the cadets in front of him say.

Holder saw the hair first: past shoulder length, dark and glossy, it was a trademark of Shanya Taylor, one of New York television's current hot stars. Taylor was an aggressive, in-your-face interviewer—"No Quarter Taylor" the tabloids had named her—who wielded her trademark, outsized microphone like a police baton.

At the moment she was using the bulbous, foam-headed mike to back a cadet against an unmoving wall of bystanders.

"But since the taxpayer is spending so much more on your education than on people who come out of ROTC, don't you think the country should get more for its money?"

The cadet—a junior named Mary Kyle whom Holder recognized from one of his classes—shifted her books from one hand to the other, her eyes clicking right and left.

"Well, yes, ma'am," she answered in the cadences of Gulf Coast Texas. "I suppose that's reasonable."

"And you said a moment ago that the Academy should continue to be funded. Therefore you must think that you're that much of a better product than, say, an officer who comes out of Penn State ROTC? Is that what you're saying?"

Cadet Kyle looked like she wanted to bolt. Shanya Taylor threw her thick mane back over a shoulder, a gesture of triumph.

A man in outrageous Bermuda shorts stepped to the front of the crowd next to Kyle and announced, "I have something to say."

A woman, also dressed in loud shorts with the megasunglasses favored by older tourists, tugged at the man's arm. She apparently didn't want the man, probably her husband, to embarrass himself—either by sparring with Shanya Taylor or by appearing on television in those shorts.

"I served in the Korean War under a few West Pointers, and they were damned good men for the most part."

He paused at the end of the sentence, but his mouth kept moving. Holder wondered if he was trying to seat his dentures properly.

"No one is disputing the history," Taylor allowed, smiling for her camera. She was a good six inches taller than the old veteran; she stepped closer so that she was looking down on him when she spoke again.

"But we're talking about today's dollars, sir. Your tax dollars."

"Well, I'll tell you what," Bermuda shorts said. "I imagine you make more than whatever it's going to cost to educate this young lady here," he said, reaching out and touching Cadet Kyle on the arm. "And I know that she's going to make a positive contribution to the country. You, on the other hand, will spend a career chasing ratings."

This comment brought hoots from the cadets gathered round. Taylor, apparently not unused to insults, tossed her hair and turned her back on the old man.

"How about you?" she said, turning on another cadet. She picked a plebe, who seemed torn between wanting to talk to this beautiful woman and not wanting to say anything that would draw attention to himself.

"What will you do if the Academy is closed?"

The plebe looked a bit stunned, as did the public affairs officer. Reverting to form, the young man stammered an honest answer.

"Ma'am, I do not know," he said, leaning into the microphone as if this were some profound development.

The cadets in the circle laughed, the camera operator took his face away from the eyepiece for a second, as if to see if this was for real. The reporter looked frazzled. She had probably rushed up from New York just after hearing the announcement from Bruckner's Washington office that the hearings would be public, hoping to scoop some of the other stations in time for the evening news. She didn't seem to be getting anywhere.

As Holder watched, Liz stepped up next to the plebe. Holder could see that she'd been nearly pushed forward by Grath.

"I'd like to say something," Liz offered.

The camera swung immediately toward her.

The long set of bars on her shirt collar shone, the wreathed star of her class standing sparkled on the breast of her dark shirt. Her smile fairly glittered; she exuded confidence, intelligence. White teeth, clear skin, eyes bright. Wayne Holder was completely smitten with her.

"The comments about the academy closing seem a bit premature, I think, ma'am," Liz said. The reporter proffered the microphone. This wasn't the panic they were looking for, but the television people knew a photogenic face and a presence when they saw one.

"It reminds me of Mark Twain's comment, 'Reports of my death have been greatly exaggerated,'" she said.

The cadets laughed; even the camera operator chuckled, but cut it off when Taylor shot him a daggered look.

"But you're aware, are you not, of Senator Bruckner's reputation as a dedicated cost cutter?" the reporter asked, pulling the microphone back to her own mouth. "Do you know his Commission has been called 'The Spanish Inquisition'?"

"Yes," Liz said sweetly. "We couldn't help but be aware of that, what with all the coverage in the press." There was the slightest indictment in her tone, as if the press—not the Senator—were responsible for the image.

"Aren't you concerned that the academy might be closed?"

"Yes, frankly, that would concern me," Liz said. "I obviously have a stake here. But it isn't something I can control," she finished. "Except to the extent that we can all do our best and hope that the public sees that."

The reporter made her mouth smile, then gave the "cut" signal to the camera.

"Way to go, young lady," the vet in Bermuda shorts said. He held out his hand and Liz shook it. The man's wife gave Liz a kiss on the cheek.

"Such a lovely young girl," the woman said.

"Good show, there," Holder said to Liz as the crowd drifted away.

"Just making it up as I go along," she said.

"Me, too," Holder said. "Except I keep making it up wrong."

CHAPTER 14

THE MESSAGE TO CALL CAPTAIN JACKIE TIMMER WAS WAITING for Holder when he got back to his room.

Holder sat down at his desk and dialed.

"Hello, ma'am," he said when Timmer picked up. "This is Cadet Holder returning your call."

"I need to speak with you, Cadet Holder," Timmer said, businesslike. "Are you free this last period?"

"I'm free right now, but I have drill right after last period, ma'am."

"Can you meet me out by the bleachers for a few minutes? I won't make you late for drill."

"I can do that, ma'am."

"Good," Timmer said. "Right by the Supe's box. Meet me there in ten."

"Yes, ma'am," Holder said.

He tapped a key on the computer, erasing the electronic mail marker blinking Timmer's message. He wished all of his troubles would go away that easily.

Holder buckled his sword belt around his waist, pulled on a pair of white gloves, and was out the door in less than three minutes. Since drill was about to start and cadets were scattered here and there setting markers on the field, Holder thought it OK to cut across the wide Plain.

Timmer was already standing by the shiny aluminum bleachers next to the Superintendent's reviewing stand by the time he got there. The sun shot off the seats in blinding darts; he squinted and saluted.

"Cadet Holder reporting, ma'am," he said.

Timmer returned his salute.

"Why don't we go back here," she said, indicating the shade behind the bleachers.

Holder nodded, grateful. The parade field was already a sauna; drill was going to be a hothouse.

When they were behind the bleachers, Timmer walked out onto the green lawn between the sidewalk and the street. There was something about West Point that made people stick to the sidewalks; the little green space around them afforded them just enough privacy.

"Do you have any idea why I wanted to talk to you?" Timmer asked.

Holder had never spoken to Timmer before; she was prettier, even, than everyone said. "The poster child," Dearborn had called her.

"I have a couple of ideas, ma'am," Holder answered. His class shirt was already damp with sweat; he removed his cap and ran one gloved hand back over his blond hair.

"I've been tasked by the Dean to work with the Bruckner Commission representatives," Timmer said. "Kind of a liaison between Claude Braintree—the Senator's advance man—and the Academy. One of Braintree's staff approached me the other day with a bit of . . . disconcerting news. Your name came up."

She paused, waiting for a reply.

"Are you talking about the incident with my Tac, Major Gates?" he asked.

"That's only part of it, apparently," Timmer said.

Holder remained quiet.

"Look, Cadet Holder," Timmer said. "By the way, it's Wayne, right?"

"Yes, ma'am."

"Look, Wayne. I'm not conducting an official investigation here. Nor am I all that interested in what you've done, short of criminal behavior. . . ."

Criminal behavior.

Holder's mind shot off on a tangent; he began a mental review of the Uniform Code of Military Justice.

"I'm not conducting an investigation, nor am I the morality squad," Timmer said. "But I've heard a few things that might get . . . that might be messy if they're dragged out before the commission, before the media. I'm trying to do a little damage control, I guess."

"Yes, ma'am."

It seemed to Holder that she was talking in circles; the more she talked, the more he sweated. He pulled at the collar of his tee shirt.

"Why don't you start by telling me what happened between you and Major Gates," Timmer suggested.

Holder started to tell Timmer that the cadets in the company called Gates "Major Mercury." Then he realized he was doing exactly what he had accused Dearborn of doing: attacking Gates to avoid other consequences.

"Friday before last, I got a call from Major Gates. He told me to roll all the firsties out of the barracks for a little spirit run," Holder said.

Timmer stood with her arms at her sides, leaning forward a bit. Holder recognized the stance from his leadership class on counseling. *Put the soldier at ease.*

"So my roommate and I met him outside a few minutes later. . . ."

"Where were the rest of the firsties?" Timmer asked.

Holder paused. He wanted to place himself in the best light, but she was already on to him.

"I sent the CQ around to kind of warn them, ma'am."

"To give them a chance to get out of the barracks?" she asked. There was no hint of a smile on her face, no disapproval either.

He told the rest of the story, right on up to the next morning's interview with the Commandant.

"And what about you and Mrs. Gates?" Timmer asked without changing her expression. "Kathleen Gates."

"I . . . uh . . . spoke to Mrs. Gates at the hospital that night."

"Did you also meet her in the library a few nights later?"

"Yes, ma'am."

"And you walked her to her car." It wasn't a question this time; Timmer was laying out the story.

Holder wanted to throw up; he wanted to run; he wanted to be quiet; he wanted to ask again if this might lead to an investigation.

He also wanted, he was surprised to realize, to tell Jackie Timmer everything.

So, in spite of the fact that he was embarrassed, he told her. He did not leave out a single detail about the meeting in the library; about his suspicions; about the fact that he knew, right there by her car, that he should have left. He told her, in intimate detail, exactly what had happened between him and Kathleen Gates.

"You said you knew you would get in trouble," Timmer said. "What, specifically, were you thinking?"

"I guess I wasn't thinking, ma'am. I mean, I know I should have left, but I just got carried away . . . you know?"

"I'm not talking about that, Wayne. Obviously it's not a good idea to have sex with your Tac's wife in a parking lot. I'm wondering what you thought would happen to you?"

"I thought Major Gates would kill me."

Jackie Timmer smiled for the first time.

"Were you afraid of criminal prosecution?"

Holder felt his mouth go open. He had stepped right into this, given her enough to hang him. And she had never actually guaranteed that she wouldn't use what he told her.

"I can be prosecuted for that?" Holder asked. "For . . . adultery?"

Now it was Timmer's turn to look surprised.

"That's not exactly what I'm talking about. But to answer your question, they could nail you for conduct prejudicial to good order and discipline. Is that what you were most afraid of?"

"No, ma'am. I was most afraid of Major Gates finding out and killing me. Literally killing me."

"Did you consider that she would tell?"

"No," he said. "I guess I thought that was the least likely thing to happen."

"Walk with me, Wayne," Timmer said. She turned and

stepped onto the sidewalk, heading toward the Superintendent's house and North Area, where Holder's D Company would soon be forming for drill.

"Kathleen Gates has accused you of forcing her to have sex."

"Jesus Christ!" Holder said, stopping abruptly. "That's just not true," he began. "Why, if anything, she was the one who . . . er . . . pulled me to her. . . ."

"Yes, Wayne, you told me the details," Timmer said.

Holder felt as if he'd just been sucker-punched. Timmer didn't believe him.

"I didn't force myself on her, ma'am," Holder said. "That's the truth."

Jackie Timmer turned her head as she walked, then looked at the ground again.

"I know it's difficult, Wayne," she said. "You've been told for years now to always tell the truth. I know it's difficult when someone doesn't believe you."

"I can't believe this is happening to me," Holder said.

"I'm sure that's what Kathleen Gates said."

"I don't need to force myself on anyone for sex," Holder began.

"Shut up, Wayne," Timmer commanded. "That's what every rapist says."

"I'm not a rapist," Holder said.

The whole scene was completely surreal. Here he was, walking next to an English professor who was accusing him of raping a woman who had all but forced herself on him.

"I didn't say you were a rapist, Wayne," Timmer said. "I'm telling you not to sound like one."

There was a steady stream of cadets walking by them now. Timmer was obliged to return the salutes of all of them, which gave Holder a moment to think.

"Don't you think it's at least as plausible that Mrs. Gates and I are equally responsible as it is that I forced her?"

"Now she's Mrs. Gates," Timmer said. "Like Mrs. Robinson."

"She used that name," Holder said, wondering what he was missing. "Who's Mrs. Robinson?"

Timmer turned to him.

"What did she say about Mrs. Robinson?"

"On the way to the parking lot she said something about her being my Mrs. Robinson. But I didn't know what she was talking about. She thought that was funny."

Timmer stopped walking, turned her back to the cadets straggling toward the reviewing stands, and folded her arms. "That's interesting."

"What's going to happen now?" Holder asked.

"I'm not sure," Timmer said. She stared past Trophy Point where the river stretched like a pewter road under the hazy sun. Behind them, buglers blew "assembly."

"Kathleen Gates hasn't reported this to the police, just to someone on the Bruckner Commission."

Timmer thought she should go to Flynn; a second later she thought she might try something else.

"Maybe I can keep this from spreading too much further if I have a talk with her myself."

Holder had a sudden image of himself waiting in his room for the military police.

"And what do I do in the meantime?" he asked.

Timmer turned to him, watched his eyes for a moment, then dropped her arms.

"For the moment, I suggest you get yourself to drill."

Wayne Holder excused himself from drill, putting one of the other seniors in charge of the formation. Alex Trainor, in the stands to grade the company's performance, suspected that something had gone wrong and went off in search of his roommate. Holder wasn't hard to find. He was lying on his bunk, white gloves still on his hands; scabbard, saber and sword belt in a pile beside him on the floor.

"What gives, man?" Trainor asked.

"You always said I'd get in trouble if I didn't stop thinking with my dick, Alex. I guess you were right."

Holder told him about Kathleen Gates's accusation.

"We both fell into temptation," Trainor said.

The roommates sat quietly, thinking about how quickly their lives had changed, for the worse.

"So now you want to quit and I'm about to get thrown out, maybe even courtmartialed."

"What did Timmer say?" Trainor wanted to know.

"I don't think Timmer believed me for a second," Holder said.

"If she didn't believe you, you'd already be in handcuffs," Trainor said, although he wasn't convinced that was true. He went to his desk and dragged the chair over so that he was seated beside Holder's bunk.

"Now, let's take a good hard look at what we know before this gets any more weird."

Holder propped himself up on one elbow.

"It doesn't matter, Alex," Holder said. "If it comes down to my word against hers, no one is going to believe me. The guy is always guilty."

Trainor watched his roommate for a few long seconds without speaking.

"You finished whining?" he said at last.

"Oh, yeah, I'm finished all right," Holder said, dropping back onto the mattress.

"Wayne, you told me you didn't force Kathleen Gates to have sex with you. You told me that she was the one who initiated it and kept it going. Isn't that what you told me?"

"That's what I told you, Alex."

"And that's the truth?" Trainor asked.

"So help me, God," Holder said.

"OK, then. I believe you. But Kathleen Gates is telling another story, and we have to figure out why. We have to figure out what she's after."

"Why do we have to figure that out?"

"Because when we find her motivation, we're going to find her weak point. And that's where we're going to find whatever it'll take to convince everyone else that you're telling the truth."

Holder turned his head to the side on the pillow. Trainor was on the forward edge of the chair, absentmindedly playing with a loose strip of the bandage on his hand.

"Besides, that's what you keep telling Dearborn, right? You get knocked down, you get up. Right?"

Although they'd called ahead of time, Jackie Timmer was still somewhat surprised when she answered the doorbell and found Holder and another cadet on her front porch.

"Evening, ma'am," Holder said. "This is my roommate, Alex Trainor."

"Come on in," Timmer said, pushing the screen door open. Holder looked as frightened as when she left him earlier. Maybe even more so.

"Would you like some iced tea?" she asked.

"That'd be great," Holder said.

"Follow me."

The cadets trailed her through the tiny dining room to the kitchen, where Timmer picked up a tray with some glasses and a pitcher of tea. She wore khaki shorts and a polo shirt, untucked. No shoes.

"Open that door for me, would you," she said, pointing with a bare foot. "I thought we'd sit outside. It's too hot in here."

They stepped out onto a tiny patio behind the brick row home. Two children playing in the yard next door said hello to Timmer, then stared at the cadets through the wire mesh fence that separated the yards.

"Spies," Timmer said.

Holder, confused, looked at the children, then back at Timmer, who let the corner of her mouth turn up in a tiny smile.

"Joke, Wayne," Trainor said. He followed Timmer's lead and sat in one of the deck chairs. Holder stood for a few seconds longer, shifting his white cap from one hand to the other; then he sat down.

"Thanks for seeing us," Holder said. "I told Alex here about our conversation this afternoon," he went on. Then, pausing, "I hope that's all right."

"Entirely up to you, Wayne," Timmer said. "Although I'd limit the number of people I tell."

"Right," Holder said.

It had to be ten degrees cooler outside the house, but Holder was sweating as if he'd run the two miles from the barracks.

"Hi, all," Rob said, leaning out of the back door.

Holder shot up as if his chair had an ejection button. Trainor stood.

"Evening, sir," the cadets said in unison.

"I'm headed out for a bit, Jackie. Need anything?"

"No. Thanks."

Rob nodded at the two cadets as he withdrew. Jackie had told her husband about the accusations and had asked him for some privacy.

"Anyway, Alex had a couple of ideas," Holder said as the young men found their seats again.

"You're the counselor?" Timmer asked.

She's smiling, at least, Holder thought.

"Something like that, ma'am," Trainor said. "Wayne is a little . . . distracted. But I wanted to propose a couple of things to you."

"I'm listening."

Trainor leaned over and placed his cap gingerly on the ground, then took a long sip of the iced tea Timmer had given him. He looked over at Holder, who was holding his glass in two hands, as if it might try to get away.

"I've been thinking of the possible scenarios," Trainor said. "At least as you'll have to look at them. For my part, of course, I believe Wayne."

Timmer sat back, crossing one long, tanned leg over the other. Trainor swallowed.

"Let's say, for argument's sake, that Wayne did assault Mrs. Gates," Trainor said. "I mean, you'll have to consider that. The meeting was her idea, then she let Wayne walk her to the parking lot. Then things got ugly, out of hand."

Trainor looked at his roommate as he spoke; Holder looked pasty.

"It's pretty far-fetched that Wayne would take that kind of chance, especially with things so bad between him and Major Gates already."

"Far-fetched," Timmer said. "But not impossible."

"Let's look at things from the perspective of Mrs. Gates," Trainor said. "A Letter of Reprimand over the first incident between her husband and Wayne here could end Major Gates's career. She told Wayne, when they met in the library, that their whole livelihood was at stake. So she's thinking: 'How can I get some leverage? How can I influence the administration to go easy on my husband?' She seduces the cadet involved, then cries foul play—suddenly she's the victim."

Timmer was about to speak when Trainor went on.

"Except it's not simple. She can't blackmail Wayne; he's already told the Commandant about the incident by MacArthur's statue. But she can go to the Bruckner Commission. She can tell these civilians—she's already started—that she was assaulted, raped, whatever, and that her husband's getting canned because she reported it. . . ."

"Except that even the most slanted interviewer is still going to ask her about the chronology," Timmer said. "The alleged sexual assault came after the fight between Holder and Gates. Looks too suspicious, even for Senator Bruckner."

Trainor sat back in his chair. Holder actually slumped in his. She had killed their theory. She knew the story was more convoluted than that, of course: Kathleen Gates had accused the Superintendent of misconduct. The cadets didn't know that.

Wayne Holder stood.

"Ma'am, I'm not sure how she plans on using this story, but that's just what it is. I did not force myself on Mrs. Gates. If anything, she forced herself on me."

Jackie Timmer sat quietly in her deck chair. The young man before her was clearly distraught, although that didn't mean he was telling the truth. After the little melodrama of his pronouncement, Holder didn't know what to do with himself. He pulled his heels together as if standing at attention, as if waiting for Timmer to take the next step.

"Sit down, Wayne," she said calmly. "Look, I know you're upset by this. I'm going to do my best to get to the bottom of it all."

Holder looked wounded. For the first time it occurred to her that he was facing jail time—hard time at Fort Leavenworth—if this turned into a rape trial in a military court. She wanted to tell him about her own suspicions, wanted to comfort him, and tell him that she also thought Kathleen Gates was orchestrating events. But she wasn't sure he needed to know all that just yet.

"There's more to this, more I need to look into. . . ."

"What's that?"

"I can't tell you right now," she said. "But I promise to keep you posted. OK? That's the best I can do right now."

Holder looked defeated. Trainor sat still, turning over the possibilities in his mind.

"I still think she's got something going on," Trainor said. "I just haven't figured out her angle yet."

"Let me know if you do," Timmer said.

The sun had dipped below the western mountains by the time Holder and Trainor left Timmer's quarters, and the darkness rolled in from the east, up off the river and onto the bluff. As they walked along Washington Road, they could see the streetlights that curved around Trophy Point. They passed Professor's Row, taking their time getting back to the barracks. Holder had his head down.

"It ain't over 'til it's over," Trainor said. He was surprisingly upbeat, as if Holder's problems had somehow eclipsed his own, as if he were happy for the distraction of someone else's personal disaster.

"I'd say it's pretty close to over," Holder said without looking up. "Timmer certainly doesn't believe me."

"I don't know if that's true or not," Trainor said. "I think she's just being guarded. But let's not talk about Timmer; let's talk about Kathleen Gates.

"This whole fabrication has to be connected to you and her husband. We haven't quite figured out, yet, what she's up to, but her goal has to be to save her husband's career. Do you agree?"

Holder was staring up the valley; the last light of evening kept the sky pale above the river, turning the lazy curves of the Hudson into a silver trail.

"Wayne, are you listening? I said her ultimate goal has to be saving her husband's butt, don't you think?"

"Sure, Alex. Oh, and don't forget steamrolling over me in the process."

"I think that's just a side effect," Trainor said. He was as detached as if they were talking about a problem in the classroom.

"I think she has an Achilles' heel, though," Trainor said. "I don't think she wants this to go public."

"What are you talking about? The Bruckner Commission is all about publicity. Once they let this thing out, it'll probably be all over the friggin' news," Holder complained.

"But that wouldn't serve her real purpose, see? Her goal is to keep her husband's career intact. It would hardly do for the two of them to become famous that way."

"So why did she tell the Bruckner Commission that I'd . . ."

Holder couldn't bring himself to say the word "raped." The crime was that abhorrent to him.

"I don't know how she's going to use all this; maybe there's more to the story than Timmer told us. Maybe there's more to it than Timmer even knows. But I still think it's a pretty safe bet that Kathleen Gates doesn't want this to get out. I think she's bluffing—she won't go all the way with this. She doesn't want to end up as the subject of a televised hearing. Not if she wants to protect her husband's career."

"So how does all this help me?" Holder asked.

"Call her bluff. Convince her that the only possible end result here is that this will become public. That she and her husband will not be able to live with this any more than you will."

"Wrong," Holder said. "Has it occurred to you that I could be court-martialed for this? I could end up in prison."

Trainor stopped under a streetlamp before one of the old stone homes. Above their heads, a halo of summer insects whirled around the light. Trainor put his hand on his friend's shoulder.

"Let's take it a day at a time," he said.

"A disaster at a time, more likely," Holder said.

"Maybe we can convince Kathleen Gates to tell the truth, or at least to withdraw the story she's told."

"Why would she do that?"

"Because she's not going to want this to go public."

Holder suddenly felt dizzy.

The reality of what he was doing—this conversation, the threats, the possible consequences—was only apparent to him in waves, like nausea. He could only talk about it if he pretended it were all something else: a case study in leadership class, for instance.

"Look, Timmer is already working on this, and you know she's sharp. She'll do the right thing," Trainor said.

Holder nodded.

"I think we should also try to open up a communication channel with Kathleen Gates," Trainor went on.

Holder thought to mention something about the communication channel that didn't exist between Trainor and Ruth, but then thought better of such a cruel comment.

"I don't want to talk to her," Holder said. "Hell, I don't even want to think about her."

"We'll figure out a way," Trainor said. "Let's sleep on it."

At ten o'clock the following morning, Kathleen Gates stood in her living room, looking out the wide front window for Dorothy Sayer. Sayer was prompt—that was good—but she'd brought along someone else.

Gates watched the young woman unfold herself from the car, long legs, a beautiful cream colored suit, that confident smile. She pushed her hair back with that practiced gesture Gates had seen her use before, then she stood and pointed at the brick quarters, where a sign below the house number read MAJOR TOM GATES.

The man with her was also beautifully dressed in a lightweight, dark suit, a lightblue shirt with a white collar. He was not handsome, but was so impeccably groomed that he couldn't help but make a good impression. No doubt he was Claude Braintree, Sayer's boss.

Gates looked quickly about the room. She had taken her children to a neighbor for the morning, but she had left a few of their toys lying about to give the house the domestic feel she had cultivated with Sayer in the first interview. For that meeting, Gates had chosen to look a little bedraggled, a little helpless. Now her clothes were clean, crisp, prim—a long cotton skirt, a white blouse with patch pockets. Hot as it was, she had even put on a camisole lest her bra show through. She would dress this way, the very picture of propriety, until the drama was played out.

She checked her appearance in the mirror, ran her hands over the front of her skirt, pushed at her hair, and took several deep breaths. Braintree's appearance—and the elevation it signaled—meant that things were happening quickly. She told her reflection that she would remain in control.

She did not want the little story she'd told about Flynn to be widely known. Her plan was complicated, with lots of moving parts that could go spinning out of control—so she had mentally prepared herself for the fact that Tom would eventually find out what had happened—her version of the events in the parking lot. She had no doubt that he would believe her. In all their years of marriage she had never failed to be able to influence him when she needed to, but she had never faced a test like this one.

She was a little afraid of her husband's temper. Once, in a club outside Fort Campbell, a suit with a few too many drinks on his bar tab had complimented her on her hair. She'd smiled and turned away, but the man stepped closer to her and, just as Tom returned from the men's room, had said something about how her long curls would be great "lap hair." Tom had picked the man up by the collar and the back of his belt and slid him along the bar, plowing glasses, ashtrays, money, and pitchers of beer up in a dramatic rooster tail of destruction.

She was a little worried what Tom might do to Wayne Holder. She even toyed with the idea of telling Tom that the cadet had not done anything wrong (she would not tell him she had seduced the cadet) but that she had fabricated the story to apply a little pressure to West Point. He would have to understand—she would make him understand—that she was doing all of this out of love.

Sayer and Braintree were at the door. Gates passed her hands over the front of her shirt once more.

"Hello, Dorothy."

"Hello, Mrs. Gates," Sayer said. "This is Claude Braintree, my boss."

She was about to say something more when Braintree stepped past her into the tiny living room. He was almost as tall as Tom, though not nearly as good looking. But his clothes were beautiful and he smelled of soap and cologne. Kathleen wondered how he could bear to wear a suit during these hot days.

"I apologize for dropping in unannounced, as it were," he said, taking her hand in his. His grip was firm, his palm dry and warm.

"But I wanted to talk to you myself."

"That's fine, Mr. Braintree," Kathleen said. "Won't you come in?"

The three of them sat in the living room. Like everything else about the quarters, the room was tiny. Kathleen got a sudden mental picture of how ridiculous they looked, all dressed up and sitting around the living room on a weekday morning. Normally, her kids would be crawling over this furniture and piles of toys, watching brightly colored cartoon characters dash back and forth across the television screen.

"I wanted to come and speak to you in person . . . may I call you Kathleen?"

"Certainly."

"First of all, let me say that I'm terribly sorry for what you've endured," Braintree said, "and that we are concerned about these very serious accusations you've made.

"Senator Bruckner has expressed a personal concern and wants to make sure that we—that is, my staff and I—are both responsive to your needs and respectful of your privacy. This is a very delicate matter."

"You told Senator Bruckner what I said to Dorothy, here?" Kathleen asked.

This was an unexpected development. She pictured Bruckner, whom she'd seen often enough on the television news, standing in a big Washington office, phone pressed to his ear as he listened to her story.

"Ms. Sayer told me that you hadn't reported this incident to the authorities," Braintree said. "May I ask why not?"

"I was frightened," Kathleen said. "And then after the incident with General Flynn, I couldn't."

"Have you told your husband about this?" Braintree wanted to know. He spoke softly, but it was not clear to Kathleen that he had sided with her.

Kathleen began to speak, caught her breath, forced a few tears. The performance wasn't as difficult as she'd expected. She was genuinely afraid.

"No. I've been afraid of that, most of all. I feel as if I've gotten him into some kind of awful mess."

There was a large element of truth in that. She had launched something big and was now wondering if she could control it. Maybe she'd gone too far, made up too many lies to keep track of. She had no guarantee about Tom's reaction, no way of predicting whether her plan would work. All she knew was that she had to do something; she wasn't about to stand by and watch the Army screw her husband as the Navy had screwed her brother. She had set the course, and she was going to see it through.

"It's not your fault, Mrs. Gates," Sayer said. She reached over and patted Kathleen on the knee. "You're the victim here."

Braintree might have given Sayer a look that said *enough,* but Kathleen wasn't sure.

"Can you recount for me exactly what General Flynn said to you, Kathleen?" Braintree asked. His tone made it clear to Kathleen that he was going to be harder to sell than Sayer had been.

Kathleen told the story again, sticking to the facts as far as possible, then keeping the fictitious dialogue simple. She didn't want to contradict herself.

When she had finished, Braintree nodded, then asked, "Would you be willing to testify to this in front of the committee?"

Kathleen took a deep breath. This was the point she needed to control, and it was going to be her toughest challenge.

"I . . . uh . . . that is, I was hoping it wouldn't come to that," she managed.

"In order for us to reach some sort of resolution," Braintree said, "we would more or less have to get this out in the open. That would mean telling the committee."

"In public."

"Well," Braintree said, sitting back in the chair and picking a tiny piece of lint from the leg of his trousers, "most of the hearings will be public, yes. I suppose that would mean you would talk in public."

He looked up at Kathleen and smiled.

"I assure you that you wouldn't have to worry about reprisals, Mrs. Gates. Once we establish what General Flynn offered you, he won't be in any position to touch you or your husband."

"But it would be very difficult for me to say all these

things in public. You're talking about a setting like one of those committee meetings you always see down in Washington, right?" She gestured at the television as she said this. "Cameras, spectators, all that?"

"Well, probably not so many spectators," Braintree said, smiling as if this were some sort of inside joke.

"I don't know that I'm willing to go that far, Mr. Braintree," Gates said. "I need some time to think it over."

"Senator Bruckner could probably get you and your husband transferred, if you're worried about staying here."

Kathleen nodded. She hadn't thought of this possibility, and she was pleasantly surprised that Braintree brought it up. She thought for a moment about asking if they could go to Hawaii, but it was no more than a diversion. She didn't want to get to a new post only to have people refer to her as the woman who'd had sex with a cadet while her husband was stationed at West Point.

No, television was a bit too much.

"I really feel this is the best way we can help you, Kathleen," Braintree said. He leaned forward, put a hand on each knee as if preparing to stand.

"Frankly, it's the only way I see; I hope you'll give it some serious consideration."

"There is the matter of another action—an unfavorable action—pending against my husband," she said.

Braintree held up a hand.

"I'm sure that we could persuade the right officials that the whole incident, beginning with the letter, needs to be reevaluated in light of the assistance you've offered us," he said. "We'll take care of you."

"I can't afford to talk to the whole community about this," Kathleen said. "I have a reputation, after all. I mean, I made a mistake, perhaps, in talking to that boy. He was very upset and I was trying to be nice to him. Tom and I take very seriously our roles as mentors to these young men and women."

Braintree touched the perfect knot on his tie. "Of course you do," he said.

Kathleen continued. "I'm even more afraid—and I don't think that's too strong a word—of what might happen if I take on General Flynn in public. The Army is a very small community. There is no place my husband and I could go that we wouldn't be followed by this."

Sayer nodded amiably. She was in Kathleen's corner.

Kathleen Gates had a sudden image of herself sitting at a table covered with green felt, sweating under hot lights, leaning into a microphone and telling the lies she'd told about General Flynn while television cameras and photographers roamed about before her.

If it came to that—if that were the only way—she could do it.

But it didn't have to come to that.

Simon would have to come through for her first.

CHAPTER 15

THE TELEPHONE ON THE DEAN'S DESK BUZZED AS HE WAS finishing a call to one of the professors. David Simon fingered the lighted button and heard his secretary's voice.

"Mrs. Gates on two," she said.

"Thank you," Simon said, suppressing a sigh.

"Oh, and . . . sir," Sarah Wiley continued. "She sounds awfully upset."

Wiley had occupied the desk outside Simon's office for seven years. Fiercely loyal and the very soul of discretion, she had earned Simon's confidence in almost all of his official dealings. He rarely felt it necessary to conceal something from her.

This, suddenly, seemed one of those occasions.

"Thank you, Sarah."

Simon hit the line button before Wiley could reply, then looked at the lights banked on the phone, and wondered if there was some way Wiley could listen in without his knowing it.

"General Simon," he said.

"Claude Braintree just left my house," Kathleen Gates said without preamble. "He wants me to testify at a public hearing."

Simon had known it would come to this, of course. The titillating little story about Kathleen Gates and her cadet lover wouldn't do the Bruckner Commission any good if it was kept under wraps. It only became useful if it was out in the open.

"Just what does he want you to say?" Simon asked, trying to match the sound of panic in Kathleen Gates's voice with a measure of control in his own.

"It doesn't matter," she insisted, her voice rising. "I don't want to say anything. I won't testify in public."

"Maybe you could offer to make a deal with the commission so that the incident with the cadet wouldn't have to . . ."

"I'm not talking about the cadet, General," Kathleen interrupted. "I'm talking here about me and the Supe. I'm talking about what happened when I talked to General Flynn about all this."

David Simon felt a sudden dryness in his throat; he remembered clearly his first impression of Kathleen Gates as a dangerous woman.

"I'm afraid I'm not following you," Simon said. He suspected that he knew more than he wanted to about what Kathleen Gates was up to; he wanted to hear it from her.

There was a pause on the other end of the line, maybe the sound of Kathleen Gates drawing a long breath. When she began to speak again, Simon pictured her speaking through clenched teeth; her voice sounded like glass being ground underfoot.

"I met General Flynn at the alumni building," Kathleen said, speaking slowly now, measuring her words. "I told him how upset I've been about all that's been happening to us.

"He knew about the assault, and he offered to remove the letter of reprimand from my husband's file if I would consider dropping the accusation against the cadet."

It was a lie, of course. A bold lie.

Kathleen Gates had all but told him, during her visit to his office, that she was planning to go after Flynn; but Simon hadn't thought she would have the nerve to see it through. Yet in two quick strokes—one with the cadet and the other with Flynn—and because of the timing of Bruckner's visit, she had set herself up to rock the Academy with a tremendous scandal at its most vulnerable time. All over one little letter of reprimand. It was the equivalent of killing a rhinoceros to get its horn. She could doom the career of a thirty-year veteran and cut off, before it even got started, the career of another young man. All with a few well-placed and well-planned lies.

Something told him to pull away from Kathleen Gates, leave her hanging out there with her fantastic story.

"What did Mr. Braintree say about all this? About General Flynn's . . . offer?"

"He wants me to testify to this in front of the Commission."

"Weren't you expecting that?" Simon asked. For all her viciousness, he thought, Kathleen Gates was not all that savvy.

"You're not fucking reading me here, General," Kathleen said, all pretense of control gone. "It doesn't need to go that far. You and I had a deal: Flynn needs to resign to save the Academy the embarrassment of having this out in public. You need to get these civilians on board about that, and you need to make sure that there are no bad letters in my husband's file."

Simon swallowed hard. Kathleen Gates was a live grenade, and the pin was missing. Handled well, she could be most useful. Handled poorly, she'd kill him and anyone else standing too close.

"Once again, Mrs. Gates, I'm afraid you overestimate my usefulness," Simon said cheerfully. He was smiling, trying to lighten up the conversation a bit. "Even if General Flynn were to resign to save the academy some embarrassing publicity, I'm not likely to be the first candidate that comes to mind when the Chief of Staff starts considering a replacement."

"Jesus Christ, you really are a spineless thing," Kathleen said. "Of course no one's going to *give* it to you. You have to go and get it. You can't sit around waiting for things to come to you; you'll never get anything that way."

Her words tumbled out rapid-fire, and Simon got the impression he was speaking with someone who was hanging on to control by the slimmest of threads.

"I mean, look at me. If I had waited for your precious Academy to make things right for my husband, I'd still be waiting around, wouldn't I? I had to go out and *make* things right. You have to do the same thing here. You have to go out and bend things to the shape you want. Do you get what I'm saying?"

Why should I put my head on the chopping block when you're doing all that for me? Simon thought.

"I'm not sure it would be prudent of me at this time to approach the Bruckner Commission with anything suggesting my appointment. . . ."

"Too late," Kathleen interrupted. "I knew you'd turn out to be a wimp, so I took the liberty of making a little tape recording of our last conversation in your office, the one in which we talk about your becoming Supe. You remember that, General? Or should I refresh your memory a bit? We talked about the Naval Academy and the plans they're developing. Then I mentioned that you would be the Supe in time to remove the letter from my husband's file."

Simon stood up abruptly, pushing his chair back against the credenza. He wanted badly to yell into the phone, to curse Kathleen Gates for a manipulative liar. But his years at West Point had put a thick coat of civility on him, and he wasn't even sure he was capable of a good fit anymore. He just couldn't get the prissiness out of his voice. And besides, maybe she had such a tape. He sputtered into the phone.

"Mrs. Gates, I think you're in over your head here. Furthermore, you have completely misinterpreted my comments on your situation. I could never promise such a thing, such a quid pro quo, because I don't have the power to do that. And besides, what good would such a tape do you? It would reveal that you'd planned this all along."

"Oh, put a lid on it, will ya?"

Simon shook his head. *What the hell am I dealing with here?*

"Of course the tape won't help—except to give me the satisfaction of seeing all of you gutless wonders go down the tubes. If my husband is forced out of the service, look for me—and this tape—on Oprah."

Simon fell back into his chair. Outside his window and several stories below him, a crew worked to repair the surface of the road that wound beneath Taylor Hall. The hammering sounds of their compressors rose and fell, rose and fell according to no discernible pattern. David Simon felt as if the sound were drilling into his skull. He didn't remember relinquishing control, but he couldn't think of an option.

"What do you want me to do?" he asked.

"I don't want to testify," Kathleen said. "Go to Braintree, tell him you don't think it would be a good idea for this to come out in public. Propose a compromise; tell him about your plan to reshape USMA. Reinventing the whole academy should garner enough publicity to satisfy his boss. Tell him you'll support all that if he spares West Point the bad press."

Simon rubbed his eyes. He had wanted Flynn gone; it looked as if he was going to get his wish. He worried about this connection with Kathleen Gates. If he pulled the letter from her husband's file, Kathleen would always have that on him, always be able to point out that they'd been in league.

"You still there, General?" she asked.

"Still here."

"It's time to act," she said.

"Yes," Simon said. "Apparently it is."

Kathleen Gates began to tremble as soon as she hung up the phone. Still dressed in her prim white blouse and longish skirt, sweating now, her breakfast doing barrel rolls under her rib cage. She thought she might throw up.

How did things get this screwed up? If she had just stayed home the Friday before last, she could have kept Tom from trying to get the cadets together for a run, avoiding the whole embarrassing incident with Holder and the escalation that followed.

She walked into the small powder room at the back of the house. Outside, she could hear three or four neighbor kids squealing as they played in an inflatable pool. She turned on the overhead light and stared at her reflection in the mirror under its harsh glare.

The skin below her eyes seemed to have loosened, and there were tiny lines, like check marks, at the corners of her mouth. She put the pads of her fingers on each cheek and massaged her face in small circles.

Simon is a dolt, she thought to herself. *Probably the wrong man to get mixed up in this with.*

She wondered if he would do what she'd told him; there had to be a limit to his ambition. And what did she have left if she needed to turn up the heat, apply more pressure?

Not much.

She leaned forward, resting her head against the cool glass of the mirror, and began to cry.

Just tears at first, dripping off her cheeks and into the shiny sink. She kept her eyes open, and felt the tightness spread across her shoulders, across her chest as she pushed back the sobs she knew were waiting there. All the anxiety of the last two weeks had built up to a point right behind her eyes, and she felt that if she let it out she might never be able to stop, and if she didn't she might be stuck right here in this position, paralyzed, unable to move forward or back.

She stayed that way for nearly ten minutes, alternating between telling herself to let it go, let it all go—the plots, the schemes, the desperate maneuvering, and the sleepless nights—and just let Tom sort things out as he might. But then she would glance up at herself in the mirror and see her brother's face in her own. And she was determined not to let the system steamroller her and her family.

She gripped the sides of the sink tightly.

"I will win this," she told herself. It had the force of an order. "I will be stronger than Flynn, stronger than Simon, than Tom, than Holder, or Trainor, or any of the others. I will win. I will not lose."

But there was no recovering the confidence she'd had when she first brought her idea to Simon. No way to go back, even as far as she'd been this morning, before Braintree's visit, before she pictured herself in front of the commission, in front of the television cameras.

She could not go back. She could not stay where she was. The only thing left to do was to go forward.

The phone rang in the kitchen behind her.

Kathleen Gates straightened, used both hands to push the hair away from her face and swipe at the wet streaks on her face, then turned to the room behind her. By the time she'd walked the few feet to the wall phone, she had composed herself. She would be strong. No matter what happened, no matter who got in the way.

She picked up the receiver and practiced her smile, because you could hear that over the phone.

"Hello," she said. And she could hear it. Clear, purposeful. The voice of a winner.

All through his last period class, history of the Military Art, Alex Trainor stared at the map depicting Napoleon's Austerlitz campaign and thought about Wayne Holder having sex with Kathleen Gates.

He wasn't intentionally calling up the image, of course, but he seemed powerless to stop it. A few facts about logistics in early nineteenth-century warfare did manage to worm their way into his consciousness, but mostly he imagined Kathleen Gates in the half dark of the parking lot, her long skirt pulled up around her waist. . . .

"Alex."

Trainor blinked. Turned his head to the side. His instructor, a Major Reagan, stood beside the map, arms akimbo, looking at him expectantly.

"Are you with us?"

"Uh . . . yes, sir," Trainor managed.

Reagan waited patiently. Trainor could feel his classmates, seated around the half circle of desks in the room, looking at him. Apparently, Reagan had asked him a question and was now expecting an answer.

"I'm sorry, sir," Trainor said, owning up. "I guess I wasn't paying attention."

"I guess not," Reagan said, still managing a smile. "Let's get back to the task at hand, shall we?"

Trainor held his pen over his open notebook. The period was twenty minutes old and he had written down exactly nothing.

Before Holder's problem, it had been Ruth. He had spent a good part of the spring semester daydreaming about her and fighting off those daydreams. He remembered writing in a notebook at the beginning of May an injunction from Scripture: *If thine eye is an occasion for sin, pluck it out.*

He had sat through classes torturing himself with exquisite guilt over his relationship with Ruth, especially after it turned physical. He thought constantly about his family, about the disappointment they would feel; and he thought about Ruth, about her pink and willing mouth, about the unexpected pleasures she had visited on him with those lips, things that he'd heard other cadets talk about.

When Ruth had finally taken him to her bed—and she had been the one leading the way—it was as if someone had turned up the volume on the banshee voices. There was no stopping the tumble of images that played on his conscience at all hours of the day and night. Pray as he might for some relief, there was none to be had.

Until Wayne Holder had fallen.

Alex Trainor could sit and think about Kathleen Gates without the same sense of guilt because, after all, he had not touched her. It had been Wayne. Yet the same images played constantly on the grainy screen of his imagination. The little voice that might have warned him of his sin was telling him that it was OK, he was trying to think of ways to help his friend.

"Cadet Trainor."

Trainor snapped back to the present. It was Reagan again, using the much more formal address that spelled trouble. Trainor glanced down at the page again. Still nothing there. Up at Reagan, who normally wore a smile.

"Stick around after class, Alex. I need to talk to you."

"Yes, sir."

Trainor dragged his concentration around during the last few minutes of the period, copying, almost verbatim, whatever Reagan and the other cadets had to say about Napoleon's dash for the Austrian supply lines. He wrote without thinking. If nothing else, he looked as if he were paying attention.

"You want to tell me what's going on with you, Alex?" Reagan said when the other cadets had cleared the room.

"I'm sorry, sir. I know I haven't been participating much lately," Trainor said.

Two cadets entered the room for the next class period. Reagan raised a hand to them and they retreated back into the hallway.

"You've been out to lunch since the first class," Reagan said. "Based on your class standing and your reputation with the other instructors, I thought you'd be a better student than that."

"I am, sir," Trainor said. "I've been distracted. . . ."

"Personal problems?"

"You could say that, yes, sir."

"Well, don't be afraid to ask for help," Reagan said. "In my experience, we sometimes miss the obvious solution, the one that's right in front of us the whole time."

"Thanks, sir. I'm sure I'll get a grip on things. One of my classmates is having some difficulty and I'm trying to figure out a way to help him."

"Don't let yourself go down the tubes in the process," Reagan offered. "No more daydreaming through a whole class period. Right?"

"Roger that, sir."

As he left Thayer Hall, Trainor thought about Reagan's comment. The simple things.

How could I have missed it? he thought. *How could I have not seen that all I need do was turn to the Lord?*

He came out into the sunlight of the early afternoon, the bright shards glinting off the crenelated buildings, the glass, the statues, and felt a clear vision for the first time since learning that Ruth was pregnant. Alex Trainor had spent too much time worrying about himself.

I need to put my faith in the Lord. He'll help me see what to do about Ruth. And in the meantime I can help Wayne Holder.

Wayne Holder had fallen; Wayne Holder had sinned. There was redemption for Alex Trainor in helping his roommate.

It's time to look outward, to take note of the suffering around me, he thought as he made his way in front of the library. He smiled at a few cadets he recognized, snapped off a sharp salute to a couple of instructors walking in the opposite direction.

Yes, that was it. Stop worrying so much about your own difficulties, Alex. Wayne Holder is in trouble, too.

It was amazing, he thought as he crossed the street near

Eisenhower's statue, amazing how he had allowed himself to be distracted.

"Put your trust in the Lord," he said aloud.

A cadet coming up behind him turned.

"What's that?"

"I said, 'Put your trust in the Lord,'" Alex repeated.

"Yeah, whatever," the other cadet said, lowering his head and walking faster, putting some distance between himself and Alex.

An unbeliever. One who couldn't see, refused to see, the possibilities.

"All things are possible through Jesus Christ," Alex said to the cadet's back. He might as well have been talking to the bronze Ike.

It was all right there for anyone to see. Open your eyes. The truth will set you free.

By the time he reached the door to MacArthur Barracks, Trainor had achieved a state of self-induced ecstasy. He wanted to hug each of the cadets he saw on the way. His brothers and sisters in Christ. Even the unbelievers. Even the ones who called him a thumper and a Jesus freak.

Blessed are you who are reviled for my sake. . . .

"Hey, Alex."

A D Company yearling, dressed for intramurals, passed Trainor on the stairs.

"Praise the Lord," Trainor said.

There was a glow to the day. Today Trainor would not see the smirks, did not care even to think about them, though he knew they were there. He was the butt of jokes among the other cadets. But today it did not matter.

Service and witness. That's what it was about. It wasn't about worrying over what Ruth wanted. He would put his trust in the Lord. The Lord would help him solve his problems. And in the meantime, he could turn to Wayne. Holder needed him. He had to come through for his friend.

Trainor pushed open the door. Holder wasn't there. Wayne's class shirt, with nametag and collar insignia attached, was hanging in his locker, slightly ripe from a long day of classes. Holder had already been in the room and changed for athletics.

"No matter," Trainor said out loud. "The Lord can reach out to you even if I can't find you."

He sat at his desk, pulled his Bible from the shelf above his head, and just let it fall open. He did not read it; sometimes the words he found there confused him, or contradicted his ideas. So he put his hand on the open page and imagined himself drawing strength from those words without reading them. There was such a thing as truth, he believed, and it extended from these very pages and could touch everyday lives. It could touch the lives of Kathleen Gates and Wayne Holder and Major Tom Gates. And if he didn't think about Ruth, well, the Lord, after all, was going to take care of that.

He sat at his desk, alone in his room, the fingers of his good hand entwined with the fingers sticking out of the bandage on his other hand. The door was closed, the barracks quiet for a few moments at the end of the class day.

"Dear Lord," he began, as he always did. He pressed his eyes tightly closed.

"Please let me see clear to help Wayne in his time of trial," he said.

He prayed for nearly ten minutes. Not once did he think of Ruth. Or the baby.

Alex Trainor had not heard from Ruth all week. He usually called her every other day, depending on how much time was available to him; but Wayne had convinced him that it would be best to let things cool a little bit.

At first he thought it would be difficult to stop calling Ruth. It wasn't that he found their conversations all that stimulating, it was just that they had become a habit. Yet he had passed the whole week and hadn't even been tempted to pick up the phone. Instead he had allowed himself to become absorbed in Holder's problem, and some part of his mind had shoved the picture of Ruth to a back corner of his consciousness.

Alex Trainor stood up and looked out the window.

Kathleen Gates was walking along the road in front of the gym, heading toward the barracks entrance nearest her husband's office.

This was not chance; this was not coincidence. This had to be the hand of God providing him an opportunity.

Trainor turned excitedly back to his desk, picked up his Bible, and pressed it to his lips.

"Thank you, Lord, for this chance to serve you and your children. Help me to do the right thing."

He tucked the worn book under his arm and headed out into the hallway, his steps light, his purpose—if not his course—firm.

Kathleen Gates had not picked up the kids from the sitter. She had called her neighbor with a story about something coming up and could you, oh, would you please, I'd be so indebted to you, and yes, thank you very much.

She had driven north along the valley, winding through the little towns spotted among the hills. The river was there, always off to the east, exquisite views made fuzzy by the late summer humidity. Calmed down after an hour, she had driven back, passing her house at the last moment, overcome with a sudden urge to see her husband.

She almost never visited him unannounced, and Tom rarely called her during the day. Too busy. He did not call her to say hello, or I'm thinking about you. If he called her at all it was to ask her to do something for him. And if she called him, she realized, it was to ask when he would be home. The nag's question.

Tom didn't like to be pinned down. And she knew that, for the most part, his schedule was genuinely unpredictable. But she had expected things to be different at this post. She expected him home at a decent hour. But Tom Gates was unwilling, or afraid, to fall into a pattern, especially one Kathleen established. The moment he stuck to a schedule, he gave up control.

Those were the lines that had formed stealthily in their marriage, like a coral reef, built up over time. You couldn't actually see it grow, but these things were there, and they became solid.

She had once presented herself to this man, dressed in wedding white and full of promise. And he had turned to face her before the altar of a little church in Pennsylvania, handsome in his dress blues, innocent of all the sins she would accuse him of, ignorant of all the petty squabbles about who was supposed to clean the dishes, how many times this one or that one had gotten up with the baby. All that sludge, the mire, the sediment at the bottom of the pool that was their marriage.

But for all the tedium of running a life together, the events of the last few days had convinced her of something else: she loved her husband. Not in that goofy, eye-rolling way that had struck her when they first met. She was beyond all that. Share a bathroom with someone for more than a decade and you lost your illusions.

Driving the snake-track roads of the valley, thinking about the course she had set for them and asking herself why, there had been one clear answer. No matter what she thought about Tom, she did love him, and she was loyal to him, and she would do whatever she could to help him.

Kathleen Gates wandered down to the cadet area, to the barracks where Tom's office was located, for some reassurance. She wanted to talk to him, see him face to face, as if to convince herself that this man was really there, that there was a flesh and blood someone who needed her.

Kathleen walked around the end of the barracks and into North Area, the paved quadrangle formed by MacArthur and Scott Barracks. There were three or four pick-up games of basketball going on; other cadets in class uniform, rifles at high port, hurrying to drill; still others jogging toward the gym in small formations. She was the only person in civilian clothes. She paused a moment, looked out at the activity and felt, as she knew her husband did, buoyed by it. It was from this that Tom drew his strength, watching these kids or the soldiers at Bragg or Campbell, plugging into their energy, taking from it and giving it back.

Just a few yards away, in front of a rollaway basketball goal, a tall cadet broke away from his defenders and executed a beautiful lay-up, feet, arms, hands, everything gliding forward and up at the basket nearest where Kathleen stood. Eyes on the prize, graceful as a dancer, he tipped the ball in, landed at a run and jogged back onto the court, nodding at Kathleen as he went by.

"Hello, ma'am," he said.

Kathleen smiled.

Then she turned and saw Alex Trainor opening the door behind her.

"Good afternoon, Mrs. Gates," Trainor said, smiling widely. He had a thick black book in his good hand, and it took Kathleen a moment to realize it was a Bible. Probably on his way to some sort of meeting at the Chaplain's office, him and all the other soft-spoken ones, the do-gooders.

"I saw you coming into the barracks area," he said, smiling his missionary smile. "May I speak with you for a moment?"

"I'm on my way to see my husband," Kathleen said, pushing past him in the doorway.

"This will only take a moment," Trainor insisted, still smiling, still following her. "I just want to tell you about this wonderful revelation I had today."

He was crowding her, trailing her through the double doors and staying right at her side. At the bottom of the stairwell, they ran into a gaggle of a dozen or so cadets hurrying out to the gym, all dressed in athletic shorts and tee shirts, all of them loud, excited, talking at once. The crowd surged off the stairs, split like the sea to make way for Kathleen, but still managed to hold her up, push her back toward the far wall so that she couldn't escape Trainor.

"I came out of class today and was just struck, struck hard, by the beautiful day the Lord has given us," Trainor was saying.

Kathleen looked at him to see if he was serious. He had that wide, healthy smile, the one that radiated friendliness. Praise the Lord.

"And I went up to my room and was praying over these little problems my good friend Wayne has been having lately. . . ."

Kathleen Gates grabbed him by the arm, just above the bandage, and dragged him into the hallway in front of Tom's office.

"You need to learn when to keep your mouth shut," she whispered fiercely.

She twisted his arm as she sidestepped to look inside the office. The door was open, the light was off; she pulled Trainor into the room behind her.

"See, that's just it," Trainor was saying as he followed her. "That's exactly what I found today. The relief for all of this anxiety is right there in front of us. There is no need for all this pain, all of this wasted, misdirected energy."

He stood before Kathleen, holding his Bible out in his good hand like some roadside preacher, smiling like an imbecile.

Kathleen put her hands on her hips, narrowed her eyes, wondered if this kid was for real.

"The truth shall set you free," he said.

"What the hell are you talking about?"

"The truth shall set you free," he said again.

"I didn't say I couldn't hear you, you idiot," she said. "I asked what the hell you meant."

She stepped close to him, widened her eyes, as if that might help her see more clearly what Trainor was talking about. Normally she would have been happy to dismiss these ramblings. But Trainor knew too much. He was dangerous. And here they were, right in Tom's office, talking about those very things she wasn't ready to tell her husband. What would she do if Tom came back?

"All we need to do is tell the truth, the absolute truth, and put our faith in the Lord," Trainor said again. "Wayne and I know that you must be very concerned about what Major Gates is going to think of all this, and so you're afraid. And perhaps that has distorted your clear vision of what really happened out there."

He was looking straight into her eyes, unwavering. A true believer. The most dangerous kind. And he was talking, she became sure in a moment, about Tom finding out. About *telling* Tom what happened.

"But I really believe that if we all just come clean, if we all just speak the truth, that the truth *will* set us free. Major Gates can't fail to see your sincerity if you tell the truth, whatever that is. And I know Wayne will be better off for it."

Kathleen stood quietly for the few seconds that Trainor held this running commentary; she could hear herself breathing. This kid had dropped in from outer space.

"I think we should pray on it," he said, reaching out for her hand.

"Don't touch me!" she yelped, trying to control her voice, pulling her arm back as if he might bite her.

Kathleen looked out in the hall, half expecting some-one—Tom, maybe—to come to the open doorway to see what the shouting had been about. No one appeared.

"You self-righteous little prick," she said, poking Trainor in the chest. "Are you threatening me?"

Trainor actually laughed.

"Not at all," he said. "I just wanted to tell you where I found help. Right here, with the Lord. And I think you and Wayne can find help, here, too. Help in resolving this conflict. . . ."

"We don't have a conflict," Kathleen said, moving even closer to him, dropping her voice to something barely above an angry whisper. "We have a crime. Your roommate committed a crime, and now he's getting nervous because the axe might just fall on his head. And I think he sent you here to scare me off."

"That's just not the way it is," Trainor said. His I-am-saved smile—still in place—was beginning to piss off Kathleen Gates mightily. She wanted to punch him right in the middle of his shiny teeth.

"No, I'll tell you how it is," Kathleen said. "You and your roommate are toying with the wrong girl. You have no idea. . . ."

At that moment Kathleen Gates thought she heard her husband's voice in the hall, and here she was, practically nose to nose with this smiling little Bible thumper who was just crazy enough to break into his routine when her husband walked into the room.

"But I'm trying to help," Trainor whined. "And I think if you'll take a minute, a calming minute to pray with me on this, you'll see that the truth is the only thing that can provide you relief from this torment, from your worries."

Kathleen Gates felt a sputtering rage inside her, wordless, dangerous.

"You need to back off, Trainor," she said.

"I can't." Still with that smile. "My friend needs me, and I think you need me, too," he went on. "And we all need the Lord."

Clearly there was no reasoning with this one. Kathleen just wanted away from him.

"Go away," she said.

Trainor lowered his Bible, brought it to his chest, holding it there, stroking the back cover with one thumb.

"OK," Trainor said. "Maybe I've hit you with too much all at once. I know that you must be distraught. After all, it took me a few days to see what I needed to do. I think that you'll come around.

"If you want to talk, you can always call me at the barracks," he said to her. He leaned over and hugged her, patting her on the back, the Bible between them. She was too stunned to do anything but stand still.

"God bless you," he said.

He smiled again, turned, and walked out of the room.

Kathleen Gates stood quietly in the space before her husband's desk, trying to make sense of what had just happened.

As best she could figure, Alex Trainor had just threatened her even as he offered her a solution. All that talk about coming clean, about the truth and freedom . . . it had to mean he was planning on telling her husband about the rendezvous with Holder. But he had decided not to confront her directly. It was clever, really; he was giving her a chance to save face. All she had to do was to pretend to find Jesus, to grab this line he was throwing her. Then she and Holder could hang on it together, come clean about the truth, mourn their sins, and everything would come out all right in the end. A win-win situation, as Tom liked to call it.

Kathleen Gates actually smiled. It was brilliant.

But of course, she was not about to let it happen.

She walked around behind her husband's desk and toyed with the the clutter there as she admired Trainor's plan. She had to give him points for originality.

Kathleen shoved some papers around, put the pencils and pens back in the 82d Airborne Division mug, touched the phone log.

And there was her answer.

Ruth Rhodes.

A New York City number. Trainor's pregnant girlfriend. The one who wanted to get married. Or maybe she had changed her mind about this family thing after all.

Kathleen Gates looked out the window, still watching for her husband. He wasn't around, and she would have to find her own strength.

Hell, if she was in it this far, what difference would it make if she pushed a little more? She had already cornered a three-star and a one-star general, she had already manipulated one of the investigators and her boss, and she was well on her way to lying to a Senator and his commission. It hardly seemed like a great deal more to make a few phone calls to a distraught and no doubt lonely little pregnant girl in the city. See what might shake loose. Something to get Alex Trainor's mind back on his own problems.

On Friday morning Brigadier General David Simon waited, knuckles drumming the tablecloth, in the high-ceilinged dining room of the Hotel Thayer. Simon was dressed for work in a class "B" uniform of short-sleeved green shirt and darker green trousers with the parallel black stripes, alongside the leg, of a general officer. He had come into the room smiling and ten minutes early for his breakfast with Claude Braintree. Now, twenty minutes later, he drained the last of his third cup of coffee and scanned the room again. His stomach, empty except for the coffee, churned.

Goddamn civilians, he thought to himself. *Think they can play with me like this.*

He coached himself to a self-righteous huff, never a long journey for him.

Flynn lets them get away with this, he thought. *But they won't treat me like this when I'm Supe. I won't stand for it.*

"Good morning, General," Braintree said, gliding up to the table. A young man in slacks and a blazer was following Braintree, scribbling on a notepad. A retainer.

"So sorry to keep you waiting," Braintree continued. He held up his hand, though Simon had made no move to stand, then turned to his assistant.

"Check those requirements with Washington before you commit us to anything," he said as he installed himself in the chair across from the Dean. The young man nodded, mumbled a barely audible "yessir," and vanished.

"Trying to find the right venue for the committee hearings," Braintree said to Simon. "The Senator likes pomp and circumstance, even if there will be no press there, even if the hearings are closed."

He picked up a menu, set it aside without looking at it.

"Are the hearings going to be open to the public?" Simon asked.

"That hasn't been determined yet," Braintree said, smoothing his tie, tucking it into the folds of his open jacket. This morning he wore a light gray suit, some sort of pattern barely visible in the weave, white shirt, dark tie with tiny paisley print. His hair shone; his fingernails were smooth, polished. Simon had heard about men getting manicures; one just didn't see it all that often around West Point.

"Is that Senator Bruckner's decision?" Simon asked. He had a sensation that he was blundering through some protocol minefield, as if he were asking questions to which he should already know the answer, or questions he shouldn't ask at all. But the nature of the hearings was Kathleen Gates's major concern—and a way, perhaps, to control her.

Braintree paused, weighing an answer. A waitress appeared.

Simon looked up at the woman, whom he recognized from some of the official functions he'd attended at the hotel. He thought her name was Angela. Be a good idea to show Braintree just how well known he was around here.

"Good morning," Simon said. "Angela, isn't it?"

"Good morning, General," she answered. "It's Donna, actually. What can I get for you gentlemen this morning?"

"Decaf coffee, toasted English muffin with margarine, not butter," Braintree rattled off. He didn't look up at the woman.

"And *please* make certain it's decaf. And *margarine,* not butter," he repeated.

Donna looked at Braintree, then at Simon. She smiled as if to say, *Isn't this pleasant?*

Simon ordered a light breakfast. When he'd handed the menus over, he looked back over the table and found Claude Braintree watching him, giving him the wide smile.

"I'm so glad we're getting this chance to talk, General," Braintree said. "Things are moving along rather swiftly now, and I doubt I'll have much time to spare once the Senator arrives."

"When will that be?" Simon asked.

"End of next week, I suspect," Braintree said.

"And did you say that the meetings will be closed?" Simon pressed.

"Actually, I didn't say," Braintree smiled. "That will depend on a lot of factors." He smiled again. Clearly Simon was not getting any more information about the format for the hearings.

"Is that what you wanted to talk to me about?" Braintree asked. "The hearings?"

Simon shook his head, shifted in his seat, trying to appear comfortable. He regretted the coffee. "No. I wanted to talk to you about some plans we've been working on here."

Simon led off just as he'd rehearsed in his head a dozen or so times between three and five in the morning, when he finally gave up on sleep and dragged himself out of bed.

"These discussions about the shape West Point should take are nothing new up here," Simon said. "We are constantly evaluating ourselves to make sure we're doing the best possible job, and we're always on the look-out for ways to improve."

Simon paused, watching for some feedback. Braintree wore the same look of mild amusement Simon had seen in each of his meetings with the man.

"In fact, we even have what you might call contingency plans, alternatives for the Academy."

"Why?" Braintree asked.

"What's that?"

"Why would you have contingency plans?"

"Well, let's say Congress comes down and says 'increase the size of the Corps'; it would be better for everyone if we'd thought that through."

Braintree laughed, but there was a bit of mockery there.

"Yet you don't expect that Congress is going to call for a larger military, do you?"

Simon tried smiling. Big joke. We're all in this together. His lips seemed stuck to his teeth; the smile felt crooked.

"Well, I guess that's the least likely scenario," Simon allowed. "But let's say, for argument's sake, that the word came down that we had to reduce the academy by some significant percentage. Let's say we had to cut strength by one third or one half. Well, that would mean a change in the way we did business, everything from the letting of contracts to recruiting faculty members from the active Army. We have people in graduate school now who would have to be sent back to the field Army. We would have to retool our admissions process.

"These contingency plans—not much more than brainstorming in some cases—are the initial groundwork for those kind of changes."

"And where are these contingency plans developed?" Braintree wanted to know.

"How's that?"

"I mean, is there one person or office at the academy responsible for putting all these plans together, keeping them all on a shelf somewhere, updating them? Or is it up to each individual department to do that?"

A small voice in Simon's brain was trying to incite panic. Maybe Braintree was a step or two ahead of him, had already talked to Foster at Navy and knew about the Two Star Plan. Simon felt as if he'd just stepped out into an open area and was waiting for the crack of the sniper's rifle.

"No, there is no central clearing house. In fact, there is no official mandate to come up with such plans."

Simon leaned back in his chair, tilted his head back a bit. "It's just that those of us who've been around for a while know that it's good to be prepared."

Simon and Braintree watched each other across the table, two powerful men and their unspoken secrets.

"There are two schools of thought," Simon continued. "One is to change the academy to something like what the British have at Sandhurst, their military college. A sort of finishing school that all officers, no matter what their source of commission, would attend for a year to learn the basics of their professional responsibilities. Not the technical stuff, but the philosophical stuff. Law, history, those kinds of things."

Braintree was looking at his tie again. He had pulled it from his jacket and was smoothing it. When the ends went back into the coat, Simon began to speak again.

"The other school of thought says to keep the Academy as a four-year institution—one that continues to offer a degree—but reduce it in size."

Simon took a sip of water, then brushed the back of his hand along his eyebrow. Braintree was giving him nothing in the way of feedback. No nod, no smile, no twitch. A blank look.

Maybe, Simon thought, *he isn't even following this.*

"In either of these cases, the leadership is going to have to be strong and experienced. If the Academy is reduced in size, there will be no call for a three star to command. It will probably be a two star billet."

Braintree was quiet, nothing moving, barely blinking. Simon felt a tiny bead of sweat move down his back, like a cold ball bearing inching along under his shirt.

He wanted to jump up, pound Braintree on the back and say, *I'm that man.* Get it all over with all at once. *Oh, and by the way, there's this little matter of what we're going to do with General Flynn. Well, when you hear what he's been accused of, you'll know the place is going to need a new leader. I'm the one.*

Donna brought the plates with their paltry breakfasts. A big china dish with a lonesome English muffin in the middle of it for Braintree, a large bowl of oatmeal for Simon. An old man's breakfast.

And at that instant he saw what was happening.

It was almost over for him. He'd retire in a few years; then, a couple of years down the line, no one would even remember that he'd been Dean.

But that wouldn't be the case if he became the Supe, the man who'd led the Academy through its biggest transition in the last century. He'd be another Sylvanus Thayer, Father of the New West Point. With a statue out there, not as big as MacArthur's, of course, or Patton's or Eisenhower's. Maybe just a marker. But he'd be remembered.

All he had to do was speak up.

"If that becomes necessary," Braintree said, dabbing at

the corners of his mouth with a napkin. "West Point would need someone at the helm with a lot of experience, lots of institutional knowledge."

"Exactly," Simon agreed. He was so relieved he felt like crying.

"Someone who can deal with the alumni, the press. Someone who's been around the block a few times," Braintree went on. He sipped from his coffee cup, folded his napkin, placed it alongside his plate.

"And would you be willing to take the job under those circumstances?" he asked.

"If it would help West Point, yes, I would," Simon said.

"General Flynn just arrived this summer, though," Braintree said. "I don't think it would be a good idea to change that position right away. I mean, he could probably stay on just to get the Academy through a transition period, don't you think?"

"Yes," Simon said. "As long as everything is . . . going well with General Flynn."

Braintree looked up, his mask falling aside for a second.

Simon leaned his elbows on the table; the cold ball-bearings were rolling down his back again.

"Your boss," he said to Braintree, "is looking for exposure up here. Press. But he already has a reputation for being a trouble-maker. Half the voters in America think he's just a publicity hound, that he'll do anything for a sound byte. And what he does is usually negative.

"And unless I miss my guess this is why you're up here," Simon went on. "Sort of the diplomatic corps. Get things done without setting the house on fire. Show a little good-will. Am I right?"

Braintree nodded slightly, a tiny acknowledgment.

"This is a chance for him to do something positive. If he wants to appeal to the conservative vote, he's going to have to develop a reputation as a visionary. This is going to be his chance to do something good for the country and still get the exposure he wants."

Braintree was very still, palms pressed flat on the table.

Not picking at your tie, now, are you? Simon thought.

"I know about the accusation against General Flynn," Simon said. "Very sad. A terrible mistake. Obviously it won't be good for the Academy if this comes out. My argument is that it won't be good for Senator Bruckner, either. He doesn't need to be center stage at another scandal; he needs to be seen doing something positive. I'm offering a win-win situation."

"I'm listening," Braintree said.

"General Flynn resigns in lieu of an embarrassing public scandal, a pissing contest with Mrs. Gates. Senator Bruckner recommends me to the Secretary of the Army to become acting Superintendent. If he then wants to propose a plan for a smaller version of West Point—save the taxpayers millions, become a visionary for defense in the twenty-first century—I'll support him among the alumni. I'll come down to Capitol Hill and tell everyone what a good idea I think it is."

Braintree studied his hands, still flat on the table, palms down. The dining room was nearly empty; Simon thought he could hear his own heart beat. He had no guarantee, of course, that Braintree wouldn't go immediately to General Flynn. That would be the end of Simon.

But the Dean had resolved to dare great things. And besides, if he didn't, Kathleen Gates was ready to make life miserable for him. Simon leaned back in his seat, trying his best to look calm.

"Well, General, you've given me quite a bit to think about," Braintree said. He stood, buttoned his jacket. "You're a very perceptive man."

Braintree put his hands on the back of his chair, shoved it under the table, met Simon's eyes. Gave him the big smile. "Ambitious, too."

"Because I don't believe her, Senator, that's why."

Claude Braintree was in a small office off Ninninger Hall, the tiny hearing room used by the Cadet Honor Committee. Behind the long wooden conference table, on a wall of exposed brick, hung an oil painting of Sandy Ninninger, USMA Class of 1941, centered beneath a single spot. Ninninger had been killed in the Phillipines in 1942. Won the Medal of Honor.

Beneath Ninninger's smile and forever-young face, Senator Bruckner and his minions would conduct hearings meant to move the academy onto the budget gallows—all so that the Senator could garner some free press.

The room was on the top floor of the First Division, the only remaining barracks from a set that dated to the nineteenth century. The middle floors were a museum. On reunion weekends the old grads dragged their families up the narrow stairs to the crowded two- and three-man rooms, complete with fireplaces.

This is how we used to live, back when things were better, all the brothers valiant, all the sisters virtuous.

"Because her story isn't plausible," Braintree went on. "General Flynn is too savvy to make that kind of offer and expect that no one would find out."

"But didn't you say she was a mousy little thing?" Bruckner asked, a sharp impatience in his voice. He'd already gotten excited by the possibility of a bloodbath in front of the TV lights; now Braintree wanted to take it away.

"Didn't you say she was out of her league, confused by everything that's happening?"

"Actually, that was my assistant's description, Senator."

"Ah, yes," Bruckner said. "The lovely Miss . . . what's her name again?"

"Sayer."

"Yes, Miss Sayer. I remember meeting her," Bruckner said.

Braintree could feel the leer over the phone.

"Isn't it possible that such a senior officer thought he could easily bully this woman?"

"Yes, Senator, it's possible. I just don't think that's what happened."

"What do you think happened?"

"I think Mrs. Gates is trying to develop some leverage on the Academy to keep her husband from getting canned. It's just too convenient. And I think the Dean is part of this deal."

"You think they're in this together? That's quite a conspiracy theory, Claude. Maybe you should call Oliver Stone to cover these hearings."

Claude Braintree looked down at the yellow legal tablet on top of the desk before him. On the top page he'd written the name "Simon," then drawn a circle around it. Across from that he'd written the name "Kathleen Gates" and drawn a circle around that. Claude Braintree knew there was a connection between the two, he just couldn't prove it.

"I'm thinking we should go to Flynn with all this," Braintree said.

"No. He'll just come up with some other maneuver."

Bruckner would rather have a scandal in hand, ready to play for the cameras, than the possibility of some truth that required all that complicated investigating and thinking about what was right.

"So for now, we keep Mrs. Gates in the line-up," Bruckner said on the other end of the phone. "We're going to see how the opening of the commission hearings plays in the press. We'll keep her in reserve, call her up to the big leagues if we need her."

Meaning, Braintree thought, *If you don't get enough media attention without her.*

"She doesn't want to testify," Braintree reminded his boss.

"That's because you haven't turned on the charm, yet, Claude," Bruckner said. "You're not with the program. I think you're getting chickenshit on me. I'd better get up there before you lose the killer instinct."

When Braintree didn't answer, Bruckner went on.

"There are ways around her protest," Bruckner said. "Private testimony. One on one with me. I can be very persuasive, Claude."

Another leer.

"Anyway, we'll get her in there and dazzle her with the power of her own words. Maybe we'll even tape it and use it at some other time."

Claude Braintree sat down at the desk and drew a line connecting the Gates and Simon circles.

"Let's at least hold her off a bit, Senator. Give me a chance to explore this a bit more. We wouldn't want to put this woman up there only to find out that we'd been duped. Am I right?"

"Sure, sure, sure. Whatever," Bruckner said. "Just make sure you keep the goal in mind, OK, Claude? Maximum exposure."

"Right, sir," Braintree said.

When he was off the phone, Braintree studied the sheet of paper in front of him. He had to admit that the story did sound fantastic. Kathleen Gates accuses the Superintendent of making her an offer in exchange for her silence, then she gets the Dean to go along with her. Simon approaches Braintree and lobbies to be the next Supe, knowing that Flynn is about to sail into a shitstorm.

If all that were true, he was dealing with some pretty unscrupulous bastards. Not that this was anything new to Braintree, he was just surprised to find it here, right out in the open.

He walked out into the conference room, placed his palms on the table and studied the painting of Ninninger, who had been chairman of the Cadet Honor Committee. Ninninger had lived only twenty-three years. Probably never told a lie. Beneath his portrait, the Bruckner Commission would traffic in the worst kind of unfounded accusations, the most vile lies.

Senator Bruckner was intent on making the biggest splash he could; Kathleen Gates filled that ticket nicely. The old man—no great moral beacon himself—wasn't likely to give her up. But there were times when the Senator had to be protected from his own ambition. If they gave Kathleen Gates and General Simon what they wanted and all the machinations came out later—exposed, somehow, in the press—the Commission would be a bust. Bruckner wouldn't take the heat, of course; he would only go so far as to admit that perhaps he'd let his subordinates run a little too freely. Claude Braintree would be hung out to dry. Bruckner would head back to Washington, maybe even off to the White House, without him.

That's not going to happen because of little old Kathleen Gates, Braintree told himself.

News Leaks Indicate Surprising Discoveries at West Point

Washington, DC. (AP) The Bruckner Commission, sent to study the U.S. Military Academy, has already unearthed some surprising discoveries, according to sources on Capitol Hill. One legislative assistant has hinted that the Commission, once it is in session, will reveal corruption and malfeasance at the highest levels.

Senator Bruckner, who plans to visit West Point personally in the next week, said that comments from him "at this time would be premature and irresponsible."

"If there's something going on up there that shouldn't be, you can bet we'll uncover it," Bruckner said. "For now, we're going with the assumption that West Point is serving the nation well—if expensively—just as it has for the last two hundred years."

Academy supporters, both in and out of uniform, as well as its powerful alumni association, have long known that West Point is vulnerable from an economic standpoint. Even the most generous interpretations of the cost-per-graduate still put the estimate higher than the cost of educating a new lieutenant at a civilian university for commissioning through the Reserve Officer Training Program, known as ROTC.

A Department of the Army spokesperson said that the academy is constantly under this kind of scrutiny. "West Point is careful about how it does business and is mindful of the public trust. We are confident that the academy will shine even under the closest scrutiny."

Some members of Congress chose to focus on another aspect of the current inquiry: the naked ambition of its head, Senator Lamar Bruckner. Just last month Senator Sandy Erwin (D-CA), herself a graduate of the U.S. Naval Academy, criticized the appointment of Senator Bruckner to head the investigative committee, calling him a "publicity-seeking, self-aggrandizing, camera hound."

"The Department of Defense is trying to design the forces that will guard our nation in the next century," Erwin went on to say. "We think that the service academies are part of that force. Senator Bruckner is out to get his face in front of a television camera. If it takes burning down West Point to do that, he'd come running with the gas can."

When asked whether or not the hearings will be

televised, Senator Bruckner's office responded that "a decision hasn't been reached yet. We'll be discussing some very sensitive issues. Senator Bruckner is concerned about fairness to all concerned parties and wants, as much as possible, to protect the privacy of the people involved."

Reached at West Point, Claude Braintree, the Bruckner Commission's lead man at the Military Academy, would say only that "testimony has not begun."

∽∾ ∾∽

Wayne Holder cut through Central Area on his way back from last period class. There was a big panel van parked in front of the First Division steps; several civilian workers were unloading what looked like audio and video equipment.

"What's all this stuff for?" Holder asked.

"Setting up some kind of hearing room up there."

This from a young guy, maybe early twenties, who wore his hair back in a short, unruly ponytail.

"I think it's those people from Washington," he said. Then, turning to an older coworker, a fattie straining with a black box that looked like an amplifier, the ponytail asked, "That right, Richie? This for those people from Washington?"

"No, this is for my fuckin' movie debut," Richie said in a sitcom New York accent. The big man was sweating heroically. His stomach peered out from where his tee shirt might otherwise have met his pants, a crescent of white flesh. "You wanna gimme a hand here?"

The ponytail jumped from the lift gate of the truck to the steps, took one end of the big box from Richie, kept up his banter.

"Yeah, but this is all for those people who are planning on shuttin' this place down, right? I mean, maybe we oughta set up a bomb or sumpin'."

The ponytail, who didn't seem to be straining under his end of the box, winked at Holder as he said this.

"I mean, they close this place, we're out of a job, right? Right, Richie?"

"Is there anyone from the committee up there?" Holder asked.

"Yeah, there's a couple of 'em up there," Richie said. "Gabbin' and gettin' in the fuckin' way."

Richie backed into the doorway, blowing harder as he strained. Holder wondered if the ponytail knew CPR.

The cadet stood on the porch and watched through the door, which was propped open. Richie and his partner had gone about a half dozen steps up the narrow staircase when several young men—their blazers and striped ties so similar they looked like members of a glee club—came down and tried to squeeze past.

"Can you people see that we got a heavy box here?" Richie demanded.

But the suits kept coming. When they reached Richie, they looked at him as if surprised that he couldn't just step aside.

"Sorry, we're in a hurry," one of the men said. "Can you just back down a few steps there?"

"Sure, sure," Richie said. "There's nothing I'd like better than a chance to haul this big fuckin' thing up the same stairs again."

He dropped the end of his box on one of the stairs, shot a withering look at the threesome. The functionaries, oblivious, squeezed by.

"Is one of you Mr. Van Grouw?" Holder asked, slipping inside the doorway.

"I'm Sandy Van Grouw," one of the men said. He stared at Holder from behind round glasses. "Do I know you?"

"I'm Cadet Wayne Holder."

Van Grouw's eyes widened. He reached up and touched his hair, which was piled on top of his head like a wave.

"Oh," he said.

"I wonder if I might talk to you for a minute or two," Holder said.

"Well, I . . . that is, we're awfully busy," Van Grouw tried.

Just what I expected to hear, you little weasel, Holder thought. He had seen this guy around the gym, around the boxing room. Hatching his plot, no doubt, to use Chris Dearborn.

Van Grouw looked around the little vestibule. Another worker was bringing in a big box, the doorway was blocked.

"This will only take a minute, Mr. Van Grouw," Holder said. "Maybe we could step outside as soon as these guys come in."

Holder put his hand out to indicate the door. Once the workmen were clear, Holder stepped out through the open door and onto the old-fashioned porch that fronted the narrow building. He stood by the railing; Van Grouw came up beside him.

"I came to talk about Chris Dearborn. I think you're using him to get some recognition with your committee. I think you're trying to get him to say something about Major Gates, something that will win you points with your boss."

Van Grouw looked surprised.

"That's what you came here to talk about?" he asked. He chuckled, then looked out over the quadrangle. "I would have guessed you had a few other things to worry about, Cadet Holder. In fact, I would think that protecting Major Gates would be one of your last concerns."

"You know about me and Major Gates?"

"Sure," Van Grouw said. "I know lots of things."

"Let's forget for a moment that my conversations with Cadet Dearborn are privileged, confidential. Let's even assume, for the sake of argument, that Major Gates has attracted some attention. Why would you care? I would think you'd be happy to see him get whatever he had coming to him."

"Because I don't think you're doing the right thing," Holder said. "I don't think you care about Chris Dearborn or Major Gates or any of us. This is just a photo op for you guys."

"Did Major Gates put you up to this?"

Holder screwed up his face; the suggestion seemed ludicrous. "No."

"So you're going to run interference for Major Gates . . . because it's the right thing to do?"

"Isn't that good enough?"

Van Grouw stared at Holder for a moment, until the cadet became uncomfortable.

"What?" Holder asked.

"You've got stones, I'll say that for you."

Sandy Van Grouw considered that perhaps he should

have gone to Wayne Holder with the little story about Kathleen Gates's accusation. This was a kid who'd take things on, who'd fight back. Jackie Timmer didn't have the same personal stake Wayne Holder did.

"Would you like to know how I know who you are?" Van Grouw asked.

Holder suddenly felt light-headed; there was a big gob of something at the back of his throat. He was afraid that if he tried to swallow, he'd throw up. Van Grouw wasn't talking about the incident by MacArthur's statue. He wasn't talking about Major Tom Gates.

"Kathleen Gates," Van Grouw said.

Holder leaned against the railing.

"Kathleen Gates accused the Supe of offering her a deal," Van Grouw said. "She told a woman on the committee, Dorothy Sayer, that Flynn offered to pull her husband's letter of reprimand if she'd keep quiet about . . . what happened between the two of you."

"Who the hell would believe that shit?" Holder said.

"Senator Bruckner, if he wants to," Van Grouw answered.

"You're kidding me."

"This isn't anything to kid about," Van Grouw said. "Bruckner loves big scenes. If he gets Kathleen Gates up before the committee, gets her to tell this story about the Supe, you can bet this will be all over the national news. And there's nothing the Senator likes better than that."

"Is she going to say all that? Will she testify? I mean, under oath?"

"From what I've heard, there's very little the woman *won't* do to get her way," Van Grouw said. "Of course, you'd know more about that than I would."

"Who else knows about this?" Holder asked.

"Besides the committee, just Captain Timmer, as far as I know," Van Grouw answered. "I told her."

Holder looked up at the civilian.

"Quite the little courtier, aren't you?" he said.

"I watch out for myself," Van Grouw sniffed. "I wouldn't think a hothead like you has a lot of room to be smug, though."

Holder smirked.

"Did I say something funny?"

"Nah. It's just that I went from being uninvolved to being a hothead," Holder answered.

Van Grouw stepped up to the rail beside Holder, facing the huge, paved quad. Around them, hundreds of barracks windows stared out at the teeming courtyard filled with cadets hurrying, always hurrying on their treadmills.

"Well, if Senator Bruckner gets his wish, your days here might be numbered anyway."

Jackie Timmer figured out what was going on with Kathleen Gates and General Flynn before the cadets showed up at her house, before Holder's roommate offered his theory. But the whole scenario—one woman setting out to blackmail an entire institution, and putting the career and reputation of a senior officer in jeopardy—seemed so preposterous that she had to sleep on it before she approached the Dean.

It seemed to her that Simon was the logical choice for this next move. He was the one who had chosen her to work with the Bruckner people in the first place; problems should be brought to his attention.

She'd thought about telling Rob, but only for a second or two. She hadn't had a conversation with him in over a week. Or maybe it had been a few years. Compared to the things she shared with Layne Marshall, her interaction with her husband was painfully shallow. What did you teach today? How was your run? What do you think about the new policy on . . . blah, blah, blah. She wasn't sure if she was becoming more distant from him because she was spending so much time thinking about Layne Marshall, or if her time with Layne Marshall was just casting light on the true character of her relationship with Rob. To call what she had with her husband superficial would be generous.

She considered telling Jon Hillard about it, but Jon seemed to be pissed off at her. Part of her mind told her it was because she'd missed a few appointments with students, because she hadn't been spending as much time in the office working—she'd been spending her spare hours at Layne's apartment. When Layne wasn't there, she worked at his desk, wore his shirts, waited for him to come home.

When they were there at the same time, they spent their time making love—in the bed, on the couch, the kitchen table, the floor.

"Is General Simon in?" she asked Ms. Wiley, the Dean's secretary. Timmer smiled sweetly, her preacher's-daughter smile. She did not have an appointment, and Wiley guarded Simon's door with a fervor that would make a Secret Service agent jealous.

"Just a moment please," Wiley said. She did not return Timmer's smile.

"There's a Captain Timmer out here to see you, sir," Wiley said into the phone. "She doesn't have an appointment," she sniffed, opening the Dean's appointment book.

"Now, you know you have Colonel Peters coming by in fifteen minutes," the woman went on in the tones of a den mother. "Ten minutes really, because he's always early, and you wouldn't want to . . ."

Apparently Wiley was trying to talk the Dean out of seeing her.

Thanks, lady, Jackie thought.

Jackie stood close to the desk and looked down at the Dean's appointment book—upside down as she faced Wiley's desk—to see if the Dean had any openings. There, early in the week, "K. Gates 1100" was written in pencil.

What the hell?

Wiley turned around, the phone pressed to her ear, and noticed Timmer looking at the appointment book. She pulled her lips together tightly and pulled the appointment book toward her, out of Timmer's view.

"The Dean will see you now," Wiley said, putting the phone back in its cradle.

"Thank you," Timmer mumbled, suddenly feeling disoriented. She knocked on the door, which was not closed all the way.

"Come in, come in, Jackie," Simon said, standing behind his desk. "Good to see you."

"Thank you, sir," Timmer said. She moved awkwardly behind one of the chairs, her brain buzzing with questions about why Kathleen Gates would have come to see the Dean.

"What can I help you with?" Simon asked.

She had been looking right at him, without seeing him. She was suddenly nervous about sharing what she'd brought to the meeting.

Kathleen Gates and the Dean . . . what could they have talked about?

"Uh . . . sorry to drop in on you unannounced like this, sir," Timmer managed. "It's just that . . . something has come up, and I thought I should run it up the flagpole."

Simon sat back down at his desk, still smiling at her. His neck looked tiny inside the collar of his uniform shirt, his arms birdlike.

"Have a seat, have a seat," he said. "What is it?"

The Dean looked at her expectantly; he had no idea of the bomb she was about to drop.

K. Gates. 1100.

Or maybe he did.

She started with the visit from the cadets, Holder's explanation about what had happened. As she spoke, she watched Simon's face for some sign of surprise. Something—a raised eyebrow, an exclamation—that would indicate he'd heard none of this before. Instead, the old man just looked tired. He sat further back in his chair, his shoulders slumped a bit more than usual.

She told him about a source on the commission, leaving out Van Grouw's name, who'd told her that Kathleen Gates was going to accuse the Superintendent of offering her a deal. That Kathleen was prepared to testify in front of the committee. She told General Simon that she believed that Kathleen Gates had engineered the whole thing, all to get that letter removed from her husband's file.

"I thought about going right to General Flynn," Timmer said. "But I came here instead. After all, you were the one who gave me the job of working with the Bruckner people."

"You did the right thing, Captain Timmer," Simon said. No more Jackie.

The Dean pushed his chair back from his desk. He was perfectly centered on the big window behind him, the one above the credenza. The glass soared fifteen feet up the oak paneled wall, making Simon look even smaller.

"I can appreciate your concern, even your alarm about all

this," he said. "And I can assure you that I'll take care of it from here."

Timmer wanted to jump up and leave the office, and it was clear that Simon wanted her to leave. But something had her pinned to her seat. Curiosity, perhaps. Some new attitude—fostered by her late indiscretions—that made her a little more careless, a little less circumspect.

"What will you do, General?" she asked.

"I haven't decided yet," Simon answered.

"Do you want me to go to the Supe with you? Explain all this, how I came up with all this theory?"

"I'll let you know if I think that's possible."

It seemed to Jackie that Simon should be more upset, more distracted by what he'd heard. He should ask her more questions. There was a terrific silence in the room. Outside, she could hear Wiley's fingers flying across the keyboard of her computer.

Timmer tried swallowing; her mouth was like ash. "I noticed that Mrs. Gates's name was in the appointment book," she said.

Now Simon's face registered surprise. Finally.

"Yes, I did speak to Mrs. Gates the other day," Simon said cautiously.

Timmer's stomach flipped over. Her good-little-girl instincts told her to leave. But Simon, even with the intimidating stars on his shoulders, seemed backed into a corner. If she was going to find out anything, it had to be now.

Timmer smiled at the Dean.

"Is she going to tell stories about you, too?" she asked, remembering to laugh.

"I don't think so," Simon said, not returning her smile.

"Well, I just want you to know, sir, that I'm ready to go to the Bruckner Commission. . . ."

She was about to say "whenever you think it's appropriate," but she left that off. Let him think she might go on her own.

"I'm sure you are, Captain Timmer."

There was another awkward pause, another long, uncomfortable silence. Jackie Timmer felt a wetness on the back of her neck, under her arms.

"If there's nothing else, sir," she said, standing.

"Actually, there is," Simon said. He pulled his chair close to his desk again, put on his reading glasses, picked up a paper, and pretended to read it.

"I'm pulling you off the Bruckner Commission detail," he said.

Timmer wasn't sure she'd heard right. "Why is that, sir?" she asked.

And just as she was thinking that her morning was turning out an awful lot like a B-movie script, David Simon cracked open Jackie Timmer's life.

"There have been rumors of some . . . indiscretions on your part."

Simon looked over the top of his glasses, the disapproving principal.

"I don't understand, sir," Jackie said, stammering.

"I'll be blunt with you, Captain," Simon continued. "There have been rumors going around that you've been having an affair with a civilian visiting professor, Layne Marshall over in the History Department. Now, I'm not asking you to confirm or deny these rumors. That is not even necessary, not even germane, really, to the question of your working with the Bruckner Commission. Even the appearance of impropriety, even false rumors, would be enough to pull you from the work at this point."

Jackie Timmer felt her face go a hot crimson; she looked down at her lap, at her fingers twisted there. She was struck dumb.

Simon continued to speak.

"I am not going to investigate these rumors," he said. "I have decided just to make you aware so that you can figure out, on your own, what you might want to do about them."

Timmer looked up. No tears, just a dry, uncomfortable calm.

Simon stood; the interview was over.

"I know that this is going to be a difficult time for you," he began, falsely solicitous. "If there is anything I can do, anything at all, please don't hesitate to ask."

Timmer nodded in response, stood before her own chair.

"What about the other thing, sir?" she asked. "General Flynn and Mrs. Gates?"

"Don't think any more about that," Simon answered. He came around to the front of the big desk and lightly touched Jackie on the arm. "At this point you need to concentrate on keeping your own life together."

Jackie nodded again, still numb, and stepped to the door. She might not have figured out what was happening until much later, after she'd had a chance to go over the conversation in her mind. But General David Simon, who might have been repeating himself out of habit, who might have been looking for a little extra insurance, who might have been unsure that this distraught woman really understood him, tipped her off when he said again, "Don't give a second thought to that other. In fact, keep all that to yourself. Take some time to straighten things out in your own life. Keep these rumors from spreading."

Jackie Timmer was still just inside the Dean's office when she realized what he was doing. She pulled her arm away from his touch and turned quickly toward him.

The Dean stood facing her squarely. Dropping his voice to a whisper, he said, "You wouldn't want your husband to hear what I've heard."

CHAPTER 16

WAYNE HOLDER SAT THROUGH LUNCH QUIETLY. AT THE FOOT of the ten-person table sat three of the company's plebes, filling glasses, cutting the dessert into ten equal pieces, and passing the family style serving plates handed off by the waiter. They worked without smiling—which was not allowed—and with a minimum of talking. The rest of the cadets at the table—yearlings, cows, and one other firstie, all arranged by seniority—added to the general low roar of conversation that always filled the cavernous mess.

"Hey, Wayne," Mike Viegas called from the next table.

Holder looked over; Viegas was turned almost completely around in his chair. The boxer's plate was empty in front of him; he was trying to drop weight, go down to a lighter weight class. Holder figured that Viegas dropped weight out of habit—it was what fighters did. He could easily pummel most of the men one or two weight classes above him.

"You hear about my man Dearborn in yesterday's practice?"

"No," Holder said. He glanced around quickly, sighting Dearborn one table farther away.

"He kicked some ass in boxing practice, man," Viegas said. "Turned into a real fire-eater there for a few minutes."

"You serious?"

"Abso-freakin'-loot-ly, man," Viegas finished. "I guess he figured out that it's better to give than to receive."

"That's great, Mike," Holder said flatly.

Viegas watched him for another few seconds; Holder knew he was expecting more of a comment, a little more enthusiasm.

"Really great, Mike," Holder said, failing to muster anything more.

"Yeah, I can see you're ecstatic," Viegas said, turning back to his glass of ice water.

Holder pulled a few slabs of cold cut off the serving tray, then decided against eating. All he could think of was Kathleen Gates.

He had no idea what to do next. The only person he might have asked for advice was Alex Trainor. He could see his roommate behind the plebes at the foot of the table. Trainor looked happy, animated. He was smiling and even laughing at the next table.

"Hey, Wayne, you look like your dog just died."

Rebecca Hollings, a junior, sat on Wayne's left behind a sandwich that was a minor engineering marvel. Slabs of tomato, lettuce, meat, and cheese on a triple decker platform. As she spoke, she speared three long pickles from a metal serving dish. Wayne Holder stared at her plate.

"A girl has to watch her figure," she said, smiling. Rebecca stood five feet two inches tall, weighed about one hundred pounds, and ate like two men. Her classmates, tired of trying to figure out where she put all this food, called her Becky Calories.

"So anyway, what's with you?"

"Long story, Becka," he said.

"OK," she said. "Whatever you say. Just make sure you keep it all bottled up inside you. That's good for your health."

Rebecca finished her construction project and folded her hands in front of her. None of the upperclass cadets at the table would eat until the plebes were ready. The lowest ranking person did most of the work and also ate first.

The plebe at the foot of the table occupied the "gunner" seat; when he and his classmates had their food and had completed their table duties—filling glasses, passing condiments, asking the waiter for extra dessert—the gunner asked permission to eat. Wayne nodded.

"What's up with Alex?" Rebecca asked around a mouthful of food. "He's passing out 'Praise the Lord' like it was candy."

"Just one of his states of agitation, I guess," Holder said. He wondered if his roommate had talked to Ruth.

Wayne Holder sat glumly through the rest of the meal, watching Rebecca work her dainty way through the huge sandwich she'd constructed. He only half-listened to the stories told by the cadets in this little family: comparing notes on professors, courses; discussing which intramural teams had the best chance of winning the various championships; talking about the opening of the Army football season the next day.

"Attention to orders." The deep, bigger-than-life-sized voice rolled down on them from speakers in the ceiling.

"I think it's God," Rebecca whispered.

"He wants to talk to you about gluttony," another junior at the table said.

The voice, amplified by the sound system, rolled through the six wings of the mess hall, quieting the four thousand cadets. Knives, forks, spoons, napkins, glasses—all went to the table. Four thousand college students, near instant silence.

"One fifty football goes this afternoon against Colgate," the voice said.

On cue, four thousand fists struck tabletops throughout the mess in a single, tremendous crash.

"Beat Colgate!"

This was a warrior tribe. Absent drums, they used what was handy.

The voice was that of the Brigade Adjutant, a senior on the staff that ran the Corps. Wayne Holder had always thought the kind of cadets who were chosen for the brigade staff were a little self-important, a little too serious. The Academy called such budding luminaries "Emerging Leaders." Less reverential cadets—such as Wayne Holder—called them Bulging Leaders. All that was before he met Liz Wrenson.

The adjutant stood on a little balcony called "the poop deck," which had been part of the facade of the old Cadet Mess, built in the twenties. With the additions added to the Mess Hall in the sixties to accommodate an expanded Corps, the front of the old mess stood squarely in the middle of the huge interconnected rooms. Announcements boomed down from the poop deck during meal time. VIPs who lunched with the Corps often ate up there with the Superintendent and other important guests.

"There will be a spontaneous pep rally tonight at twenty-two forty-five hours," the adjutant said, apparently without irony.

This met with catcalls and hoots from the hundreds of tables. Next to Holder, Rebecca Hollings rolled her eyes dramatically. Somewhere off in an adjacent wing, several hundred voices started to pick up the chant.

"Goooo, Ar-may. Beeee-at Colgate."

As the chant spread, the pace picked up, the words coming faster and faster until the words disappeared in a frenzy of foot-stomping, table-pounding, clapping, shouting, and whistling.

"A spontaneous pep rally, planned to the minute," Rebecca Hollings shouted at Holder. "Just the kind of thing you'd expect from the little Mortimers on Brigade Staff."

The adjutant was calling for quiet, but the cheering didn't let up. Wayne Holder suspected that the other cadets were thumbing their collective noses at the notion of a "spontaneous" pep rally planned days ahead.

The adjutant gave up. At the end of the announcement, a set of lights dismissed the various classes in order of seniority. When the lighted numeral "1" came up, releasing the first class, Wayne Holder stood and buckled on his saber.

Rebecca Hollings looked at the untouched food on his plate.

"Seriously, Wayne," she said as he bent over to retrieve his hat from the rack under the chair. "If you want to talk, I'm a good listener."

"Thanks, Becka," he said.

Holder caught up to Trainor on the steps leading to North Area.

"You're not gonna believe what I found out," Holder said as he came up behind his roommate.

"Wayne," Trainor said, reaching his good arm around to embrace his friend. "I talked to her a little while ago."

Holder stopped short. A cadet hurrying behind bumped into him, nearly knocking him down.

"To . . ." Holder dropped his voice, mouthed the words *Mrs. Gates.*

"None other," Trainor said. He wore a big, vacant smile. "I think we're about to reach a breakthrough."

"You don't know what I just learned," Holder said.

"She's ready to put her trust in the Lord," Trainor went on, as if he hadn't heard.

"What?" Holder stopped again. This time he thought to look behind him; the traffic out of the Mess was increasing as the second and third class lights came on.

"I told her that all we have to do is put our trust in the Lord and tell the truth. Christ will take care of the rest," Trainor said.

"What the hell are you talking about, Alex?" Holder asked. The day was turning out to be a series of surreal conversations.

"I told her we were wasting a lot of energy fighting each other. All we have to do, Wayne . . . and I really believe this. . . ."

Trainor put his hand out and touched Wayne on the shoulder.

"All we have to do is tell the truth and put our trust in the Lord."

"Don't give me that shit, Alex," Holder said, surprised at the flash of anger.

He looked up; several passing cadets had turned to see what was going on. Chris Dearborn saw the two seniors, started toward them, then moved away. He and Holder were still on the outs.

Holder took Trainor by his good arm and dragged him off to one side, where they could stand close to the towering wall of the Mess, out of the traffic pattern and out of earshot of most of the passing cadets.

"You're talking a lot of that bullshit mumbo jumbo again and this woman is trying to cut my nuts off."

"See what I mean, Wayne? That's negative energy. We've all been spending our time with negative energy. And we need to get away from that if we're going to get anywhere."

Trainor leaned closer to Holder. He looked like a man who had a secret to share.

"And the first step is to come clean."

"And what the hell does that mean, Alex? Am I supposed to march into Major Gates's office and tell him my side of the story? You think she's going to cut me any slack?"

"I think if you really put your trust in Jesus, Kathleen will see that and she'll be moved by the Holy Spirit," Trainor said. He was a bit slack-jawed; there was an odd light in his eyes. "She's going to want to tell the truth, also."

"That's rich, Alex. That's really good. You think she's going to go in there and tell her husband what happened?

"You have no idea what this woman is really up to, man. She's a nut case, Alex."

"She's one of God's children, Wayne. And God can touch her and help her move in the direction she needs to go. . . ."

"What the fuck you talkin' about?" Holder said. His voice had grown louder still.

Two cadets had actually stopped to watch, like kids waiting for a schoolyard fight to break out.

"There's no need to swear, Wayne," Trainor said.

"Let me tell you what I just found out about little ol' child-of-God Kathleen Gates," Holder said.

But Trainor had his eyes closed, his chin lifted. He might have been humming.

"What are you doing now?" Holder demanded.

"I'm praying for you, Wayne."

"Praying for me?"

Trainor opened his eyes; he was still wearing that simple smile, the one that reminded Holder of old paintings of saints.

His roommate had stepped out beyond where Holder could reach him. Wayne Holder no longer wanted to confide in Trainor.

Holder pivoted, began to walk toward the barracks.

"Where are you going, Wayne?" Trainor asked.

Holder shook his head, held a hand—palm flat—up over his shoulder.

"Forget it, Alex. Just forget it, OK?"

But he could hear Trainor following him, calling him.

"Wayne. Wayne."

Holder ignored him, hurried up the stairs and into their room, where he threw his saber onto the bed and grabbed the stack of books for his afternoon class. He had forty-five minutes, and he wanted to make it to Lincoln Hall and Captain Timmer's office first.

Trainor entered the room before he could get out.

"I knew you'd resist me at first, Wayne," Trainor said.

"Hey, don't take it personally, Alex," Holder said. He approached his friend, tapped his temple to help him enunciate each word. "I mean, it's only because you've *lost your fucking mind.*"

Holder straightened. "As soon as I lose mine—which could be any day now—I'm sure I'll come over to your way of thinking."

"Don't you see, Wayne, that you're just afraid of the truth? And the truth. . . ."

"Yeah, yeah, yeah, Alex. Let me guess. The truth will make me free."

Trainor smiled at him.

"I gotta go, man," Holder said.

Trainor was beginning to look scared. "Where are you going now? We need to talk," he said.

"No, I need to talk to Captain Timmer," Holder said. "She's holding out on me with some important info, but at least she's got both her oars in the freakin' water."

Jackie Timmer remembered leaving the Dean's office, because Ms. Wiley gave her a gloating smile as she walked out. The bitch.

But Timmer did not remember how she got to Layne Marshall's office; yet there she was, sitting at his desk in Thayer Hall. When she closed the office door, she thought she might cry, but she didn't. There was still that hot, dry numbness she'd felt in the Dean's office. And she felt exposed. If Simon had heard about her and Marshall, who else had figured it out?

Worse, Captain Jackie Timmer was certain that she was being blackmailed by the Dean.

You wouldn't want your husband to hear what I've heard.

"Jesus," she said aloud. "Holy fucking shit."

What was the Dean's involvement with Kathleen Gates? Obviously the two of them had to be close enough so that Simon would want to protect her. . . .

Which meant he was probably also protecting himself. . . .

Timmer pushed back in the desk chair.

"How did I get here?" she asked herself out loud.

But no answer came. Maybe Layne Marshall would have one for her.

She stood up and paced around the small space, trying to clear her mind. There wasn't much in the way of the personal in this little office: no pictures, no college mugs, no travel posters, or mementos on the desk. There were his books, of course, and piles of journals and papers and newspapers crowding the corners and the floor and every horizontal furniture surface. But there was nothing that would identify the space, give clues to the personality of its occupant. Nothing like Jon Hillard's tank poster or the family reunion photo she kept on the bookshelf in her office.

There were voices in the hallway, murmurs; Jackie sat on the forward edge of the desk. As the voices drew closer they differentiated themselves: one was clearly Layne's—and she felt her heart beat a little faster in anticipation. The other voice belonged to a woman. Jackie watched the closed door, saw a shadow figure through the glass. Just before it opened, the woman outside laughed—a lovely, flirtatious giggle.

Jackie suddenly wanted to be anywhere but where she was. Then Layne had the door open, but he wasn't looking inside. His head was turned; he was looking over his shoulder at the woman, a cadet senior. The young woman smiled, her whole face alight with . . . something. Lips parted, eyes bright. She wore the same gray uniform every other cadet at the academy wore, but she was so vibrant, so alive and young and fresh that she made even that drab outfit look sexy. Just before the woman noticed her, Jackie saw what was in her eyes. It was adoration.

"Jackie," Marshall said, turning toward her. If he was surprised he didn't show it. He kept the same smile in place, all those teeth, those sparkling eyes. The cadet was standing close.

"What a pleasant surprise," he gushed. "Do you know Cadet Claire?"

Cadet Claire made no move to enter the office. She tamped her smile down a notch, nodded at Jackie, and said, "Pleased to meet you, ma'am."

"Hello," Jackie said. She did not move, but stayed at the front of the desk, leaning there, her arms crossed across her chest. There was a long second, like the pause of a pop fly at the top of its arc.

"So, I'll see you day after tomorrow. OK, Professor?" Cadet Claire said.

"Certainly, certainly. Thanks for walking down with me," Marshall said. He'd put his books down and stood, one hand on the doorknob, the other hand in his pocket. Casual cool.

Cadet Claire turned away, then looked back over her shoulder, little of her smile left. "Afternoon, ma'am," she said to Timmer.

When Marshall had turned to her, Timmer said, "You won't get away with that here."

"What?"

"Flirting with the little college girls."

Jackie hated the way she sounded. Like a jealous wife.

"Oh, please, Jackie. Spare me, will you?"

"They aren't coeds here," she went on in the same tone. "They're cadets. And you'd be hard pressed to find a school that took a dimmer view of little flirtations between professors and students."

"My, we've become awfully Moral Majority, considering what you and I have been up to for the last two weeks," he said, smiling, trying to keep it light.

Marshall walked around behind the desk, put his hands on her shoulders. Jackie felt the heat there, then, in the next instant, thought that Marshall had been stirred up by the sweet young thing who'd just left his door.

Jackie stood up abruptly, turned to face him.

"Don't fuck around with me, Layne," she said. "I've put myself at risk for . . . you."

She had wanted to say "for us" but wasn't sure there was anything that could be called by that name. She had not asked Marshall for anything because she had not wanted to become a cliché, the clinging mistress, demanding promises he couldn't keep and didn't want to make.

"We're both taking risks, Jackie," he said. "I thought you'd decided it was worth it to you."

"What are you risking?" she asked, her voice more shrill than she wanted it to be.

"My professional reputation," he said solemnly.

"You wouldn't be kicked out of your profession," she challenged him. "You might get sent home from West Point without a glowing report, but no one is going to take your life away."

"Is that what would happen to you?" he asked, a patronizing little smile on his lips. "Firing squad at dawn, perhaps."

"Let's start with the end of my marriage," she said.

"You decided to take the risk," he said abruptly. "We can stop any time."

"It may be too late," she said. Timmer walked around behind the desk again and fell into the chair.

"What do you mean?" Marshall asked. It was the first time she'd heard alarm in his voice.

"The Dean just threatened to tell Rob what's been going on."

"The Dean? How the hell did he get involved?" Marshall said.

Now there was a clear note of panic. The Dean was one of two people who would write Marshall's performance evaluation when it came time to leave West Point and return to Louisiana.

"Have a seat," Timmer said, slumping further into the chair. "It's a long story."

Marshall settled himself on the desktop. "Fire away," he said.

Jackie told him about her work with the Bruckner Commission, how the Dean had called on her to be a liaison, how she'd met Van Grouw. She told him about Tom Gates and Wayne Holder, tussling by MacArthur's statue, Gates half in the bag. She told him about Kathleen Gates and Holder's fling in the parking lot; about Holder coming clean; about the two cadets visiting her quarters, clearly upset, Holder looking at some serious charges. She told him about the accusations about to be leveled against General Flynn—that he had offered Kathleen Gates a deal, the letter of reprimand in exchange for her silence. Timmer presented her theory—that Kathleen Gates had engineered the whole thing, taking advantage of the Bruckner Commission's visit. At each little piece of the puzzle, Layne Marshall's eyes grew wider.

"That's an *incredible* story," Marshall said when Timmer finally paused. "And those are some pretty incredible accusations you're making about this Mrs. Gates."

"No kidding," Timmer went on. "So I go in to see the Dean, fill him in on what Van Grouw had to say about these charges against Flynn. And Simon tells me to forget what I heard. And in the next breath he relieves me from the detail with the Bruckner people and tells me about some rumors about our affair. And when I'm headed out of the office he says 'You wouldn't want your husband to find out.'"

Marshall paused, fingered some papers on his desk.

"I'd say he has you between a rock and the proverbial hard place."

"What do you think I should do?" she asked, hating the uncertain tone in her voice.

"I don't see where you have much choice," Marshall said, standing. He paced back and forth in the small space in front of his desk, his hands clasped behind his back. Timmer sat in his chair.

"The most important thing is that you don't want Rob to find out about us," he said. "It seems to me the best way to ensure that is to do exactly as the Dean says."

He stopped walking.

"And of course, we must stop seeing each other."

He said it with a sort of finality, a professor handing out facts to students who were not in a position to contradict him.

"For the time being, at least," he added.

Jackie Timmer put her head down on the desk. It was all too much for her. She had been stunned by the Dean, then frightened by the thought of Rob discovering her infidelity. And now her lover was pushing her away.

She wanted to let go, to cry, but she held on to her control. She couldn't possibly leave Marshall's office on the first floor of the most crowded academic building on post, wiping tears from her eyes. Besides, Rob's office was only one floor up.

Jackie Timmer stood, testing her legs behind the desk.

"I guess you're right," she said. She had to concentrate on getting out of the building without making a spectacle of herself. It would take whatever self-discipline she still had.

"I guess I'll talk to you later," she said.

Layne Marshall, who'd spoken ten thousand sweet words to her, leaned against the front of his desk and said nothing.

Claude Braintree watched General Flynn all through the quarterback luncheon at the Officer's Club, trying to get the measure of the man. Braintree's staff had brought him a few of the Trojan Horse cartoons, and he had heard one or two comments about Flynn's being sent to dismantle West Point. But Braintree had a feeling those comments were dying as Flynn adjusted to his new job and as the community got to know him better.

There was certainly no shortage of people trying to get a moment of his time at the end of the luncheon: officers and civilians pressed around him, waiting to be noticed. Flynn waded through the crowd to shake hands with the Army football coach and wish him luck. As Braintree watched the crowd, a tall major came up beside him.

"Sir?"

Braintree turned on the wide smile.

"General Flynn asked if he could meet you out front in a few moments. He has to shake himself loose from the crowd."

"Very well."

Braintree walked up the stairs and out the main entrance of the club. As he waited, he thought about his first meeting with Flynn, where he left the general standing on his own front porch while he, Braintree, pretended to have a conversation on his cellular phone. He had wanted to establish the hierarchy early on, wanted to let the general know that he, Claude Braintree, was not impressed by the array of stars.

Since then, things had changed, and if Braintree didn't quite respect the Superintendent yet, he no longer assumed the soldier was a fool.

"Sorry to keep you waiting, Mr. Braintree," Flynn said as he came down the stairs.

"Not at all, not at all," Braintree said. "I could see you were very busy. And please, call me Claude."

"The football program here takes up a lot more of my time than I would have imagined," Flynn said. Then, holding his arm out, "Shall we walk?"

They turned north, headed away from Flynn's office and toward the athletic fields and beyond that, Trophy Point.

"Are you a big football fan?" Braintree asked.

"Not really, but it pays the bills for all the other sports. And it gets West Point's name out there—at least it does when we win. And that helps with recruiting."

"Recruiting more football players?"

"Football players, other athletes, and just talented young people. That's part of my job. Get the best kids possible interested in coming to West Point."

Braintree smiled.

"Something funny?"

"No. It's just that the popular perception of you has you more concerned with tearing the place down than worrying about the future."

"The Trojan horse, you mean."

"You've seen the cartoons?" Braintree asked.

"Sure," Flynn said. "But I'm not overly concerned. I think people will figure me out after a while, see that I didn't come here to close the gates. I think the staff and faculty are already coming around, with a few exceptions among the old timers. Eventually, they'll all figure out what I'm about."

They were in front of Cullum Hall, an ornate memorial building constructed on a grand scale at the end of the last century. The tall bronze doors were propped open. Inside, they could see some cadets moving about and hear what sounded like a tour.

"What are you about, General Flynn?" Braintree asked.

Now it was Flynn's turn to give an enigmatic smile. "Have you been in here?" he asked.

"No."

"Why don't we continue the conversation inside," Flynn said, stepping into the dark interior.

When Braintree's eyes had adjusted he saw yet another marble lobby, more tall ceilings, and grand-scale rooms decorated with oil paintings of dead generals.

"Very nice," he said.

Flynn, still smiling, led him down the hallway where the little flock of cadets had disappeared. They climbed wide stairs; around them the walls were decorated with nineteenth-century cannons, all standing upright, embedded in the thick walls. The barrel of each bore an inscription of some sort. Braintree put on reading glasses and studied one gun in the light from a outsized window.

"Captured at Chapultepec by the 12th Infantry," he read.

He looked at Flynn, who said, "Mexican War."

At the top of the stairs the cadets gathered; they did not notice the two men below. Braintree looked up and could see one officer, a big major, with ten or twelve plebes. Behind them, an ornate ballroom decorated with dozens more oil paintings of generals in blue.

"Who knows why there are so many Union generals hanging in that room?" the captain asked his charges.

"Because the people who paid for this building wouldn't allow portraits of Confederates, sir," one cadet said, drawing laughter from his peers.

"That's part of it," the officer said. His voice was almost too big for the building; he was also having fun.

"Years and years passed after the war before any former Confederates were invited back to West Point. Why else are there so many portraits of Union generals?"

There was no response for a moment. Braintree studied Flynn, who also seemed to be enjoying the lesson.

"Sir!"

One eager cadet shot his hand up, as if they were in a classroom.

"OK, Mister Fensel," the major said. "Why are there so many paintings?"

"Because Lincoln went through commanding generals like paper napkins, sir?"

"Exactly!" the officer said. "Good job. You've been paying attention."

The group moved toward the stairs, and Flynn motioned to Braintree that they should slip away. But before they turned Braintree heard the major direct a plebe, "Read what's on the cannon, son."

The young voice echoed down the marble stairs.

"Captured with honor at Vera Cruz, Mexico, by the Second Infantry."

"That's what it's all about, men. You get in a fight with somebody, you go over to *their* turf, you kick *their* asses, you take *their* shit, bring it home, and put it on *your* walls."

Flynn headed down the stairs; Braintree followed.

"That's the short version of what it's all about," Flynn said, still smiling.

"Quite," Braintree agreed. He wondered if Flynn knew ahead of time that the major and the cadets would be in there.

"It's also the long version."

"How's that?"

"We're in this for the long haul, Mister Braintree. Part of my job is to help people see that. Everyone wants to react to the crisis of the moment, whether it's a change in regulations or the latest budget crunch or a drawdown of the forces. . . ."

"Or a visit from the latest pack of Washington hyenas," Braintree said.

"Something like that. I have to remind people that we have to keep the big picture in mind. This place works, the Army works, because we keep some basic things in mind: we look for bright young people who are willing to learn, and who aren't afraid of hard work. We teach them how to put other people first, how to tell the truth and make hard calls, no matter what the cost. If we keep doing that, I'm convinced that all the little shit will take care of itself."

"So you're telling me you're not going to get worked up about the commission?"

"That's right," Flynn said. "I'll pay attention to it, sure. But let's face facts. Your boss is going to come up here and try to make a bunch of noise to get his name in the news. That's how he operates. Then he'll move on and, God willing, we'll still be here, doing the daily grind. The Superintendent can't afford to lose sight of that."

"You're a plain-spoken man, general," Braintree said.

"Do you find that startling?"

"I find it refreshing."

Wayne Holder left the barracks and hurried past the library and the Officers Club on his way to Lincoln Hall and the offices of the Department of English. Van Grouw had said that Timmer knew about the accusation. She must have known about it when he and Trainor had gone to see her, yet she didn't tell him.

Maybe, he thought, *she's conducting her own investigation.*

Holder fantasized that Jackie Timmer had almost wrapped the whole problem up. He would go to her office, and she would tell him how she had taken the right actions, had talked to the right people, had fixed everything, and managed to save his ass. Oh, there might be some fallout, maybe a few weekends of room confinement.

Holder rolled his shoulders back, tried to release some of the tension there.

Sure, he told himself. Timmer might already have wrapped everything up. She didn't get to be the Academy's poster child by not knowing what to do in a crisis. He would just go into her office, let her know that Van Grouw had filled him in on the gory details of Gates's plan. Then Timmer would bring him up to speed, and they could all sit around her office and laugh about how close they'd come to disaster.

"Dream on, Wayne," he said aloud.

Holder passed in front of Cullum Hall, with its huge twin cannons guarding the entrance. This was the same route he and Kathleen Gates had followed from the library to her car in the parking lot.

He stopped, momentarily disoriented, still amazed at what was happening to him. Everything spinning outward from that first little fiasco with Major Gates over by MacArthur's statue. Everything beginning, really, with his little decision to let the rest of his classmates skip out of the run Gates had planned for them.

He approached the front of Lincoln Hall. Before going in, he looked across the street at the baseball stadium and the parking lot beyond.

Kathleen Gates seduced him out there, fully knowing how she was going to use the incident: the accusations against him and then, incredibly, against the Superintendent. He had to give her credit: the woman had stones.

Then Holder began to wonder: if she was so ready to lie to further her story, why had she actually gone to the trouble of having sex with him, risking getting caught. She could have walked with him to the car, then made up an entire story about the tryst, as well.

His first reaction was vain, and he recognized that. She had seduced him because she wanted him. But Holder dismissed that thought in a moment. By going through with it, she had enlisted another witness: Kathleen Gates knew that Holder would tell the truth, no matter what the consequences.

The lobby of Lincoln Hall is all dark wood, with a fireplace—now purely ornamental—that used to greet the officers who lived in the building when it was known as the Bachelor Officers' Quarters. Holder took the stairs two at time, glancing quickly at the office directory for Timmer's name. Down the third floor main hall, checking off the room numbers, passing the plebes queued up for tutoring.

Holder knocked at the door marked with paper nametapes that said MAJ J. HILLARD and CPT J. TIMMER.

"Excuse me, sir," Holder said to a shiny head bent over one of the desks in the room. "Do you know when Captain Timmer will return?"

The head looked up.

Holder had seen this guy before; Hillard was the one who wore his Class A's to the first day of classes. His cadets called him Quasimodo.

"She just went down to the latrine," Hillard said. "Come in and take a load off."

Holder passed Hillard's desk; the officer studied his nametag.

"You the infamous Cadet Holder?"

"I'm afraid so, sir," Holder said, falling into the chair beside Timmer's desk.

"Hey, they haven't drummed you out, yet, Holder. You just might make it."

"Sir, I'm not even sure I've hit bottom yet," Holder answered.

Hillard grunted, maybe in sympathy, maybe in amazement. Timmer appeared in the doorway a few seconds later, her eyes red and puffy.

"Cadet Holder," she said. "I didn't know you were coming by."

Holder stood. Timmer looked agitated, upset over something.

Holder hadn't thought much about how he was going to deliver all this, so he launched right in.

"A few minutes ago I spoke to a Mr. Van Grouw from the Bruckner Commission," Holder said. "He told me a couple of things that really surprised me."

Hillard was watching them now. By the time Timmer reached her desk chair, her officemate was up and collecting some of the papers he'd been working on.

"I just had this sudden urge to go for a walk," he said, closing the door behind him.

When they were alone, Timmer folded her hands on the desk in front of her. "What did he tell you?"

"Well, ma'am, I was about to ask you the same question," Holder said. He was surprised to hear his voice rise to a sharp edge; he struggled to push it back down. "Seems like you're the one with all the information around here, even though it's my ass on the line. Maybe if you'd told me all you knew about what Kathleen Gates was up to, I could have found out something by now. Or maybe if I knew she wasn't going after me, I might have been able to sleep at night."

Timmer narrowed her eyes. "Let me remind you of something, Mr. Holder," she said. "You're the one who fucked up here, not me. So don't think for a minute that getting pissed off at me is the right answer."

She leaned over the corner of the desk; her face was just inches from Holder's.

"Even if we were peers, I wouldn't let you talk to me like that. And we're not peers. Got that?"

Holder swallowed; she was right, of course. On all counts.

"Yes, ma'am," he said.

"Now," she went on. "What did that little worm Van Grouw tell you?"

Holder went over the latest version of the Kathleen Gates story. When he was finished, Timmer leaned back in her chair and looked out the window. Outside in the hallway, Holder could hear muffled laughter.

"Did you know all that?" Holder asked.

Timmer nodded but did not look at him.

"You think something like that might have happened? I mean, do you think the Supe might have . . . you know. . . ."

"Not for a minute," Timmer said. "I don't think General Flynn is capable of something like that. Even if he was, he wouldn't be so stupid. No, Kathleen Gates is the common denominator in all this."

"What can we do?"

She was staring out the window; something else, Holder thought, was on her mind. He wanted to grab her shoulder, shake her out of her lethargy. He wanted to leave, just walk out the door, out of the building, right on up to the parking lot. Drive away in his car, throw his uniform out the window on the mountain roads as he looked for the highway west.

"I'm not sure there's anything we can do," Timmer said at last.

"What do you mean?"

"I've raised the issue with my superiors," Timmer said. "That's all we can do."

"You told the Supe?"

"That's not what I said," Timmer corrected him.

"Well, what's going to happen?" Holder demanded.

"I'm not sure," Timmer said. She lowered her eyes to the clean desk. "I've done all I can."

"That's it? That's all I get? I'm just supposed to sit back and let things happen to me?"

"Sometimes you just have to trust your superiors," Timmer said, the words vile on her tongue.

Holder stood and walked to the window.

"You know, when I came out to your house the other night, I was just interested in saving my own ass. I thought all this was about me. I didn't force myself on Kathleen

Gates, but I'm willing to suffer the consequences for what I did. The little story Van Grouw told me . . . hell, people will be getting into trouble for stuff they didn't do. That's worse."

Timmer had no response.

"I'm asking you what I should do, ma'am," he said. "I need some advice. Some help."

"And I'm telling you there's nothing we can do, Mr. Holder," Timmer said. She looked up at him from between slumped shoulders, her eyes dull and watery.

"Things are out of our hands."

Holder sighed, picked his books up from the floor beside the chair, and tucked them under his arm.

He walked to the door, rested his hand on the knob. "I'm kind of surprised, ma'am," he said. "You have this reputation . . . somebody who gets things done. Action. All that good stuff."

Timmer didn't speak; she merely watched him.

"Seems to me you've given up on this thing," he said.

"You should, too, Mr. Holder."

"I can't afford to, ma'am," he said.

He closed the door behind him, leaving Jackie Timmer alone with the wreck she'd made of her life.

"I'll bet I know why she's changed," Liz Wrenson said to Wayne as they walked from the cadet area around the gym.

They were on their way to meet her grandparents for a tailgate picnic before the first home football game. They had spent a long Friday evening at a Tex-Mex restaurant in Poughkeepsie, where Wayne Holder had told her everything, all the sordid details about his escapades with Major and Mrs. Gates.

Holder had come to care very much for Liz, and he figured that he'd best start this relationship with honesty. She'd been surprised at his poor judgment, but was not judgmental herself.

All that had been a great relief to Holder. Not just because he wanted to continue seeing Liz, but because he valued her opinion. And since his roommate had gone off the end of the evangelical pier and he'd been at odds with Dearborn, he had no one else to confide in.

"Now, I'm not one to spread idle gossip," she said, "but it seems this is germane to the problems you're having with Captain Timmer."

They climbed the stairs behind the gym with a throng of cadets and tourists making their way from the parade to the stadium. Liz held the rest of her story; presumably because they were within earshot of dozens of people. Holder was content to walk beside her.

Even with all the emotional turmoil he was going through, he enjoyed her company. His nerves seemed to be constantly vibrating, like a plucked string. Liz somehow made the movement harmonious.

They cut along the back of Lusk Reservoir. Liz Wrenson's grandfather, USMA '50, was a retired two star who'd made a small fortune in the stock market. He was a generous alumnus and a big supporter of the Army athletic program. For his gifts of thousands of dollars a year, he got season tickets and a premium parking and picnic spot close to the stadium in one of the prettiest spots on post.

Holder followed Liz to the small road that ran along the western edge of Lusk Reservoir. These spots had a view across the water of the stadium and the hills beyond. Walking with Liz in the sparkle of sunlight and her company, no longer worried that she was going to dump him when she heard about Kathleen Gates, Holder felt better than he had in weeks.

"Timmer is having an affair with a civilian professor."

Holder stopped. "A what?" he said.

"An affair," Liz said. "You know, doing the horizontal mambo, making the beast with two backs."

"The poster child?"

"None other," Liz said. "Miss West Point is playing hide the salami with some visiting professor named Layne Marshall."

"I can't believe it," Holder said.

"Believe it. Besides, is that any more fantastic than your little parking lot romance?"

Holder shook his head, trying to process yet another startling fact. Just a few months before, while on summer leave, he'd told a high school friend that West Point was boring and predictable. "Monastery" was the word he'd used.

"Wait," he said. "What does this have to do with her getting all squirrelly about helping me out with the Kathleen Gates story."

"C'mon, Wayne," Liz said. "This whole thing is about blackmail, about who knows what that can get somebody in trouble."

Liz waved to her grandfather, who was still some fifty feet away and standing at the tailgate of a big four-wheel drive. Rail thin with a shock of thick white hair, he wore a black and gold apron that said "BEAT NAVY."

The two cadets paused before joining the group.

"So you think someone told her to butt out of this thing with the Supe?"

"Seems a good possibility to me," Liz said.

"Who? Kathleen Gates?"

"The most likely candidate, I'd say. But you also said she'd told the Dean about her concerns. Maybe he's telling her to back off." Then, turning to him, she said, "Poor Wayne. Things are getting curiouser and curiouser."

Holder shook his head quickly, trying to clear his mind for a moment, just one clear moment.

"I'll get through it, I think," Holder said. "Thanks for supporting me."

"Of course," Liz said, touching his arm. "For now, let's go see what my grandfather is cooking up, shall we?"

Holder and Liz waded into the party: her grandparents and a dozen friends and classmates of General and Mrs. Wrenson. Judging by the proliferation of "Go Army" clothing, hats, coolers, pennants, buttons, stadium chairs, and blankets, many of the friends, it seemed, were regular fans at football games. Or at least at football tailgaters.

General Wrenson had been two years behind Holder's grandfather at West Point. When Liz announced this and her grandfather figured out that he did, in fact, know Bud Holder, Wayne became an instant member of the extended family.

"That's great," General Wrenson said, tipping a silver flask over Wayne's cup of cola.

"A little something to keep the enemy at bay," he said, winking.

The talk at the party was about good times—past and ongoing. One couple, several years older than the Wrensons, had just returned from a cruise in the Mediterranean with another group of classmates and Army friends. Still another was planning a big get-together for the Army-Navy game in Philadelphia at the end of the football season.

"Of course, if it's too cold, all the old people retreat inside," one woman said to Wayne. She was about five feet tall, with small birdlike limbs and gestures and a bright smile that couldn't have been any more full of mischief when she was eighteen.

"I spent enough time standing around in the cold for my country," one of the men said to her. He had a fringe of pure white hair and a deeply tanned, shiny dome.

"Hey, Mark, let's tell these kids some stories about Korea, shall we? Really put the fear of God into 'em."

"Be careful," Mark Wrenson answered. "My granddaughter here is going to be an Army doc. If you haul your tired old butt into the clinic one day and see her there, she might extract revenge for all the years you've made us listen to your stories."

On and on the banter went, shifting back and forth from 1951 to the present day, to Vietnam and back to Korea. Heidelberg and Washington, San Francisco and Manila. Post Little League games for children who were now in their forties. Children grown and moved away and grandchildren providing late blessings. General Wrenson hugged Liz a half-dozen times. She stayed close to him, lit up when he told his stories, and if he said something off color, she teasingly slapped him on the arm.

This was nothing like Wayne's family. Their get-togethers were polite and cool, like town meetings. Everyone came late and left early. When relatives visited from out of town, they stayed in hotels. Holder imagined that the Wrenson family slept on the floor.

Holder had long ago accepted that he didn't have the kind of television sitcom family that got along well, wrote to each other, called on birthdays. He was just coming to see that he'd been adopted into such a family when he joined the

Corps of Cadets. Here was the evidence all about him. These people were still friends, some fifty years after they roamed around together as young men and women, making their way from war to little Army posts, carrying children and memories and loyalties. And he was a part of this; he had more in common with these people than he had, perhaps, with his own father.

And the pity of it was that he might lose it all. Kathleen Gates might just take it away from him.

"How's your grandfather doing, Wayne?" General Wrenson asked.

"OK, I guess, sir," Holder answered. "I haven't seen him in a while."

"Where is he living?"

"Uh . . . San Antonio," Wayne said, not at all sure. It had been at least ten months since he'd spoken to his grandfather. He suddenly hoped General Wrenson wouldn't ask him that question.

"Well, when you talk to him, tell him you ran into me and a bunch of the other young studs from fifty. OK?"

"Will do, sir," Holder said, smiling.

"Oh, and, Wayne."

"Yes, sir?"

"Call him soon, you hear? We old people drop off at an alarming rate."

The party broke up as game time approached. The fans pulled little seat cushions—also emblazoned with the Army mule and various fighting slogans—and binoculars and sun hats and sunglasses and made their way to the stadium. Mrs. Wrenson walked ahead with some friends. Liz and Wayne stayed behind to help the general close things up before the three of them headed out to join the crowds.

When they were on the road that skirted Lusk Reservoir, General Wrenson said, "I'm not sure if I locked the car."

"I'll go back and check for you, grandpop," Liz said. She turned and jogged back under the trees, leaving Wayne alone with her grandfather.

"That's my favorite monument around this place," Wrenson said, gesturing to the huge bronze that stood across the road from them. Three soldiers in heroic pose, leaning forward as if into a heavy rain. Leaning forward into enemy fire. One of the giants had an arm raised, exhorting unseen others to follow. The statue was a gift from the classes of 1936 and 1937; dedicated to the American Soldier, it was a reminder to the cadets who passed by.

Wayne studied the inscription, which he knew well already.

To the United States Corps of Cadets
The Lives and Destinies of Valiant Americans
Are Entrusted to Your Care

"I guess because it's about the future," Wrenson said. "About what's ahead for you."

Wayne looked at the old man, who studied the heroes through narrowed eyes.

"Course, they got the statue all wrong," he said.

"How's that, sir?" Holder asked.

"Should be three guys crouched in a shell-hole that's half-filled with rain water and ice," he said. Still that far away look.

"They haven't had hot chow in ten days, haven't eaten for a day. Two of them have the GI trots and have been shitting in the bottom of the hole because it's too dangerous to get out. The other has pneumonia and has been trying to cough up a lung. They haven't seen the lieutenant in fifteen hours. Two of them hope he's dead, but the other one says they better hope the guy's alive, because that's the only way they're ever going to get out of that hole in one piece."

Wayne looked back across the road. All around them, people in shorts and tee shirts were huffing as they climbed the steep hill to the stadium. Beside him, General Wrenson had just taken a trip back in time, and he had invited Wayne along for the ride.

"That's what the statue is trying to tell you, son," Wrenson said.

Wayne wasn't sure he understood enough to make an intelligent comment, so he kept his mouth shut.

The general looked at him, smiled.

"It's telling you to always go back for your men." He leaned closer; there was a faint smell of bourbon, like some masculine cologne.

"You gotta go back because they expect you to come back for them," he said. "It's about trust. This whole ball game is about trust."

"I'm glad to see you two didn't take off without me," Liz said, catching up with them. She came up between the two men, put one hand on her grandfather's arm, one hand on Wayne's.

"Two handsome dates," she said. "Must be my lucky day. Shall we go to the game?"

CHAPTER 17

WHILE MOST OF THE WEST POINT COMMUNITY CHEERED THE
Army football team on to a victory at Michie Stadium,
Kathleen Gates worked to control what she'd set in motion.

Kathleen thought there was a chance that Alex Trainor
might take his little "truth shall set you free" campaign
right to Tom, and she was determined to stop the cadet
before it got that far. Of course, Trainor was just one of her
concerns: Holder might crack first, or Braintree might just
dump her, or Tom might find out—the list went on and on.

One thing at a time, she told herself.

Kathleen spent Saturday afternoon on the phone. She
spoke for almost two hours to Ruth, Alex Trainor's pregnant
girlfriend, even though the young woman had invited Gates
to New York in the first ten minutes. Kathleen was laying
groundwork; she didn't want to skimp on a telephone call.
She had concentrated on convincing Ruth that she was
sympathetic, that as the wife of a Tactical Officer she had
seen this kind of thing before, that she was there for Ruth, a
new confidante, an instant friend.

Kathleen pressed the children on Tom early Sunday
morning and drove to the city, gliding down a nearly empty
Palisades Parkway to the gritty Fort Lee side of the George

Washington Bridge. She took her time navigating Manhattan, fascinated as always by the sheer size of everything, before moving slowly crosstown to the Brooklyn Bridge. Forty minutes after entering the city and still holding her written directions in her hand, she found Ruth's building. It took Kathleen, suburban driver, nearly five minutes to squeeze her car into a parallel parking space.

"Hello, Ruth," Kathleen said when the door to apartment 5D opened, revealing an overweight young woman in an expensive but too-small dress. Her face was wide, even pretty, with large, dark eyes, and a cupid's bow mouth. A large hat was jammed on her head.

"Hello, Kathleen," Ruth said, holding out her right hand but blocking the door with her body. Kathleen caught a glimpse inside at a riot of clothing, magazines, trash bags strewn about.

"I'd invite you in but the place is a mess," Ruth said, indicating the chaos behind her with a slight toss of her head. "I thought we could go out for coffee, maybe some brunch."

"That would be very nice," Kathleen said, smiling sincerely. "Do you feel up to a walk? Or should we drive?"

"Oh, no, I'm up to a walk," Ruth said. Then, more tentatively, "I've been walking and exercising every day."

I'll bet, Kathleen thought.

"That's a good idea," Kathleen said.

They walked three long blocks, passing neighborhood shops, where Kathleen admired her own slim figure—dressed for the visit in a short-sleeved dress gathered at the waist—next to that of the younger, larger woman. Kathleen was glad she'd worn comfortable shoes. The streets were hot but interesting: signs in English and Spanish, a family walking to church towing three little girls in ribbons and ruffles, like little party favors with feet.

"This is a colorful neighborhood," Kathleen said. "Much more fun than the bland old suburbs."

"Yes, quite," Ruth said.

They hadn't gone a half mile and the young woman's breath was already coming in labored gasps; Kathleen was glad when they came to a small storefront restaurant and

413

made their way into the air-conditioned little room. Kathleen ordered coffee and a croissant. Ruth ordered a cheese omelette, hash browns, a large glass of milk, and two bagels—one toasted, the other, she told the waitress, "in a bag to take home for later."

"I haven't spoken to Alex in almost a week," Ruth said when the waitress finished scrawling the epic order. "We thought we needed some time to straighten things out, you know. Give us each time to think."

She fidgeted with her hat, watching herself in the uncertain reflection of the plate glass window.

"I started wearing this when I go out because I let my hairdresser positively *maul* my hair," Ruth said.

Finished toying with her hat, she moved down to her collar, tugging and pulling; then to the front of her dress, where she pulled a gold chain out of her ample cleavage.

"To tell you the truth, I don't know if I can stay in Brooklyn another minute," she gushed. "I mean, I was going to school here, but that didn't work out. And I'm just not at all . . . charmed by the neighborhood. I'd rather live in Manhattan, but Daddy won't hear of it. But, like, when my friends call and want to come to the city to visit . . . then they find out I live over here, well. . . ."

She went on like this for several minutes, changing subjects, adjusting her clothing, squirming nervously in her seat. Kathleen listened quietly, nodding from time to time. The girl was frightened; this was going to take some care.

For all her ravenous appetite, Ruth's table manners were impeccable. She took tiny bites of food and wiped her mouth every time she sipped her juice. The huge omelette disappeared slowly, relentlessly.

"So Alex told me he needed some time," Ruth repeated from behind a forkful of egg and cheese.

"That's to be expected," Kathleen said. "I mean, Alex seems like a nice young man, but even the nice ones often need to distance themselves at this point."

"Is it true that he can't get married?"

"Not if he wants to stay at West Point, graduate, and get commissioned."

"It hardly seems fair that the Army gets to run your

personal life like that," Ruth said. She twirled her fork around to catch a bit of cheese dribbling there.

"That's just the beginning," Kathleen said, "They tell you where to live, how to dress, how to act—all kinds of things."

"Is it worth it?" Ruth asked.

"I think so," Kathleen said quickly.

It felt like a lie coming out, but Kathleen Gates had told herself for so long that it was true that she couldn't even tell how she felt. Couldn't tell if she was lying.

"But there are things that one just can't control," Gates went on, tentatively. "And timing is very important."

Kathleen watched Ruth carefully, looking for some sign of the young woman's vulnerability.

"I could just scream when I think of how I let this happen," Ruth said, touching her belly.

"I mean, this has been one surprise after another for me. First I had to quit school. Then my parents got angry at me and so haven't been much help."

She put her fork down, wiped her lips, then used the napkin to blow her nose loudly.

"But the biggest surprise has been Alex. I thought he'd marry me. I mean, he's such a conservative, religiously, I mean. Always talking about wanting to do the right thing and all. Christian this and Christian that."

Kathleen nodded sympathetically. She felt as if she were about to jump into a small boat that was pitching beside the dock. She had to time her leap carefully.

"Have you thought about keeping the baby yourself?" Kathleen asked.

Ruth looked puzzled.

Kathleen reached across the table and took the girl's hand. "Or maybe putting it up for adoption."

"You don't think Alex is going to want to marry me?"

Kathleen managed to look puzzled.

"Oh, he didn't say anything about not wanting to marry you. It was the pregnancy he's changed his mind about."

Ruth put her fork down, missed the side of her plate; it clattered noisily to the table top.

"What are you talking about?"

"I guess he just thought that you two sort of . . . needed to start over. From square one, so to speak."

Ruth's mouth was open now. Kathleen could see little bits of egg between her teeth and gums.

"Now, I have to tell you that as a mother, this whole thing pains me. I support a woman's right to choose, but that's not to say these things aren't tragic."

Ruth looked quickly around her, as if they might be sharing the booth with people she hadn't yet noticed. She leaned forward.

"Are you talking about . . . what I think you're talking about?"

"Ending the pregnancy," Kathleen said.

"But Alex would never want me to do that," she said, without sounding at all convinced. "It would be against everything he believes in."

Kathleen reached across the table again, found the girl's chubby hand.

"Forgive me, but I imagine it was also against Alex's high-flying religious scruples to sleep with you before you two were married."

Ruth leaned back, and Kathleen got a look at the front of Ruth's dress. The young woman was probably unused to her new bulk; she had leaned on her plate, smearing a dark oval of grease across her breasts.

"Look, I know this is hard," Kathleen said. "You must be stunned. First you have some of your most important choices taken away from you. And you're frightened about the possibility of having to support a baby on your own. . . ."

Ruth's eyes widened at that comment.

She's more worried about money than the baby, Kathleen thought.

"And now this shock."

Ruth sat across from her, shoulders slumped, hand limp in her lap, breathing through her open mouth. Stunned. Vulnerable.

Lie big, Kathleen thought.

"I know this looks bad for Alex. Since you two haven't spoken he worried that you'd feel abandoned. But he knows you're disappointed in him, and he didn't want to leave you alone in this tough time. Which is why he asked me to help you through this."

Ruth breathed heavily through her open mouth. Silver crescents of tears welled at the bottom of her eyes, threatening to spill over.

Kathleen held Ruth's hand tightly, brought it up to her mouth and kissed it. A mother's gesture.

"There, there," she said. "It's going to be all right."

The first punch caught Chris Dearborn in the center of his forehead, but he had taken enough shots to know that the headgear would protect him from everything except the dull ringing; that would stay with him for hours. He had also learned, in the last two weeks of long practices and extra sessions in the evening with Kilo Mike, that he could ignore all but the most strident protests his body registered when he was in pain. In fact, some of the most insistent alarms, the ones that used to worry him the most, the ones that used to distract him, had stopped ringing altogether. The panicked voice in his head that was constantly screaming about the threats had been replaced by the steady, relentless coaching, like some religious chant, like some combat mantra that he had only recently learned to carry into the ring with him.

Hands up, step left, elbows tight. Breathe, relax.

The boxer across the ring had taunted him just before the beginning of the match. Not in the brainless way of playground bullies, more in the way of the Psychological Warfare people. A little condescending smile at Dearborn when the kid stepped into the ring. Leaning over to share a laugh with his coach, his corner, as Dearborn windmilled his skinny arms to loosen up.

Kilo Mike had told him—in the last few days had convinced him—that it was a good thing when opponents underestimated him. Had even dragged a textbook to Dearborn's room one night after a second, grueling practice—*History of the Military Art*. Right there, in authoritative black and white: Never underestimate your enemy.

Kilo Mike, the boxing scholar.

Dearborn jabbed, jabbed again, connecting the second time, not hurting his opponent, but surprising him.

If he watched me fight last week he didn't even see me throw a punch, Dearborn thought.

His opponent—a yearling from Company F whom Dearborn had seen around the barracks—stepped forward, almost in slow motion, dropping his right shoulder. Telegraphing. Just the way Mike said it would happen.

He's going to throw a right.

Dearborn seeing it now, like a chess player who can see three moves ahead.

Dearborn stepped left, then quickly bobbed right. Just the way Mike had drilled him last night, the two of them in the latrine for most of the evening study period.

The kid saw the left step, compensated, threw the punch, didn't have time to adjust to the next move. His right trailed out in the air, passing harmlessly an inch from Dearborn's head.

Now, now, now, Dearborn thought, not even hearing Mike at the side of the ring, not hearing the shouts along the ropes, his own Company D classmates cheering for him. He heard only the calm voice his coach had drilled into him.

Hands up, step left, elbows tight. Breathe, relax.

Dearborn had feinted right, now came back to center, continued the move, momentum bringing him around, the right hand following, all the way up from his opponent's knees, up and up and there it was, just the way Mike told him it would be: the other boxer's stomach exposed.

Dearborn landed a solid right just below the "Co. F" lettering on his opponent's shirt, the other boxer bending forward at the waist, his head almost crashing into Dearborn.

Dearborn thought the kid was trying to head butt him; then, a split second later, he realized the other fighter was winded. Dearborn had actually punched him hard enough to make him gasp. Stepping back now as the kid presented a clear shot, his head unguarded. Dearborn's left already there, coiled, ready to strike, connect with the thick red pad that covered the other boxer's temple.

Dearborn faded back.

"What are you doing?" someone yelled from the ropes. But it wasn't Mike.

As the other boxer stumbled, Dearborn shot a glance at his corner. Mike held the corner ropes; he was smiling.

"Finish him off," someone else yelled.

Blood makes the grass grow.

Dearborn waded in, hoping the other boxer would just throw up his hands. Stop the fight after one good punch. Maybe those could be the new rules: whoever lands the first good punch wins.

But Co. F came back, bent over a little more than when he started, eyes wide.

Dearborn walked straight into a jab, then another light touch, then a hard right that he didn't see coming.

Circle left, circle left, circle left.

Dearborn tossed a fist out there, found air, stepped in, and threw his right just as hard as he could. The other boxer holding his arms almost vertically in front of his face. Dearborn's big glove pushing in between, splitting them, but running out of steam before it connected with the opponent's nose.

Co. F threw a wild punch; Dearborn leaned back, stepped in closer. Jab to the head. Lean over, right to the belly.

The other boxer flailing; Dearborn feeling laces burn the side of his face.

"Keep calm," Kilo Mike's voice commanded from the side.

Control yourself and you'll control the fight, Mike had told him.

His opponent no longer boxing. Dearborn taking half a second to check his stance: leaning forward at the waist, elbows tight, head down. Bore in. Bore in.

Dearborn recognized what had happened to his opponent. He had given up. He was thrashing away now, just trying to keep Dearborn away until the bell rang. Just trying to do something to hurry the end of the fight. Dearborn had been there.

That's not your concern now, he told himself, stepping up, ready to punch again.

The other boxer stepped directly back. Not a move, not part of the little dance. He was trying to get away.

The crowd saw it. Cadets hanging on the ropes now, their arms and hands inside the ring, the judges yelling at them to get back.

"Get him, Chris."

"He's running away."

"Kill him! *Kill him!*"

He didn't recognize the voices now. They were from his company, he had heard them talk for years, but they had never cheered for him.

Dearborn threw another punch. The other boxer trying to bend backward over the rope, out of reach. Dearborn's hand fell short of his opponent's face, landed on his chest instead. The other boxer bounced off the ropes, his right straight out like a battering ram, like a telephone pole shot from a cannon. Straight into Dearborn's nose.

"Well, that had to hurt," Claude Braintree said to Sandy Van Grouw. The two men stood in a corner of the boxing room in a tiny circle of open space afforded them by the cadet crowd. It was as if the young soldiers-to-be were allergic to civilian clothes. Or maybe to the Bruckner Commission.

"Chris Dearborn tries hard," Van Grouw said, "But I'm afraid he isn't a talented boxer. Smart kid, not a fighter."

"They're all so earnest," Braintree said, looking about the room. "So serious about doing whatever the powers tell them is important."

"Yes, sir," Van Grouw agreed. He did a perfunctory look around, only because that's what the boss seemed interested in. Trying to figure out where Braintree was going with all this.

Braintree had summoned Van Grouw to his new office in Ninninger Hall and suggested that the two of them go to intramurals and Chris Dearborn's boxing match.

"Do you think this Major Gates will be there?" Braintree had asked. "The one who has so captured your attention?"

"Undoubtedly, sir."

Van Grouw was ecstatic. Until that morning Braintree

seemed not at all interested in what Van Grouw was uncovering—Van Grouw referred to it as hazing—about this officer's conduct. Suddenly Braintree had some time to spend listening, and Van Grouw was happy that the spotlight had clicked on.

Maybe Sayer cut him off, Van Grouw thought.

"That's the pity of what this Major Gates is doing," Van Grouw pressed on, confident now that he had won Braintree's respect. "He perverts that drive when he steps out of bounds, when he doesn't play by the rules.

"That's why I think the cadets—and their interaction with the faculty and staff—should be the focus of the commission's investigation," Van Grouw ventured.

"Oh?"

Braintree turned to him, flashed the wide smile.

Van Grouw swallowed, continued.

"Yes, sir. I think that all these other investigations we've tapped into may wind up more of a distraction."

"Are you talking about Dorothy Sayer's little involvement with Major Gates's wife?"

"Well, sir, that does come to mind," Van Grouw said.

Braintree still smiling, looking out at the ring again. Inscrutable.

Van Grouw was determined not to be timid. No doubt Braintree knew that Van Grouw and Sayer—and all his other subordinates—were in some sort of race for attention, all of them jockeying for position, striving to have the most newsworthy investigation going full blast just at the time Bruckner arrived amid the fanfare of press coverage. Braintree had encouraged it. The trick would be to present himself as objective, concerned only about the Commission's mandate. That was the fiction they all had to preserve, the curtain behind which Senator Bruckner was rabid for publicity.

"What Dorothy has uncovered should really be the concern of an official investigator, don't you think?" Van Grouw asked. "Alleged sexual assault . . . we're talking criminal activity here."

Braintree's smile faded; he seemed to be staring at a spot on the opposite wall. All around them, dozens of cadets were screaming at the fighters, at the referee. Van Grouw had been in this room when the noise was almost unbearable. Today it was just painful.

"I'm afraid it's more complicated than that," Braintree said, leaning closer to Van Grouw. He looked at the younger man, watching his eyes, gauging him.

"I'm afraid Dorothy is being used by some of these people."

It took Van Grouw a few seconds to get over the shock of realizing that Braintree was confiding in him. "How's that, sir?" he asked.

"I believe that Kathleen Gates and the Dean, General Simon, have been orchestrating events, have made up much of what Gates has reported to Dorothy."

Van Grouw said, "Oh?"

"You know that Major Gates already has some sort of letter in his file, a letter of reprimand that could prove career-ending?"

"Yes, sir."

"I think Kathleen Gates saw the Commission as a way of getting that letter out of her husband's file. I think, in fact, that she made up the whole story about General Flynn's offer."

Van Grouw was stunned and elated all at once. Dorothy Sayer had been duped. She wasn't going to be the golden child of the preliminary investigations after all.

And after all those romps with the boss.

Van Grouw suppressed a smile.

"Can't we just ignore her, sir?"

"And run the risk of her going to the press? No, that wouldn't work, Sandy."

Braintree brought his hands up, rubbed his temples with steepled fingers.

"General Simon, the Dean, wants to be the Superintendent. He told me that if General Flynn were forced to resign and we wanted to make a recommendation that the Academy be reduced in size, he would support us in Congress and with the alumni."

"Is that possible?" Van Grouw asked.

"Yes, it's possible. Simon knows that Senator Bruckner doesn't need any more publicity as a troublemaker. He doesn't need to be at the head of any more commissions digging up corruption and hollering for heads on pikes. He needs to be a facilitator, a peacemaker. Simon knows that, and he knows that I agree with that. That's what he's offered us. In exchange, we get the Dean's cooperation and the chance to reduce the Academy, save the taxpayer's money. West Point gets to continue.

"The problem, of course, is getting the Senator to see as clearly as Simon and I do what we should be seeking up here."

Van Grouw was amazed. He had thought himself fairly perceptive in divining that Kathleen Gates was pressuring the commission. He had no idea that these kind of maneuverings went on anywhere other than in the movies.

"Holy shit," he said.

"Exactly," Braintree agreed.

"So what do we do now?" Van Grouw asked.

"I'm not sure, to tell you the truth. This Kathleen Gates is a slick customer. I don't want to put the commission in a position of not taking her claims seriously—that opens us up to all sorts of problems. But I don't want the commission manipulated by this woman, either. I was sent up here to do a job, not to play into the hands of this schemer."

"And you don't want to say 'No' to Senator Bruckner," Van Grouw said.

"Right."

Van Grouw watched the boxing ring as he let the story sink in. On the opposite side, Wayne Holder approached the ropes, pushing his way through the crowd. He looked tired, distracted.

"Suppose someone at the Academy exposed the Dean's complicity?" Van Grouw asked.

Braintree folded his arms across his chest. Silver cufflinks on white cuffs peeked out from his sleeves.

"I suppose that would be a way of thwarting their plans," he said. "But I doubt if anyone is going to want to take on the Dean."

He looked at Van Grouw.

"Captain Timmer was removed as our liaison," Braintree said. "Any officer who wants to keep a career isn't going to be willing to jump into the middle of this."

"Well, sir. It wouldn't have to be an officer," Van Grouw said.

Wayne Holder heard the surge of noise as he pushed his way to the front of the crowd and positioned himself behind Kilo Mike. Chris Dearborn was on the mat, arms out at his sides, a crucifixion scene.

"He was going good," Mike said when Holder touched the coach on the shoulder. "Guy got a lucky punch in."

Wayne shot a quick glance around the ring. Major Gates was behind one of the neutral corners, leaning over the ropes and mouthing something to Dearborn that Holder couldn't make out from ten feet away.

Dearborn rolled over onto his side and stood up. The referee sent the other boxer to a corner and took Dearborn's hands for a standing count. The ref looked into Dearborn's eyes to see if the fight should continue; Dearborn looked over the ref's shoulder at Major Gates, still talking, smiling now.

As Holder watched, the civilian, Van Grouw, made his way from the back of the crowd to the ropes almost beside Gates. Van Grouw was watching the officer through his round glasses and was trying to hear what he was saying to Dearborn.

Dearborn leaned over and spoke to the ref, who signaled that the fight would go on just as the bell ended the first round. Dearborn hustled to his corner and Mike Viegas.

"He's going to keep telegraphing his punches," Viegas said to his boxer. "Every time he drops that right shoulder he leaves his face unprotected. And every time, I want you in there with a jab, then come back with that combination to the belly."

Viegas was talking fast, his accent—absent in the barracks—strong again amid the excitement. Dearborn was nodding continually, dancing on his toes, taking a shot of water from a bottle offered by another Company D boxer. But his eyes were on Major Gates and Van Grouw.

Chris Dearborn had told Van Grouw to show up; now he regretted the call.

He tried to focus his attention on the other boxer, who

seemed to have regained some of his composure, some of his confidence, after knocking Dearborn to the mat.

He had told Van Grouw to come knowing that Gates would probably show up. And, if the match turned out as he expected it would—him on his back and Gates yelling something cutting from the ropes—Van Grouw would have more of what he needed to make short work of Major Gates.

But now this. Dearborn had actually landed a punch. More importantly, he had taken a few without falling apart. Suddenly the outcome wasn't so certain.

He could make it easier on everyone, of course, by taking a dive. The Company F boxer hadn't expected Dearborn to fight back, nor had Gates, or Holder. Maybe Kilo Mike held out some hope for him. Certainly Chris Dearborn hadn't expected much from himself.

Co. F came out with two jabs, slower than the first round's, but straight and hard, no combinations.

Dearborn watched for the signal, and when the other boxer dropped his shoulder, just as Mike said he would, Dearborn moved in quickly and jabbed. Good punches, one to the cheekbone, one flat on the other boxer's forehead. He tried for the low right, but it didn't work.

"Good shot, Chris," Wayne Holder yelled from the ropes. Wayne was moving closer to Gates. Everyone Dearborn had to worry about would soon be collected in one corner. And for just that half second Dearborn let his mind out of the ring.

Co. F stepped in and landed a right cross to Dearborn's chin. He never saw it coming, barely saw it sailing by, only felt the crack on his jaw, in his neck as his head jerked to the right.

Then Co. F was in close. Two body punches, three, and Dearborn's wind was gone. Another shot to the head, the black shirt backing up, leaving behind another straight right. Dearborn suddenly on his knees, on all fours.

This was it. He couldn't see Van Grouw, but he knew that the civilian was there, waiting to hear whatever Gates had to say. And he knew that Gates, like some dog in Pavlov's lab, would scream at him if he could just let his arms out from under him. All he had to do was kiss the mat. Or stay down there for a few seconds.

He swiveled his head to the right, saw Gates's legs, heard something that sounded like the officer's voice—except that it was unexpectedly calm.

"You got up once, Chris," Gates said, his voice carrying amid the shouting, as if it were on some special frequency meant for Dearborn. "You can do it again."

Dearborn brought his right foot forward, leaned his weight on it. Then he was standing, slapping his gloves together. He went for the other boxer before the referee started the count.

Co. F had started for a neutral corner, but he saw Dearborn coming after him and turned, his hands going up quickly, surprised to see his opponent standing. Dearborn led with his right this time, kept moving forward, rights and lefts coming from down around his waist, forcing the other boxer to pull his arms in tight, try to protect himself.

Boom, boom, boom. Right, left, right.

Then stepping back, Dearborn taking his stance, rocking forward, all his weight behind another straight right.

The boxer in black caught the punch full on, right at the bridge of his nose, his head snapping back and staying back, the body following over backward like a tree felled from the near side.

"That's it!" the ref said, grabbing Dearborn by the shoulder, spinning him around, pointing to Kilo Mike's corner with the other hand. "You ignored my call, you're outta here."

Dearborn had broken the rules, failed to follow the ref's instructions to wait for a count, and now the fight was over. His opponent was sprawled on the ropes. He was declared the winner, but it would take a few minutes before he'd be able to stand and raise his hand.

Gates and Holder were there with Viegas when Dearborn climbed out of the ring.

"Man, you can get into big time trouble like that," Viegas said. "You can't just ignore the ref, man." Trying to be serious, the coach's role, but he was smiling. The boxer in black wasn't hurt. Company D had lost the bout, but Chris Dearborn had won something.

"Dearborn," Gates said.

Dearborn wasn't even completely through the ropes yet.

When he tried to speak he realized how hard he was blowing, his breath like a wet bellows.

"Sir?"

"You got up," Gates said. Not smiling, just calm. "That's all I wanted you to learn, Dearborn. How to get up."

The big man nodded once, twice, seemingly satisfied, as if he'd just completed some piece of work that needed doing.

"I may not have to kill you after all."

Holder watched three more Company D bouts, standing next to Chris Dearborn, not talking, the room too loud. When the last company boxer was finished, the two cadets walked out of the room together, Holder not sure what to say. Then he spotted Sandy Van Grouw waiting in the hallway outside the boxing room.

"Cadet Dearborn," Van Grouw said civilly. "Cadet Holder."

The two cadets nodded their greetings, neither of them happy to see this man.

"I heard what Major Gates said to you," Van Grouw said to Dearborn.

"You mean the part about how I got up?"

"Actually," Van Grouw said, "I meant the part about his letting you live."

"Just a figure of speech," Holder added.

Van Grouw tried to ignore Holder.

"I still want to help you, but it will be better with your cooperation," the civilian said.

The two cadets, who'd been walking slowly toward the big doors, stopped.

"Look, Mr. Van Grouw," Dearborn said. He reached up and touched his swollen lip with the tips of his fingers. "Major Gates put me on the boxing team to teach me an important lesson. I only figured out today what that lesson was."

"I'm sure Major Gates has the highest ideals in mind," Van Grouw said sarcastically. "His methods, however, are clearly outside the boundaries of what is acceptable."

"You know, Mr. Van Grouw," Dearborn countered, "I'm starting to regret talking to you in the first place."

Van Grouw smiled, no light in his eyes.

"Did Major Gates get to you, threaten you?" Van Grouw asked.

Dearborn shook his head. He had asked the same question of Holder just a few days earlier.

"You made the right choice, Cadet Dearborn, even if you're not sure of it now. You're hardly an objective observer. That's what the Bruckner Commission is for."

Holder watched Van Grouw as he spoke. He didn't so much mention the commission as invoke its name.

"I don't think I want to bother with the Bruckner Commission," Dearborn said.

Van Grouw laughed. "You already have, my friend. Did you think I was going to forget all that you've already told me? That Major Gates struck you, smacked you around by Lusk Reservoir?"

"I told you that was sparring," Dearborn said.

"That's not what you said at first," Van Grouw said smugly. "I think that's the story you came up with later."

"What if I say I don't want to talk to you anymore?"

Van Grouw stepped closer to Dearborn, trying to appear intimidating. It didn't work. Dearborn, sweat-soaked, bloody, and fairly buzzing with what was, for him, a victory, exuded a new confidence.

"I'll call you to testify and ask you all the right questions," Van Grouw said. "I have no doubt you told the truth in all your testimony. We'll just bring it all out again. You're not suggesting that you'd lie to the commission, are you?" Van Grouw asked.

"I wouldn't lie to anyone, and you know it."

"Fine, then," Van Grouw said. He had a superior look on his face, as if he'd just won some important argument before a court.

"Chris," Holder said. "Why don't you let me have a moment with Mr. Van Grouw?"

Dearborn walked away, keeping his eyes on the civilian until he was outside in the afternoon sunshine.

"Let it go," Holder said. "Chris doesn't want to play anymore."

Van Grouw and Holder stepped to the side of the hallway, let the throngs of cadets spilling out of the gym go past them. They stood beside the big glass case that contained photos of the top performers in physical education for each of the four classes. Four women and four men—PE Poster Children, other cadets called them—smiled from inside the big glass case.

"You tried to get Chris to go along with you in this vendetta you have against Major Gates just so that you could grab a little notoriety with your boss," Holder said.

He wasn't sure he had things nailed down exactly right, but he was no longer afraid of pissing people off. Too many things could go wrong that would wind up forcing him out of West Point. He was beyond the point of worrying.

"Major Gates was trying to accomplish something here with Chris. Sometimes you have to make up ways to handle a need."

Van Grouw sniffed. "And does that include going outside the boundaries of legal behavior? Does that include his punching your friend? I would think you'd be the first one to come to Cadet Dearborn's aid."

"I am," Holder said. "But the best course was the one you saw played out here today. Chris learned what he needed to learn when he got up from the mat. Not every leadership question is answered in the books."

"I'm so sick of hearing all this talk about leadership from you people," Van Grouw said. "You're all so high and noble and self-righteous, you're convinced you have a corner on the market when the truth is . . . you can't even see what's going on right in front of you."

He stepped closer to Holder, trying—once again unsuccessfully—to look menacing.

"This is the most legitimate investigation going," he said. "What does that mean?"

Van Grouw looked over his shoulder; dozens of cadets were spilling out into the afternoon sunshine. Braintree was gone; he'd left Van Grouw to do his bidding, to protect the Bruckner Commission.

"Let's go outside," Van Grouw said. "Somewhere we can talk without all these people around."

"That explains a lot," Jackie Timmer said.

She and Holder were sitting on her back patio again,

Holder in his summer white over gray uniform, Timmer in shorts with an oversized tee shirt that said "Key West Diving." Holder had just finished reporting what Van Grouw had to say outside the gym: that General Simon wanted to be the next Supe and that he and Kathleen Gates were working together.

"Damn," Timmer said. "It was weird enough when it was just Kathleen Gates as the only loose cannon. Now the Dean is involved."

"So you believe this Van Grouw, ma'am?" Holder asked.

"I'll admit it sounds pretty wild," Timmer admitted. "But some other things have been going on that now make sense."

The window behind her was open; inside the house, Holder could hear her husband whistling tunelessly as he cleaned the kitchen. Holder had interrupted a late supper. When she'd brought him through the house, he looked for some sign that things were not right between Major and Captain Timmer. Her husband seemed fine; Jackie Timmer looked distracted.

"You know of something that can corroborate this?" Holder asked.

"I saw Kathleen Gates's name in the Dean's appointment book," Timmer said. "That in itself doesn't mean much, but I can't imagine why the wife of a Tac would be going to see the Dean. General Simon isn't even in Major Gates's chain of command."

"Can we get a copy of that appointment book?" Holder asked.

"I doubt it. The General's assistant is a woman named Wiley. It'd be easier to get it from the CIA. Besides, what would you do with it when you had it?"

"I have no idea," Holder admitted. "But at least I'd feel like I was doing something, you know?"

Holder slumped in the chair, legs straight out in front of him. Hardly the posture for a cadet guest at an officer's house. Something else he didn't care about.

He had spent the last few hours lying on his bunk, trying to think of something he could do, some next step, that wouldn't include coming here to talk to this woman. In the barracks, he had been nervous. In her home, he figured he would be even more afraid. But he had reached some desperate point, some resigned sense that things couldn't get much worse anyway.

He had come to Timmer because he didn't know what else to do. He knew of her connection with the Bruckner Commission; he was hoping she would come up with a fresh idea. But as he watched her sit across from him in the dying light, he knew that he'd come here on a fishing expedition, looking for clues that what Liz Wrenson had told him was right: that she was having an affair with some civilian professor and so wouldn't be willing to stick her neck out for Wayne Holder.

"I asked General Simon about this thing between Gates and Flynn," Timmer admitted. "Whether he believed it was true. He told me to forget about it; said that he would handle everything."

"But if he's really in league with Mrs. Gates," Holder said, "then he's the last one who'll fix anything." He was stating the obvious, and he knew it. He chewed his lip.

"Maybe you could talk to this Braintree guy, ma'am. Tell him your concerns about Kathleen Gates. Or General Moro. The Commandant might help."

Timmer dropped her eyes to the deck, pulled her legs closer to her.

"I can't," she said.

"Because the Dean told you to drop it?"

Timmer looked up, met his eyes. Dearborn was right, she was a beautiful woman.

"I just can't," she said.

Holder stood, looked into the kitchen window. Rob Timmer, wearing running shorts and a white tee shirt, was bent over the kitchen table, wiping it with a sponge.

Holder's back was to Jackie Timmer now. He was having difficulty believing that it was to come to this. He had come to this officer's home and, without a shred of evidence, was about to accuse her of having an affair—all because he was desperate and couldn't think of another way out of his predicament.

Timmer was behind him.

"Does General Simon have something on you?"

He dropped the question quietly. He had no right, even, to ask. It was a gamble at best.

Timmer did not answer right away. Wayne Holder turned around so that he could watch her; she still had her head down. From where he stood behind her, he could see the ridge of bone at the base of her neck, the clean line where her hair was cut. He wanted to reach out and put his hand on her shoulder.

"What do you mean?" she said, just as quietly.

Holder walked around in front of her, pulled his chair closer; they were almost knee to knee. No one could hear their conversation. He leaned forward, elbows on his knees, surprised as he took this stance. All the power had shifted to him.

"If General Simon and Kathleen Gates are in this to the extent we think they are," he began, "it wouldn't surprise me in the least to know that they would do anything—threaten anyone, make up any story . . . blackmail anyone—who might get in the way."

Timmer's face looked softer; she wanted to cry.

"Look, Captain Timmer," Holder said, trying to give her back some of her dignity. "I'm not here to make judgments on anyone. Given my behavior, I'm hardly in a position for that."

"What do you know?" she whispered.

"I don't know anything, really," he said. "Just some rumors, gossip, speculation."

"Cadets are talking about . . . this?"

Holder nodded.

"Oh, Jesus," she said, turning her head to the side and pressing her fist to her mouth.

"Jackie," her husband called from in the house. "I'm making some iced tea. You guys want some?"

Timmer took a second to collect herself before she answered.

"No, thanks, Rob," she said.

She looked at Holder, shook her head.

"I can't," she said. "I can't let all this come out. I can't hurt my husband like that."

It's already out, he thought. *It just hasn't reached your husband. Yet.*

Holder sighed. Back in his room, he had thought that maybe they'd fight. She'd yell at him, try to throw him out of the house. Then he'd bring up the affair, tell her that her problems didn't mean she could turn her back on doing the right thing. Whatever that was.

But the woman sitting across from him was in as big a mess as he was in, on the verge of tears, heartbroken, by the looks of things. And scared. What the hell could he do to her that would be worse than what she was facing?

"I'm sorry that you're in a tough spot, ma'am. I really am," he said. "I know what it's like to be in a tough spot because of something stupid I've done."

He pulled his chair closer to her still; he could have reached out and embraced her.

"But you still have to do the right thing," he said.

Timmer didn't answer, didn't shake her head or nod. She sat, quiet and beautiful as a churchyard angel. Then she shook her head. No.

Holder stood, unconsciously ran his thumbs along the tops of his trousers to smooth his uniform shirt against his stomach, picked up his white hat, and tucked it under his arm.

"You know, I've been spending all this time worrying about graduating, worrying that I was going to get thrown out and not get commissioned," he said.

"But after seeing you and General Simon in action, I'm not sure it's any big deal to be an officer. Hell, I'd rather be like Major Gates. I mean, he's an asshole and a wildman, but at least he's consistent. He doesn't pretend to be something he's not."

Holder put his cap on, brought his heels together, arms at his sides, touched the brim of his hat.

"Good evening, ma'am."

As darkness seeped into the valley from the eastern hills, Alex Trainor found a quiet spot in the cemetery. He settled on a bench-shaped monument just down the graveled path from the obelisk marked "Brevet Major General George Armstrong Custer."

He had taken the call from Ruth as he was dressing for dinner. It took her only a few sentences to destroy everything he believed to be true about his life, about this world he had fashioned around himself, about himself.

"Alex, I had an abortion today," she said as soon as he came on the line.

"I know that you didn't want this baby, and just yesterday I found out how much of a burden the two of us would have been to you. I know you wouldn't have asked me to do this in a million years, but I think it's what you really wanted. You're free now. Please don't call me."

That was two and a half hours ago. Trainor had walked out of the barracks and wandered around the post, walking for miles through housing areas, back along the river, down among the rocks and trees of Flirtation Walk, the riverside park where cadets were allowed some privacy with their dates. He walked out of memory, had no recollection of where he went or what he'd been thinking about. No sounds reached him; the familiar sights of the river valley didn't reach him either.

He had been living a lie. He had lied to his parents, lied to Ruth, lied to Wayne and to himself and to God. He had sinned and forgiven himself without asking God's forgiveness. And for a while he had thought that this child, this baby he had never seen, had not felt stir in its mother's womb, was a sign of his absolution, that out of his sordidness would come something good. He had lied to the child, in a way.

And like some terrible story of Old Testament justice, the child had paid.

When the curtain came down on this day, when he was fully enclosed in darkness, he began to weep. He sat, face in his hands, unable to do anything except draw in breath, squirt it out again in great sobs.

"Oh, Jesus, what have I done?"

When he was eleven, Alex's mother had taken him and his siblings to a protest outside an abortion clinic in Kansas City. They stepped off the bus into a buzz of excitement; the adults were talking about Christian soldiers and the good fight, and Alex had been genuinely stirred. Then the pastor had opened the cargo bay of the bus and pulled out a stack of signs, posters that the believers could hold. Alex's mother chose a half dozen for her brood, handed them out after she had placed the kids in a long line of children along the driveway that led to the clinic. She was solemn when she handed Alex his sign, and he pretended it was the shield of a Christian soldier. He held it in front of him and yelled as the cars drove past. He yelled louder when the news crew arrived, when the television cameras showed up. This was their big moment, his mother had told her children, this was the way to get the message out. And Alex had yelled long and hard, straining to be the loudest, the most Christian, the best soldier.

And it had seemed to work, the camera found him, a young man with a ponytail and a huge shoulder-held camera, the lens like the cannon's mouth pointed right at him. And Alex screamed harder still, imagined his righteous message shooting through the lens and the wires and out over the airwaves, invading all those homes where the people would surely turn to God if they could just hear his word. Alex was his messenger.

But the camera was focusing on his sign, not on his face. And then a reporter had come up to stand next to the operator; she held her microphone at her side, an unused weapon. She shook her head and stared at the poster Alex held. And that's when Alex looked, for the first time, at the placard his mother had given him.

It looked like a rabbit. A tiny, skinned rabbit laid out on a white sheet. There was a ruler in the picture, and though the numbers were fuzzy, Alex could see that the ruler—marked up to six inches—was longer than the little red wiggle. Then he saw the hands. Tiny, red as the rest of the thing, attached to a tiny arm and a tiny shoulder and nothing else above that.

And eleven-year-old Alex Trainor had thrown down the poster, and his mother had come to him and hugged him and said yes, oh, yes, my child, that's what we're fighting against. That's what we must stop.

But Alex had pretended to be sick so that he could sit in the shade of the bus for the rest of the day, holding his stomach.

And because of his base lust, he had brought about another abortion. On his knees in the cemetery, he cried out his sin, until his eyes were dry. He had no idea what time it was, but the streetlights were on. He left the cemetery and walked along Washington Road, hatless, back to the barracks.

He did not talk to anyone. The hallways were busy as cadets roamed around—it was study barracks, a minor social time. A few friends in his company noticed him, spoke to him, but he did not answer them. He kept his eyes firmly ahead.

Wayne was not in the room. Alex took off his uniform and sat down, dressed only in his underwear, at his desk. In his drawer he had a box of fine stationery he was planning to use to write letters to the relatives who would attend his graduation in the spring. The box was still sealed when he pulled it from the drawer. He wrote a short note, sealed it in an envelope, and put it on Wayne's desk. Then he washed his face, combed his hair, and changed his sweat-soaked tee shirt. He opened the wooden locker and put on a pair of starched white pants, then he pulled out the full dress coat they wore on the most formal occasions, the one the seniors would wear for the last time on graduation day, when they threw their hats in the air and headed off down the bright tunnel of the future.

The tunic wouldn't go on over his bandages, so he cut off the dressing. There was still a roadmap of stitches in his hand, along his fingers, across his palm, where the surgeons had opened him up then put him back together. He thrust his hand into the tight sleeve, relishing the pain. When he had buttoned the big brass buttons, he took one quick look around the room. He put his dirty uniform in the laundry bin, then put the box of stationery away in the drawer. Force of habit: a quick inspection glance around the room before he walked out, closing the door behind him.

Wayne Holder dragged himself back to his room at ten-thirty, utterly exhausted. He fell onto his bunk, still dressed in the white over gray uniform he'd worn to Timmer's house hours before. He'd spent the intervening time with Liz Wrenson, brainstorming what he might do next.

"The count is one and one," a voice in the hallway said. He looked between his black uniform shoes, past the foot of the bed, to the big door, which he had not shut on his way in.

A white plastic ball sailed by. Then the rushing-air sound of a plastic bat.

"Swing and a miss," the voice said again.

"Pitch it to my head, why don't you." This, no doubt, from the batter.

"Your head is so big it has its own gravitational field," another voice said. "He can't help but hit you."

There was too much noise in the hallways, too many cadets talking at full volume. This was still study barracks; there was supposed to be some quiet so that cadets could work. Wayne had been on the receiving end of a slew of warnings about too much noise in the hallways over the last two years. But that was then. A few months ago he had pinned on the black collar brass of a first class cadet and the four bars of a company commander. With that role had come some responsibilities.

"You clowns want to knock it off out there?" Holder said.

A yearling named Thomas appeared in the doorway.

"Sorry, Wayne. The lights were off in here, we didn't know you were here."

Thomas peered into the darkened room, trying to figure out what was going on, why Wayne Holder was lying on his bunk in the dark, fully dressed, when he should be doing some course work.

"Yeah, well, it shouldn't make a difference if I'm here or not," Holder said. "People are trying to study."

A yearling named Cupit, who did indeed have one of the largest heads Holder had ever seen outside of the circus, filled the rest of the doorway. Cupit swung a yellow plastic bat back and forth in front of him.

"Sorry, Wayne," Thomas said, then turned away.

Cupit squinted into the dark room, shot his hand up in a fascist salute, executed a sharp about face, and marched off down the hallway.

Holder got up and shut the door. He turned on the overhead light, then turned it off. He rolled onto his bunk again, still fully clothed. He was thinking about something he'd once read about people suffering from depression, that they sometimes didn't get out of bed for days at a time.

I'm not giving up, he told himself. *I just need a little sleep, is all.*

The telephone jolted him awake some twenty minutes later. It was Liz.

"I've got an idea, Wayne," she said. "And I'll help you with it."

"Huh?" Wayne said. He was surprised at how sleepy he sounded.

"You there?"

"I'm here," he said. "Sort of. I dozed off."

"You and I will go over to the Dean's office and make a photocopy of the Dean's appointment book, the page that shows his meeting with Kathleen Gates."

"Oh, yeah, right, Liz. We'll just waltz right into the office and say, 'Hey, we're doing a little project on time management and we wonder if you'd let us make a copy of the Dean's personal appointment book. And while we're at it, could we see his expense account and the academy budget as well?' That's just the kind of thing they're likely to give cadets."

"We don't have to ask," Liz said.

Holder laughed. "Stealing the Dean's appointment book would solve my problems, for sure. Then I could just turn myself in for an honor violation and be done with this whole thing. I'll be headed out to the 101st Mess Kit Repair Battalion by the end of the week."

"We're not going to steal the appointment book, Mr. Paranoia. We'll just make a photocopy of that page."

Holder sat up, turned so that his legs dangled to the floor. With the door closed, the temperature in the room had climbed. His shirt was matted with sweat.

"Even if we could pull something like that off, Liz, what the hell would I do with the page?"

"It's time for you to go to the Supe, Wayne."

"Share with him my wild-ass theories. 'Sir, there's a coup brewing, a mutiny in the ranks. And to prove it, I have this photocopy of a page from the Dean's appointment book. . . . What's that, sir? How did I get it? Well, well, well, funny you should ask. . . .'"

"Wayne, you can't just sit by and do nothing."

Holder was about to give her another comeback, but he couldn't argue with her last point. Senator Bruckner was due to arrive in thirty-six hours. The games were about to start.

"I don't know, Liz. I'm beginning to think that maybe I have this all wrong. I mean, maybe Van Grouw was wrong, or was deliberately lying to me."

"Timmer believed him."

"And look at what a stand-up Joe ol' Captain Timmer turned out to be."

"Are you giving up, Wayne?"

The overhead light came on suddenly. Out in the hallway, the scratchy public address system played the first notes of "Taps."

"Wayne, you know where Alex is?"

It was Will Carey, the company first sergeant, doing a bed check.

Holder brought his hand up to his eyes to shield them from the glare. He looked over at the empty bunk across from him, as if noticing it for the first time.

"No," he said. "Is he in the latrine?"

"I didn't see him," Carey said. The junior pulled his head back out into the hallway, looking up and down for Holder's roommate.

"I gotta check these other rooms," Carey said. "How about looking in the latrine and I'll come back in a minute."

Holder nodded. "Liz," he said into the phone. "I need to go look for Alex so he doesn't miss bed check."

"OK," she said. "Call me back."

By the time Holder checked the three latrines that ran down the length of the wing, the last notes of "Taps" had rattled through the speakers and Alex Trainor was officially absent without authority.

"Any idea where he is?" Carey asked.

Wayne shook his head. "Haven't seen him since before dinner."

Carey leaned against the wall. "Damn," he said.

There was no doubt about the right thing to do at this point; Carey had to turn Trainor in as absent, and Alex would have to suffer the consequences, which could be considerable.

The culture among the cadets at West Point was such that the peer pressure was on the offender. Carey would not lie to cover for Trainor. Everyone expected Trainor to be on time so as not to put another cadet into the position of having to turn in such a report. In the family that was the cadet company, it was Alex who would be embarrassed.

"Alex has seemed a little spacey lately," Carey said. "Is he having some kind of personal trouble?"

"You could say that," Holder admitted.

He went back into their room, opened Trainor's locker. At first glance, everything seemed to be there. Carey followed Holder into the room, looked over the senior's shoulder.

"His full dress coat is missing," Carey said. "He send it out to the cleaners?"

Holder didn't answer. He turned to the windows and walked to Alex's desk. It was clean save for a framed picture of Alex's wholesome family: mom, dad, six children.

"Damned if I know where he is," Holder said.

Then he saw the envelope on his own desk. His name written in Alex's handwriting. He tore open the message.

Dear Wayne,

Sorry to do this to you, but it's the only way I can see to straighten out the mess I've made of things.

Ruth called me this afternoon and told me she had an abortion. She said that Kathleen Gates told her how much I really didn't want this child, that the baby and Ruth were in the way of my career and my plans. I was so blind that I didn't even see that myself, but I suspect that Ruth was right.

I've been a liar and a hypocrite, quick to condemn other people for sins I was guilty of. And now, because of that, I have the blood of an innocent on my hands. I turned away from the Lord. I wonder if He'll even have me.

You'll get through this trial, Wayne. Keep your face turned to Jesus.

Yours—
Alex

"Oh, shit," Holder said.

"What is it?" Carey asked, coming closer, nodding to the paper Holder held in a trembling hand.

"Oh, my God," Holder said. "Oh, Jesus."

They found him amid the rocks below the high roof of Thayer Hall. A young soldier, a private wearing a Military Police brassard and carrying an oversized flashlight, called to the other searchers from up among the thin trees that covered the rocks to which the great building clung.

Wayne ran to the spot where the beams of the flashlights converged, wild fingers of light spiking through the undergrowth.

Alex Trainor lay on his back in the crevice of a cleft rock. His hips and legs were twisted at a vicious angle, so that he looked to be running backward. But his face was turned up, and in the pale white of the MP flashlights, he appeared to be sleeping.

Wayne Holder walked away from the base of the building to the middle of the soccer field that stretched from the bluff to the river's edge. He sat cross-legged in the dark, his back to the comings and goings of investigators, the headlights playing across the fields. Major Tom Gates found him by following the dim reflection of light off Holder's rumpled white shirt.

"Hello, Wayne," Gates said. The big man came up behind him and sat down on the grass. Out on the river a tugboat pushed a barge against the current. From this distance the bow wave looked like a misplaced snowdrift.

"I'm sorry about Alex," Gates said.

Holder kept his silence.

"The investigator will want to talk to you in the morning. I convinced him to give you a few hours."

"Thanks, sir."

"I know this is a terrible time for you, Wayne, but I have to ask. Was there any indication that Alex was thinking of doing something like this? I mean, I'm assuming this has something to do with his girlfriend."

"She had an abortion."

Gates didn't say anything. Holder sat quietly for another minute before he spoke again.

"Funny thing is, I'm not even sure she knew him well enough to figure out that this would be his reaction. They haven't even known each other a year."

"When did he find out about the abortion?"

"Tonight."

"Did you talk to him afterward?"

"No, I got a note," Holder said.

And your wife's name is in it, he thought. *She as good as pushed him.*

Holder looked up at Gates, a big shadow discernible in the reflected lights of the MP cars.

"May I see it?"

"I'll have to get it for you, sir," Holder said. "I dropped it on my desk when I ran out."

He was afraid that Gates was going to walk back with him. If Gates saw the note, the whole story would come spilling out. He wanted to talk to Timmer first.

"The investigators will want to see it in the morning," he said. "I'll be in my office by zero seven. I'd like to see it first."

Gates turned to look over his shoulder at the activity by the cliff.

"I imagine I'll have to go to the morgue," he said. "But you can call me at home—no matter what time it is—if you need me. OK?"

"OK, sir," Holder said.

"Want me to walk back to the barracks with you?"

"I'll be fine, sir. Thanks."

The conversation was finished, but Gates lingered; he wanted to say something more.

"You know, Kathleen was supposed to give that girl a call. Trainor's girlfriend. She was going to try to help her out, you know. Give her someone to talk to."

Holder didn't trust himself to speak.

"Oh, well," Gates said. With that he stood, bent over to dust off the legs of his trousers, then turned and walked into the darkness.

CHAPTER 18

WHEN LIZ WRENSON HEARD THE NEWS THE NEXT MORNING AT breakfast, she left her seat at Brigade Staff tables and walked over to the adjacent wing, where D Company tables were located. Holder's seat was empty.

"Where's Wayne?" she asked another firstie.

"Outside," her classmate told her, gesturing to the door. "He was at formation, don't know where he went after that."

She headed for the big doors and found Holder as he was coming in. He looked as if he'd walked guard all night; his uniform hung slack; he had done a poor job shaving—there was a swath of blonde along his jawline. His eyes were red-rimmed and a bit wild.

"I'm so sorry, Wayne," Liz said. The little vestibule was filling with first and second class cadets hurrying to pick up books for class. Liz hugged him.

Holder took her by the arm and led her into the cavernous mess hall. There were now hundreds of cadets heading out the door, a sea of gray, many of them still not fully awake, some of them noticing Wayne and Liz, Wayne leaning close, whispering to her.

When they were off to the side, Holder took out a sweat-stained and creased paper from his pocket and pressed it into Liz's hand.

"Read this," he said, looking around the room as if they might be ambushed.

Liz read quickly, then sat down in a nearby chair. The cadets at the table—heads down, still eating—looked up at her briefly, then went back to their food.

"Oh, God," she said. "He left this for you?"

Holder nodded. "It's time to do something," he said. "You still with me?"

"Yes," she said.

Holder tried a smile. When it didn't work, he let it go.

"I'm supposed to meet with the investigator in a few minutes," he said. "But I'm not going to."

"What can I do to help?" she asked.

"Make a call for me."

An hour later Liz Wrenson walked into Taylor Hall, where the Dean's office was located. She took off her hat as she crossed the threshold, pressed a stray hair back into place, took a deep breath, and headed up the stairs.

Plan A, as she and Wayne had worked it out, was for Liz to get Ms. Wiley away from her desk.

"Timmer told me the woman's an attack dog," Holder said. "And big as a house, too."

"Well, maybe I'll be able to charm her," Liz answered.

"If she goes for your throat," Holder said, "I'll institute plan B."

"What's that?"

"Don't know. I hope I'll figure that out by the time I need it."

When she reached the landing, Liz saw Wayne in the little anteroom outside the Dean's office, just out of sight of the woman inside. He gave Liz a wink and a thumbs-up sign as she passed him without speaking.

Ms. Wiley sat hugely behind her desk, overflowing the chair. Liz thought it unlikely that Wiley would get up for the general, much less to help a cadet.

The Dean was out; Wayne had determined that by calling just a few minutes earlier. Plan A was for Liz to lure Wiley away from her desk with some story about being confused about medical school versus applying for a fellowship.

"Hello, ma'am," Liz said, turning on her brightest smile. "My name is Liz Wrenson, and I was wondering if I could make an appointment to see the Dean."

Ms. Wiley did not smile back at her.

"What do you need an appointment for?" Wiley asked. "Did you go to your chain of command first? I mean, you can't just waltz right into the Dean's office. There are procedures to be followed."

As she spoke she shoved file folders around her desk; she looked as if she might be building a nest.

"Yes, ma'am," Liz said sweetly. "I didn't expect to get an appointment today. I wanted to ask the Dean for advice. I'm sort of in the middle between applying to medical school and applying for a fellowship, and I have to figure out how to proceed from here."

Liz was playing her smart-girl hand, the same one she played from time to time with instructors, the parents of boyfriends, or anyone else from whom she needed something.

"I don't see why you have to bother General Simon with these things," Wiley said. "Certainly you must have other advisors."

Liz kept smiling as Wiley turned around to retrieve a tablet from the credenza. When the woman's back was turned, Liz looked out in the hallway; she could see Wayne there. She put her hands up to her throat and made a panicked face.

Guard dog.

Wayne smiled at her, then disappeared around the corner.

"Give me your number," Wiley said, copying "Wrenson" from the nametag on Liz's pocket.

Liz opened her mouth to speak, was drowned out by the clanging of the fire alarm.

Wiley looked up at the door, as if the fire might be standing there.

"Oh, my," she said, all trace of vehemence gone.

"Guess we'd better go," Liz said helpfully. "Is the quickest way down the front stairs?"

"Oh, my," Wiley said again. All her arrogance was gone; fear had taken over.

"Are you all right, ma'am?" Liz asked.

"I . . . uh, I may have some trouble getting down the stairs," the woman said. "I usually take the elevator."

Oh, great, Liz thought. *No sign of Wayne, and now I'm going to be doing CPR on this fat lady.*

"I'll help you," Liz said, walking around behind the desk and taking hold of Wiley's chair.

The woman pushed at the floor with her feet, moving the chair back an inch at a time. Liz saw something move across the open door, looked up. It was Wayne. When he saw her struggling with the bulky Ms. Wiley, he ducked back out into the hall.

"It's going to be OK," Liz said. She tried to roll the chair back, but Wiley had it cemented to the floor with her bulk.

Liz helped Wiley find her feet. She could hardly believe the woman got here under her own power every day. She had to hurry her out into the hallway. She looked at the desktop, considered taking the appointment book with her, but sensed Wayne hovering outside.

They made it only as far as the door of the office when Liz heard the fire trucks pull up. At most, they had only a minute or two until the firefighters came running up the stairs.

"There, there, that's it," Liz said, over and over. "You're doing great, that's it, keep it up, one foot at a time now, that's it."

"Oh, I feel faint," Wiley said

"DON'T FAINT!" Liz said sharply. Then, calming her voice, she added, "There's no need to panic. I don't even smell smoke. I'm sure we'll be outside in a few moments, safe and sound."

The stone-floored hallway magnified the sounds of the firemen two floors below them. Liz steered Wiley out the door, saw, out of the corner of her eye, a shadow pass behind them as Wayne went into the Dean's office. So far, so good. But when she turned to the front, she saw three firemen coming up to them.

"Keep going, ladies," a handsome firefighter said. He had

an oxygen mask slung across his face, unfastened, and a fire ax in one hand. He looked like a recruiting poster for the Fire Department.

"Keep going," he said to his companions. "Murray, check the second floor, Dusty, you take the third and I'll head up. . . ."

Liz turned around. Wayne had not come out of the office; the firefighters were almost past her.

"She's going to faint!" Liz said suddenly.

Two of the firefighters came up short, stopping their headlong run up the stairs. One of the men actually looked behind him, as if to make sure the escape route was clear. The suggestible Ms. Wiley obligingly started to weave back and forth, a boulder in an avalanche. The firefighters were directly below her and none too happy about it.

"Help me, here!" Liz shouted at them, more of a command than a plea. Wiley looked at her, possibly to see if there was some reason Liz knew of why she should be even more panicked. The firefighters, if for no other reason than to save themselves, stepped forward and put out six hands to help keep Wiley from bowling down the stairs.

The cluster made it down to the landing on the first floor without incident when the alarm stopped ringing.

"You people all right?"

A middle-aged man in a turnout coat stood at the foot of the stairs, two-way radio pressed to his cheek.

"We might need a stretcher here, Chief," one of the firefighters said. Liz had let go of Wiley's hand and was about to turn around when Wayne appeared on the other side of the knot of men.

"Anything I can do to help?" Holder asked.

"You cadets get outside," the chief told them.

Liz and Wayne hustled into the courtyard, where they had to squeeze past more firefighters, more equipment, and a growing crowd of spectators in gray and green.

"I heard you say she was going to fall," Wayne said to her when they had made it to the street. "Pretty smart."

"Wish I could say the same about your pulling the fire alarm," Liz said.

"I wish I had another choice, but I couldn't think of any at the moment."

"Did you copy the page?"

Holder held up two sheets of paper. "I even got an extra."

"The suicide of that cadet is a tragedy, of course," Senator Bruckner said to Claude Braintree. "But from a strictly practical standpoint, it couldn't have come at a better time for us."

Braintree stared out the window of the limousine as they rolled out of the gates at Stewart Airport, eighteen miles north of West Point. He hoped that the driver couldn't hear his boss through the glass partition.

This is what it's come to, Braintree thought. *All the work, all the years, all the scrambling. I get to sit in the back of a limo with this parody of a man and celebrate the death of a twenty-year-old.*

Bruckner twirled his trademark cowboy hat in his hand. "The media got wind of some connection between this suicide and the beginning of the hearings," he said.

Braintree turned his head slowly; the Senator was smiling.

"Yet there is absolutely no connection, as far as we know," Braintree said.

"As far as we know," Bruckner repeated. "But we can't rule it out. Nor can we be responsible for assumptions the media makes."

"And just where would they have gotten such a notion?" Braintree asked.

Bruckner ignored him. "Besides, it does seem remarkably coincidental, don't you think? I mean, this kid . . . what'd he do? Jump?"

"Jumped," Braintree said.

"This kid jumping the night before our opening press conference."

The Senator sipped the coffee provided by the limousine service, made a face.

"Whoa, that tastes like cow piss," he said. Then, cheerfully, "I hear all four major networks will be here this morning."

You'd have pushed that kid off the roof yourself to guarantee that kind of exposure, Braintree thought.

"It's critically important that we keep the public's attention focused on us up here. These kind of committee hearings can be boring, drop right into ratings oblivion if we're not careful about orchestrating them."

Braintree was looking out the window again, bracing himself for what he knew was coming.

"That's why I want to lead off with this Kathleen Gates," Bruckner said. "She's going to be here this morning, right?"

"She agreed just this morning to come in and meet with you. I still think her testifying is a bad move, Senator," Braintree said as calmly as he could. He was about to add "You already have a reputation," but he took a deep breath, paused for one beat, two.

"The media has this perception of you, that you're always stirring up dirt, always going for the sensational. I don't think that's going to serve you well in the future. You get coverage in the short run, sure. But the people are not going to want to elect a talk-show host into the White House."

Bruckner put his cup down carefully, then shifted in his seat so that he was nearly facing Braintree. The limousine glided along under an arch of trees, the road climbing steadily now, the beginning of the last hill that would roll down to West Point.

"Are you trying to hurt my feelings, Claude?" Bruckner asked. "Or is it that you've become so enamored of the military in your time up here that you'd just as soon we forget the whole thing?"

"Neither of those things, sir," Braintree said. "I told you that I don't think much of Mrs. Gates's credibility. I don't want to see her use the commission for her own ends and then have us shown up later for being gullible. I don't think sensationalism is the way to the White House."

"For us," Bruckner said.

"Sir?"

"For us, I said. You don't think sensationalism is the way for us to get to the White House. Am I right?"

"I've never deceived you about my ambitions, Senator. I think you can win the Presidency in six or ten years. And I want to be there when it happens."

"But you're not willing to do what's necessary," Bruckner said. "To get the public's attention."

Bruckner put the big hat down on the seat between them.

"The country wants a plainspoken man in the White House, Claude. Someone who isn't afraid to take on these big elitist institutions."

"Is that what you think of West Point?" Braintree asked.

"It doesn't matter what I think, Claude. What matters is that the people think that. They want to see the old institutions get taken apart. People are tired of the way things are. We're talking about a revolution here, a complete reworking of the way the government spends money. But none of that is going to happen unless we get people's attention."

"And we can do that by closing West Point," Braintree said. It wasn't a question.

Bruckner reached over and patted the back of Braintree's hand. Braintree recognized the gesture; he had used it with the lovely Captain Timmer, who'd found it annoying. Now he saw why.

"Trust me, Claude. I know what I'm doing."

They passed through Washington Gate, rolled by the hospital. Traffic stopped as two big fire trucks backed into the station house; Bruckner kept checking his watch.

"We have plenty of time, sir. Once the traffic clears, it's only a few minutes to the main cadet area."

"I'm not worried about being on time, Claude. I want to be a few minutes late. Make my entrance, you know."

The limousine rolled around Trophy Point, and Claude Braintree looked out at the parade field, the river view, the vast expanse of barracks. Bruckner had his head buried in a newspaper, looking for his own name.

The press brief was set for Central Area, right on the steps of the Old First Division Barracks. Braintree had chosen this spot because it made sense—the hearing room and the Senator's temporary office were upstairs in Ninninger Hall—and because the hundred-year-old building made a picturesque yet serious backdrop. He had chosen this spot over one near the river because he thought it looked more like the commission was getting down to business. The plan was for the Senator to go right upstairs after he spoke to the press, heading off to do the nation's work. Gotta run. Lots to do.

The limousine pulled up to the chain that blocked access to Central Area. A young Military Police officer, apparently well briefed, unhooked the chain and let it drop so they could drive through. There were a half dozen television vans and cars parked haphazardly in what was supposed to be an area for cadet formations. Braintree looked out the darkened window of the limo; Bruckner had been right: the major networks were all represented.

"I'll want to talk to this Mrs. Gates as soon as this thing is over," he said as he straightened his tie.

Braintree tried not to watch. Bruckner tended to wear ties in unfortunate colors with double breasted suits. But he left the jacket open, as if it were single breasted. The result was a pair of long creases down the front where the jacket hung open. Claude Braintree, impeccably turned out—as always—in a tightly woven black and white check, could hardly stand to look at his boss's clothes.

The heat and the questions barreled into the car as soon as the door opened.

"Senator, is it true the cadet suicide last night is connected to the hearings?"

"Senator Bruckner, was your committee talking to the cadet who killed himself last night?"

"Senator Bruckner, are Academy officials cooperating in your investigation?"

"Senator Bruckner, are you going to recommend closing the Academy?"

Braintree stayed in the back seat of the limo for a few moments, until the worst of the melee had moved away when Bruckner passed around the corner. He used the phone in the back of the car to place a call to the Gateses' quarters; he got the machine.

Braintree set the phone gently back in its cradle and got out of the car. Part of him wanted to find Kathleen Gates right where she said she would be—in the front row of the press conference—and part of him hoped he'd never see her again.

There were lots of places Tom Gates needed to be at the beginning of this bad day. Alex Trainor's body was in the morgue at Keller Army Hospital. Trainor's parents—whom he'd called in the middle of the night to deliver the terrible blow—were flying in from Kansas City in a few hours; there was an investigator from the Army's Criminal Investigation Division waiting back at Gates's office and a psychiatrist who'd soon be calling to begin work on a suicide profile and psychological autopsy.

And Wayne Holder, who probably knew more than anyone else about why Trainor jumped, was nowhere to be found. The morning report, sitting on Gates's desk when he arrived, showed that Holder was present at breakfast formation, but he had missed his meeting with the investigators. A call upstairs to a couple of the other firsties revealed that he had skipped breakfast and at least one class this morning. It was so unusual for a cadet to miss class—let alone a meeting he'd been ordered to attend—that Gates wasn't even sure how he would handle such a development.

All that crap and Holder could get bounced for skipping class, he thought.

Tom Gates had all of this on his mind as he moved across Central Area, trying to spot his wife amid the crowds of cadets and faculty members gathering for the circus of Senator Bruckner's appearance.

The big quadrangle had a carnival air. Cadets, normally in a constant state of agitation as they hurried from or to class, stood about in the bright September sunshine, joking and pointing and waiting for the main event. Gates moved through a sea of gray, of flashing brass and quick salutes, tracing a big circle around the steps of the First Division.

Most of the spirit posters for the following week's football game were gone. There was a large banner hanging from Bradley Barracks, directly facing what would be the speaking platform for the press conference. It showed Army's mascot, The Black Knight, being pursued by a larger, darker rider trailing a banner that read, "The Inquisition." Below the painted figures, "I'm from the government, I'm here to help."

Gates could see, suspended from a barracks window, another ten-foot high black horse with a fair likeness of the Senator from Texas. In the painting, Bruckner wore a maniacal smile and held a giant sword over his big hat. As

Gates watched and some photographers snapped photos, two cadets were busy pulling the poster inside.

"Good morning, sir."

Cadet Will Carey, the lean-forward-in-the-foxhole First Sergeant of Company D, stood beside Tom Gates.

"You seen Holder this morning?" Gates asked, returning the young man's salute.

"Not since formation, sir," Carey answered.

"You have any idea why he would disappear?" Gates asked. "He missed a class this morning."

Carey's normal demeanor was a model of self-restraint: arrow straight, tightly tucked, as squared away as a statue. When he blinked twice at the question, Gates knew the cadet was suddenly uncomfortable.

"I'm sure he was upset about Alex," Carey said.

"Is that why he went AWOL?" Gates asked. Sixteen years of dealing with young soldiers told him this one had something more to say.

Carey looked him in the eye. "He was probably also upset about the note, sir. The one Alex left for him."

"What did it say?"

"I don't remember it word for word, sir," Carey said. "I only got a glimpse of it." He swallowed before speaking again. "But it pretty much said that Mrs. Gates helped Alex's girlfriend get an abortion."

Tom Gates felt a sudden, painfully sharp awareness of his surroundings, as if he would remember this moment for a long time: Carey fidgeting in front of him, shifting his weight back and forth on the balls of his feet; the background noise of the crowd; the sun bouncing off the white side of a nearby television van.

Gates pulled himself up straight, raised his right hand in salute. "Carry on," he said to Carey. The cadet saluted, hurried away.

There was some commotion on the steps of the old building, and Gates spotted Kathleen right up front, talking to a guy in jeans and a polo shirt who was armed with a clipboard and festooned with wires, a headset, and several battery packs.

"Kathleen," he said as he approached. The sound tech gave him a curious look; Gates pulled himself up to his full height, flexed his shoulders, and returned a scowl and the civilian turned away without speaking.

"I tried calling you at home; the babysitter told me you'd come down here."

"Did she also tell you I came to talk with Senator Bruckner?"

Tom Gates didn't trust his voice; he nodded.

Several of the cadets standing closest had become interested in their conversation. It would have been hard to miss the tension. Kathleen didn't look at her husband; he stood to her side, facing her like a petitioner. To the observers, it looked like a marital battle was about to break out.

"Why didn't you tell me about this?" he asked after a pause.

"You came and went without waking me up," she answered.

"I spent the night with the MPs and the doc at the morgue," he said, rubbing his big hand across his chin. "I came in and grabbed a clean uniform around five, then headed back to the barracks. You got my note, right?"

"Yes," she said. "I was sorry to hear about Trainor."

Gates stared at his wife. "His girlfriend had an abortion," he said, testing her knowledge.

Kathleen turned to him, meeting his gaze for the first time. Her eyes were clear, her face untroubled.

"You asked me to get involved," she said.

"I asked you to call her," Gates said. "What did you talk to her about?"

He sounded like a nag, but Gates reminded himself that this was part of the investigation into Trainor's death. And Kathleen would be part of the official investigation once Holder showed up with the suicide note.

"She asked me about being an Army wife, about the kinds of sacrifices involved. She also asked me if it were true that Trainor wouldn't be allowed to marry her."

The sound tech passed close by again; Kathleen flashed a smile at him.

She's trying to piss me off, Gates told himself. But the knowledge did him little good, and he could feel his anger roiling inside him.

"Did you tell her that Trainor didn't want this baby?"

"Now how would I know something like that?" Kathleen snapped. "Although I have to say that the way he acted, it didn't look like he wanted this baby."

"Did you bring up the possibility of an abortion?"

There was a disturbance around the side of the building; Gates thought he saw a limousine roll by. The crowd moved in that direction, like the surge of a wave, and Kathleen began to walk away from him.

"Kathleen," he said sharply.

She had taken some six or seven steps. She stopped, and the cadets moving past her parted, water flowing around a midstream boulder. Some of them, Gates saw, were bold enough to look directly at the couple, and wouldn't it make great table conversation: *and then this Tac and his wife got into it, right there in the middle of the crowd.*

"That young girl made up her own mind," Kathleen said testily.

A half dozen cadets were listening. Tom Gates didn't care.

"It's sad that Trainor reacted the way he did, but that was a choice he made."

Kathleen had moved into the narrow alley between the First Division and Pershing Barracks. The crowd of cadets was pushing behind them and a half-dozen reporters jostled their way through the tightly packed mass. It was the equivalent of having an argument in a crowded elevator.

"You sound like one of those pop psychology books, Kathleen," Gates said. "This isn't an academic exercise, or a discussion around someone's cocktail party. One of my cadets is dead."

Now the cadets and faculty members around them stared unabashedly. Kathleen moved toward her husband, something burning in her eyes—anger, maybe, or defiance.

"Why are you quizzing me?" she asked.

Tom Gates put his hand on his wife's arm and led her out of the narrow space. The crowd was deep here; they had to wend through dozens of cadets, all pushing toward them. When they'd found a little space, Gates turned on her, took his hand off her arm.

"Trainor left a note for Holder," he said, glad to hear he'd regained some control of his voice. "Said you helped her get an abortion. I want to know what's going on, what all this has to do with Holder and Trainor."

Kathleen dropped her eyes, shook her head slowly. When she brought her eyes back to his, the hot look was gone.

"A sad mistake," she said. "It's all a very sad mistake."

"Well, that tells me a whole helluva lot," Gates said. "The investigators will want to talk to you, you know."

"Everyone wants to talk to me," she said.

"What's that supposed to mean?"

"I'm meeting with Senator Bruckner this morning," she said, looking over her shoulder. They were twenty or thirty yards from the First Division steps, close enough to see the little forest of microphones.

"What are you going to say to Bruckner? What is it that you have to say that's so interesting?" Gates asked. He spoke slowly, measuring his words to conceal the growing panic.

Kathleen pushed her hair back over her shoulder, a practiced gesture that meant she wasn't worried.

"Try not to sound so surprised, Tom. I do have a thought now and then," she said, turning to face the limo.

"Don't be so mysterious," he said. "The last thing I need is any more notoriety."

Kathleen turned quickly on him. She dropped her voice, but a few cadets nearby noticed the sharp move and glanced over.

"I'm perfectly aware of what you need and what you don't need," she said. "Maybe more so than you."

Gates looked at his watch. There were dozens of other questions he wanted to ask Kathleen, but absolutely no guarantee that he would get a single straight answer.

There was a stir in the crowd, a disturbance that spread like ripples on water; in the distance, the sounds of reporters' insistent questions. A tall man in a suit and a ridiculous cowboy hat was the center of attention. Kathleen stood on her tiptoes.

"I don't want you to get involved with this commission, Kathleen," Gates said.

"I already am," she answered. "And so are you."

As he considered the possible meanings behind her latest cryptic remark, Tom Gates looked around the crowd. Wayne Holder was there, some forty or fifty yards away, standing next to a dark-haired woman cadet.

Gates's first sensation was relief: Holder hadn't jumped off a building himself. His second sensation was anger: Holder wasn't where he was supposed to be that morning.

"I gotta go," Gates said to his wife. He couldn't figure out what was on her mind; he might as well attack one of the other problems on the morning's long list.

The big officer waded through the crowd again. On the steps of the old Barracks, Senator Bruckner was saying something about the recent tragedy. A few camera crews mingled with the cadets watching the speech, a few reporters with notebooks, some with microphones, ready to record the crowd's reaction.

Gates moved quickly, the cadets stepping aside to give him room. He caught a glimpse of the cadet Holder had been talking to, recognized her as a striper from Brigade Staff, Wrenlin or Wrendon or something.

Gates shot a glance over his shoulder. Behind him, the Senator droned on about the need for a completely open investigation and his hopes that, with the help of Academy officials, this commission would result in a better, stronger West Point to serve the nation well into the twenty-first century as it has for the last two.

When Gates turned back to the front, Holder was gone.

There was no sign of the woman either. When he got to the spot where they'd been standing, he did a little pirouette. Nothing. Holder had seen him coming and had taken off.

What the fuck?

Gates spotted one of the juniors from his company, a woman named Rebecca Hollings. He motioned her toward him.

"Morning, sir," she said, saluting sharply.

"Rebecca," Gates said by way of greeting. "Are you on your way to class?"

"No, sir. Headed back to the barracks. I just cut through here to see a bit of the show." She smiled and raised her hand to indicate the podium, then twirled her index finger beside her temple.

"Right," Gates said. "Did you see Wayne Holder here just a minute ago?"

"No, sir. Saw him at breakfast formation, but not since then."

"OK. If you see him, ask him to come to my office right away. It's very important. And if you see anyone else from the company, tell them I'm looking for Cadet Holder and that they should give him the same message. Got that?"

"Yes, sir," Hollings said, saluting and moving away.

"Major Gates?"

"What?" Gates snapped. When he turned, he didn't find a cadet, but a civilian, a young woman in a rumpled business suit standing beside him. A heavy briefcase tugged at one of her shoulders, a big pass marked PRESS dangled from the strap.

"I'm Marjorie Sams from the *New York Post,*" she said, switching a wire-bound notebook to her left hand so that she could offer her right.

"Do I know you, ma'am?" Gates asked, shaking her hand.

"Saw your nametag," Marjorie Sams said. She took a step closer to him, moving out of the way of a group of cadets surging toward the sally port and their next class. She was about twenty-two, he thought, with brown hair, brown eyes, and an intense, no-frills look that Gates had come to associate with print reporters. She looked as if she'd slept in her suit; her shoes were scuffed and dirty. He wondered if she'd walked from New York City.

"The Public Affairs officer said you'd be available later to talk about the cadet who committed suicide," she said, surprising Gates. He wasn't aware that the Academy's Public Affairs officer knew who he was. The man had certainly not asked him if he'd be available.

"I understand he was in your command," Sams continued, producing a small recorder as she spoke.

If her clothes were any indication of how hard she went after a story, Gates figured the woman would soon know— if she didn't already—about Trainor's hand being smashed in the door. He wondered how that story would look in the

Post's famously oversized—and overcute—headlines: *Bone Crushing Discipline at West Point.*

"That's right. Alex Trainor. He was a senior," Gates said.

"I'm sorry to hear the bad news. Was there any indication, anything in his behavior to make you think this cadet was a suicide risk?"

"No," Gates said.

Sams smiled at him, then put one hand on her hip, as if to signal how ridiculous this answer sounded to her.

"No? That's your whole answer? Well, that'll make a great story."

She was smiling, but Gates felt the joke was at his expense.

"Let me just get my notebook out quickly here to make sure I get all of that down."

"I'm not really sure I should be talking to you about this, Ms. Sams," Gates said. He sounded a bit more gruff than he'd intended, but he'd been frustrated all morning.

Sams pressed her lips together, then flipped open her notebook. The recorder dangled from a wrist strap.

"I tried to contact his roommate," Sams said. "Cadet Wayne Holder."

She looked up from the book. "Called him in his room, asked around the dormitory or barracks or whatever."

Gates was tempted to walk away; he saw what was coming.

"One of the—more helpful—cadets told me that Holder missed class this morning, that no one has seen him since breakfast. One of the cadets also mentioned that missing class is a serious offense here."

"Yes," Gates said. "A soldier has to show up where and when. Period."

"So you've determined that Holder missed class?"

"I'll know for sure when I get the attendance reports from the professors, Ms. Sams," Gates said.

"Are you being evasive, Major?" she asked.

This woman has balls, Gates thought.

"Did you get a report that Holder had missed class?"

"One or two of his classmates did tell me that, yes."

"Aren't you worried that he might have done something to hurt himself?"

"No," Gates said. "I'm not worried."

Sams let her notebook fall to her side, tapped her pen against her leg.

"Is that because you're such an excellent judge of how your subordinates are handling pressure? Or do you just know Wayne Holder better than you knew Alex Trainor?"

The woman reminded him, just a little, of Kathleen.

"I know that because I saw him a little while ago," Gates said.

"You spoke to him?"

"No, I saw him. I didn't get a chance to speak to him."

"So one of the principals in this suicide is AWOL. . . ."

"He's not AWOL, ma'am."

"OK, so he's missing, or missing in action, whatever it's called. But you don't know where he is or why he's hiding."

"Who said he was hiding?" Gates demanded, a little louder than he'd intended. A few cadets nearby stopped to watch.

She was running with it now.

Is this what it looks like? he thought. *Some hundred-pound woman in a bad suit starts throwing around these headline words, and I'm fodder for the press? Jesus. . . .*

He wanted to run away.

Control yourself, he thought.

"Has Holder ever missed class before? Is he in trouble a great deal?"

Gates remained quiet. He was thinking about ways to murder the Public Affairs Officer. Slowly.

Gates saw another of his cadets, a pathologically talkative senior named Heydrich, approaching. The next act, no doubt, in the comedy his life had become. Gates twisted his head to the right, trying to warn Heydrich off. The cadet glanced to the side, as if Gates were trying to draw his attention to something there. Then he came straight ahead.

"Hello, sir," Heydrich said in his happy voice. "Good morning, ma'am."

He waited for Sams to acknowledge him; gave her the Wholesome West Point Cadet smile.

He's here to check out this woman, Gates thought. *The little horndogs would try to make time with lightposts if they could figure out which ones were female.*

472

The officer allowed himself the briefest hope that Heydrich would stumble through a little flirting—and be stuffed by Sams—then wander off harmlessly.

No such luck.

"I just saw Wayne Holder out in front of Eisenhower Barracks, sir. I passed the message Rebecca Hollings gave me, told him to get to your office right away."

"Why, thank you, Stacy," Gates said pleasantly.

Sams looked at Gates, then back at the cadet.

"Excuse me, cadet," she said.

Heydrich turned around, smiled at her.

Always ready to help, Gates thought. *Thrifty, loyal, brave.*

"Which way was Cadet Holder headed? Back to Major Gates's office?"

"Well," Heydrich said. "As a matter of fact, they headed off in the other direction, sort of toward the library and the academic buildings."

"Who's 'they'?" Gates asked.

"Wayne and his friend Liz Wrenson," Heydrich said.

Sams scribbled in her notebook.

Heydrich, ever the helpful cadet, leaned closer to her. "That's W-R-E-N-S-O-N," he said.

"That's all, Heydrich," Gates said.

Jackie Timmer had called Layne Marshall at home, in his car, and in his office. No answer. She knew his teaching schedule; he wasn't in the classroom. There was a chance he was sitting in someone else's office, drinking coffee and trading stories. But there was also a chance, she realized, that he was avoiding her.

She tried to develop a good healthy anger, muttering "bastard" under her breath a few times, but it worked like wet kindling. Nothing catching. Instead, she sat at her desk behind a huge pile of ungraded papers she was supposed to hand back to her cadets today. She had rubbed her eyes red and raw—again.

"Well, if it isn't my long lost officemate," Jon Hillard said as he breezed in the door. He dropped a stack of cadet papers on his desk, then picked up a light blue mug with "UNC Chapel Hill" on the side and headed for the coffee pot. "How are you, darlin'?" he asked.

"How do I look?" Timmer said.

"Well, truth be told, you look like shit," he answered. He sipped his coffee noisily, studying Jackie over the rim.

"Just the way you've looked for the last few days, in fact. *Not* that you've confided in me, or asked for my help." He was smiling at her, but it was a tender rebuke.

Jackie Timmer felt as if she'd just run—and lost—a long, hard race.

"I've gotten myself into quite a mess, Jon," she said. Her elbows were on the desk, palms pressed flat to the side of her head.

Hillard shut the door, walked to the student chair beside Timmer's desk, and sat. He placed his mug carefully on the corner of her desk, staring at it as if it held the key to what he should say next.

"I've heard some things about the trouble you're in," he said, smiling sadly.

"Oh, Christ." She put her hands over her eyes. "Have I become the hot gossip item?"

"You could say that."

Timmer stood up abruptly, knuckles on the desk, head down between her shoulders. "Do you think Rob knows?" she asked without looking up.

"You probably have a better handle on that than anyone else. Do you think he knows?"

"Not yet," Timmer said. "He asked me this morning what was wrong—which surprised me. It's unusual for him to notice."

"You gonna tell him?"

Timmer looked over at her officemate, who sat quietly in the chair, thick hands folded in his lap, his homely face a picture of concern. Jon Hillard, who cared so much for her, who probably loved her as much as her own husband, certainly more than Layne Marshall.

"Are you nuts?" she said without conviction. "That would kill Rob."

"It would kill Rob to find out from someone else," Hillard said quietly.

Timmer sat down hard in her chair.

"Maybe it would send Rob a wake-up call," she said. "Maybe he'd realize that our marriage is superficial."

She turned in her chair so that she was facing Jon Hillard.

"Oh, let's make this about Rob, shall we?" Hillard said. "Let's talk about all of Rob's shortcomings. In fact . . . what the hell . . . let's make him responsible for the whole thing."

Hillard stood; he'd lost some of the gentleness in his tone.

"Spare me the moral platitudes, will you, Jon? You don't know what it's like to be married to Rob."

"I don't know what it's like to be married to anyone. But we're not talking about me here, Jackie. We're talking about you, about the kind of person you used to be. Do you like this change in you? Ducking out on your students, letting your work slide, lying to Rob . . . and to me? Is that who you really are?"

Timmer felt color in her throat, her cheeks. She pulled her hair back in a short ponytail, held it there with two hands while she spoke.

"I thought I knew who I was," she said, her lips only inches from the desk surface. "But then I started to think that other people had made all these choices for me. I was the good little girl, the good little cadet, the good little Army officer, the loyal wife. I'm not sure I ever considered that these might not be the things I wanted."

Hillard stood before her, hands at his sides.

"Well then," he said. "I'd say it's time to decide. Because your experimenting is hurting people. And that's just irresponsible."

She was crying now, softly, her shoulders not shaking yet. She looked up, wiped her nose with the back of her hand. Jon Hillard went to the bookcase behind her desk and picked up a box of tissues she kept there. Timmer took one when he offered.

"Look, Jackie. Whether this affair was right, wrong, moral, immoral, your fault, Rob's fault, Marshall's fault . . . whatever, that doesn't matter right now. You did it. What matters now is whether it's right for Rob to hear it from you or from someone else."

"It gets worse," she said. "The Dean is holding it over my head to keep me quiet about something else."

Timmer explained the tangled story of Kathleen Gates, Wayne Holder, and Sandy Van Grouw. She told her friend about the Dean's role and the why and how of his black-mail.

Talking about it helped. Laying it out on the table let her see the parts in daylight. Let her see more clearly what she had to do if she was going to become—once more—the kind of woman who took responsibility.

"What about Marshall?" Hillard asked, all but spitting the name out.

"Marshall won't even take my calls. He's afraid that if this comes out, he'll lose his spot as a visiting professor, and that will affect his career."

"Tough shit," Hillard said. "He should have thought of that when all this started. You wanna run with the big dogs, you gotta learn to pee in the tall grass."

Timmer looked over at her officemate. He had his hands on his hips now, blood up, color rising, sweat glistening on the top of his head, the ridiculous mask of his face set in a scowl—but for the sharp twinkle of light in his eyes.

"What the hell does that mean?"

"Damned if I know," he said. "My grandfather used to say it all the time, though."

And with that, he smiled. And Jackie Timmer managed to smile back; then the two of them were laughing, guffaw-ing, and snorting and rolling around on the wheeled chairs, laughing so as not to cry, laughing at the sheer idiocy of it all.

Wayne Holder stepped up to the closed door; just before he knocked, he heard laughter from inside. Not chuckles, but deep, uncontrolled belly laughs. He stepped back, his fist still raised, and checked the nameplates once more. Timmer and Hillard. He gave the door two hard raps.

"Come!" a man's voice commanded.

Holder opened the door; Hillard and Timmer were slumped in their chairs, feet out. Timmer swiped at her eyes. Her laughter fell away to the occasional burst.

"Well, if it isn't Cadet Holder, the other member of the All-Fucked-Up Club," Timmer said. "Come in, come in. Take a seat."

Holder watched the two officers from the doorway for a few seconds.

"Oh, come on in, Holder," Hillard said. "We're just indulging in a little inappropriate laughter. A little gallows humor. . . ."

"Before we start jumping out the window," Timmer added. "But don't worry, we probably won't push you."

She doesn't know, Holder thought.

He walked to Timmer's desk and dropped a folded piece of paper on her desk. When she reached for it, he spoke.

"My roommate, Alex, killed himself last night."

Timmer's hand was almost to the note. She stopped, met Holder's eyes, then pulled back.

"I'm so sorry, Wayne," she said.

"Kathleen Gates was in on it," he said. "It's right there in the note."

Timmer picked up the paper. As she read, her officemate asked, "Should I leave?"

"Actually, I'd rather you stay, Jon," she said. "Unless Wayne here has some objection."

Holder shrugged; he was beyond caring who knew what.

"Why would Kathleen Gates bother with Alex?"

"Because she thought he was going to tell Major Gates about what happened in the parking lot. This was a way of hitting him first."

"You think Kathleen Gates knew what effect this would have on Alex?" Timmer asked. "You think she knew he'd jump?"

"I think she knew it would tear him up," Holder said. "Alex is . . . *was* a conservative Christian from this super-straight family. When he was a kid his mom would take them all—Alex, his brothers, and sisters—to march in abortion protests.

"She thought Alex was going to mess up her plan," Holder went on. "And then I got this from the Dean's office."

He held out the photocopy of the appointment book page that said *K. Gates 1100.*

Hillard stood and came up beside Holder, looked down at the desk.

"You took that from the Dean's office?" Hillard asked.

"It's just a photocopy of the appointment book," Holder said. "I didn't steal anything."

"What does it prove?" Hillard asked.

"Nothing, really," Holder said. "I mean, it's not enough."

"The Dean and Kathleen Gates are in this together," Timmer said. "There has to be a way to get that out in the open."

"Before this Gates woman talks in public to the Bruckner Commission," Hillard added.

"What are you proposing we do?" Timmer asked.

The "we" was not lost on Wayne Holder.

"Go straight to the Superintendent," he said. "Dump it all in his lap and let him sort it out. I'm tired of sneaking around . . . I'm hiding from my Tac right now."

"Why is that?"

"Because I was supposed to meet with the investigators this morning," Holder said. "But I didn't want to show them this note just yet, so I kept moving until I could find you. I want to give the note to the Supe first."

"Well," Timmer said. "We still don't have much. This meeting, a few comments from Van Grouw."

"As soon as Kathleen Gates starts to testify, she'll give us all the proof we need."

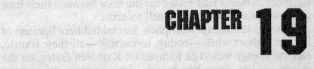

CHAPTER 19

KATHLEEN GATES IDENTIFIED HERSELF TO THE MP WHO STOOD guard beside the entrance to the First Division; when he found her name on his list, he opened the door for her. She climbed the three flights to the top floor, the temperature and noise level rising with each step. She expected the scene in Ninninger Hall to be one of calm control, some orderly approach to carrying out the business of Congress in this outpost. There would be measured tones and sensible procedures and the calm demeanor of people who were following a master plan.

What she found instead looked like a command rescue center after a train wreck. Fifteen or twenty men and women in shirt sleeves raced about, waving sheaves of paper and sounding off in loud, important tones to—as far as Kathleen could see—no one in particular. Technicians in shorts and the logo shirts of news organizations wrestled thick black cables across the floor. The whole room measured only forty by thirty feet, and huge chunks of that real estate were eaten up by a couple of conference tables big enough to double as raised dance floors, each sporting a bank of laptop computers. There were sound consoles and a little forest of tall director's chairs and some sort of witness stand and a choir of arm chairs arranged along one wall. A black box with important-looking gauges and dials blocked the entrance. Two burly young men, tanned, unshaven, biceps straining against shirt sleeves, stood straddling shoulder cameras that rested on the floor between their legs, giant weapons awaiting the call to arms.

This was the media wolf pack, assembled here because of her. In a short while—today, tomorrow—all their frantic, electric energy would be focused on Kathleen Gates, on the words spilling from her mouth. True or false they would believe her, for no other reason than she was at the very epicenter. They would believe, all those people at the far reaches of the black cables and the satellite dishes and the camera eyes, they would believe because they wanted to believe, they were desperate for the minute and nauseating details of scandal, they all wanted to see the darkest secrets dragged into the daylight. They would believe whatever she had to say because she was on-camera. And even the ones who would call her a liar to her face, even they would not change the channel, but would anoint her with some kind of importance. Even the unbelievers would be mesmerized by her presence on the electronic stage. The medium would make truth out of her falsehood.

It was intoxicating; it scared her to death.

Kathleen recognized the worker bees who followed powerful men like a cloud, flitting importantly from place to place. Dorothy Sayer was one of these: linen skirt, white blouse opened to a deep V, standing with her weight on one leg, foot cocked half out of her shoe, unglamorously chewing a pencil as she studied a clutch of papers. Kathleen Gates steered through the crowd, avoiding her.

Claude Braintree sat regally at one of the dark conference tables, perfectly tailored as always, smiling coolly at some amusing tidbit kept to himself while all about him aides and staffers and technical support people and other lesser beings rushed and sweated and drove the temperature in the room up by the minute. He rested his hand on the table before him; his fingernails gleamed like the polished wood, the white cuffs of his shirt were as stiff and sharp as typing paper.

"Mrs. Gates," Braintree said, standing, smiling that odd, mile-wide smile. "Won't you have a seat? May I get you a glass of water? Some coffee perhaps?"

"Water would be great, thanks," Kathleen said. She allowed Braintree to pull out a chair for her.

Kathleen looked over at a bank of lights some technicians were assembling only four or five feet from the table. The room was stifling already; she couldn't imagine what the lights would do to the temperature.

"Looks like you're getting ready for a big production," Kathleen said.

Braintree watched her for a few seconds, as if looking for signs that she was being sarcastic.

"Indeed," he said at last.

He sat down next to her, adjusting the creases of his trousers as he settled in the chair. Kathleen wore a sleeveless blouse and a cotton skirt, turquoise, that came to a demure spot just above her knees. She couldn't imagine that Braintree was going to sit beside her with his coat on.

"The Senator will want to talk to you straight away," Braintree said. Then, leaning close to her, he added, "I'm sure he's going to want you to testify as soon as possible."

"Well, no one said anything to me," Kathleen said. "There are a few things I'd like to get straightened out first; I may not be ready yet."

"That's what I told him," Braintree said. He reached across and patted the back of her hand; his palm was cool and dry. "But the Senator has his own schedule."

Kathleen felt a bead of sweat collect just below her collar bone, at the base of her throat. It rolled down her chest and disappeared into her cleavage; she resisted putting her finger down the front of her shirt.

A knot of noisy humanity approached the table; at the center was one tall man. He was handsome, but in a overfed way; she could imagine him eating huge meals, measuring his drink by the bottle. He had a wide forehead, thick hair that threatened to make its own way. Thick lipped, heavy lidded—like the heavy in a gangster movie.

As he walked, he dictated to a woman who trailed him, writing furiously on a steno pad. The big man tugged at the knot of a silk tie. When it was just loose enough to pull over his head, he yanked it off quickly, as if escaping from a noose. He unbuttoned his cuffs as he reached the edge of the table.

Braintree stood.

"Mrs. Kathleen Gates, I'd like to present Senator Lamar Bruckner of Texas."

Bruckner stuck out his right hand and said, "Very happy to meet you." With his left hand he began to unbutton his shirt.

Kathleen Gates was disoriented; the United States Senator standing before her was undressing.

"I don't think I'm overstating the case, Mrs. Gates. . . ."

His shirt was undone to the waist; still using just one hand, he yanked the sweat-stained tails from his trousers.

"When I say that the public appreciates your candor in coming forward like this. I believe you can only serve justice and the truth by being absolutely forthright. . . ."

He pulled at the tail of the shirt, tearing off a button, which skittered across the polished table and clattered to the floor. No one, Kathleen noticed, looked down.

Bruckner had on a V neck tee shirt. A thick copse of brown and gray hairs sprouted in twisted bundles from the deepest part of the crevice. He was ferociously hairy; another ring of curly hair seemed attached to the back collar of his shirt. What had once been an athletic build was going soft—he swelled roundly just above the line made by his belt; he was shaped like an urn.

". . . absolutely forthright even when the news you bear isn't pleasant. I admire your courage in coming forward."

Kathleen was just about to say something about how far forward she was willing to step when the bank of television lights came on. The sudden white glare was startling, and it was only a second or two before she felt the heat roll over her. She felt moist sweat between her shoulder blades, on her upper lip.

A young woman with oversized glasses was behind Bruckner, trying to unbutton a packaged shirt that had been starched to the consistency of sheetrock. Her glasses slid down her nose, which was shiny with sweat, and she kept tapping herself between the eyes, pushing her glasses back as she beat the starched shirt against her leg. Bruckner thrust his arms straight out behind him and the young woman slipped the sleeves over his hands.

"Claude has filled me in on the terrible circumstances surrounding your coming here today, and I want you to know that I sympathize with you in this difficulty and am ready to stand beside you."

"Senator. . . ." Kathleen began, but Bruckner had turned to face the young woman who was assisting him. He tugged at his sleeves and tried to find the buttons on the cuffs while she fussed with the front placket. Their hands and arms were crossed and no one was making any progress, Bruckner muttering, frustrated. The woman actually seemed to shrink, even though her fingers never stopped moving.

"If you *please,* Anna," Bruckner said fussily. The woman dropped her hands immediately. Two other aides, white-bread bookends in earnest ties, stood in front of the Senator, talking at once even as Bruckner gave instructions to Anna about what suit to get ready for his next appearance. There were two reporters pressed into a small space to Kathleen's left, speaking into handheld microphones. One of them appeared to be doing voice exercises as he alternately opened his mouth into a wide circle and said "Ahh," then snapped his lips shut and hummed "hmmmm."

Kathleen scooted up tight against the table as a technician swung a long metal boom, with a klieg light at one end, in a dangerous arc that nearly hit her in the chest. The boom was now between her and the Senator. There was no room; Kathleen felt as though the walls were collapsing on her. She could feel the panic right beneath the surface.

"Mrs. Gates."

Dorothy Sayer stood at the far end of the conference table.

Kathleen took a step toward Sayer, but it was also closer to the lights, which were pumping out heat like a house fire. Gates tripped over a thick black cable.

"Sorry," a technician said as she caught herself on the sharp corner of the table.

"I have the questions and responses here for your interview," Sayer was chattering before Kathleen had even gained her footing. "And we're in kind of a time crunch. I was hoping you'd go over them very quickly."

"What responses are you talking about?" Kathleen Gates said.

Her skirt had slipped when she stumbled, so that now her blouse had worked its way out of the waistband. Kathleen tucked her shirt in, but now it was too tight on one side. She looked down at her foot and saw that she'd broken a strap on one sandal, which now trailed behind her.

Sayer was talking quickly now, and though a few hairs were glued to her forehead and there was a sheen of perspiration on her chest, she seemed to be thriving on the chaos in the room. The presence of the television cameras, or maybe the strong lights, had whipped everyone into some kind of frenzy, like overstimulated lab rats.

"The questions for your interview. In front of the cameras. Except that we're not going to have time to rehearse," Sayer said, breathlessly, rapid fire. "The crew will be setting up here so we have to move don't you wish they'd chosen a bigger room than this isn't it god-awful hot in here I feel like I'm positively *wilting* and this skirt was definitely *not* the thing to wear. . . ."

Kathleen Gates dropped her purse, sending change and keys rolling and jangling into the tangle of electrical cables on the floor. A technician shot her an evil look; Kathleen considered giving him the finger. Bruckner was yelling at the hapless Anna for some other infraction, and just behind her the noisy reporter had increased the volume of his voice exercises.

Ahh. Umm. Ahh. Umm.

Kathleen Gates was hot and sick to her stomach and more than a little claustrophobic and feeling as if she were being rushed to some destination she didn't know and hadn't chosen.

She stood up straight, spread her feet, and said, as loudly as she could, "Will someone please tell me what the *hell* is going on."

If she'd been in a mood to laugh, she might have. The effect was that comic.

The technicians were suddenly silent. The voice student turned to her, his mouth still open in a silent *ahhh*. Dorothy Sayer looked more than a little shocked. Senator Bruckner peered over his shoulder as if a pupil had suddenly spoken out of turn.

The only person in the room who didn't stop in freeze-frame was Claude Braintree.

"Kathleen," he said, gliding around the end of the conference table, his hand extended, touching her gently on the arm. There was still no trace of perspiration on his face, although he had unbuttoned his jacket.

"I know that this is terribly upsetting," he said, almost cooing. "And you probably weren't in any way expecting this circus."

Braintree raised his chin in what must have been a secret signal. Two aides leaped out of the way and opened the door to a tiny side office. Braintree ushered her inside and closed the door.

This space was no cooler but a great deal quieter than the main room. There was an overnight bag on the table, an opened laundry box of starched white shirts and two silk ties—Bruckner's baggage train. Braintree closed the door, then pulled out a chair for her.

"Let me explain to you what's going on here today," he said pleasantly, as if they were talking about the receiving line at a garden party.

As he spoke he poured a glass of water—no ice—and set it in front of her. Kathleen gulped half of it down before pausing to say, "Thanks."

She dipped two fingers into the glass, pressed the wet tips to her temples. When she opened her eyes, Claude Braintree sat on the other side of the table, relaxed, legs crossed, hands resting on a knee, smiling at her. That wide smile.

"I guess you've figured out that the Senator wants you to testify."

"Today?"

"This morning, as a matter of fact," Braintree said, watching her carefully.

"That's not possible," Kathleen said. "I haven't even had a chance to tell my husband what happened."

Braintree did not seem surprised by this fact. He raised his eyebrows and made a face closer to *No kidding*.

"You've been playing this close to the vest," he said. He leaned toward her, still smiling, but not friendly anymore, not the gallant who'd saved her from the crush of the other room. She could smell the cloying citrus of his cologne.

Kathleen Gates's pulse hammered away; her heart was suddenly too big for her chest. The corner of her mouth twitched involuntarily, a nervous tic she hadn't experienced in a long time. Braintree noticed, looked at her mouth for a second.

"I didn't want to tell him until I'd decided if I was going to come forward with this," she said.

"Ah, my dear Mrs. Gates," Braintree said. "Did you honestly think you could put all this in motion—accusations about the Superintendent, the sexy little story about you and this young man—did you honestly think you could just tease us with all this and it wouldn't come back until you were absolutely sure that you wanted it to? Didn't you see that once you got things rolling, this whole nasty scene took on a life of its own?"

Kathleen felt as if she'd just been wrapped in a heavy blanket. The room got smaller, hotter.

"I can't do that until I talk to my husband," she said again.

"Mrs. Gates, I understand your position completely," he said with mock sympathy. "You started all this without really thinking through what was going to happen at the end.

"The problem you've created is this: the cameras are out there, the networks are here today, but there's no guarantee that they'll be interested tomorrow."

Braintree placed his palms flat on the table, leaned even closer.

"And my boss wants the network air time."

Kathleen wanted out of this room. She'd thought she was coming this morning for a private talk with the Senator. It had all been very exciting, if a bit dangerous.

She had a sudden mental image of Alex Trainor in the morgue. And Tom's sad face when he talked about the dead cadet, the dead soldier. For a painful moment her resolve shimmered. Would her husband ever see what she had tried to do? How pure her motives had been?

"The problem is that my boss doesn't always know what's best for his political life."

Kathleen latched on to something that had always served her well in the past. She became indignant.

"So this is all about ratings for you and Senator Bruckner," she said, as if uncovering some juicy secret.

"Of course it is," Braintree said unexpectedly. "What did you think it was about? The truth?"

"That's what you keep talking about," she answered.

"And you keep talking about all these terrible things that happened to you," Braintree countered. "All these coincidences that fell into place after your husband received his letter of reprimand."

Braintree walked around to her side of the table. He paced the small space between the desk and the wall, a lawyer before the jury box. Behind him hung a framed academy crest, with "Duty, Honor, Country" rolling out in gold on the scroll.

The game was clear to Kathleen Gates.

"You don't believe me, do you?"

Braintree turned on her.

"Not for a minute," he said. "I know Simon is in on this, too."

Oh Christ, she thought. *Simon talked to someone. Maybe to Braintree. Maybe to Flynn, and where would that leave me?*

There was a long silence then. Outside, she could hear Bruckner's booming voice as he greeted one of the reporters.

"In fact," Braintree went on, all trace of civility gone from his voice. "I told Senator Bruckner that I thought it was dangerous to bring you before the Commission. I think you're using us, using the timing of these hearings to salvage your husband's career. And I don't want the Commission embarrassed if it comes out later that you made up this whole story."

He was speaking quickly now. He wanted to finish, Kathleen saw, before Bruckner came in.

"Give yourself a few minutes to think about the consequences, about what you're about to do."

"You want me to tell the Senator that I've changed my mind, that I'm not going to testify?"

"Tell him whatever you want," Braintree said. "Tell him

you've got stage fright, tell him you don't want to embarrass your husband."

Braintree fixed her with a hard stare.

"Tell him you lied."

"I want my husband's record cleared. You said you'd help see to that."

"That's not going to happen," Braintree said. "All that was before I learned the extent of your scheme."

"I'll still go through with this," Kathleen said, fighting to keep the desperation out of her voice. She had set this thing in motion, and would take the bumpy ride right to the end.

"Is that what you want? For your husband to hear on the national news that you did this cadet in the parking lot?"

She stood up behind the little table, the two of them ridiculously close together in this tiny, heated space. She took a step closer to Braintree and was surprised when she looked up and saw a single, glistening bead of sweat at his hairline.

"Senator Bruckner wants me to testify. . . ."

"Lie under oath and I'll have you prosecuted for perjury," Braintree interrupted, his silly smile gone.

"You're assuming that you'd be able to prove that I lied," Kathleen said. "Yet you've seen for yourself how much people want to believe me."

"Not everyone."

"Perhaps not," she conceded. "But your boss believes me."

Braintree leaned against the table, allowed his shoulders to go slack.

He was beaten, at least for the moment.

The door swung open and Senator Bruckner stepped into the room. He looked at Kathleen, then at Braintree, then back at Kathleen as he spoke.

"I trust Claude has briefed you on what's going to happen this morning," he said.

"Yes, Senator, he certainly has," she answered, forcing a smile. "I'm ready to take a look at those questions now. And I need to call my husband."

What Jackie Timmer felt wasn't calm, exactly. Nor was it the kind of certainty she often felt after making a tough decision. There was still too much of the unknown here. But there was relief. She had decided to fight the Dean, but first she had to make sure Simon couldn't blackmail her. She had to tell Rob herself.

She called her husband, who'd already finished teaching for the day, and asked him to meet her at home. When he didn't ask why, Jackie suspected that Rob knew what was going on.

He was sitting on the front steps of their quarters when she pulled up and parked at the curb. She thought something was out of place, then realized that Rob—who was always doing something: reading, grading papers, looking at one of his runner's magazines—was sitting quietly on the top step, hands folded, elbows on his knees.

"Hi," Jackie said as she got out of the car and made her way up the short walk. Rob didn't answer.

She sat down beside him, the two of them quiet for a moment. Across the street, some toddlers played in a fenced playground; a young mother, pregnant, sat on one of the benches, fanning herself with a magazine.

Rob spoke first. "I was sitting here thinking about that café in Heidelberg. Remember? The one you used to go to with your friends."

She saw it all, quickly, at once, a photo pulled from memory's drawer. The thin metal chairs and tiny tables, the giant beer steins, the streetlights that came on so late in the northern summer, like a line of torch bearers marching through the streets.

"I went there three weekends in a row," Rob said. "Sat at tables nearby, until I got up the nerve to introduce myself."

Jackie nodded; she did not trust her voice.

"I wasn't much of a romantic to start with," he said. "And I certainly didn't get any better over the years."

He kept his eyes to the front, watching one child who straddled a swing seat, belly down. Jackie reached over, touched his arm. He gently lifted her fingers off of him.

"I guess there's no good way to find out something like this," he said.

Then he turned to her for the first time. She leaned against the railing, half facing him now. She tasted salty tears at the corners of her mouth.

"But hearing it from someone else has to be one of the worst."

"I'm so sorry, Rob," she said. "So sorry."

Rob Timmer stood and brushed his uniform pants. Then he tucked his thumbs into the tight front of his trousers and ran them back along his sides. The shirt was pressed flat to his belly.

"It's over," she said, meaning the affair, looking up at him.

He smiled, reached out and touched her cheek with the back of his hand. Then he settled his uniform cap on his head.

"Yes, I suppose it is." Then he turned and walked toward his car.

Chris Dearborn found Sandy Van Grouw outside of the First Division.

"Mr. Van Grouw," Dearborn called.

Van Grouw turned to the crowd of gray; Dearborn raised his arm to be seen.

"Well, Chris," Van Grouw said, raking his hand through his hair. "Did you come to cause me more trouble?"

"You could say that," Dearborn answered. "But every obstacle is an opportunity."

"Gosh," Van Grouw said sarcastically. "Let me write that down."

The two men were forced to stand close to each other by the crowd. Van Grouw folded his arms across his chest.

"I guess you know I'm not going to testify," Dearborn said. "I'm not going to help you put Major Gates away."

"I can always call you and ask you to recount the conversations we had earlier," Van Grouw countered. But his heart didn't seem in the threat.

"And I can always say that I thought from the beginning you were just out to find something sensational. But let's not get into that, shall we? I know that there is something else going on here. Something that will make you a lot more valuable to Mr. Braintree."

"Oh?" Van Grouw said. He looked left and right; a theatrical move that made Dearborn smile.

"Wayne told me all the details you revealed to him, everything that Kathleen Gates is about to say up there. Braintree told you all that, am I right?"

Van Grouw reached up and adjusted his glasses. "Maybe," he sniffed.

"Mr. Braintree doesn't want Gates to testify. He thinks it would be bad for the commission. He told you all that so you could sidetrack her."

"You're a very perceptive young man," Van Grouw said. "Or perhaps you just have a vivid imagination."

"A little of both, I like to think," Dearborn said. "At any rate, I know a way you can help Mr. Braintree."

Van Grouw gestured over his shoulder. "I don't think it's going to make a difference," he said. "Kathleen Gates is up there, and I think she's getting ready to spill her guts. Senator Bruckner is just about foaming at the mouth in anticipation of the news coverage."

Dearborn looked up at the front of the building, watched the techs rush in and out, stepping over thick cables that wound down the staircase and out to the trucks.

"We boxers have a saying," he said, looking at the civilian and smiling his crooked smile. "It ain't over 'til the last bell."

Wayne Holder jumped when the phone rang on Timmer's desk. He looked at it, then looked over at Major Hillard, who swiveled his big head around to stare at the instrument again, as if to make sure he'd heard it ring. When it jangled again, Hillard reached across the space between the desks and picked it up.

"It's for you," he said to Holder.

"Wayne, it's me," Liz Wrenson said. "Major Gates just called here looking for you, asked if I knew where you were."

"And?"

"Well, at first I said no, which was true. But then he asked me where I'd look if I had to guess, so I had to tell him the truth."

"Is he on his way here?"

"That'd be my guess."

"Shit," Holder said.

"And I just heard that the Bruckner interviews—on camera—are going to start this morning."

"On television?"

"I talked to one of the sound techs who was running some power lines," Liz said. "He told me the Senator is afraid that the news teams will leave if he waits until tomorrow. I'm betting he'll want to start with something big."

"Alex?"

"Maybe Alex," Liz said. "But the sound tech told me there's a civilian woman in Ninninger Hall. Blue eyes, red hair."

"Kathleen Gates," Holder said.

"None other."

Holder looked at his watch. It was eleven ten.

"When are they going to start?"

"The sound tech said they had to be ready by eleven thirty; they may want a live feed at noon to the New York stations. He said they're definitely shooting for the evening news."

"Thanks, Liz," Holder said.

"What are you going to do?"

"Same thing I've been doing," Holder answered. "Making it up as I go along."

Holder put the phone back and scooped up his hat.

"Where you going?" Hillard asked.

"Major Gates is probably on his way here," Holder answered. "I've got to find Captain Timmer before Gates finds me."

"I'll fight a rear guard action," Hillard said.

Holder slipped down to the side entrance of Lincoln Hall and looked out into the street without opening the door. No sign of Gates. No sign, either, of Timmer.

He came back inside and slumped against the wall.

He felt a fuzzy-edged exhilaration. He had not slept the night before, yet the adrenaline told him to prepare for battle.

He was amazed that over the past three years he had done what he was supposed to do—with an occasional minor slip now and then. Even as recently as two weeks ago, his big worry was that he hadn't perfected his saber manual. Now his roommate and friend lay dead in the morgue, and Wayne Holder was running around like a supporting actor in a bad spy movie, cutting class, hiding from his tactical officer, making secret photocopies of an appointment book belonging to one of the most powerful men in this little world. He'd had a sexual tryst with the wife of a violent lunatic, and now the woman was probably going to accuse him of assault—on television. He had argued with and insulted the only other officer who seemed interested in helping him, and he had spied on the Dean.

From the narrow window in the door he could see the Cadet Chapel. Beyond that was the football stadium, and up the hill from that his car waited in one of the lots. All he need do is walk up there, shedding his uniform on the way, and keep running.

Some part of him wanted to leave and not look back. Hell, he was already AWOL, he might as well go the whole way and disappear from the Academy and the mess that had started with Major Gates out by MacArthur's statue.

Holder leaned back, resting his head against the wall, eyes closed. Then the door screeched open, and a woman in rumpled civilian clothes was beside him.

"Excuse me," she began, then looked at his nametag. "Cadet Wayne Holder? Company D?" she asked.

"None other," he said.

"I'm Marjorie Sams, from the *New York Post*," the woman said. She had a clutch of material in her right hand—a notebook and pen, a tourist map of West Point that showed the buildings by name, a small tape recorder. She shifted all of this to her left hand, then shook Wayne's right.

"Are you looking for me?" Holder asked.

"Wasn't it your roommate who committed suicide last night?"

When Holder nodded, Sams said, "I'm sorry for your loss. I know this must be a tough day for you. I wonder if you're up to answering a few questions."

"Absolutely not," Holder said.

"Did your roommate," she began anyway, glancing at her notes. "Did Alex show any signs that he might be a danger to himself?"

"I don't want to talk about it," Holder said again.

Sams seemed to relent for a moment, and Holder glanced out the window in the door.

"Did you know that Major Gates is looking for you?" Sams said.

Holder didn't answer. Sams tried another approach.

"I heard from another source that there is a Kathleen Gates meeting with Senator Bruckner this morning. Would that be the major's wife?"

Holder nodded.

"Is all of this stuff connected? Her testifying, your roommate, the fact that you're hiding from Gates?"

"Who said I was hiding?"

"Well, for starters, I know that you skipped class this morning," Sams began.

"How do you know that?"

"That's my job," she said, allowing herself a small grin. "I find stuff out."

When Holder didn't respond, she continued. "Then I find you here, skulking in the stairwell while this officer is looking for you . . . I guess I'm just naturally curious."

"I really don't want to talk about all this, ma'am," Holder said.

"If there's some sort of disagreement between you and Gates—he is a little scary looking—I might be able to help you out."

Holder smiled. "I'll keep that in mind. For now, I think I'd better keep my mouth shut."

"Is that how you got into trouble? By not keeping your mouth shut?"

Holder was tempted to say he should have kept his zipper shut, just to see what kind of note-taking frenzy he might inspire, but the moment passed quickly.

Sams stood quietly for a few seconds, then reached into a battered shoulder bag, and pulled out a dog-eared business card.

"My cell phone number is right on there. You can reach me anywhere, anytime," she said. "Good luck."

She turned and put her hand on the bar that opened the door, then turned back to him.

"I really am sorry about your roommate," she said. "I lost a close friend to suicide when I was in college. It'll be rough on you. Call me if you want to talk."

Holder watched her walk back toward the barracks and the main show at First Division. He was still watching her when Timmer's car pulled to the curb across the street. Holder watched from inside the vestibule as she wiped at her eyes with the back of her hand, then fumbled for a tissue, and blew her nose. When she got out of the car and crossed the street, Holder stuck his head out the door just far enough for her to see him.

"Did you see Major Gates looking for me?"

"No," Timmer said.

Jackie Timmer was a wreck. Her face was puffy and there was a thin line of what looked to be streaked makeup that shot straight back from the corner of her eye. Her nose was red from the tissues, and she sniffed and seemed on the edge of crying all over again.

Wayne Holder doubted he looked much better, but at the moment he wished he had another ally.

Timmer honked into a balled tissue.

"Don't we look like the fucking walking wounded," she said.

"What's next?"

"We could go back to the Dean again," Timmer offered.

"With the page from his appointment book?"

"That's one new development," Timmer said. She moved to the wall on the other side of the doorway and mirrored Wayne's fugitive stance: back to the wall, legs stuck out in front of her. "He doesn't have as much leverage now. And Alex's suicide note mentions Kathleen Gates."

"Yeah, but that still doesn't connect her and the Dean," Holder said. "I think we should just cut to the chase and go to the Supe."

"I've thought about that," Timmer said. "The advantage, of course, is that we'll have alerted the person with the most power to do something about this mess."

"And the disadvantage?" Holder asked.

Timmer turned to answer him, then spotted Tom Gates coming up the sidewalk.

"It's Gates."

Holder didn't even look out the narrow window. He pivoted on the landing and headed down the staircase, taking the steps two at a time. He had just turned the corner when Gates pulled the door open. Jackie Timmer ducked into the first floor hallway. As she hoped, he went up the stairs to the third floor and the English Department.

Timmer came back out onto the landing and looked up. When she heard Gates go into the hallway, she leaned over the railing beside her and said, "Let's go."

Wayne Holder came up the stairs and the two of them hurried out the door.

"He's going to kill me when he finds out I've been hiding from him," Holder said.

"Maybe the Supe will kill both of us and we won't have to worry," Timmer answered.

They walked quickly past the Officers Club, cutting across between the library and the bronze of Georgie Patton, Wayne Holder glancing back over his shoulder every few steps to see if Major Gates was pursuing them.

"This week, on *America's Most Wanted.* . . ." Holder said.

"Very funny," Timmer answered.

"Can I ask you a question, ma'am?"

Timmer walked a few more paces before answering. "As long as it's not about me and my husband," she said.

Holder nodded, kept silent.

They were about to turn toward the administration building when Timmer, watching the crowd of television vans visible in Central Area, stopped short and squinted.

"Isn't that the Supe right there?" she asked, pointing.

Holder scanned the crowd some fifty yards away. There were plenty of cadets, some Military Police, a couple of green shirts here and there.

"I don't see him."

And then he did.

Flynn was short and powerfully built, and the crowd parted as he surged forward, snapping return salutes.

"He must be on his way to the hearings in First Division," Timmer said.

"Liz told me that testimony starts this morning," Holder said. "I forgot to tell you."

"Starts with Kathleen Gates?"

"Right."

Timmer held her hat down with one hand and jogged across the street. Holder followed, nodding at the cadets whose salutes Timmer ignored as they closed in on the broad back of General Flynn.

"Holder."

Wayne knew the voice, of course. It was Major Gates, somewhere behind him. Holder did not look back. People were looking at them now, this captain and this cadet running, hands on their hats.

Holder and Timmer crossed Washington Road and entered Central Area. Here the space between the buildings narrowed, the crowd became more dense. They jogged left and right around spectators, excusing themselves, Holder watching Flynn as the general stood talking to a cadet near the rear door of the First Division.

When they closed to within a few yards of Flynn, they slowed to a walk, Holder tucking his shirt at the front, setting his hat squarely on his head. A few yards past Flynn, near the statue given West Point by France's L'Ecole Militaire, Holder saw Marjorie Sams. She stood with Chris Dearborn, who winked at him, and a man in a short-sleeved polo shirt who held what looked to be a big plastic dish.

He turned away from Dearborn and Sams and concentrated on Flynn.

This is it, he thought. *It can all end right here.*

Holder and Timmer came up behind the general, who paused in his conversation and turned around.

"Sir," Timmer said as she and Holder saluted.

"Captain Timmer and Cadet Holder," General Flynn said, returning the salute. The cadet behind him faded away into the crowd.

Far from being reassured as they were about to unburden themselves, Holder was alarmed that Flynn knew him immediately. It was almost as if the general expected to see him and Timmer standing there.

"Sir, Cadet Holder and I would like to talk to you if you

can spare a moment," Timmer said. Then she added, "It's very important, sir."

"I imagine it is," Flynn said. He was not smiling; he did not move. "Go ahead, I'm listening."

"Sir, I wonder if we could go somewhere private," Timmer said. "These are sensitive issues."

"I'll listen to you two right here."

Oh, shit, Holder thought.

It was there in the tone of his voice, in the way he responded to Timmer's comments. He knew what they were going to say, and he already didn't believe them. This was the possible disadvantage of going to the Supe, the one Timmer hadn't mentioned.

At that moment, General Simon came through the back door of the First Division. The Dean paused at the top of the stairs and looked down at the little tableau.

Holder glanced at Timmer, who was clearly shocked at the Dean's appearance. She wasn't ready to confront Simon. She hesitated; Holder jumped in.

"Sir, we believe Mrs. Gates, Kathleen Gates, the wife of my Tac, is going to tell the Bruckner Commission that you offered to remove a letter of reprimand from her husband's file in exchange for her silence . . . about an alleged sexual assault."

Flynn looked at Holder as if the cadet had a third eye in the middle of his forehead.

"There's more to it than that, sir," Timmer said, recovering. She was talking to Flynn but watching Simon, who was coming down the stairs slowly. There was a hint of a smile on the Dean's face.

"I believe the Dean and Mrs. Gates are in league with each other," Timmer continued. "She made up this story with his knowledge and wants his help in making it believable."

"General Flynn," Simon said, reaching the bottom step and saluting the Superintendent. "I see our cast of characters has appeared just as we thought they would."

There was a moment, just a second or two, when Wayne Holder thought Flynn might believe them. Then the moment passed.

"Captain Timmer was just telling me how you and Mrs. Gates are in league, General Simon. Fellow mutineers."

"Today West Point," Simon joked, "tomorrow the world."

Flynn smiled, looked back at Holder.

"Kathleen Gates made up the whole story about what happened in the parking lot," Holder blurted. "She's lying—she seduced me out there. She practically attacked me. . . ."

"A novel defense," Simon said in an aside to Flynn.

"She did it all so that the academy would be at risk and she'd be able to make a deal for the letter in her husband's file. . . ."

"Seems to me you were involved in that original incident, too. Isn't that correct, Mr. Holder?" Simon was sidetracking, blowing a smoke screen.

"Yes, sir. That's where it all started. . . ."

"So you figured you'd already tangled with Major Gates, it would be OK to take advantage of his wife?"

"Sir," Holder sputtered, "I did no such thing."

Holder was getting creamed, and he knew it. What's more, Jackie Timmer seemed to be fading into the background.

"So you defied your Tactical Officer, forced yourself on his wife, and now you're AWOL, if I'm not mistaken. Is that correct?" Simon asked.

"I didn't go to class this morning, sir," Holder said. "My roommate committed suicide last night."

"I'm very sorry about that," Flynn said. "But you didn't ask for relief or bedrest or anything—all of which Major Gates would have arranged. Instead you took it upon yourself to just skip class. And now you come up with this fantastic story and expect everyone to believe it."

"Sir . . ." Timmer began.

"And you, Captain Timmer," Flynn said, turning on her. "The Dean chose you for a highly visible and sensitive assignment, and you. . . ."

For a sickening moment Holder thought that Flynn would say something about Timmer's affair, drag everything out right here in the equivalent of the public square.

"And you put yourself in a compromising position," Flynn said after a frightening pause. "And you expected to keep your job with the commission? What's more, you expect that you have some credibility left when you come up to me with this outrageous story about the Dean and Mrs. Gates," Flynn said. "You should be worried about a court-martial for conduct unbecoming an officer."

Timmer rocked back on her heels. Holder thought she might fall. She was beaten; the incident with her husband had taken too much out of her.

Holder wanted to back up, go back to the first reel. They'd made the wrong choice, staking everything on this meeting with the Supe, hoping that Flynn would provide the magic bullet, the cure-all. What had made them think Flynn would believe such a story about the Dean?

"You'll both get a chance to talk to an investigating officer," Flynn said.

"By then it'll be too late, sir," Timmer said. "Bruckner will never let go of the spotlight. You'll be accused on national television; that's as good as being convicted."

"Captain Timmer," General Simon said. "I'm afraid I'm going to have to talk to the head of your department about relieving you of your teaching duties. I'm no longer satisfied that you can carry out those tasks."

Simon stood with his hands folded primly in front of him. Flynn, arms at his sides, had squared off with them, the bulldog standing his ground.

Timmer was devastated. Kathleen Gates was upstairs, getting ready to testify, to bring down the house. And Flynn didn't even want to be helped. It was all over for Wayne. Even the Supe had used the term "sexual assault."

Holder looked over Flynn's shoulder; Marjorie Sams was there, waving her notebook at him, at something behind him. When he turned around, he saw Major Tom Gates walking quickly toward the little group, head down, face an angry mask.

Simon was droning. "And as for you, Mr. Holder. . . ."

Wayne felt disconnected from his surroundings, as if he were watching this all in slow motion, from a remove, while all around him the walls were closing in.

"While I sympathize with you over the loss of your

roommate," Simon continued, "I have to point out that your behavior . . ."

Holder watched the Dean's mouth, saw it moving, heard the words, could not listen for another moment.

"What about this?" Holder interrupted, whipping the papers from his back pocket.

Simon stopped talking; his face registered shock that this cadet was yelling at him.

Holder shook the papers until they fluttered open; Alex's note fell to the ground.

"Why you impertinent little . . ."

"What about this?" Holder demanded again. He was wide-eyed now, angry; he wanted to punch Simon right between his eyes.

"This is Alex Trainor's suicide note," Holder said, waving the paper. "Mrs. Gates talked his girlfriend into an abortion. That's why he jumped."

Flynn took the note from Wayne's hand; he did not look at it.

"I know you're very upset about your roommate, and you should be. There will be an investigation into the suicide and a psychological autopsy. We'll let the doctor straighten this out."

Holder was losing the battle.

"What's that?" Simon asked, indicating the other paper in Holder's hand.

"This is a copy of a page from your appointment book, the one your secretary keeps."

"How did you get that?" Simon snapped. He glanced quickly at Flynn; Holder thought he saw fear there.

Over the edge now, Holder said, "Never mind," and handed the paper to Flynn, tapping the entry with his finger.

Flynn said, "Watch your tongue, mister," but took the paper.

"This is the book his secretary keeps. Kathleen Gates came to visit him in his office."

Beside the Supe, Jackie Timmer surprised them all by sitting—almost falling—to the curb, where she put her head in her hands. Sitting down, uninvited, in the presence of a three-star general.

"What does this prove?" Flynn wanted to know.

"They talked about General Simon becoming the next Supe," Holder said.

Flynn turned to his Dean, who smiled as if to say, *It's tough dealing with lunatics.*

"Let me be sure I understand you, Cadet Holder," Flynn said. "You're saying that General Simon and Mrs. Gates got together and plotted the takeover of the Military Academy?"

"That's exactly what I'm saying sir," Holder replied, sounding more confident than he felt in his theories. "They made a deal. Kathleen Gates would put you in some sort of compromising position; you could save the academy bad press only by resigning. General Simon wanted to step in and become interim Superintendent."

"And you know this . . . how? You were privy to this conversation?"

"No, sir. We heard about it from one of the Bruckner staffers, a guy named Van Grouw. . . ."

"Secondhand? Third hand? Fourth?" Flynn said. "Do you have even a shred of evidence to back up anything you're alleging here?"

Wayne sputtered. Simon jumped in with another diversion.

"You pulled the fire alarm in the building, didn't you?" the Dean said.

Without waiting for an answer, Simon turned to Flynn. "Sarah Wiley noticed something was wrong with her desk when she came back in that day. Her appointment book had been moved and the copy machine used during the evacuation. The fire department said someone had pulled the alarm just outside my office, but had wiped the prints off."

Flynn turned to Holder.

"Did you pull the alarm?"

A cadet will not lie, cheat or steal. . . .

"Yes, sir," Holder said.

There's the end of my cadet days, he thought.

"Did you pull it with the express purpose of making a copy of the Dean's appointment book?"

"Yes, sir, I did." Holder made it sound as if he were proud of this.

Go out with a little panache, he thought.

Flynn handed the paper to the Dean.

"For your information, Mr. Holder, General Simon can meet with whomever he chooses. He doesn't have to clear it with me, and he certainly doesn't have to clear it with you."

"We talked about the command environment," Simon said. "Not a single fantastic story came up."

Holder looked at Flynn. "And you believe that, sir?" he dared.

"Are you calling me a liar?" Simon said, stepping toward Holder, his voice sharp.

Flynn held up a hand.

"Mr. Holder is under a lot of stress after the events of last night. He's probably not even aware of what he's saying," Flynn said.

Gates reached the group, saluted.

"Have you been looking for Mr. Holder here?" Flynn asked the big officer.

"Yes, sir, I have," Gates answered.

"General Simon and I are going upstairs," Flynn said. "We can deal with all of this later. I trust you can take care of Cadet Holder."

"Yes, sir," Gates said.

"Will you be coming upstairs, Major?" Flynn asked.

Gates hesitated, looked at Holder.

"What for, sir?"

"Well, I believe your wife is going to talk to the commission this morning," Flynn said. "Maybe even wind up on television."

Now it was Gates's turn to look sick.

"Yes, sir," he said after a considerable pause. "I think I will."

The two general officers climbed the narrow steps; Gates clamped a vise grip on Holder's arm and pulled the cadet into the sally port, the covered passageway through the ground floor of the barracks.

"You want to tell me what the hell is going on?" Gates said. He made an effort to control his anger, clenching his teeth, holding his arms stiffly at his sides.

"You don't show up for class. You don't show up for your meeting with the investigator. You run away with the note from Alex, which is an important piece of evidence the CID needs to close this case—which would be nice to do before his poor parents arrive. And now I find you running away from me and confronting the Supe."

Gates seemed only one tiny shove away from grabbing Holder by the throat, but Wayne Holder didn't care at this point. He had done everything he could, and Flynn hadn't believed him. And in a little while Kathleen Gates would tell her fantastic story, and the lies would beam from the television vans and then it wouldn't matter if a hundred angels lined up to testify on Wayne's behalf—or on behalf of General Flynn, for that matter. Wayne would go down in flames. So would Flynn. So would Alex's memory.

It was over.

"What the hell is going on, Wayne?"

Holder looked up at Gates, who stood now with his hands on his hips. He had relaxed his jaw; his rage seemed to have subsided a tiny bit, like a wave that has peaked.

"It doesn't matter anymore, sir," Holder said. "It's all over anyway. Maybe you should just take me back to the barracks, put me under arrest, whatever you're going to do to me."

"Wayne, you little worm. You still don't get it, do you?"

Gates straightened, looked around the sally port as if noticing for the first time that there were other people walking by.

"Do you know that Van Grouw character has it in for me?" Gates said. "Chris Dearborn might be called and asked about my . . . technique in coaching, in sparring."

Holder nodded.

"But Dearborn came to me, told me he'd made a mistake in telling Van Grouw anything. Told me he'd learned something from me that he had managed to avoid for his whole cadet career so far."

"What's that, sir?"

"Damn, Wayne. Haven't you been paying attention? He learned to get back up after he'd been knocked on his ass."

Holder leaned back against the wall, his shoulder against the cool stone. Gates stood beside him, blue eyes squinting at sunlit Central Area. They were only a few yards from the

First Division, could see all the windows. Across the narrow space between the buildings, Jackie Timmer stood shakily and leaned on the railing that climbed to the back door of the old barracks.

"I'm going inside, see what the hell my wife has cooked up," Gates said. "You get yourself back to the barracks. Don't move out of your damn room until I tell you to, you copy?"

Holder nodded, pulled himself upright, and saluted. Then he watched Gates climb the stairs to the room where his wife was going to lay her lies on the table. And he had no idea. Wayne Holder saw some unfinished business there.

Kathleen Gates could see them—Holder and her husband—from the window in the little office Braintree had taken over. Holder was doing the talking. Tom stood, shaking his head slightly.

Kathleen Gates tried to pull the window open, but it was painted shut.

What the hell was Holder saying to him?

"Mrs. Gates?"

It was one of the sound techs.

"I need to fit you for a microphone," he said, holding up a little black box and a tiny wire with a lapel clip. While he worked she looked back out the window; Tom was gone.

She had tried to call her husband at his office several times in the last hour and a half, but he wasn't around. Bruckner had told her not to leave the room, told her that the testimony would not be carried live, that she would have a chance to talk to Tom and explain everything before anyone saw this in the news or on television.

Out in the conference room, the bright lights were on. Bruckner was answering questions in front of a bank of microphones. Kathleen could hear some of the reporters calling out General Flynn's name.

Bruckner had told her that the general did not know about her accusations. That he, Bruckner, would ask Flynn to leave the room if she became uncomfortable.

"Shouldn't you tell him ahead of time what's going to happen?"

"Why, Kathleen?" Braintree had said from behind the Senator's shoulder. "If the story you told us is true, he already knows what he said to you. It's just that it's going to come out in the open here."

"Of course," she'd said.

Wayne Holder crossed to where Jackie Timmer stood leaning on the iron rail.

"You gonna be sick?" he asked.

"No, I think I'm finished embarrassing myself for the day," she said.

"So you think Flynn will believe us after Gates testifies and everything we talked about out here turns out to be true?"

"Sure," Timmer said. "But by then it'll be too late. Flynn will be tried and convicted in the press."

"Were we wrong about the Dean? I mean, how could he be so chummy with the Supe if he knows that Gates is going to trash Flynn in a little while?"

"He's setting Flynn up, leading him to the slaughter," Timmer said. "This way, he gets to look like the loyal subordinate right up until the end. He and Kathleen Gates probably had all this figured out from the start."

When Holder didn't answer, Timmer studied his face.

"You feel bad for her husband, don't you?" she asked.

"I suppose I do," Holder said. "He's no prince, but he doesn't put up a facade. He's consistent. And he's about to be blind-sided."

The two of them were silent for a moment. All around them, cadets went about their business.

"There's one way you can prevent that," Timmer said.

Holder had been studying the stone wall before him; he met her eyes.

"Yeah. Thought of that myself."

Ninninger Hall was packed with bodies, equipment, lights, heat. Holder found a tiny piece of floor along one of the narrow walls, opposite the podium where Senator Bruckner was making some remarks to the press. He scanned the room, spotted Major Gates standing behind and towering over Generals Simon and Flynn, like some caricature of a bodyguard. He watched Gates's face for a sign that the officer had spotted him. The reaction—rage—was fairly predictable, since Holder had defied Gates's order to return straightaway to the barracks.

"Some juicy stuff out there."

Holder looked to his left. Marjorie Sams, pressed close by the crowd, stood nearly on top of Holder.

"You were eavesdropping," Holder said, as if that might make a difference.

"Directional microphone," she said. "Your buddy Chris Dearborn made the suggestion."

Sams leaned closer to him.

"Do you really believe that the Dean over there is in league with this Gates woman?"

Holder studied her for a moment, the keen, intelligent eyes.

"I do," Holder said. "Unfortunately I can't prove it, and in a few minutes it won't matter much anyway."

"Why don't you give me the details—an exclusive. We might be able to stir up enough interest in your side of the story to protect you."

Holder thought about what Gates had said. Get up when you're down. But he didn't think he had it in him.

Funny thing was, it turned out Chris Dearborn was the tough one after all.

Holder looked again at the woman beside him, tried to put on a smile.

"I might need a job soon, Ms. Sams," he said. "Maybe you'll be able to help me out."

Holder turned his attention back to the front of the room. Gates spotted him, made eye contact, drew a single finger across his throat.

Just a few feet away from Major Gates, Holder saw a door open; Kathleen Gates peered out. When she saw Simon and her husband standing with Flynn, her face registered shock. She pushed the door shut quickly, slamming it loud enough so that Bruckner, still at the podium, paused for a moment and glanced in that direction.

Holder put his hand on Marjorie Sams's arm and made ready to squeeze past her, head for that door. But he saw

Gates, hemmed in by Simon and Flynn, watching him, waiting for him to come close.

"You still want that exclusive?" Holder said to the reporter.

Kathleen Gates paced in the small office while Bruckner prepared her dramatic entrance into the larger conference room. She had not expected to see the Dean, had certainly not expected to see him with Flynn. What could that mean? Had Simon double-crossed her? And Tom was out there, too. If she went ahead with everything her husband would hear, in a news conference instead of from her, that she'd had sex with Wayne Holder.

Panic clawed at her throat, made it hard to breathe. Kathleen had had enough. Flynn had to leave, so did Tom.

She reached for the door handle, but the door swung open toward her and a young woman in a badly wrinkled suit came in the door.

"Oh, hello," the woman said. "Are you Kathleen Gates?"

"Who are you?" Kathleen demanded.

"Marjorie Sams from the *Post,*" the woman answered. She had a great bundle of papers, pencils, pens, and notebooks in her hand, all of which she dropped on top of a filing cabinet before offering her hand.

"I wanted to meet you, Mrs. Gates, and see if you'd agree to give me the first interview after your testimony."

"Jesus," Kathleen said. "Can't you people just leave me the hell alone? I haven't even gone out there yet. Suppose I don't have anything to say that's worth printing?"

"Well, I suppose we'll discover that when you start talking," Sams countered.

"Please, Miss. . . ."

"Sams."

"Please, Miss Sams. This is a very nerve-wracking time for me. Maybe you could just give me a few moments to myself."

Sams looked disappointed. "Of course," she said, turning slowly for the door. "Is there anything I can get for you?"

"No," Kathleen said. Then, "Yes. Would you do me a big favor and ask . . ."

Kathleen Gates walked to the door, which was ajar.

"Ask that man," she said, pointing at the Dean, "to come in here for a moment."

Holder watched as Claude Braintree made some remarks about how the commission's investigators went about their work. He wondered how much time they had before the Kathleen Gates show. On the other side of the room, Marjorie Sams loitered by the entrance to the small office General Simon had entered seconds earlier.

Suddenly Holder's upper arm was seized in a powerful grip. When he turned his head, Tom Gates's face was only inches from his own.

"What the fuck are you doing here?" Gates whispered. "I told you to get your ass back to the barracks."

Holder met his eyes; it was time to come clean.

"You also told me to get up when I got knocked down."

"What are you talking about, boy?"

Holder glanced to his right; Simon had just emerged from the little office. Holder could see Kathleen Gates in the doorway. Marjorie ducked inside. Kathleen Gates confronted the reporter, but Sams came out, head down, holding something to her ear.

"Sir," Holder said to Gates. "Do you have any idea what your wife is going to say this morning about General Flynn?"

Gates loosened his grip, relaxed his features a bit. He wasn't expecting this.

"Do you know what she's going to say about me?" Holder asked.

"Got it," Sams said as she came up beside the two men and held out a small voice-activated tape recorder. "Just like you said it would be, too," she said to Holder.

"Lucky guess," Holder said, reaching for the recorder.

"Aren't you going to take this to Bruckner first?" Sams asked. She appeared somewhat alarmed that the tape had left her control.

"No," Holder said. "First I have some things to talk about with my Tac."

Kathleen Gates did not want General Flynn in the room when she began to testify, which meant he had to be told why he was being asked to leave. To Claude Braintree fell the duty of telling the Superintendent he was about to be accused of offering to tamper with official records—Tom Gates's Letter of Reprimand—in order to cover up an alleged sexual assault by a cadet in his command.

Braintree chose one of the many lulls caused by uncooperative technical equipment and waded into the mob. He had no doubt, now, that Kathleen Gates was lying; he was about to accuse an innocent man. As he focused on Flynn and made his way through the pack, it occurred to Claude Braintree that he could just keep going, walk right on out the door, down the stairs, and out of Lamar Bruckner's life.

If I had any balls at all, that's what I'd do, he thought.

Instead, he approached Flynn, adjusted his jacket, and tugged the snow-white cuffs out to the perfect length. He smiled his widest smile, called Flynn's name and thought about how much he hated his life.

"That's what this is all about?" Flynn said after Braintree had sketched the outline for him. "All this hoopla over one woman's *lies?*"

His voice rose sharply. "She *dares* accuse me of such a thing, accuses me of lying?"

Two or three of the reporters closest to them edged closer still; the crowd in the already packed room seemed to take up the available oxygen.

"I'm afraid so, General," Braintree said. Simon stood just behind Flynn. Braintree allowed his eyes to click to the Dean's, then forced them back again.

"I'm sure you can see that we'll have to take this allegation very seriously," Braintree said. "In fact, Senator Bruckner has asked if you would consider leaving so that your presence doesn't upset the witness."

"The witness? The *witness?* Witness to what? There was no crime here." Flynn bulled his way through the technicians and camera crews. The reporters were following his every move now.

Bruckner was seated at one of the conference tables, Kathleen Gates next to him. Flynn stood opposite the Senator and, ignoring the woman, put his hands on the table.

"I see what's going on here," Flynn said, struggling to control his voice. "This is just a headline grab, pure and simple. . . ."

"I'm afraid I'm going to have to ask you to leave, General," Bruckner said.

"You can't be serious about allowing this woman to air these charges. You haven't even asked me what happened, haven't even considered that there is another side."

Bruckner stood, drawing himself up so that he looked down on the shorter officer. Flynn felt the eyes—and the cameras—of everyone in the room on him. The general straightened. He felt a powerful temptation to reach across and punch this soft civilian in his belly. Instead, he glanced at Braintree, who looked as if he'd just lost a battle.

This is what they want, Flynn thought. *They want me to make a scene, get it all on tape so that it will be even more sensational.*

"I have my reasons for proceeding this way," Bruckner said.

Flynn did not answer. Behind him, he could hear the *click-whirr* of still cameras rolling off the shots. He was playing right into Bruckner's ambush by losing his temper.

Flynn looked down at Kathleen Gates, seated at the table. She tried to hold his gaze, faltered, then looked back up.

"Shame on you," he said.

Then the Superintendent turned on his heel and walked out of the room. He did not look for General Simon, who was hiding up against a wall.

The questions started immediately.

"Senator, what was General Flynn talking about?"

"Has General Flynn been a subject of investigation?"

"Did you ask the Superintendent to leave the room?"

"Ladies and gentlemen," Bruckner said as he held up his hands, as he waited for all eyes in the room to come to rest on him. "Ladies and gentlemen. . . ."

Wayne Holder and Major Tom Gates walked into the room together and threaded through the crowd. Flynn was headed in the opposite direction.

"Sir," Wayne Holder said to the Superintendent as he held the tape recorder. "You might want to hear this."

Flynn paused in the doorway.

Tom Gates, quiet now, approached his wife, leaned over, and whispered something to her. She began to shake her head.

There was only a tiny, hotly lit space between Senator Bruckner and the television cameras; Wayne inserted himself there, only a few feet from the big Texan. The reporters were now in a frenzy. One of them, a handsome young man eager for the story, leaned closer to Tom and Kathleen Gates, stretching across the table, trying to hear their conversation.

"What's going on?" the reporter asked loudly. "Are you going to testify, Miss? Who are you, Major? Can someone please tell me. . . ."

Gates turned his face to the man, extended one big hand to the reporter's collar, and hauled him off the floor to the table's polished surface. When the reporter's feet were dangling, Gates said, "Do you mind, pal?" and slid the man away to the end of the table.

The camera jockeys, seeing a confrontation, were trying to get in front of Wayne Holder, trying to get a face shot.

"Who the hell are you?" Bruckner demanded. "What are you doing, young man?"

"Me?" Holder asked, producing a small black tape recorder and placing it on the table in front of the Senator. "I just got up for round two."

CHAPTER 20

THE DEAN HAD BLINDSIDED LIEUTENANT GENERAL PATRICK Flynn, who started to leave Ninninger Hall out of a sense of frustration and because he knew his anger would cloud his judgment. But as soon as he heard the first few sentences from the tape recorder Wayne Holder set on the conference table, Flynn took charge again. He reached past Holder, hit the stop button, and said to Senator Bruckner, "Why don't we step into that little office."

Holder wasn't sure his legs would carry him; the relief left him weak-kneed. The cadet glanced around for General Simon. Flynn, seeing this, turned to spot the Dean headed toward the door.

"General Simon," Flynn called out. A dozen reporters turned toward the Dean. "A moment of your time please, sir."

Kathleen Gates, still at the conference table, stood and turned to Bruckner.

"Wait," she said. "I can explain."

She turned sharply, raised her arm and pointed at Simon. "It was his idea, his plan."

She was hysterical, eyes streaming tears, voice cracking, finger stabbing the air.

"He came to me."

But the others were ignoring her, filing into the room behind General Flynn. Kathleen Gates tried to fight her way past a cordon of reporters who were pressing around her. She pounded her fist on the table, walked into her chair, grabbed it, and threw it aside.

"God damn it!" she shrieked. "You people pay attention to me! I said . . ."

Tom Gates came up behind her and put his hand on his wife's shoulders.

"No more lies, Kathleen," he snarled at her. She seemed to wilt, and he became more gentle, though he still had his hands on her shoulders, still guided her to a chair. "No more lies."

Tom Gates stepped around from behind the chair and faced her.

"How could you? You caused so much pain."

"I did it for you!" she screamed. Then, quieter, crying. "I did it for us. I did all of this to help you keep your career. I love you, Tom. You have to believe me. . . ."

Tom Gates leaned over and put his hands on the arms of the chair; his face, twisted, pained, was inches from his wife's.

"You're killing me here, Kathleen. Don't you see that? I don't want anything I have to lie for."

Kathleen tried to stand, tried to put her arms around her husband, but he held up his hand and said, "Just go home, Kathleen."

Then he turned, went into the room with the others, and closed the door behind him.

Holder was packed into the tiny office with Senator Bruckner, Claude Braintree, Major Tom Gates, Generals Simon and Flynn. Gates was about to close the door when Marjorie Sams shot a hand in.

"May I come in?" she asked Flynn, who was obviously in charge.

Flynn looked at Holder.

"That's her recorder, and she already has half the story, sir," the cadet said. "She'll probably do a more fair job if she has the whole thing."

Flynn motioned Sams in. The woman closed the door on the other reporters and produced a notebook.

"General," Bruckner began. "I want you to know that I am outraged at this interruption to these very important proceedings and I will take whatever steps I deem necessary. . . ."

"With all due respect, Senator," Claude Braintree said, smiling his wide smile and smoothing his tie. "General Flynn is about to save our collective asses. So why don't you put a lid on it."

Bruckner sputtered a bit, then, with an eye to the reporter by the door, fell silent.

"Senator Bruckner," Flynn said. "This is Cadet Wayne Holder. Mr. Holder came to me this morning with . . . a fantastic story."

Holder looked at Simon, who had slumped into a chair in the corner.

"Mr. Holder has been under a lot of stress lately. In fact, it was his roommate who committed suicide last night. So I chose not to believe him. Turns out that I decided too hastily to dismiss him."

There was a knock at the door. Marjorie Sams peeked out, then turned to Flynn.

"It's a Captain Timmer," she said.

"Let her in."

When Sams opened the door, Holder saw Chris Dearborn in the press of reporters behind Timmer. He gave Holder a goofy look and shot him a thumbs-up.

Flynn nodded at Timmer, then turned on the tape recorder. The first sound they heard was a door closing, the door to the office they now occupied. The first voice they heard was Kathleen Gates's.

"Don't you turn on me," she said.

"What did you expect me to do?"

At the sound of this voice, General Simon put his head in his hands. Marjorie Sams scribbled furiously.

"I could hardly treat Flynn as if he'd already been relieved," Simon said.

Kathleen Gates's next comment was unintelligible.

"All you have to do is go through with your testimony," Simon assured her.

"What about my husband?" she pleaded. "I haven't even had a chance to warn him and he's standing right out there."

Wayne Holder stood beside Major Gates, who had a glassy-eyed look. Holder had given him the whole story, so this wasn't news. But it didn't make it any less painful.

"Emphasize the other," Simon's taped voice went on. "Talk about your meeting with Flynn. Make it sound like he approached you, but keep the details simple; you don't want to get caught up later on trying to remember a complicated story."

"I've decided I want Tom to have a transfer," Gates said on the recorder.

"As soon as the dust settles," Simon assured her. "I already let Braintree know that I'd support plans for a downsized Academy. He went right along with it. As soon as I'm acting Supe, we'll have orders cut for you. I think that would be best for all of us."

There was some shuffling on the tape, then Simon's voice again.

"The fewer people around here who know about this, the better off we'll both be."

"What about Wayne Holder?" Kathleen Gates asked Simon.

At the sound of his name, Holder stiffened. Braintree, he noticed, was watching him.

"He's got to go," Simon answered, the pronouncement clear on the tape. "Timmer, too."

"I never meant for that boy Trainor to get hurt," Kathleen Gates was saying.

"That was hard," Simon answered her. "But you had no way to know what he would do."

There was a pause, some static on the tape. Then Simon's voice again, clear.

"West Point will be better for all of this."

Flynn pressed the stop button. There were eight people in the room, and for a few seconds, the only sound was their breathing.

"My staff knew that Mrs. Gates was trying to use us," Bruckner said. "Mr. Braintree here was monitoring her at all times."

When Marjorie Sams looked up from her notebook, Bruckner smiled at her. Damage control.

"We'll have a full statement ready shortly," the Senator said. "And then we'll get back to business, once this little distraction is cleared."

Bruckner smiled at Sams, then made his way toward the door. Braintree followed. When he drew abreast of Holder, Braintree put his hand on the cadet's shoulder.

Simon stood, faced Flynn.

"I had nothing but the best interests of West Point in mind, General," he began.

"Have your resignation on my desk within the hour," Flynn said crisply.

Simon started to speak, then nodded, and shuffled out to the waiting reporters.

"Captain Timmer, Cadet Holder," Flynn said. "I owe you each an apology. I found your story simply too fantastic to believe."

"So did we, sir," Timmer said.

Flynn looked to the door. "Miss?" he said.

"Marjorie Sams," the reporter answered. She was still writing on her tablet even as she looked Flynn in the eye.

"Why don't we retire to my office," he said. "It's a little less crowded there, and I have an interest in what you're going to write."

"Certainly, General," Sams said.

When Timmer, Flynn and Sams were gone, Major Tom Gates sat in one of the chairs, kicked his big legs out before him.

"You know something, Wayne," Gates said. "When I first met you I wondered why your outgoing Tac had made you company commander. He admitted to me that there were other people who deserved it more."

Holder sat on the table.

"He told me you didn't take this business seriously, that you spent too much time goofing off and chasing skirts."

Gates paused. "Turns out he was right."

Holder felt as if he should say something, but he could not think of an apology that would give this man—whom he'd come to respect—his life back.

"But I guess he saw some potential there."

Gates put his hands behind his head, lifted his big feet to the conference table. He looked like he'd just come in off a ten-day combat patrol.

"I'll say this for you, you don't give up."

"Thank you, sir," Holder said.

Gates stood, rubbed his hands across his face. "Keep that," he said. "And your sense of what's right and what's wrong. If you do that, and you remember to take care of your soldiers, hell, you'll be an OK lieutenant."

EPILOGUE

THEY CAME OUT OF THE SALLY PORTS IN SOLID BLOCKS OF GRAY and white, out into the green arena of the Plain, into the rolling applause of their families and friends who had come to this place to watch the Graduation Parade. A hot June breeze stirred the guidons, ruffled the black feathers on the tarbucket hats of the cadet officers. Bayonets and sabers flashed in the sunshine, and the heavy *thump-thump-thump* of the big drums carried across the new-cut grass, echoing the heartbeats of those seniors marching in their last parade as cadets.

Wayne Holder marched in the front rank of his company with the other seniors. The second semester company commander and guidon bearer were out front, in the position of honor. That was just fine with Wayne, who wanted to watch Liz Wrenson, still out front with the Brigade Staff, wanted to scan the bleachers for his family. His grandfather was out there somewhere, wearing a black, gold, and gray alumni arm band that said "1948." His father had told Wayne that he would wear a white Panama hat, "so that you can see us in the stands."

Alex Trainor's parents were out there, too, sitting with

Wayne's family. Holder had invited them to Graduation Week. The evening before the parade and two days before graduation, the Trainors had participated in a ceremony in the Cadet Library, orchestrated by Wayne with help from the Superintendent. They placed Alex's West Point ring in a display case that held one ring from each class dating back to the mid-nineteenth century. In the twentieth century, it had become customary that the ring belonged to a graduate who died young: in combat, in accidents, taken by disease or, in Alex's case, by suicide.

Wayne remembered Alex saying that his father was the emotional one. Mr. Trainor had cried quietly at the ceremony while Alex's mother made a few remarks and said a prayer. Afterward, General Flynn had gone over to shake hands with the family; the general had hugged Alex's father.

The first class—who would become new lieutenants the next day—marched away from the companies that had been their families for the last three years to form a reviewing line. This parade, their last as cadets, reversed the course of their first at the end of plebe summer. In that ceremony the new plebe class is on the field when the Corps takes its position. The freshmen then march forward to join their companies—their new families. Four years later the seniors march onto the field with their companies, then walk away and form a reviewing line to receive the salutes of the passing cadet formations.

"Pass in review."

The order was greeted with rattling bayonets in the ranks. The plebes were especially excited; the end of this parade marked the end of plebe year. Afterward, back in the barracks areas, they would shake hands with a line of upperclassmen, exchange first names, and leave behind a memorable—and often painful—year.

Holder watched Liz Wrenson, some seventy yards away, turn sharply with the rest of the stripers and move into position beside the reviewing party. He had blown her a kiss when he passed. They would spend most of their graduation leave together before reporting for more schooling, Wayne at Fort Benning for the Infantry Officers Basic Course, Liz at Fort Sam Houston for medical school. The separation would be difficult on both of them, but they were determined to make the relationship work.

Among the deep ranks of seniors arrayed in front of the reviewing stand, the atmosphere was relaxed. As the cadet companies wheeled by on the bright carpet of spring grass, the seniors from each unit greeted their friends with a salute and cheers. Elsewhere in the mass of gray and white seniors congratulated each other and looked over their shoulders for their families, now behind them in the stands.

Wayne Holder saw Tom Gates in the crowd.

It was only a glimpse, and then someone was in the way. When Holder recovered, shifting left and right, Gates was gone.

The announcer's voice boomed through the public address system. "Company D is commanded by Cadet Will Carey, of Philadelphia, Pennsylvania."

Holder turned to the front, saw Chris Dearborn in the front rank, confident, at ease with himself. It had been Dearborn's idea to enlist Marjorie Sams in those last desperate moments the previous fall. Dearborn had made his peace with West Point and was ready for the increased responsibilities of senior year and the challenge that lay beyond that. Dearborn had Tom Gates to thank for that.

Mike Viegas was there, too, and Rebecca Hollings.

"Eyes . . . *right!*" Carey called, and the cadets marching by snapped their heads and eyes to face the reviewing party, the seniors who were no longer a part of the old company. The next rank of leaders had stepped forward.

Wayne Holder watched them, saluted with his classmates, held the salute as D Company turned the corner and headed back toward the barracks. The familiar strains of "The Army Song" rolled across the parade field.

And that was it.

The class was dismissed. His last parade as a cadet had passed, it seemed, more quickly than any of the hundreds that had gone before. Wayne Holder left his friends and waded into the crowd. Leaving all this behind would provide him a relief he hadn't known in the wake of the scandal; he could escape his fame.

Marjorie Sams had done a sensitive and thoughtful piece

about Alex Trainor, about Tom Gates, about the pressures of duty. Holder had become something of a celebrity in his own small world, and West Point hadn't suffered greatly at the hands of the press.

Senator Bruckner and his commission had conducted a tactical withdrawal from West Point; Bruckner was currently beating his chest before the doors of the Central Intelligence Agency. Claude Braintree had left the Senator's staff to become chief counsel for the National Democratic Committee. Lieutenant General Patrick Flynn would, in a few days, mark his first anniversary as Superintendent. With his firm guidance the academy had weathered the troubles of the past year and had come out better in the end. Flynn told his wife that their second year at West Point might be boring in comparison.

Brigadier General David Simon had resigned in lieu of court-martial and had moved to France, where he taught English at a small university. Captain Jackie Timmer was still teaching, though this was to be her last assignment. An unfavorable comment on the "moral judgment" block of her efficiency report meant she would not be promoted. Timmer was living in the Bachelor Officer's Quarters; her husband had requested early reassignment and had left at the end of the spring semester. Timmer's officemate, the memorable Major Jon Hillard, had received a verbal reprimand—a slap on the wrist—from the Superintendent for punching a civilian history professor in the O'Club lunch line. Some seniors had reported seeing Timmer and Hillard at the local movie theater.

Major Tom Gates had left West Point within a few days of the opening salvos of the Bruckner Commission the previous fall; Wayne had heard that Gates had resigned from the service in order to take care of his wife and children. Kathleen Gates had suffered a nervous breakdown and spent nearly a month in a Pennsylvania mental hospital. She had wrecked her husband's career, had helped derail Simon's, had contributed to a suicide, had lied and cheated and cut a wide swath of destruction in a few wild weeks. Wayne Holder sometimes wondered what ghosts visited her at night.

Tom Gates had sent a Christmas card to Holder; in it, the

former officer said he was concentrating on taking care of his family, and that the service—the service he so loved— was not the best place for that. Gates had not given up his fight, he had chosen his family over his career.

Holder pushed through the crowd, keeping an eye out for the big man. Scores of cadets were jostling in the happy throng. People were snapping pictures, video cameras were rolling, cadets in tall parade hats were surrounded, hugged, and kissed by proud families.

"Can I take your picture?"

A little boy in shorts and a Yankees tee shirt stood before Wayne, holding a small camera and looking up expectantly. He was about ten.

Holder wanted to find Gates; his family was to meet him near the flagpole; he had fifteen things to do all at once. But this was a habit learned early on by cadets: be nice to the tourists.

"Sure, pal," he said.

Holder put his hat on and stood straight, smiling at the boy, who aimed the camera too low. The picture would be of a decapitated cadet body.

"I'm supposed to give you this," the little boy said, holding out a folded piece of paper.

"What is it?" Holder asked.

"Don't know. Some big guy said you'd let me take your picture. Then he said to make sure I give you this."

Holder took the paper from the boy's hand.

"Is it a secret message?" the boy asked, his eyes wide.

"I don't think so," Holder said.

The boy looked disappointed; clearly he expected something more from this fancy-dress soldier.

"But if it is secret, I wouldn't be able to tell you anyway, right?"

The boy's eyes grew wide. He was smiling when a woman put her hand on his shoulder.

"Let's go, Michael," she said.

Michael stood up straight, pushed his shoulders back, and touched his fingers to his forehead in a salute. Wayne came to attention and returned his own sharp salute as Michael went off with his mother.

Holder recognized the handwriting. He looked around to

see if Gates might be watching him, did not see him in the crowd.

Congratulations, maggot, the note began.

Holder smiled.

> *Seriously, Wayne, congratulations. This has been a hard road for you (some of that your own doing, of course), but you made it. Remember what it means to fight for something you know is right.*
>
> *I'm going to take off before you get this. I don't want to interfere with your family celebration. I also don't want to be introduced as "my former Tac, Major Mercury" (you probably thought I didn't know all the nicknames).*
>
> *As I write I can hear you guys forming for parade. I'm sitting on Trophy Point, one of my favorite spots at this strange place. Did you ever notice how we try to capture things in these great statues, and then people come and expect to see, in these big piles of stone, what the service is all about. But it can't work that way. The statues can't tell the story because they're not alive. The only things we can pass down—from me to you and from you to whatever soldiers you come in contact with—are things that are alive. We define ourselves by our actions, and we do that every single day, in a hundred tiny choices made by thousands of people at every moment. Tell the truth. Work hard. Don't be discouraged. Help your buddy. Tend your duty. Believe. Obey.*
>
> *Every time you put on your boots, every time you talk to a soldier, every time you get up and move when you want to sit and stay warm and dry, you get to make a choice to serve your country well.*
>
> *Take care of your soldiers, Wayne. And good luck.*
>
> *Yours,*
>
> *Tom Gates*

Wayne Holder tucked the note into the red sash he wore around his waist, then touched his eyes with his white gloves.

"Wayne. *Wayne!* Over here."

His father was across the street, standing by the flagpole, wearing a big white hat, and waving as if to a rescuer.

Holder waved back. His mother was there, too, aiming a camera at him. Beside them, straight-backed as a plebe, smoking, stood his grandfather, who had been through all of this years before.

"I'll have to talk to the old man," Wayne told himself.

And above his family, the huge garrison flag billowed and rolled over slowly in the sharp light.

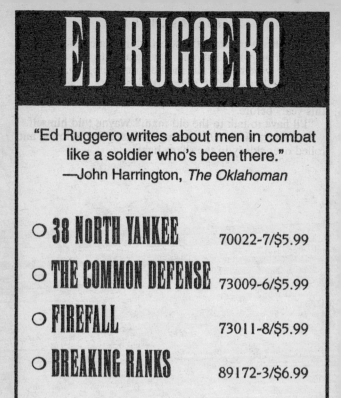

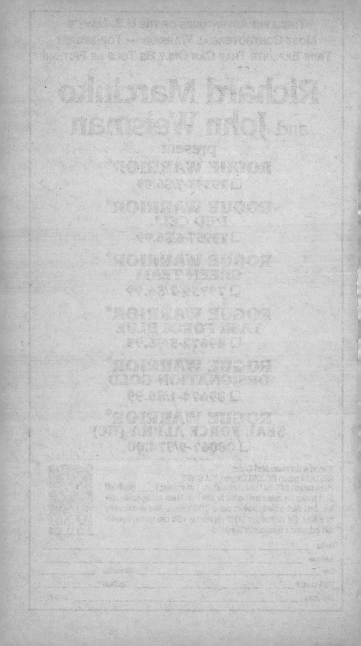